THUCYDIDES, BOOK I

HISTORY OF
THE PELOPONNESIAN WAR

THUCYDIDES, BOOK I

HISTORY OF THE PELOPONNESIAN WAR

Edited by E.C. Marchant, M.A.

WILDSIDE PRESS

HISTORY OF THE PELOPONNESIAN WAR

Published by Wildside Press LLC.
www.wildsidebooks.com

THUCYDIDES, BOOK I

PREFACE

THE Greek text of this book I. is reprinted, by
kind permission, from that of Mr. Stuart Jones
in the Oxford series. Some years ago I prepared
a text; but, on comparing the Oxford text with
my own, I found that mine seldom differed from
it, and it seemed better to follow the new text
as it stands, merely noting the few passages in
which I am unable to agree with Mr. Stuart
Jones. For the permission so readily accorded I
tender my best thanks.

Fifteen years have passed since the first
instalment of this school edition was published.
It was intended to include books I., II., III., and
the Sicilian Expedition. In this long period
blind admiration of the author has sobered down
into a clearer appreciation, as I hope, both of his
greatness and of his defects. I do not think now
that the adverse portions of Dionysius' criticism
can be dismissed as absurd. Where he goes
wrong, he is misled by his rhetorical instinct, as
when he makes the startling statement that the

Proem would have been better if it had consisted
of the head and the tail without the body. This
is perhaps about the most disturbing thing that
he says ; and, after all, if Thucydides had been
making a speech, even that criticism would have
been quite true. Dionysius did not understand
how history should be written ; but he did most
thoroughly understand the qualities of the austere
style in composition ; and he appreciated the best
qualities of Thucydides on the artistic side—his
consummate power in narrative, his fertile invention in the speeches, his dignity and unsurpassed
pathos. Modern editors, even Poppo, owe a debt
to him that they do not always acknowledge.

In the introduction to this book I have only
attempted to suggest lines of thought or investigation ; and so I have touched on those
points that seem to me, at least, to be the most
interesting. In writing the notes, my sole object
has been to arrive at a clear understanding of
the text myself, and to present what I take to
be the meaning as clearly as possible and in a
simple form. I could wish that my notes might
be thought illuminating ; but have no ambition
whatever that any one should think them learned.

CONTENTS

vii

INTRODUCTION

I. LIFE OF THUCYDIDES

THE sources of information about his life are :—
1. *References to himself* in the Histories. Owing
to his reserved and impersonal manner these
references are but few.
2. *Traditions.*
(*a*) Three ancient 'biographies,' two of which are
found in some MSS. of the Histories, while the third
is in the lexicon of Suidas. Of the first two the
longer is ascribed to an unknown Marcellinus[1]; but
it consists of three separate parts by different writers
arbitrarily joined together, perhaps in the sixth
cent. A.D. The shorter life, which is anonymous,
adds nothing of moment, and is a mere collection of
excerpts. The writer confuses the historian with
Thucydides son of Melesias. Suidas uses good

---

[1] Schumann, *de Marcellini quae dicitur vita Thucydidea*
(Colmar 1879), points out inconsistencies between §§ 26 and 46,
§§ 53 and 56, §§ 31–33 and 46, 56. Of the three parts the
first ends at § 44, the second at § 53. It is assumed that the
first part is by Marcellinus, and his date is placed by some in the
third, by others in the fifth, cent. A.D. Marcellinus cites good
authorities, e.g. Hellanicus, Androtion, Philochorus, Demetrius of
Phalerum, Hermippus, Polemon ; but it is thought that he did not
know these authors at first-hand.

authorities, but he too gives little that is not found in ' Marcellinus.'

(*b*) Statements about Thucydides' family, his death, and his tomb are found in Plutarch's *Life of Cimon* c. 4.

(*c*) A statement about his recall from exile and assassination occurs in Pausanias i. 23.

1. What we know of Thucydides from his own statements is as follows :—

He was the son of an Athenian citizen named Olorus. He had an interest in Athenian gold-mines in Thrace. He was in the full vigour of life, during the Peloponnesian War (431–404 B.C.), and was engaged throughout the period on his history. He suffered from the plague at Athens (430–428 B.C.). In 424 he was one of the ten strategi, and commanded a squadron off the coast of Thrace. He failed to relieve Amphipolis, which was pressed by Brasidas; but he succeeded in saving Eion. From 423 to 403 B.C. he was in exile—presumably in consequence of the loss of Amphipolis. During his exile he was able to observe all that was done by both sides.

From these facts we may draw the following inferences :—The youth and early manhood of Thucydides were passed during the period of Pericles' supremacy. We know from his book that he felt a profound admiration for Pericles as the πρῶτος ἀνήρ, though we should judge from his attitude towards the Athenian democracy that he cannot have approved of all Pericles' internal administration. The life of Pericles closed in 429 B.C. But alike in style and opinion Thucydides belongs always to the Periclean era.[1] Partly in consequence of his exile, and partly

---

[1] So far as concerns opinions, the fact is much the same with Sophocles, who lived till 406 B.C.

as the result of his detached, independent habit of thought, he remained outside the current of Athenian politics, and he was unaffected by the rapid progress of Attic style and thought. Thucydides wrote at a time when Attic prose was not yet fully developed; and during the long period of his exile he was shut out from participation in the intellectual life of Athens. Consequently he owes nothing to any one whose *floruit* falls later than the peace of Nicias, unless we except Antiphon, who equally with him belonged to the older school. It is difficult to realise that Lysias and Isocrates were already before the public when Thucydides was still writing.[1]

2. As for the three 'biographies,' their claims to authenticity have been disposed of by Petersen[2] and Wilamowitz.[3] All three consist of inferences drawn from the statements of Thucydides himself, from the unfinished condition in which he left his work, and from his style. One other important piece of evidence was available, and was used for at least as much as it was worth. The gravo of Thucydides stood hard by those of Cimon and his sister Elpinice in the quarter called Κοίλη, lying SW. of the Acropolis, and was seen by Plutarch there (*Cimon* 4). On the grave was the inscription Θουκυδίδης 'Ολόρου 'Αλιμούσιος ἐνθάδε κεῖται. From the inscription and the locality of his grave we know that he belonged to the deme Halimus, on the coast between Phalerum and Colias, and we may safely infer that his father Olorus must have been nearly connected with a

---

[1] Dionysius naturally connects Pindar, Aeschylus, Antiphon, and Thucydides as representative of the 'austere' style. See Jebb, *Attic Orators* i. 22.

[2] *De vita Thucydidis disputatio*, Dorpat 1873.

[3] 'Die Thukydideslegende,' *Hermes* 12 p. 326.

Thracian prince of that name, whose daughter
Hegesipyle was married to the great Miltiades and
became mother of Cimon. The latter inference is
stated as a fact by Plutarch, and may be accepted as
such. More doubtful is the statement of Pausanias,
that a decree for the recall of Thucydides from exile
was carried on the motion of one Oenobius. It
happens that the names Oenobius and Eucles occur as
those of father and son. A strategus named Eucles
was in command with Thucydides on the Thracian
coast; and it has been plausibly suggested that the
Oenobius who proposed the recall of Thucydides was
son of this strategus.

II. Predecessors and Contemporaries of Thucydides

1. It is true that Thucydides began to write before Attic prose style was completely developed, and that for the rules of composition—the grammar, as they say, of style—he is indebted to Gorgias, Antiphon, and Prodicus, and perhaps in a less degree to his own study of the poets. As regard peculiarities of his syntax, it is a mistake to suppose that his freedom is accounted for by calling him 'a primitive.' It is not true that he lived 'before the age of grammar' in any other sense than the statement is true of Xenophon or of any other of the classical writers. Of course Thucydides is answerable for his own manner of writing. That his genius was unique, without predecessor and not to be imitated, is best realised by comparing with his work the first two books of the *Hellenica*, in which Xenophon evidently meant to write like him. Xenophon is a writer possessed of great and varied talents ; but he is altogether unequal to the task of writing in the manner of his great predecessor[1]; and where so accomplished a man failed it is not to be supposed that any one else would have succeeded.

[1] Of course mere slavish copyists of Thucydides need not be considered.

2. The following dates will help us to understand where Thucydides comes in the history of Greek literature :—

(a) For *tragedy*, three convenient dates are—

B.C. 468, the first victory of Sophocles, aged 28.

458, production of the *Oresteia*, the last work of Aeschylus.

448, production of the *Alcestis* of Euripides, say half a century before Thucydides ceased writing.

(b) *Rhetoric and Sophistic*; here we may notice—

465, the rise of Rhetoric at Syracuse. Corax writes the first τέχνη, or treatise on Rhetoric, and distinguishes the parts proper to a speech —*introduction, discussion, peroration* (probably also *narration*, which follows the introduction).

455 onwards, *floruit* of Protagoras, the founder of the study of grammar.

435 onwards, *floruit* of Prodicus, first to lay stress on precision in the use of words.

427, Gorgias of Leontini visits Athens (perhaps not his first visit).

417, earliest *extant* speech of Antiphon (but he was born *c.* 480).

3. That Thucydides was well acquainted with the works of earlier writers on history we know from several statements of his : e.g. c. 97 τοῖς πρὸ ἐμοῦ ἅπασιν ἐκλιπὲς τοῦτο ἦν τὸ χωρίον κτλ. The opinion that he had formed of his predecessors was not high :—

(a) They possessed no critical faculty, and accepted traditions without taking the trouble to investigate their truth, c. 20.

(b) They were too anxious to please their audience, c. 21.

(c) They did not exclude myths, c. 22, 4.

4. Of these predecessors only Hellanicus[1] of Mitylene is mentioned by name. Referring to his Ἀττικὴ ξυγγραφή Thucydides remarks (c. 97) that his account of the period between the Persian and the Peloponnesian wars lacked chronological exactitude. In style he did not differ from the many other Ionian 'logographers' who lived earlier than or about the same time as himself. They all wrote simply, without artificial ornament, but with a certain attractive naïveté, to which Dionysius attributes the survival of their works to his own time. The scanty fragments of Hellanicus show that he touched on many matters that are mentioned also by Thucydides. The only other historical writer before Herodotus who is important to us is Hecataeus of Miletus, author of *Genealogies*[2] and a *Description of the Earth*. He was born about 540 B.C., and lived through the Persian wars. He was a great traveller; he treated the myths already in a rationalising spirit; and his style was clear and at times graceful.

5. *Herodotus and Thucydides*.

(a) Though Thucydides nowhere mentions Herodotus, it is impossible to avoid the conclusion that he was acquainted with his history.[3] Two of the errors corrected in i. c. 20 occur in Herodotus. The account of Cylon's conspiracy in c. 126, 7 is an amplified and corrected version of Herodotus v. 71,

---

[1] The quantity of the *i* in the name is doubtful.

[2] Compare the opening words of his *Genealogies*, quoted by Demetrius: 'Hecataeus of Miletus speaks as follows: I write these things as they seem true to me; for the accounts of the Greeks are many, and, as it seems to me, ridiculous.'

[3] The arguments of Dahlmann, K. O. Müller, and others of the older critics have been abundantly refuted by Krüger, Lemcke, etc.

the conduct of the Alcmaeonidae being put in a less favourable light by Thucydides. As regards the corrections made in c. 20 : they are (1) The idea that each of the Spartan kings gave two votes— this comes in Herod. vi. 57 ; the text there may mean that the kings jointly gave two votes, and not that each voted twice. (2) that a Πιτανάτης λόχος exists in Sparta—this is in Herod. ix. 53, who may have meant that the λόχος was a body raised only on one occasion, and not a permanent unit of the army.

The other mistake, namely that Hipparchus was older than Hippias and was actually tyrant at the time of his murder does *not* occur in Herodotus. He narrates the famous events in v. 55 f., but his version of the story tallies with Thucydides so far as the seniority and position of Hippias are concerned.

(*b*) *The Pentecontaetia* (c. 89) begins just where Herodotus ˙leaves off, and this can scarcely be a coincidence.

(*c*) Sparta demanded that Athens should 'drive out the curse.' Thucydides explains that this is an allusion to the attempt of Cylon to seize the tyranny, and he relates the story of the attempt. Athens retaliated by calling on Sparta to drive out her 'curse'; and this demand gives occasion to Thucydides to relate, at greater length than his ostensible purpose required, the treason and fate of Pausanias. This passage may very well have been intended to supplement Herodotus, whose history does not extend so far. The appendix about Themistocles (see below p. xxxii) in one aspect fulfils a similar object. But it is also intended, in all probability, as a correction. Herodotus belittles the services of Themistocles to Athens and to Greece,[1] and he emphasises the weak points in his moral character; he failed, in short, to appreciate Themistocles. Thucydides had not the moral bias of Herodotus. Faults of character he does not disguise; but they do not lead him to underestimate a man's intellectual greatness.

(*d*) On the famous sentence κτῆμα ἐς αἰεὶ μᾶλλον ἢ ἀγώνισμα ἐς τὸ παραχρῆμα ἀκούειν ξύγκειται the Scholiast remarks αἰνίττεται τὰ Μηδικὰ Ἡροδότου, 'a hint at the Persian wars of Herodotus.'

Lucian also states that Thucydides intended a criticism of Herodotus in this passage. Dionysius on the contrary considers that the λογογράφοι are meant; but it is not unlikely that Thucydides regarded Herodotus as one of these. What accounts for a criticism so unjust to Herodotus is that the two writers regard history from a wholly different standpoint. Philosophy and epic have never found each other congenial company.

---

[1] See especially Stein's note on Herod. viii. 4 ; and cf. the note on c. 14 § 3 below.

III. ANALYSIS OF THE FIRST BOOK (AFTER POPPO)

i. Προοίμιον, cc. 1–23 :—

1. The reason for writing this history : the war was ἀξιολογώτατος τῶν προγεγενημένων.

2. Importance of this war : proof drawn from a comparison of the early condition of Greece
   - (a) *before* τὰ Τρωϊκά, cc. 2–8.
   - (b) *during* τὰ   ,,   cc. 9–11.
   - (c) *after* τὰ   ,,   ˙cc. 12–19.

   (Cf. Schol. on c. 12 τριχῶς διεῖλε τὴν ἀρχαιολογίαν, εἰς τὰ πρὸ τῶν Τρωϊκῶν, εἰς αὐτὰ τὰ Τρωϊκά, εἰς τὰ ἐχόμενα αὐτῶν.)

3. Men too readily accept the accounts of poets and annalists, and admire τὰ ἀρχαῖα : character of the period, and the manner in which it is dealt with.

ii. *Causes of the war*, cc. 24–65; 88–118.

A. Causes alleged, cc. 24–66.

   1. τὰ Κερκυραϊκά, cc. 24–55.
      - (a) War between Corinth and Corcyra, cc. 24–31.
      - (b) *Speech of Corcyrean ambassador* at Athens, cc. 32–36.
      - (c) *Speech of Corinthian* in reply, c. 37–43.
      - (d) Intervention of Athens in the war, cc. 43–55.

Note on Analysis of the Proem.—The period of
Greek history that Thucydides contrasts with the
Peloponnesian War and considers insignificant is
denoted by the words τὰ πρὸ αὐτῶν καὶ τὰ ἔτι παλαίτερα
(c. 1). In the following chapters it is clearly
implied that under this period he includes (*a*) τὰ πρὸ
τῶν Τρωϊκῶν (c. 3); (*b*) τὰ Τρωϊκά (c. 4); (*c*) τὰ μετὰ
τὰ Τρωϊκά (c. 12). It is clear that the last phrase is
not meant to take in the years between the Persian
and Peloponnesian wars. For Thucydides was of
opinion that the history of all these periods was
obscure and difficult to discover (c. 1, § 2); and this
was certainly not his opinion about the history of the
years that separated the battle of Plataea from the
Peloponnesian War, which he has himself described in
the *Pentecontaetia.* But are the Persian wars included
in the 'obscure' and 'insignificant' period? Probably
not. Though the Persian wars form the subject of
c. 18, an attentive reading will show that this passage
(c. 18) stands outside the main line of the argument,
and forms a sort of appendix to what has preceded,
quite after the manner of Thucydides, who is much
given to after-thoughts.[1] The argument that has
run through all the Proem down to c. 17 is dismissed
for the time being in the last sentence of that
chapter—οὕτω πανταχόθεν ἡ Ἑλλὰς κατείχετο κτλ.
It will be noticed also that nothing is said about the
relative insignificance of the Persian wars in c. 18.
If Thucydides meant to include them in the period
described as τὰ μετὰ τὰ Τρωϊκά, the absence of any
such reference would be inexplicable. At c. 23 he
recurs to the Persian wars, and here only he
points out (*a*) that the struggle with Xerxes was

[1] Compare, for example, the relation of the passage in which
the last years of Themistocles are described to what precedes it.

the greatest effort of the Greeks before the Peloponnesian War, and (*b*) that even that struggle, in certain definite respects, does not compare with this war.[1]

i. The *Exordium* (Προοίμιον),[2] cc. 1–23.

1. The name Ἀρχαιολογία is often given to cc. 2–23. This name occurs in the scholium on c. 12. Dionysius (περὶ τοῦ Θουκ. χαρακτῆρος c. 20) hazards the startling criticism that it would have been better if the whole of the ἀρχαιολογία (cc. 2–21 init.) had been omitted: after οὔτε ἐς τὰ ἄλλα (c. 1 end) Thucydides should have continued οὔτε ὡς ποιηταὶ ὑμνήκασι etc. (c. 21). This criticism does not mean that Dionysius undervalued the ἀρχαιολογία. In the preceding chapter he well describes the *Exordium* as ἱστορία τις αὐτὴ καθ' αὑτήν. But all his criticism of Thucydides is for us vitiated because it is written entirely from the standpoint of a rhetorician. From the rhetorical standpoint a large part of the *Exordium* really is irrelevant; for the object of the exordium in oratory is to secure the goodwill of the audience and, if need be, to indicate the subject[3] of the speech.

2. Echoes of the Ἀρχαιολογία[4] are heard in several ancient authors. Though Aristotle nowhere

[1] This note was written without knowledge of Herbst's article in *Philologus* 38 ; he argues (*a*) that τὰ παλαιά occupy cc. 2–17, and (*b*) that the adverse criticism in cc. 20–22 applies only to the writers who dealt with τὰ παλαιά, and thus he excludes Herodotus from the authors to whom the adverse criticism applies. In his *first* point I believe that he is right.

[2] The title προοίμιον occurs first in Dionysius (reign of Augustus), and is applied also by Lucian.

[3] Contrast the praise that Dionysius bestows on the προοίμια of Lysias because they are entirely προσήκοντα (*de Lys.* c. 17).

[4] Schrader, *de archaeologia* Thuc. apud veteres auctoritate, Hamburg 1891.

mentions Thucydides by name, many passages in his works show that he was well acquainted with the Proem—and this fact lends additional importance to the differences in the accounts given of Harmodius and Aristogeiton in c. 19 and *Ath. Pol.* c. 18. Aristotle does not accept a statement made in the Ἀρχαιολογία without independent investigation. Thus Thucydides (c. 11) speaks of the wall built by the Greeks round Troy (see *Iliad* vii. 436 f. ποτὶ δ' αὐτὸν τεῖχος ἔδειμαν κτλ.); whereas Aristotle declared that this wall was a fiction ! Probably, however, Thucydides was really thinking here of some other wall, built at some time long anterior to that at which the action of the *Iliad* begins. Several passages in the *Politics* take us back to Thucydides (see note on c. 6 § 1 ; *Pol.* p. 1285 b ; 1271 a ; 1311 a). The only other writers of the first rank who are known to have made use of the Ἀρχαιολογία are Sallust and Lucian.

3. The historian's purpose is not to give a summary of early Greek history, but to bring out the transcendant greatness of this war by contrasting with it the previous doings of the Greeks. Hence we have here a compressed philosophy of early history rather than history proper. From the knowledge that he had gathered from poets and 'logographers' and increased by personal observation, he has by reflexion extracted the lesson that he seeks to convey. Thucydides is a philosopher as well as a historian. Having a passion for truth, he omits nothing that is part of the war, however trifling. But when an event has no significance from the philosopher's standpoint, he narrates it in a summary fashion, and lapses into the bare manner of an annalist. Dionysius finds fault with him for

dwelling on some events at undue length, and passing rapidly over others. The explanation of this
seeming disproportion is that it is not on the mere
occurrence that Thucydides will lavish all his powers.
He selects for full treatment what is somehow
typical or illustrative of opinion, of a people, or of a
movement. Even the most splendid descriptions,
the parts of his history that every one remembers,
such as the plague at Athens, the troubles at Corcyra,
the departure of the fleet for Sicily, the last battle in
the Great Harbour, are intended not for pleasure but
for edification : these are events importing something,
they 'end in a moral'[1] which, however, is more often
implied by the writer than expressed.

4. *The Subject.*—What Dionysius says about this
is to the following effect :[2] 'The first, and one may
say the most necessary, task for writers of history is
to choose a noble subject, and one pleasing to their
readers. In this Herodotus seems to me to have
succeeded better than Thucydides. He has produced
a national history of the conflict of Greeks and barbarians . . . Thucydides, on the other hand, writes of
a single war, and that neither glorious nor fortunate ;
one which, best of all, should not have happened, or
(failing that) should have been ignored by posterity,
and confined to silence and oblivion.' This criticism
suffers from the defect that mars all Dionysius' work
on Thucydides: it is written from the rhetorician's
standpoint, not from the historian's. Little is to be
gained, in any case, from a comparison of two histories
in respect of their subject matter ; but it must

---

[1] Thuc. would scarcely have assented to the well-known dictum
in Aristotle's *Poetics*, that Poetry is *more philosophical* than
History.

[2] The translation follows Prof. Rhys Roberts' version.

certainly be conceded that Herodotus had by far the
fairer (καλλίων) subject to treat than Thucydides.
Moreover, the latter certainly exaggerated the importance of the Peloponnesian War. At the very
beginning of it he formed the opinion that it would
prove ἀξιολογώτατον τῶν προγεγενημένων, more remarkable than any that preceded it. This anticipation was only confirmed by the course of the war;
events, as he holds, justified his forecast. Exaggeration there is; but we must not over-estimate it.

(a) The past fifty years had seen a great increase
in the strength of Athens and Sparta (c. 14, 3; 18,
3); Thucydides in making his estimate thinks only
of the strength of the Greek states involved, and of
the length of the war. He does not take into
consideration the magnitude of the interests involved.
He is fully aware that the very existence of the
Greeks had been involved in the Persian War. But
the war was short: for τὰ Μηδικά, τὸ Μηδικόν in this
connexion refer only to the conflict with Xerxes
(cf. c. 14, 2; 18, 2); and that struggle was decided
'by four battles.'

(b) In the Persian War a large part of the Greek
world had remained passive. In the Peloponnesian
War all the Greeks were conscious that they were
interested.

Still we can see that Thucydides was trying to
find reasons for magnifying his subject; and no
doubt, in doing this, he was influenced partly by
tradition and partly by the sophists, who were
careful to insist on the importance of the lesson they
had to teach and who were skilled in making the
weaker argument appear the stronger.

5. *Attitude towards Myth and Tradition.*—Thucydides is not the earliest author to throw doubt

on the myths. The 'logographers' until Herodotus had subordinated fact to myth. Herodotus adopts a tolerant attitude towards prehistoric traditions, neither affirming nor denying their truth: ἐγὼ δὲ περὶ μὲν τούτων οὐκ ἔρχομαι ἐρέων ὡς οὕτω ἢ ἄλλως κως ταῦτα ἐγένετο (i. 5) is what he says about them. But belief waned; philosophy declared against tradition; the sophists preached scepticism; Anaxagoras turned myth into allegory. Comedy did not shrink from parodies on the stories of the gods, and Euripides did at least as much to bring them into disrepute. Thucydides has no liking for τὸ μυθῶδες. Yet he does not reject myth entirely. Agamemnon and Pelops, Hellen, Pandion, Tereus are to him real persons; but he believes in the accounts of them only so far as the accounts appear to him credible. What is incredible is due to the poet's exaggeration and his desire to please. Sometimes, without expressing any opinion, he just gives the story: as in iv. 24 ἔστιν ἡ Χάρυβδις κληθεῖσα τοῦτο, ᾗ 'Οδυσσεὺς λέγεται διαπλεῦσαι.[1] Such cautious statements come when he can base no probable conclusion on the poet's words, and can apply no test to them. What is really scientific in his treatment of the myths is this, that he never draws any conclusion from them that would not be justified even on the assumption that they were altogether fictitious. For example, from the story of the siege of Troy he correctly infers the early method of warfare among the Greeks. The wealth of Corinth in early times, affirmed by the poets, is rightly accounted for (c. 13). The soundness of his method in deriving con-

[1] Cf. Herod. vii. 26 τὸν (Μαρσύαν) ὑπὸ Φρυγῶν λόγος ἔχει ὑπ' 'Απόλλωνος ἐκδαρέντα ἀνακρεμασθῆναι. Xen. Anab. I. ii. 8 ἐνταῦθα λέγεται 'Απόλλων ἐκδεῖραι Μαρσύαν.

clusions from Homer may best be tested by reading
cc. 9–11 from this point of view. The example of
Thucydides was not followed by the historians who
came after. Xenophon, indeed, kept on the safe
side by avoiding mythology altogether. But
Philistus, who is said to have imitated Thucydides,
introduced legends for their own sake. Ephorus did
not go back beyond the 'return of the Heraclidae';
but Theopompus, we are told, revelled in anecdotes,
fables, and local legends. In later ages only Polybius,
and apparently Posidonius, who numbered Cicero
among his pupils, and stood to Polybius in the same
relation as Xenophon to Thucydides, rigidly kept
legend out of history.[1]

6. *Composition of the history.*—Thucydides tells
us that he began to work on his history immediately
the war broke out. Was the first book as we
have it put into shape after the end of the *whole*
war, or was it written during the peace of Nicias?
In other words, are we dealing in the Proem with
the twenty-seven years' war or with the ten years'
(or, as it was called in later times, the 'Archidamian')
war only?[2] Round this question a controversy has
raged ever since 1846, when F. W. Ullrich published
a remarkable work,[3] in which with great skill he
sought to prove that Thucydides regarded the
war as terminated by the Peace of Nicias (421
B.C.), and wrote his history down to the middle of
the fourth book under that impression. We

---

[1] This is what we should expect of Posidonius, who was a 'man
of science' in the modern sense, and conducted his varied in-
vestigations in the Baconian spirit.

[2] Cf. v. 24 ταῦτα δὲ τὰ δέκα ἔτη ὁ πρῶτος πόλεμος ξυνεχῶς
γενόμενος γέγραπται.

[3] Whether the main thesis of this book is true or not, it marks
an epoch in the criticism of Thucydides.

cannot do more than indicate the nature of the
controversy. Classen's opinion was that the first
book was not written before the fall of Athens.
Among those who maintain that the history of the
Archidamian War was written during the Peace of
Nicias, there are some who think that the Ἀρχαιολογία
and Πεντηκονταετία (cc. 97–118) were added, and the
rest revised, after 404 B.C.[1] The problem admits of
no certain solution; but it is worthy of notice, that
the three speeches in this book that give forecasts of
the course which the war will take[2] almost certainly
contain some examples of 'prophecy after the event';
and at least the passages about ἐπιτείχισις and the
desertion of Athenian slaves seem to have been
written after the fortification of Decelea in 413 B.C.
It is to be noticed that some parts of the history
show much greater elaboration than others; and I
cannot help thinking that Thucydides worked on
different parts at different times. The famous
condensation of Thucydides in his highly wrought
passages gives an effect of great rapidity; but it is
not likely that this concentration of thought and
language was achieved rapidly. In the speeches,
in particular, we seem to have the work of a
laborious and careful writer; the very complication
of the grammar is the outcome not of haste, but of
elaboration. A hasty writer does not pen tortuous
periods.[3]

---

[1] G. Meyer, *Quibus temporibus*, etc. Ilfeld, 1880. The biblio-
graphy of this controversy is very extensive.
[2] Archidamus, cc. 80–83; Corinthian envoy, cc. 121–122;
Pericles, cc. 140–144.
[3] The unfinished eighth book is perhaps in its first state.
This is probably the simple reason why it contains no speeches.
The episode of the Four Hundred may be more finished than the
rest.

ii. Causes of the war : the *Pentecontaetia*.

1. As to the alleged causes of the war, Thucydides says (c. 23, 6) τὰς αἰτίας προύγραψα πρῶτον καὶ τὰς διαφοράς. The true cause, however, he adds, was the growth of Athenian power, which alarmed the Lacedaemonians.[1] The danger is put bluntly by the ephor Sthenelaidas (c. 86)—μὴ τοὺς ᾿Αθηναίους ἐᾶτε μείζους γίγνεσθαι. At c. 88 the true cause is related. The Lacedaemonians, we read, decided in favour of war, not so much because they were convinced by the arguments of their allies, but rather because they feared the Athenians would wax yet stronger. It is here that Thucydides goes at length into the ἀληθεστάτη πρόφασις, taking occasion to write the passage (cc. 89–118) known to ancient commentators as the πεντηκονταετία. The πεντηκονταετία was probably added after the main part of the book had been written, for in c. 146 we again read αἰτίαι αὗται καὶ διαφοραὶ ἐγένοντο πρὸ τοῦ πολέμου, and in this brief summary of the causes we miss a reference to the long account of the ἀληθεστάτη πρόφασις. First it occurred to Thucydides to insert after c. 88 an explanation how the Athenians came by the hegemony—ἦλθον ἐπὶ τὰ πράγματα ἐν οἷς ηὐξήθησαν. This explanation extends from c. 89 to c. 96. Then he decided that it was desirable to state what passed between the beginning of the Athenian hegemony and the outbreak of the war. At c. 23, where he first mentions the 'true cause,' he would probably have told us that he intended to go into the matter after stating the alleged causes, but at that point he

---

[1] Dionysius is mistaken when he blames Thuc. for not dealing with the 'true' cause first. When Thuc. wrote c. 23, 6 he considered that he had said enough about this cause. Later on he changed his opinion, and inserted the *Pentecontaetia*.

had not any intention of doing so, and at a later
time, when he decided to add the Pentecontaetia
after c. 88, he did not modify either c. 23 or
c. 146.

2. An indication is not wanting that the second
part of the *Pentecontaetia* (cc. 96–118) is added as an
after-thought to the first part. In c. 89, 2 the
account of the transference of the hegemony starts
from the battle of Mycale. Thucydides did not
then notice that he was about to deal with a period
bordering on fifty years, and so he started at the
natural place, viz. where Herodotus had left off.
Now when he has arrived at the end of his survey
of events down to the war, he recapitulates ; and in
order that he may be able to put the number of
years that he has covered in the two parts of the
Pentecontaetia at the round figure of fifty, he shifts
the *terminus a quo* from the battle of Mycale to the
retreat of Xerxes after Salamis. And he concludes
as if he had given a complete list of events from
the earlier date ! In reality, of course, his list
only begins with 476 B.C., the formation of the
confederacy of Delos (c. 98) ; contrast c. 118, 2
ταῦτα δὲ ξύμπαντα ὅσα ἔπραξαν οἱ Ἕλληνες, etc.

3. *The Pentecontaetia.*

The chief events noticed are as follows :—

B.C.

480 Battle of Salamis ; flight of Xerxes.

479 Battle of Mycale. Siege of Sestos.

478 Athens rebuilt and fortified.

477 The fleet under Pausanias takes Byzantium.

476 Treachery of Pausanias ; the hegemony
    transferred to Athens. Formation of the
    Confederacy of Delos.

475 Capture of Eion by Cimon.

B.C.

466 (very doubtful). Naxos reduced to subjection.

466 Battle of Eurymedon.

465 Death of Xerxes.
Revolt of Thasos.
Beginning of third Messenian War.

461 Athens breaks with Sparta, and forms alliance with Argos and Thessaly.

459 Athens helps Inaros in his revolt from Persia.

457 Reduction of Aegina.
Battles of Tanagra and Oenophyta.

453 Destruction of Athenian force in Egypt.

450 Five years' truce between Athens and Sparta.

449 War resumed against Persia.
Death of Cimon.

448 Sacred War in Phocis.

447 Battle of Coronea.

446 Revolt of Euboea and Megara.

445 Thirty years' peace.

440 Revolt of Samos and Byzantium.

Most of these dates are more or less uncertain, because Thucydides has not fixed the date of any of the events, except the thirty years' peace (ii. 2 τέσσαρα μὲν γὰρ καὶ δέκα ἔτη ἐνέμειναν αἱ τριακοντού- τεις σπονδαὶ αἳ ἐγένοντο μετ' Εὐβοίας ἅλωσιν), and the revolt of Samos and Byzantium (i. 115). And even the former event is not dated in the *Pentecontaetia*, but only fixed relatively to the other events. Indeed, we might almost apply to Thucydides the very criticism that he makes on Hellanicus, the one author who had dealt with the period: τούτων βραχέως τε καὶ τοῖς χρόνοις οὐκ ἀκριβῶς ἐπεμνήσθη. The chronology would have been much clearer if he had adopted fully the annalistic method, and catalogued the events under the names of the archons. We must suppose that Hellanicus had got some of the events in the wrong order.

A want of proportion has been noticed in this ἐκβολὴ τοῦ λόγου. Small and big events are treated alike ; nay, the battle of Eurymedon is dismissed in a sentence, whereas much more room is given to the Egyptian affair (c. 104 ; 109), and to the third Messenian War. Dionysius with good reason expresses surprise that Thucydides says so little of Eurymedon. No adequate account of the battle or battles existed, and it was left for Ephorus and Theopompus [1] to fill the gap.

4. The object for which the two sides fought is stated incidentally in several places ; nowhere more clearly than by Pericles in his speech before the war and by the Corinthian envoy at Sparta. We have in these the final speech delivered on either side before the war. But at Sparta—two votes were taken, one from the Lacedaemonians only (c. 87) and another shortly afterwards from the whole of the confederate cities. The Athenians were resolved μὴ ξὺν φόβῳ ἔχειν ἃ κέκτηνται. In his 'laconic' speech Sthenelaidas puts the matter from the Spartan point of view. The Peloponnesians determined to ensure their security from Athens and the liberation of those already 'enslaved.' In other words the Athenians fought for ἀρχή, the Peloponnesians— so they declared—for ἐλευθερία. The catch-word of the Peloponnesians brought them the εὔνοια of the

[1] The account of Ephorus is partly extant in the Στρατηγήματα of Polyaenus i. 34. Theopompus was the chief authority used by Plutarch in the *Life of Cimon.*

majority in the Greek world; but it did not bring
their confederacy any marked accession of support.
For the Greek world knew well enough that in
reality Sparta was the controlling force on the confederate side as soon as it came to war, and that
'both leaders,' as Herodotus puts it (vi. 98), 'were
fighting for empire.' The Athenians stated their
object frankly, too frankly indeed for their own
interests [1]; the Spartans, on the contrary, wrapped
up their selfish purpose in fine words, which did not
deceive many outside the Peloponnesian alliance.
The contrast between this Athenian candour and
this Spartan deception runs all through the earlier
part of Thucydides. From the beginning of the
κίνησις Sparta played the part of a hypocrite.
Xenophon, who seldom soars, who hated Thebes and
had strong reasons for taking a favourable view of
the Spartan ἀρχή, rises to impassioned eloquence
when, through the mouth of a Theban envoy at
Athens, he tells of the nemesis that followed on this
career of deception. Surely he was thinking of
Thucydides when he wrote of Sparta the burning
words : ἀλλὰ μὲν καὶ οὓς ὑμῶν ἀπέστησαν φανεροί
εἰσιν ἐξηπατηκότες· ἀντὶ γὰρ ἐλευθερίας διπλῆν αὐτοῖς
δουλείαν παρεσχήκασιν.

5. The end of Pausanias is narrated at greater
length than is warranted by the occasion. Ostensibly
Thucydides brings in the passage to explain what
was meant by τὸ τῆς Χαλκιοίκου ἄγος (c. 128). But
from the mass of detail that he gives, we can see that

---

[1] Compare the Melian dialogue, and the ὡς τυραννίδα ἤδη ἔχετε
αὐτὴν (i.e. τὴν ἀρχὴν) ἣν λαβεῖν μὲν ἄδικον δοκεῖ εἶναι, ἀφεῖναι
δὲ ἐπικίνδυνον (ii. 63) with the speech of the Mitylenaeans,
especially μὴ ξὺν κακῶς ποιεῖν αὐτοὺς (τοὺς "Ελληνας) μετ'
'Αθηναίων ἀλλὰ ξυνελευθεροῦν (iii. 13).

he must have gained new information on the subject
from Spartan sources. This information he is
anxious to give to his countrymen. But, if the
account of Pausanias' end is lengthened out until
it becomes practically independent of the main
narrative, what are we to say of the appendix about
Themistocles? This is wholly irrelevant; and one
of the motives for bringing it in is plainly revealed
in the sentence with which the passage concludes :
τὰ μὲν κατὰ Παυσανίαν . . καὶ Θεμιστοκλέα, λαμπροτάτους
γενομένους τῶν καθ' ἑαυτοὺς Ἑλλήνων οὕτως ἐτελεύτησεν.
Having arrived at the death of Pausanias, Thucydides
wanted to round off the passage by relating the last
events in the life of his great contemporary.

The chronology and the details of the flight of
Themistocles are uncertain. Plutarch (Themistocles
27) tells us that according to Ephorus and many
other authors Themistocles went to the court of
Xerxes. But Thucydides and one of the λογογράφοι
(Charon of Lampsacus) represent him as arriving
at the Persian court after the death of Xerxes.
Plutarch finds the dates as given by Thucydides
more probable; but he says they are not settled.
The death of Xerxes is placed in 465 B.C. But
Thucydides (c. 137, 2) says that the Athenian fleet
was blockading Naxos when Themistocles crossed
the Aegean. Unfortunately the date of the siege of
Naxos can only be inferred from c. 99. But it is
quite plain that Thucydides supposed it to have
occurred a considerable time before the revolt of
Thasos and the Athenian disaster at Drabescus (c.
100). Now we happen to know from iv. 102 that
this last affair occurred twenty-nine years before the
foundation of Amphipolis, i.e. before 437 B.C.
Therefore the disaster at Drabescus happened about

465 B.C., or about the time of Xerxes' death. It is impossible that the siege of Naxos can have happened so late as 466 B.C. ; and so Themistocles must have fled from Argos some time before the death of Xerxes. Thucydides had obtained his information from the relatives of Themistocles (c. 138, 6) ; and it is evident that we cannot rely on the details. For example, there is no ground for supposing that the letter of Themistocles[1] (c. 137, 4) is genuine. Evidently Thucydides had no Persian source of information to draw upon (cf. c. 138, 1 βασιλεὺς δέ, ὡς λέγεται). All indications point to 470 B.C. as the date of Themistocles' flight[2] ; and if this be so, we must place the reduction of Naxos in that year, and conclude that Thucydides is wrong in saying that Artaxerxes was king when Themistocles arrived at the court.

iii. *The two Debates at Sparta.*

1. The influence of Corinth in the Peloponnesian league is so great that she has it in her power to force the hand even of Sparta. A bustling, trading city, in close contact with the outer world, she contrasted strongly with the supine, self-centred leader of the league ; and, as the natural champion of the more active members of the league, and especially of the cities on the coast, she was bent on compelling Sparta to show herself determined to counteract the aggressive spirit of Athens.[3] Her

[1] The text of it differs in Plutarch, but the drift of the letter is the same.

[2] Wilamowitz, *Aristoteles und Athen* i. 144 f. Themistocles, as W. points out, cannot have been regarded as a traitor up to the time when the *Persae* was produced, i.e. 472 B.C. It is unfortunate that the date of the *Prometheus Vinctus* is uncertain : Hermann's opinion that 1068–70 τοὺς προδότας γὰρ μισεῖν ἔμαθον κτλ. allude to Themistocles is highly probable.

[3] Already in 524 B.C. Corinth had impelled Sparta, though reluctant, to send an expedition against Samos. Corinth was then

hatred of Athens was traditional. It arose, according to Thucydides, out of an event connected with Megara, and at a time when Corinth and Megara were enemies (c. 103, 4). After Megara revolted from Athens in 445 B.C., she naturally threw in her lot with Corinth, and actually fought on her side in the battle of Sybota (c. 114). The Megarian decree was, of course, a menace to Corinthian trade. It is strange that no direct allusion to Megara is put into the mouth of the Corinthian speaker in either of the two debates at Sparta. Already during the Persian wars Corinth had opposed Athenian policy; she had been especially violent in her opposition to Themistocles before the battle of Salamis. The opposition may, even so early as that, have been a tradition; but it may be that the notices of it in Herodotus are to some extent influenced by later events, and especially by that later-born σφοδρὸν μῖσος of Corinth towards Athens, the origin of which is told by Thucydides.

2. How far do the speeches stated to have been delivered in these debates tell us what was really said?[1] Take the first debate. An Athenian envoy must, of course, have intervened in it. But we cannot suppose that he was capable of delivering, on the spur of the moment, any such speech as Thucydides puts into his mouth. Neither can he have used arguments of such a general character as

influenced by anxiety about her trade. She again opposed Sparta, and gained the support of the Peloponnesian allies, when there was a project at Sparta to restore the tyrant Hippias.

[1] Of the speeches in general Thuc. says he gives τὴν ξύμπασαν γνώμην τῶν ὡς ἀληθῶς λεχθέντων. The ξύμπας, which is so often contrasted with καθ' ἕκαστον, shows that we must not expect that the separate arguments he puts into the mouth of a speaker shall in any case be those that were actually used by him.

are attributed to him. He must have replied with definite answers to the particular complaints of the previous speakers. Thucydides has elevated the discussion into a conflict of opposing ideals and incompatible temperaments. We are reminded of the rhetorical battles in Euripides, where the combatants are really embodied abstractions—Theseus for Λόγος δίκαιος, Herald for Λόγος ἄδικος. Of the several attacks delivered by the allies in this battle of words we witness only the last. It is directed at the policy both of Athens and of Sparta. And so it must needs be repulsed by an Athenian and a Spartan orator. Neither of them alludes to the particular grievances laid before the assembly by the representatives present. And even among the general and common complaints only one, that referring to the restriction of the right of litigation which was imposed by Athens on her allies, is answered.

At the time of the second debate no Athenian envoys were conveniently present in Sparta. Had Xenophon been describing the scene, no doubt he would have recorded the speech delivered by the representative of some city opposed to the war, an Elean perhaps or Mantinean. Opposition there was to the declaration of war, and it was not merely silent (c. 119). But Thucydides is too philosophical to trouble himself with the words of those whose actions did not count in the result. Therefore in the scene as he represents it, the speaking parts are confined to the leading characters; the others remain silent, and so the speech of the Corinthian is not answered. But if Thucydides was to make clear the attitude of Athens, a reply to the speech was imperatively called for. Accordingly, as the reply could not be given as part of the debate at Sparta,

it is put into the mouth of Pericles, who spoke at
Athens; and, although he cannot in reality have
known just what the Corinthian envoy had said, he
is represented as replying to his forecast of the war
step by step.   This speech of Pericles is singled out
from among many that were delivered at the same
meeting (c. 139).

IV. Mind and Style

It is very difficult to arrive at a just appreciation of a genius so complex as Thucydides; and to deal adequately with so large a subject in a few pages is of course impossible. All that we can attempt here is to lay down lines of approach towards an understanding of his excellences. His faults are clear enough and strike even superficial readers who remain blind to the magnificence of his descriptions, the appropriateness and depth of his moral maxims, the pathos that so impressed the Greek critics, and even his originality. The judgment of Dionysius was warped by his rhetorical training. Yet on the whole no fairer criticism of Thucydides' style has been penned than a passage in the περὶ τοῦ Θουκυδί-δους χαρακτῆρος[1] in which he rises for a moment above details and takes a comprehensive view of the matter. After blaming Thucydides for his frequent use of the 'figures of language' (see p. xlv), Dionysius says :—

'What is most conspicuous in him and most characteristic is the attempt to express the greatest number of facts in the smallest number of words, to

---

[1] This passage is repeated in the second letter of Dionysius to Ammaeus, which may be consulted in Prof. Rhys Roberts' edition. Cf. Marcellinus §§ 50, 51.

combine many thoughts, and to leave a listener in the lurch while he is expecting to hear something further: in consequence his brevity becomes obscure. Putting the matter shortly, I say that there are four instruments by which Thucydides fashions his style : the use of poetical words, variety of construction, roughness of composition, brevity of narrative. The "colours" of his style are harshness, succinctness, pungency, austerity, gravity, vehemence—but above all these the power of stirring the emotions.'

The *brevity* of Thucydides[1] manifests itself in various ways. It is much more frequent with him than with other authors to leave words to be 'supplied' from the context : e.g. c. 70 πεφυκέναι ἐπὶ τῷ μήτε αὐτοὺς ἔχειν ἡσυχίαν μήτε τοὺς ἄλλους ἀνθρώπους ἐᾶν (sc. ἔχειν αὐτήν) ; c. 90 ἠξίουν αὐτοὺς μὴ τειχίζειν, ἀλλὰ καὶ . . ὅσοις ξυνειστήκει (sc. τὰ τείχη) ξυγκαθελεῖν. This is the grammatical figure called ἀπὸ κοινοῦ. But often a whole clause is condensed into a single word, generally an adverb, as in c. 21 τὰ πολλὰ ὑπὸ χρόνου αὐτῶν ἀπίστως (= οὕτως ὥστε ἄπιστα εἶναι) ἐπὶ τὸ μυθῶδες ἐκνενικηκότα ; c. 140 ἐνδέχεται τὰς ξυμφορὰς τῶν πραγμάτων οὐχ ἧσσον ἀμαθῶς (= ὥστε μὴ προμαθεῖν αὐτὰς τοὺς ἀνθρώπους) χωρῆσαι. As for *obscurity* it results most commonly from compression, and especially from his habits of omitting a step in an argument, and of suggesting ideas without developing them. For a clause omitted take c. 120 χρὴ γὰρ τοὺς ἡγεμόνας . . τὰ κοινὰ προσκοπεῖν, which follows immediately on τοὺς Λακεδαιμονίους . . οὐκ ἂν ἔτι αἰτιασαίμεθα ὡς οὐ καὶ

---

[1] e.g. Cicero, *de Oratione* ii. 56 *ita creber est rerum frequentia ut verborum prope numerum sententiarum numero consequatur.* Every one knows Quintilian's *densus et brevis et semper instans sibi Thucydides.*

αὐτοὶ ἐψηφισμένοι τὸν πόλεμόν εἰσι καὶ ἡμᾶς ἐς τοῦτο νῦν ξυνήγαγον. Between the two sentences, in order to complete the sense, we have to supply: 'In acting thus they are only doing their duty.' This kind of ellipse is, of course, especially frequent with γάρ. The other principal cause of obscurity is touched on under the section on the speeches.

Examples of *Poetical* and *Ionic* forms and words :[1] pref. pass. 3rd plur. in -αται, pluperf. in -ατο, found also in Herod. ; ἐπειρασάμην beside ἐπειράθην, epic, Herod. ; ἐμέμφθην beside ἐμεμψάμην, poets, Herod. ; ἀλκή, poets, Herod., Xen. ; ξυμφορά = 'occurrence,' drama, Herod. ; ὁμαιχμία Herod. ; τιμωρία = 'help,' Herod., Hippocrates ; πολέμιος = 'belonging to war,' Herod., Hippocrates ; νεοχμοῦν Herod. ; ὀτρύνω poets, Herod. ; φονεύω, Herod., Xen. ; Τρῳάς, Ἑλλάς as adjectives for Τρωικός, Ἑλληνικός, poets, Herod. Among *poetical constructions*[2] may be mentioned the dative with verbs of motion, giving the goal, as c. 13 ὅτε Ἀμεινοκλῆς Σαμίοις ἦλθε ; dat. with ἐπί, of hostile intent, c. 102 τὴν γενομένην ἐπὶ τῷ Μήδῳ ξυμμαχίαν ; dat. of agent with other tenses than perf. and pluperf. see c. 44, 7 ; 51, 3 ; neut. plur. of adjectives and especially of verbal in -τέος as predicate ; neut. sing. of partic. with article as abstract noun, e.g. τὸ δεδίος c. 36 ; τὸ βουλόμενον c. 90.

The rough, archaic style of composition (τὸ τραχὺ τῆς ἁρμονίας) allows of harsh sounds and hiatus, arranges the words in a sentence according to their importance, without regard to the ear,[3] 'so that each word may be seen conspicuously'; does not strive

---

[1] O. Diener, *de Sermone Thucydidis*, Lips. 1889.
[2] C. F. Smith, 'Some poetical constructions in Thuc.' *Am. Journ. of Phil.* vol. xxv. p. 61.
[3] Blass, *Attische Beredsamkeit* 222.

after a rounded period, but places the short clauses
side by side. All prettiness, τὸ κομψόν, is foreign to
its nature, and so when Thucydides indulges in the
mere mechanical 'figures of language,' πάρισα and
παρομοίωσις (p. xlvi) he is making a concession to a
prevalent bad fashion. As a rule it is not by sentences,
but by the effective position of single words that he
strives to give dignity to his style. Closely bound
up with the prevailing disregard of sound and form
is the *variation of construction* that appears in many
forms. A characteristic example occurs already in
c. 3, 2, where the moods change rapidly (see note).
The co-ordination of dissimilar clauses is very
common, as in c. 1 ὅτι . . ᾖσαν καὶ . . ὁρῶν. The
thought is more important to him than the *form*.
From this preference of the sense arise the numerous
small irregularities of grammar such as (*a*) the
enlargement or contraction of the subject in the
course of a sentence, as in c. 49, 4 ; and (*b*) the
'anacoluthic' δέ, generally after a parenthesis, as in
c. 11 ἐπειδὴ δὲ . . ἐκράτησαν . . φαίνονται δ' οὐδ'
ἐνταῦθα κτλ.; but sometimes without parenthesis, as
in ii. 65 ἐπεί τε ὁ πόλεμος κατέστη, ὁ δὲ φαίνεται καὶ ἐν
τούτῳ προγνοὺς τὴν δύναμιν. (*c*) Here we may place
the habit of joining two forms of construction as in
c. 72 τῶν δὲ Ἀθηναίων ἔτυχε γὰρ πρεσβεία . .
παροῦσα, καὶ ὡς ἤσθοντο κτλ.; c. 14 ὀψέ τε ἀφ' οὗ . .
ἔπεισεν . . τὰς ναῦς ποιήσασθαι. Constructions of the
kind called κατὰ σύνεσιν are naturally frequent. A
good example of these may be found in the freedom
with which a nominative partic. is used, where
strictly a gen. abs. is required, and conversely a gen.
abs. for the nom. or other case: contrast, for instance,
iii. 34 ὁ δὲ Πάχης προκαλεσάμενος ἐς λόγους Ἱππίαν . . ὁ
μὲν (Hippias) ἐξῆλθε παρ' αὐτόν, ὁ δὲ ἐκεῖνον ἐν φυλακῇ

I   ´B2

ἀδέσμῳ εἶχεν, with iii. 13 βοηθησάντων δὲ ὑμῶν προθύμως, πόλιν προσλήψεσθε, or i. 114 διαβεβηκότος Περικλέους . . ἠγγέλθη αὐτῷ.

As an illustration of the 'colours of style' enumerated by Dionysius, we shall refer to one sentence only. It contains all the qualities mentioned—disregard of smoothness, a pregnant brevity, incisiveness, grave dignity ; and for its tragic solemnity it could not have been intensified by the addition of any detail. Any one can test Dionysius' list by thinking over c. 23, 2 οὔτε γὰρ πόλεις . . . στασιάζειν.[1]

[1] Especially the emphasis thrown on the long words ἠρημώθησαν, ἰλισκόμεναι, ἀντιπολεμούντων, στασιάζειν, and for the intrusion of the parenthesis which breaks the symmetry should be noticed. Thuc. makes his greatest effect by apparently simple means.

V. The Speeches

1. Already in ancient times Thucydides is commended as the first historian who composed true speeches—δημηγορίαι.[1] He has told us what method he followed: 'I have made every speaker say what seemed to me most appropriate on each occasion, taking care to keep as close as I could to the spirit of what was actually said.' If it is asked why Thucydides inserts these set speeches, the true answer is probably that oratory was in his day advancing rapidly in importance and in technical excellence, and that the δημηγορία, the λόγος, held in Athenian life a place as important as that held by the πρᾶξις or ἔργον. Already in Herodotus the persons speak, but in an informal, conversational manner. Direct speech in history was but a legacy received from epic poetry. Naturally, influence and power of political discourse were enormously enhanced by the appearance of rhetoric. The age of Pericles did not regard Themistocles as a great orator (see c. 138, 3); even Pericles did not, so Plutarch says, write out his speeches for the assembly; but he was probably the last great statesman who did not do so. Rhetoric found direct speech already existing in Ionic history;

---

[1] αἱ δημηγορίαι αὐτοῦ, ἐν αἷς οἴονταί τινες τὴν ἄκραν τοῦ συγγρα-φέως εἶναι δύναμιν Dionys. περὶ τοῦ Θουκ. χ. c. 34.

and naturally it exerted as powerful an influence in the domain of Attic history as it exerted on Attic oratory.

2. In manner, too, Herodotus had followed the usage of epic. His speeches and dialogues have the simplicity and grace of the Homeric discourses; even the longer ones 'have the conversational tone rather than the rhetorical.'[1] It cannot be said that there is no display of rhetoric in the discourses of Herodotus; but it is quite clear that his preference was for the ample colloquial manner of the epic heroes. He professes to give the actual words of the speakers; and in the main he makes them talk not that he may present in this way an analysis of motives, but that he may diversify the narrative and retain the attention of his listeners. Thucydides was the first writer to introduce δημηγορίαι proper into history; and the writers on rhetoric regarded him, and him alone, as an orator as well as a historian, thus bearing emphatic testimony to the importance of his speeches in the history of their art.

3. The speeches in Thucydides occupy more than a fifth of the whole work. The occasion chosen for their introduction is always a notable conjuncture in the development of the war; not *necessarily*, as Sir R. Jebb points out, an occasion of much importance in relation to the war; but always, as we should expect to find in Thucydides, the occasion of some event that he can treat as 'typical of its kind.' In the first book, indeed, all the occasions on which a speech is inserted are in themselves of the first importance. But here, as always, he makes the speeches the means of affording us an insight into the inner motives of action, or into the character and policy of

[1] Jebb in *Hellenica* p. 169.

whole states or of political parties. He condenses in a single speech or in the speeches of opposed orators all the reflexions that *he* thinks appropriate to the situation ; and thus the speakers become personifications of that political idea which inspired them. The words in which they express the idea are for the most part supplied by Thucydides [1] ; the form, the topics, and the structure alike are largely dependent on the popular rhetoric of the day.

4. As regards the form, it is easy to blame Thucydides for the excessive use of the rhetorical figures of language. These are the σχήματα Γοργίεια remarked by the Scholiasts and the ancient commentators in general ; μειρακιώδεις σχηματισμοι and θεατρικὰ σχήματα Dionysius calls them. The commonest of these figures is, of course, the *antithesis* : a conspicuous example of its use is c. 70. Now it is hardly reasonable to complain just because this figure is frequent in Thucydides ; and perhaps nobody would do so had it not received a bad name as one of the 'Gorgian' tricks. Thucydides deals with a subject that is full of contrasts. There is the contrast between Ionian and Dorian, Athenian and Spartan ; between pretence and reality, promise and fulfilment; and Thucydides was bound to bring these contrasts out. But in the speeches where all the 'figures' are naturally most frequent, he sometimes lets a feeling

[1] Poppo's statement has not been improved upon and is specially appropriate to the speeches of the first book : 'Consilium Thucydidis in eo positum erat, ut orationes vere habitas imitarentur et vitam publicam exprimerent. Continentur enim iis aut descriptiones civitatum formarum atque commodorum et incommodorum ex iis orientium aut adumbrationes ingeniorum atque morum populorum et virorum principum, aut expositiones cur aliquid suscipiendum et quomodo laetus eius eventus sperandus . . . omnino, quae commentatus est scriptor de rerum rationibus hominumque consiliis.'

for antithesis carry him into verbal contrasts that
contain little or no substance. It was the fashion
of the day, and Thucydides followed it at times only
too faithfully.[1] Unfortunately, too, he does not
always rest content with the antithetic form pure
and simple. With antithesis he occasionally combines those less desirable 'figures,' such as *paromoiosis*
or jingle in the sound of whole clauses,[2] and *parisosis*
or equality in the length of clauses; but such
trivialities are less common in him than in Antiphon,
for example, or Isocrates, and they are certainly not
numerous enough to warrant us in saying that
Thucydides deliberately aimed at them. It would
be fairer to say that he does not always avoid them.
One of the minor figures, *paronomasia*, or jingle in
the sound of words,[3] is undoubtedly common even in
the descriptions. But it must be remembered that
in all Greek literature, from Homer downwards,
this *paronomasia* is common.[4] The practice is so
notorious and constant that it may be enough here
to point out that ὀδύσσομαι occurs in Homer only and
always as in *paronomasia* with the name Ὀδυσσεύς.[5]
On the whole, in spite of Gorgias, the minor 'figures

<hr/>

[1] Dionysius, as Blass says, declares the figures to be unworthy
of the grave, austere dignity of Thucydides. They can hardly be
excused *altogether* on the ground that fashion required them.
This excuse makes the κτῆμα ἐς αἰεί into an ἀγώνισμα ἐς τὸ
παραχρῆμα ! On the other hand, I do not think we can say that
antithesis is foreign to the nature of the grave style. We must
distinguish between this and the minor σχήματα λέξεως.

[2] e.g. c. 70 καὶ παρὰ δύναμιν τολμηταί | καὶ παρὰ γνώμην
κινδυνευταί.

[3] e.g. c. 33 καὶ προεπιβουλεύειν αὐτοῖς μᾶλλον ἢ ἀντεπιβουλεύειν.

[4] Nieschke, *de Thucydide Antiphontis discipulo*, Münden 1885.

[5] *Il.* iv. 140 Πρόθοός θοός; but by no means only with proper
names: e.g. *Il.* xviii. 541 πίειραν ἄρουραν εὐρεῖαν : *Od.* ix. 415
ὠδίνων ὀδύνῃσιν.

of language' are no commoner in Thucydides than
they are in Homer. Of course Gorgias did not
invent the figures; he first taught them. Suidas
mentions books περὶ τῶν παρ' Ὁμήρῳ σχημάτων ῥητο-
ρικῶν: Aristotle in the *Rhetoric* goes to Homer (*Il.*
ix. 526) for his example of *paromoiosis*: and in the
tract *de vita et poesi Homeri*, attributed to Plutarch,
several examples of the minor figures are collected
from the *Iliad* and *Odyssey*. As for the other class of
'figures,' the figures of thought, such as irony, the
rhetorical question, asyndeton, anaphora, they are so
seldom used by Thucydides that they do not count
as characteristic of his style.

5. In the choice and arrangement of his subject
matter he is never the slave of rhetoric. He gives
us, of course, the ordinary *exordium* [1] (προοίμιον),
argumentatiu (ἀγῶνες), and *peroratio* (ἐπίλογος). He
uses too the rhetorical commonplaces, such as *honour*
(τὸ καλόν), *interest* (τὸ συμφέρον), *justice* (τὸ δίκαιον);
and in handling these he has always at command an
extraordinary abundance of arguments and aphorisms
that surpasses anything to be found elsewhere in
Greek oratory. His power of invention wrings from
Dionysius an emphatic eulogy; to us it becomes at
times actually wearisome,[2] the same materials being
grouped again and again in different shapes, as in a
kaleidoscope.

Ipsae illae contiones, says Cicero of Thucydides'
speeches, *ita multas habent obscuras abditasque sententias,
vix ut intelligantur*. In the speeches much more often
than the narrative, ἀσαφὲς γίγνεται τὸ βραχύ. The
sentences are overloaded with ideas, they are compli-

---

[1] This may be omitted to produce an effect of abruptness and
vehemence, as in the case of Sthenelaidas' 'laconic' speech, c. 86.
[2] Cf. Mahaffy, *Greek Prose Literature*.

cated by the intrusion of numerous clauses which stand in various relations to the main construction. It is not that he is incapable of writing clearly when he comes to write a speech ; nothing, for example, could be more clearly expressed than the last speech in his history, the magnificent address delivered by Nicias during the retreat from Syracuse. But unfortunately he shows too often a preference for the complicated over the simple form of expression ; he likes to write in long, straggling, ill-balanced periods that contrast strangely with their machine-turned antithesis, and the rhymes and jingles in the clauses.

VI. Manuscripts and Text

The seven MSS. that are of importance for determining the text of Thucydides fall into two groups:—

1. *Laurentianus*, C, in the Laurentian library at Florence, on parchment, 27 lines to the page. Date between 900 and 950, the oldest MS., and, on the whole, the best. The first six pages, down to c. 15, 1 νήσους are by a later hand.

Monacensis, G; in Munich library, quarto on paper. 13th century. The upper margin of the page is destroyed; hence the sign [G] means that in the place referred to, the reading of this MS. is lost.

2. *Vaticanus*, B; in the Vatican library; small folio on parchment, 30 to 32 lines on a page. 11th century. Not decisively inferior to C, but with its companions derived, in the first two books, from a different recension of the text. From iii. to vi. c. 92 it does not differ nearly so often (the proportion is 1 to 4) from the C group, and is probably a descendant of the same recension. From vi. c. 92 to the end B differs widely from *all* the other MSS.

Augustanus, F, large folio on parchment. Dated 1301. Formerly at Augsburg, now at Munich.

Cisalpinus or *Italus*, A; at Paris, large folio on parchment. 11th or 12th century. It was lost from 1815 to 1869, and rediscovered by R. Prinz in the National Library.

Palatinus, E, at Heidelberg; large folio on parchment. 11th century. The only good MS. that contains the two Lives.

Britannicus, M, in the British Museum, quarto on parchment, 27 lines to the page. 11th century. This MS. belongs on the whole to the second group, but it often agrees with the first against BAEF.

In fixing the text, the readings of B and C are of course the most important. It happens that C is more often confirmed by the text of Dionysius than B; and there is a suspicion that readings peculiar to B are sometimes the result of conjecture. In a passage where CG have one reading, BAEFM another, it is best to choose the reading of CG if both are equally acceptable; and if, as sometimes happens, E or M agrees with CG, the claims of the reading to preference are strengthened.

The other sources from which the text can be occasionally corrected are the long quotations in Dionysius, the Scholia (only a small portion of which are of any considerable authority), and the numerous citations from Thucydides or else imitations in later writers, rhetoricians, grammarians and the Scholia to Homer, Aristophanes, and other authors. There is no sufficient reason for supposing that the MSS. of Thucydides are specially corrupt. There are very numerous small mistakes; the insertion or omission of short words, such as τέ, δέ, ὅτι, is frequent. But the MSS., are an average lot; not one of them is of great merit—there is nothing like the Bodleian Plato, for example, or the Paris *Anabasis*; but we may be confident that they yield between them a very fair text exhibiting in general only those forms

of error that become familiar to readers of Greek
manuscripts. The present editor, at least, readily
confesses that a larger acquaintance with MSS. has
caused him to withdraw entirely from the opinion of
those who detect incessant interpolations and whole-
sale corruptions in these very ordinary MSS.

ΘΟΥΚΥΔΙΔΟΥ

ΙΣΤΟΡΙΩΝ Α

Θουκυδίδης Ἀθηναῖος ξυνέγραψε τὸν πόλεμον 1
τῶν Πελοποννησίων καὶ Ἀθηναίων, The reason for
ὡς ἐπολέμησαν πρὸς ἀλλήλους, writing this history. This
ἀρξάμενος εὐθὺς καθισταμενου καὶ war is greater than any that
5 ἐλπίσας μέγαν τε ἔσεσθαι καὶ ἀξιο- preceded it.
λογώτατον τῶν προγεγενημένων, τεκμαιρόμενος
ὅτι ἀκμάζοντές τε ἦσαν ἐς αὐτὸν ἀμφότεροι
παρασκευῇ τῇ πάσῃ καὶ τὸ ἄλλο Ἑλληνικὸν
ὁρῶν ξυνιστάμενον πρὸς ἑκατέρους, τὸ μὲν
10 εὐθύς, τὸ δὲ καὶ διανοούμενον. κίνησις γὰρ 2
αὕτη μεγίστη δὴ τοῖς Ἕλλησιν ἐγένετο καὶ
μέρει τινὶ τῶν βαρβάρων, ὡς δὲ εἰπεῖν καὶ
ἐπὶ πλεῖστον ἀνθρώπων. τὰ γὰρ πρὸ αὐτῶν 3
καὶ τὰ ἔτι παλαίτερα σαφῶς μὲν εὑρεῖν διὰ
15 χρόνου πλῆθος ἀδύνατα ἦν, ἐκ δὲ τεκμηρίων

c. 1. 1—c. 15. 1 κατεστρέφοντο suppl. c foll. ii–vii
c. 1. 1—c. 3. 2 τοῦτο suppl. m fol. i
7. ἦσαν Fg Schol. Plat. *Rep.* 449 A Suid. Phot. : ἦσαν cett.
11. δὴ μεγίστη F Dion. Hal.   15. ἀδύνατον F¹G Dion. Hal.

Ⅲ

ὧν ἐπὶ μακρότατον σκοποῦντί μοι πιστεῦσαι
ξυμβαίνει οὐ μεγάλα νομίζω γενέσθαι οὔτε
2 κατὰ τοὺς πολέμους οὔτε ἐς τὰ ἄλλα. φαίνεται γὰρ ἡ νῦν Ἑλλὰς καλουμένη οὐ πάλαι
The greatness of βεβαίως οἰκουμένη, ἀλλὰ μετανα- 5
this war will
appear from a στάσεις τε οὖσαι τὰ πρότερα καὶ
consideration of
early Greece. ῥᾳδίως ἕκαστοι τὴν ἑαυτῶν ἀπολεί-
ποντες βιαζόμενοι ὑπό τινων αἰεὶ πλειόνων.
2 τῆς γὰρ ἐμπορίας οὐκ οὔσης, οὐδ' ἐπιμιγνύντες
ἀδεῶς ἀλλήλοις οὔτε κατὰ γῆν οὔτε διὰ 10
θαλάσσης, νεμόμενοί τε τὰ αὑτῶν ἕκαστοι
ὅσον ἀποζῆν καὶ περιουσίαν χρημάτων οὐκ
ἔχοντες οὐδὲ γῆν φυτεύοντες, ἄδηλον ὂν ὁπότε
τις ἐπελθὼν καὶ ἀτειχίστων ἅμα ὄντων ἄλλος
ἀφαιρήσεται, τῆς τε καθ' ἡμέραν ἀναγκαίου 15
τροφῆς πανταχοῦ ἂν ἡγούμενοι ἐπικρατεῖν, οὐ
χαλεπῶς ἀπανίσταντο, καὶ δι' αὐτὸ οὔτε μεγέθει
3 πόλεων ἴσχυον οὔτε τῇ ἄλλῃ παρασκευῇ. μάλιστα
δὲ τῆς γῆς ἡ ἀρίστη αἰεὶ τὰς μεταβολὰς τῶν
οἰκητόρων εἶχεν, ἥ τε νῦν Θεσσαλία καλουμένη 20
καὶ Βοιωτία Πελοποννήσου τε τὰ πολλὰ πλὴν
Ἀρκαδίας, τῆς τε ἄλλης ὅσα ἦν κράτιστα.
4 διὰ γὰρ ἀρετὴν γῆς αἵ τε δυνάμεις τισὶ μείζους
ἐγγιγνόμεναι στάσεις ἐνεποίουν ἐξ ὧν ἐφθείροντο,
καὶ ἅμα ὑπὸ ἀλλοφύλων μᾶλλον ἐπεβουλεύοντο. 25
5 τὴν γοῦν Ἀττικὴν ἐκ τοῦ ἐπὶ πλεῖστον διὰ τὸ
λεπτόγεων ἀστασίαστον οὖσαν ἄνθρωποι ᾤκουν
6 οἱ αὐτοὶ αἰεί. καὶ παράδειγμα τόδε τοῦ λόγου
οὐκ ἐλάχιστόν ἐστι διὰ τὰς μετοικίας ἐς τὰ

11. ἑαυτῶν Schol.   29. μετοικίας ἐς] μετοικήσεις Ullrich

ἄλλα μὴ ὁμοίως αὐξηθῆναι· ἐκ γὰρ τῆς ἄλλης
Ἑλλάδος οἱ πολέμῳ ἢ στάσει ἐκπίπτοντες παρ'
Ἀθηναίους οἱ δυνατώτατοι ὡς βέβαιον ὂν
ἀνεχώρουν, καὶ πολῖται γιγνόμενοι εὐθὺς ἀπὸ
5 παλαιοῦ μείζω ἔτι ἐποίησαν πλήθει ἀνθρώπων
τὴν πόλιν, ὥστε καὶ ἐς Ἰωνίαν ὕστερον ὡς
οὐχ ἱκανῆς οὔσης τῆς Ἀττικῆς ἀποικίας ἐξέπεμψαν.

Δηλοῖ δέ μοι καὶ τόδε τῶν παλαιῶν ἀσθένειαν 3
10 οὐχ ἥκιστα· πρὸ γὰρ τῶν Τρωικῶν   Greece before
οὐδὲν φαίνεται πρότερον κοινῇ ἐργα-   the Trojan War.
σαμένη ἡ Ἑλλάς· δοκεῖ δέ μοι, οὐδὲ τοὔνομα 2
τοῦτο ξύμπασά πω εἶχεν, ἀλλὰ τὰ μὲν πρὸ
Ἕλληνος τοῦ Δευκαλίωνος καὶ πάνυ οὐδὲ εἶναι
15 ἡ ἐπίκλησις αὕτη, κατὰ ἔθνη δὲ ἄλλα τε καὶ
τὸ Πελασγικὸν ἐπὶ πλεῖστον ἀφ' ἑαυτῶν τὴν
ἐπωνυμίαν παρέχεσθαι, Ἕλληνος δὲ καὶ τῶν
παίδων αὐτοῦ ἐν τῇ Φθιώτιδι ἰσχυσάντων, καὶ
ἐπαγομένων αὐτοὺς ἐπ' ὠφελίᾳ ἐς τὰς ἄλλας
20 πόλεις, καθ' ἑκάστους μὲν ἤδη τῇ ὁμιλίᾳ μᾶλλον
καλεῖσθαι Ἕλληνας, οὐ μέντοι πολλοῦ γε
χρόνου [ἐδύνατο] καὶ ἅπασιν ἐκνικῆσαι. τεκμη- 3
ριοῖ δὲ μάλιστα Ὅμηρος· πολλῷ γὰρ ὕστερον
ἔτι καὶ τῶν Τρωικῶν γενόμενος οὐδαμοῦ τοὺς
25 ξύμπαντας ὠνόμασεν οὐδ' ἄλλους ἢ τοὺς μετ'
Ἀχιλλέως ἐκ τῆς Φθιώτιδος, οἵπερ καὶ πρῶτοι
Ἕλληνες ἦσαν, Δαναοὺς δὲ ἐν τοῖς ἔπεσι καὶ
Ἀργείους καὶ Ἀχαιοὺς ἀνακαλεῖ. οὐ μὴν οὐδὲ

18. Φθιώτιδι Ef: Φθιωτίᾳ cett.   22. ἐδύνατο om. M
23. ὕστερος γρ. Schol.

βαρβάρους εἴρηκε διὰ τὸ μηδὲ "Ελληνάς πω, ὡς
ἐμοὶ δοκεῖ, ἀντίπαλον ἐς ἓν ὄνομα ἀποκεκρίσθαι.
4 οἱ δ᾽ οὖν ὡς ἕκαστοι "Ελληνες κατὰ πόλεις τε
ὅσοι ἀλλήλων ξυνίεσαν καὶ ξύμπαντες ὕστερον
κληθέντες οὐδὲν πρὸ τῶν Τρωικῶν δι᾽ ἀσθένειαν 5
καὶ ἀμειξίαν ἀλλήλων ἀθρόοι ἔπραξαν. ἀλλὰ
καὶ ταύτην τὴν στρατείαν θαλάσσῃ ἤδη πλείω
χρώμενοι ξυνεξῆλθον.

4 Μίνως γὰρ παλαίτατος ὦν ἀκοῇ ἴσμεν
Minos the first ναυτικὸν ἐκτήσατο καὶ τῆς νῦν 10
to possess a fleet. 'Ελληνικῆς θαλάσσης ἐπὶ πλεῖστον
ἐκράτησε καὶ τῶν Κυκλάδων νήσων ἦρξέ τε
καὶ οἰκιστὴς πρῶτος τῶν πλείστων ἐγένετο,
Κᾶρας ἐξελάσας καὶ τοὺς ἑαυτοῦ παῖδας ἡγεμόνας ἐγκαταστήσας· τό τε ληστικόν, ὡς εἰκός, 15
καθῄρει ἐκ τῆς θαλάσσης ἐφ᾽ ὅσον ἐδύνατο,
5 τοῦ τὰς προσόδους μᾶλλον ἰέναι αὐτῷ. οἱ γὰρ
"Ελληνες τὸ πάλαι καὶ τῶν βαρβάρων οἵ τε
Piracy in early ἐν τῇ ἠπείρῳ παραθαλάσσιοι καὶ
Greece. ὅσοι νήσους εἶχον, ἐπειδὴ ἤρξαντο 20
μᾶλλον περαιοῦσθαι ναυσὶν ἐπ᾽ ἀλλήλους,
ἐτράποντο πρὸς λῃστείαν, ἡγουμένων ἀνδρῶν
οὐ τῶν ἀδυνατωτάτων κέρδους τοῦ σφετέρου
αὐτῶν ἕνεκα καὶ τοῖς ἀσθενέσι τροφῆς, καὶ
προσπίπτοντες πόλεσιν ἀτειχίστοις καὶ κατὰ 25
κώμας οἰκουμέναις ἥρπαζον καὶ τὸν πλεῖστον
τοῦ βίου ἐντεῦθεν ἐποιοῦντο, οὐκ ἔχοντός πω

---

8. ξυνεξῆλθον Cobet: ξυνῆλθον codd.: exierant Valla
15. καταστήσας G (corr. G¹) M ‖ λῃστρικὸν GM   16.
καθῄρει] ἐκάθηρε Schol. Aristid. 87, 9 ⑴   26. τὸν] τὸ A ? G

αἰσχύνην τούτου τοῦ ἔργου, φέροντος δέ τι
καὶ δόξης μᾶλλον· δηλοῦσι δὲ τῶν τε ἠπειρω- 2
τῶν τινες ἔτι καὶ νῦν, οἷς κόσμος καλῶς τοῦτο
δρᾶν, καὶ οἱ παλαιοὶ τῶν ποιητῶν τὰς πύστεις
5 τῶν καταπλεόντων πανταχοῦ ὁμοίως ἐρωτῶντες
εἰ λῃσταί εἰσιν, ὡς οὔτε ὧν πυνθάνονται
ἀπαξιούντων τὸ ἔργον, οἷς τε ἐπιμελὲς εἴη
εἰδέναι οὐκ ὀνειδιζόντων. ἐλῄζοντο δὲ καὶ 3
κατ' ἤπειρον ἀλλήλους. καὶ μέχρι τοῦδε πολλὰ
10 τῆς Ἑλλάδος τῷ παλαιῷ τρόπῳ νέμεται περί
τε Λοκροὺς τοὺς Ὀζόλας καὶ Αἰτωλοὺς καὶ
Ἀκαρνᾶνας καὶ τὴν ταύτῃ ἤπειρον. τό τε
σιδηροφορεῖσθαι τούτοις τοῖς ἠπειρώταις ἀπὸ
τῆς παλαιᾶς λῃστείας ἐμμεμένηκεν· πᾶσα γὰρ 6
15 ἡ Ἑλλὰς ἐσιδηροφόρει διὰ τὰς ἀφάρκτους τε
οἰκήσεις καὶ οὐκ ἀσφαλεῖς παρ' ἀλλήλους
ἐφόδους, καὶ ξυνήθη τὴν δίαιταν μεθ' ὅπλων
ἐποιήσαντο ὥσπερ οἱ βάρβαροι. σημεῖον δ' 2
ἐστὶ ταῦτα τῆς Ἑλλάδος ἔτι οὕτω νεμόμενα
20 τῶν ποτε καὶ ἐς πάντας ὁμοίων διαιτημάτων.

Ἐν τοῖς πρῶτοι δὲ Ἀθηναῖοι τόν τε σίδηρον 3
κατέθεντο καὶ ἀνειμένῃ τῇ διαίτῃ Life in early
                                  Greece re-
ἐς τὸ τρυφερώτερον μετέστησαν. sembled that of
                                  Asiatics in the
καὶ οἱ πρεσβύτεροι αὐτοῖς τῶν present day.
25 εὐδαιμόνων διὰ τὸ ἁβροδίαιτον οὐ πολὺς χρόνος
ἐπειδὴ χιτῶνάς τε λινοῦς ἐπαύσαντο φοροῦντες
καὶ χρυσῶν τεττίγων ἐνέρσει κρωβύλον ἀναδούμενοι τῶν ἐν τῇ κεφαλῇ τριχῶν· ἀφ' οὗ
καὶ Ἰώνων τοὺς πρεσβυτέρους κατὰ τὸ ξυγγενὲς

27. ἐν ἔρσει (vel ἔρσει) EG Schol.

4 ἐπὶ πολὺ αὕτη ἡ σκευὴ κατέσχεν. μετρίᾳ δ'
αὖ ἐσθῆτι καὶ ἐς τὸν νῦν τρόπον πρῶτοι Λακεδαιμόνιοι ἐχρήσαντο καὶ ἐς τὰ ἄλλα πρὸς τοὺς
πολλοὺς οἱ τὰ μείζω κεκτημένοι ἰσοδίαιτοι
5 μάλιστα κατέστησαν. ἐγυμνώθησάν τε πρῶτοι 5
καὶ ἐς τὸ φανερὸν ἀποδύντες λίπα μετὰ τοῦ
γυμνάζεσθαι ἠλείψαντο· τὸ δὲ πάλαι καὶ ἐν
τῷ Ὀλυμπικῷ ἀγῶνι διαζώματα ἔχοντες περὶ
τὰ αἰδοῖα οἱ ἀθληταὶ ἠγωνίζοντο, καὶ οὐ
πολλὰ ἔτη ἐπειδὴ πέπαυται. ἔτι δὲ καὶ ἐν 10
τοῖς βαρβάροις ἔστιν οἷς νῦν, καὶ μάλιστα
τοῖς Ἀσιανοῖς, πυγμῆς καὶ πάλης ἆθλα τίθεται,
6 καὶ διεζωμένοι τοῦτο δρῶσιν. πολλὰ δ' ἂν
καὶ ἄλλα τις ἀποδείξειε τὸ παλαιὸν Ἑλληνικὸν
ὁμοιότροπα τῷ νῦν βαρβαρικῷ διαιτώμενον. 15
7 Τῶν δὲ πόλεων ὅσαι μὲν νεώτατα ᾠκίσθησαν

Origin of walled καὶ ἤδη πλωιμωτέρων ὄντων, περιου-
cities.   σίας μᾶλλον ἔχουσαι χρημάτων ἐπ'
αὐτοῖς τοῖς αἰγιαλοῖς τείχεσιν ἐκτίζοντο καὶ
τοὺς ἰσθμοὺς ἀπελάμβανον ἐμπορίας τε ἕνεκα 20
καὶ τῆς πρὸς τοὺς προσοίκους ἕκαστοι ἰσχύος·
αἱ δὲ παλαιαὶ διὰ τὴν λῃστείαν ἐπὶ πολὺ
ἀντίσχουσαν ἀπὸ θαλάσσης μᾶλλον ᾠκίσθησαν,
αἵ τε ἐν ταῖς νήσοις καὶ ἐν ταῖς ἠπείροις
(ἔφερον γὰρ ἀλλήλους τε καὶ τῶν ἄλλων ὅσοι 25
ὄντες οὐ θαλάσσιοι κάτω ᾤκουν), καὶ μέχρι
8 τοῦδε ἔτι ἀνῳκισμένοι εἰσίν. καὶ οὐχ ἧσσον

---

1. κατασκευὴ ABF   10. πέπαυνται Reiske   13.
διεζωμένοι Phot. Suid. : διεζωσμένοι codd.   19. ἐκτίζοντο καὶ
τείχεσι Herwerden   23. ἀντίσχουσαν Poppo : ἀντισχοῦσαν
EG : ἀντισχοῦσαι cett.

λῃσταὶ ἦσαν οἱ νησιῶται, Κᾶρές τε ὄντες καὶ
Φοίνικες· οὗτοι γὰρ δὴ τὰς πλείστας τῶν νήσων
ᾤκησαν. μαρτύριον δέ· Δήλου γὰρ καθαιρο-
μένης ὑπὸ Ἀθηναίων ἐν τῷδε τῷ πολέμῳ καὶ
5 τῶν θηκῶν ἀναιρεθεισῶν ὅσαι ἦσαν τῶν τεθνεώτων ἐν τῇ νήσῳ, ὑπὲρ ἥμισυ Κᾶρες ἐφάνησαν,
γνωσθέντες τῇ τε σκευῇ τῶν ὅπλων ξυντε-
θαμμένῃ καὶ τῷ τρόπῳ ᾧ νῦν ἔτι θάπτουσιν.
καταστάντος δὲ τοῦ Μίνω ναυτικοῦ πλωιμώτερα 2
10 ἐγένετο παρ' ἀλλήλους (οἱ γὰρ ἐκ τῶν νήσων
κακοῦργοι ἀνέστησαν ὑπ' αὐτοῦ, ὅτεπερ καὶ
τὰς πολλὰς αὐτῶν κατῴκιζε), καὶ οἱ παρὰ 3
θάλασσαν ἄνθρωποι μᾶλλον ἤδη τὴν κτῆσιν
τῶν χρημάτων ποιούμενοι βεβαιότερον ᾤκουν,
15 καί τινες καὶ τείχη περιεβάλλοντο ὡς πλουσιώτεροι ἑαυτῶν γιγνόμενοι· ἐφιέμενοι γὰρ τῶν
κερδῶν οἵ τε ἥσσους ὑπέμενον τὴν τῶν κρεισ-
σόνων δουλείαν, οἵ τε δυνατώτεροι περιουσίας
ἔχοντες προσεποιοῦντο ὑπηκόους τὰς ἐλάσσους
20 πόλεις. καὶ ἐν τούτῳ τῷ τρόπῳ μᾶλλον ἤδη 4
ὄντες ὕστερον χρόνῳ ἐπὶ Τροίαν ἐστράτευσαν.

Ἀγαμέμνων τέ μοι δοκεῖ τῶν τότε δυνάμει 9
προύχων καὶ οὐ τοσοῦτον τοῖς Condition of
Τυνδάρεω ὅρκοις κατειλημμένους Greece at the
25 τοὺς Ἑλένης μνηστῆρας ἄγων τὸν time of the Trojan War.
στόλον ἀγεῖραι. λέγουσι δὲ καὶ οἱ τὰ σαφέ- 2
στατα Πελοποννησίων μνήμῃ παρὰ τῶν πρότερον δεδεγμένοι Πέλοπά τε πρῶτον πλήθει

3. ᾤκισαν Β   15. ὡς . . γιγνόμενοι add. G in marg.,
om. M

χρημάτων, ἃ ἦλθεν ἐκ τῆς Ἀσίας ἔχων ἐς
ἀνθρώπους ἀπόρους, δύναμιν περιποιησάμενον
τὴν ἐπωνυμίαν τῆς χώρας ἔπηλυν ὄντα ὅμως
σχεῖν, καὶ ὕστερον τοῖς ἐκγόνοις ἔτι μείζω
ξυνενεχθῆναι, Εὐρυσθέως μὲν ἐν τῇ Ἀττικῇ 5
ὑπὸ Ἡρακλειδῶν ἀποθανόντος, Ἀτρέως δὲ
μητρὸς ἀδελφοῦ ὄντος αὐτῷ, καὶ ἐπιτρέψαντος
Εὐρυσθέως, ὅτ᾽ ἐστράτευε, Μυκήνας τε καὶ τὴν
ἀρχὴν κατὰ τὸ οἰκεῖον Ἀτρεῖ (τυγχάνειν δὲ
αὐτὸν φεύγοντα τὸν πατέρα διὰ τὸν Χρυσίππου 10
θάνατον), καὶ ὡς οὐκέτι ἀνεχώρησεν Εὐρυσθεύς,
βουλομένων καὶ τῶν Μυκηναίων φόβῳ τῶν
Ἡρακλειδῶν καὶ ἅμα δυνατὸν δοκοῦντα εἶναι
καὶ τὸ πλῆθος τεθεραπευκότα τῶν Μυκηναίων
τε καὶ ὅσων Εὐρυσθεὺς ἦρχε τὴν βασιλείαν 15
Ἀτρέα παραλαβεῖν, καὶ τῶν Περσειδῶν τοὺς
3 Πελοπίδας μείζους καταστῆναι. ἅ μοι δοκεῖ
Ἀγαμέμνων παραλαβὼν καὶ ναυτικῷ [τε] ἅμα
ἐπὶ πλέον τῶν ἄλλων ἰσχύσας, τὴν στρατείαν
οὐ χάριτι τὸ πλέον ἢ φόβῳ ξυναγαγὼν ποιή- 20
4 σασθαι. φαίνεται γὰρ ναυσί τε πλείσταις
αὐτὸς ἀφικόμενος καὶ Ἀρκάσι προσπαρασχών,
ὡς Ὅμηρος τοῦτο δεδήλωκεν, εἴ τῳ ἱκανὸς
τεκμηριῶσαι. καὶ ἐν τοῦ σκήπτρου ἅμα τῇ
παραδόσει εἴρηκεν αὐτὸν πολλῇσι νήσοισι καὶ 25
Ἀργεῖ παντὶ ἀνάσσειν· οὐκ ἂν οὖν νήσων ἔξω
τῶν περιοικίδων (αὗται δὲ οὐκ ἂν πολλαὶ εἶεν)

---

3. ἔπηλυν Stahl: ἐπηλύτην codd.   4. post ἐκγόνοις
add. οἷον Ἀτρεῖ Ἀγαμέμνονι ABEF   18. τε secl. Krüger:
δὲ Stahl   19. στρατείαν Aem. Portus: στρατιὰν codd.

ἠπειρώτης ὢν ἐκράτει, εἰ μή τι καὶ ναυτικὸν
εἶχεν. εἰκάζειν δὲ χρὴ καὶ ταύτῃ τῇ στρατείᾳ
οἷα ἦν τὰ πρὸ αὐτῆς.

Καὶ ὅτι μὲν Μυκῆναι μικρὸν ἦν, ἢ εἴ τι 10
5 τῶν τότε πόλισμα νῦν μὴ ἀξιόχρεων The Greek fleet
δοκεῖ εἶναι, οὐκ ἀκριβεῖ ἄν τις was not a large
σημείῳ χρώμενος ἀπιστοίη μὴ γενέσθαι τὸν one.
στόλον τοσοῦτον ὅσον οἵ τε ποιηταὶ εἰρήκασι
καὶ ὁ λόγος κατέχει. Λακεδαιμονίων γὰρ εἰ 2
10 ἡ πόλις ἐρημωθείη, λειφθείη δὲ τά τε ἱερὰ
καὶ τῆς κατασκευῆς τὰ ἐδάφη, πολλὴν ἂν
οἶμαι ἀπιστίαν τῆς δυνάμεως προελθόντος
πολλοῦ χρόνου τοῖς ἔπειτα πρὸς τὸ κλέος
αὐτῶν εἶναι (καίτοι Πελοποννήσου τῶν πέντε
15 τὰς δύο μοίρας νέμονται, τῆς τε ξυμπάσης
ἡγοῦνται καὶ τῶν ἔξω ξυμμάχων πολλῶν·
ὅμως δὲ οὔτε ξυνοικισθείσης πόλεως οὔτε ἱεροῖς
καὶ κατασκευαῖς πολυτελέσι χρησαμένης, κατὰ
κώμας δὲ τῷ παλαιῷ τῆς Ἑλλάδος τρόπῳ
20 οἰκισθείσης, φαίνοιτ᾽ ἂν ὑποδεεστέρα), Ἀθηναίων
δὲ τὸ αὐτὸ τοῦτο παθόντων διπλασίαν ἂν τὴν
δύναμιν εἰκάζεσθαι ἀπὸ τῆς φανερᾶς ὄψεως
τῆς πόλεως ἢ ἔστιν. οὔκουν ἀπιστεῖν εἰκός, 3
οὐδὲ τὰς ὄψεις τῶν πόλεων μᾶλλον σκοπεῖν ἢ
25 τὰς δυνάμεις, νομίζειν δὲ τὴν στρατείαν ἐκείνην
μεγίστην μὲν γενέσθαι τῶν πρὸ αὐτῆς, λειπομένην δὲ τῶν νῦν, τῇ Ὁμήρου αὖ ποιήσει εἴ

2. στρατείᾳ Aem. Portus : στρατιᾷ codd.   17. post
ξυνοικισθείσης add. τῆς Stephanus   25. στρατείαν cfg : στρατιὰν codd.

τι χρὴ κἀνταῦθα πιστεύειν, ἢν εἰκὸς ἐπὶ τὸ
μεῖζον μὲν ποιητὴν ὄντα κοσμῆσαι, ὅμως δὲ
4 φαίνεται καὶ οὕτως ἐνδεεστέρα. πεποίηκε γὰρ
χιλίων καὶ διακοσίων νεῶν, τὰς μὲν Βοιωτῶν
εἴκοσι καὶ ἑκατὸν ἀνδρῶν, τὰς δὲ Φιλοκτήτου 5
πεντήκοντα, δηλῶν, ὡς ἐμοὶ δοκεῖ, τὰς μεγίστας
καὶ ἐλαχίστας· ἄλλων γοῦν μεγέθους πέρι ἐν
νεῶν καταλόγῳ οὐκ ἐμνήσθη. αὐτερέται δὲ
ὅτι ἦσαν καὶ μάχιμοι πάντες, ἐν ταῖς Φιλοκτήτου ναυσὶ δεδήλωκεν· τοξότας γὰρ πάντας 10
πεποίηκε τοὺς προσκώπους. περίνεως δὲ οὐκ
εἰκὸς πολλοὺς ξυμπλεῖν ἔξω τῶν βασιλέων καὶ
τῶν μάλιστα ἐν τέλει, ἄλλως τε καὶ μέλλοντας
πέλαγος περαιώσεσθαι μετὰ σκευῶν πολεμικῶν,
οὐδ᾽ αὖ τὰ πλοῖα κατάφαρκτα ἔχοντας, ἀλλὰ 15
τῷ παλαιῷ τρόπῳ λῃστικώτερον παρεσκευα-
5 σμένα. πρὸς τὰς μεγίστας δ᾽ οὖν καὶ ἐλαχίστας
ναῦς τὸ μέσον σκοποῦντι οὐ πολλοὶ φαίνονται
ἐλθόντες, ὡς ἀπὸ πάσης τῆς Ἑλλάδος κοινῇ
πεμπόμενοι. 20

11 Αἴτιον δ᾽ ἦν οὐχ ἡ ὀλιγανθρωπία τοσοῦτον

Had the expedi-
tion been on a
large scale, Troy
would soon have
been taken.

ὅσον ἡ ἀχρηματία. τῆς γὰρ τροφῆς
ἀπορίᾳ τόν τε στρατὸν ἐλάσσω
ἤγαγον καὶ ὅσον ἤλπιζον αὐτόθεν
πολεμοῦντα βιοτεύσειν, ἐπειδὴ δὲ ἀφικόμενοι 25
μάχῃ ἐκράτησαν (δῆλον δέ· τὸ γὰρ ἔρυμα τῷ
στρατοπέδῳ οὐκ ἂν ἐτειχίσαντο), φαίνονται δ᾽
οὐδ᾽ ἐνταῦθα πάσῃ τῇ δυνάμει χρησάμενοι,
ἀλλὰ πρὸς γεωργίαν τῆς Χερσονήσου τραπό-

17. δ᾽ οὖν Bekker : οὖν M : γοῦν cett.   19. ξυνελθόντες G

μένοι καὶ λῃστείαν τῆς τροφῆς ἀπορίᾳ. ἦ καὶ
μᾶλλον οἱ Τρῶες αὐτῶν διεσπαρμένων τὰ δέκα
ἔτη ἀντεῖχον βίᾳ, τοῖς αἰεὶ ὑπολειπομένοις
ἀντίπαλοι ὄντες. περιουσίαν δὲ εἰ ἦλθον 2
5 ἔχοντες τροφῆς καὶ ὄντες ἀθρόοι ἄνευ λῃστείας
καὶ γεωργίας ξυνεχῶς τὸν πόλεμον διέφερον,
ῥᾳδίως ἂν μάχῃ κρατοῦντες εἷλον, οἵ γε καὶ
οὐχ ἀθρόοι, ἀλλὰ μέρει τῷ αἰεὶ παρόντι
ἀντεῖχον, πολιορκίᾳ δ' ἂν προσκαθεζόμενοι ἐν
10 ἐλάσσονί τε χρόνῳ καὶ ἀπονώτερον τὴν Τροίαν
εἷλον. ἀλλὰ δι' ἀχρηματίαν τά τε πρὸ τούτων
ἀσθενῆ ἦν καὶ αὐτά γε δὴ ταῦτα, ὀνομαστό-
τατα τῶν πρὶν γενόμενα, δηλοῦται τοῖς ἔργοις
ὑποδεέστερα ὄντα τῆς φήμης καὶ τοῦ νῦν περὶ
15 αὐτῶν διὰ τοὺς ποιητὰς λόγου κατεσχηκότος·
ἐπεὶ καὶ μετὰ τὰ Τρωικὰ ἡ Ἑλλὰς ἔτι μεταν- 12
ίστατό τε καὶ κατῳκίζετο, ὥστε μὴ Greece after the
ἡσυχάσασαν αὐξηθῆναι. ἥ τε γὰρ Trojan War.   2
ἀναχώρησις τῶν Ἑλλήνων ἐξ Ἰλίου χρονία
20 γενομένη πολλὰ ἐνεόχμωσε, καὶ στάσεις ἐν
ταῖς πόλεσιν ὡς ἐπὶ πολὺ ἐγίγνοντο, ἀφ' ὧν
ἐκπίπτοντες τὰς πόλεις ἔκτιζον. Βοιωτοί τε 3
γὰρ οἱ νῦν ἑξηκοστῷ ἔτει μετὰ Ἰλίου ἅλωσιν
ἐξ Ἄρνης ἀναστάντες ὑπὸ Θεσσαλῶν τὴν νῦν
25 μὲν Βοιωτίαν, πρότερον δὲ Καδμηίδα γῆν
καλουμένην ᾤκισαν (ἦν δὲ αὐτῶν καὶ ἀπο-
δασμὸς πρότερον ἐν τῇ γῇ ταύτῃ, ἀφ' ὧν καὶ

7. εἷλον secl. Krüger   9. δ' secl. Krüger   12. -νῇ
ἦν . . c. 20. 2 ὅτι Ἰπ· suppl. f foll. iv, v   18. ἡσυχάσασα cf
26. ᾤκισαν c : ᾤκησαν cett.   27. ἐν τῇ γῇ ταύτῃ πρότερον cf

ἐς Ἴλιον ἐστράτευσαν), Δωριῆς τε ὀγδοηκοστῷ
ἔτει ξὺν Ἡρακλείδαις Πελοπόννησον ἔσχον.

4 μόλις τε ἐν πολλῷ χρόνῳ ἡσυχάσασα ἡ
Ἑλλὰς βεβαίως καὶ οὐκέτι ἀνισταμένη ἀποικίας ἐξέπεμψε, καὶ Ἴωνας μὲν Ἀθηναῖοι καὶ 5
νησιωτῶν τοὺς πολλοὺς ᾤκισαν, Ἰταλίας δὲ
καὶ Σικελίας τὸ πλεῖστον Πελοποννήσιοι τῆς
τε ἄλλης Ἑλλάδος ἔστιν ἃ χωρία. πάντα δὲ
ταῦτα ὕστερον τῶν Τρωικῶν ἐκτίσθη.

13 Δυνατωτέρας δὲ γιγνομένης τῆς Ἑλλάδος 10
καὶ τῶν χρημάτων τὴν κτῆσιν ἔτι μᾶλλον ἢ
πρότερον ποιουμένης τὰ πολλὰ τυραννίδες ἐν
ταῖς πόλεσι καθίσταντο, τῶν προσόδων μειζόνων
γιγνομένων (πρότερον δὲ ἦσαν ἐπὶ ῥητοῖς γέρασι
πατρικαὶ βασιλεῖαι), ναυτικά τε ἐξηρτύετο ἡ 15
Ἑλλάς, καὶ τῆς θαλάσσης μᾶλλον ἀντείχοντο.
2 Advance made πρῶτοι δὲ Κορίνθιοι λέγονται ἐγγύ-
by Corinth. τατα τοῦ νῦν τρόπου μεταχειρίσαι
τὰ περὶ τὰς ναῦς, καὶ τριήρεις ἐν Κορίνθῳ
3 πρῶτον τῆς Ἑλλάδος ναυπηγηθῆναι. φαίνεται 20
δὲ καὶ Σαμίοις Ἀμεινοκλῆς Κορίνθιος ναυπηγὸς
ναῦς ποιήσας τέσσαρας · ἔτη δ' ἐστὶ μάλιστα
τριακόσια ἐς τὴν τελευτὴν τοῦδε τοῦ πολέμου
4 ὅτε Ἀμεινοκλῆς Σαμίοις ἦλθεν. ναυμαχία τε
παλαιτάτη ὧν ἴσμεν γίγνεται Κορινθίων πρὸς 25
Κερκυραίους · ἔτη δὲ μάλιστα καὶ ταύτῃ ἑξήκοντα καὶ διακόσιά ἐστι μέχρι τοῦ αὐτοῦ

3. μόγις cfG   5. ἐξέπεμπε cfG   10. γενομένης GM
20. πρῶτον ἐν Κορίνθῳ BcEf ‖ ἐνναυπηγηθῆναι cf suprascr. G¹
26. καὶ ταύτῃ cf: om. codd., add. G¹

χρόνου. οἰκοῦντες γὰρ τὴν πόλιν οἱ Κορίνθιοι 5
ἐπὶ τοῦ Ἰσθμοῦ αἰεὶ δή ποτε ἐμπόριον εἶχον,
τῶν Ἑλλήνων τὸ πάλαι κατὰ γῆν τὰ πλείω
ἢ κατὰ θάλασσαν, τῶν τε ἐντὸς Πελοποννήσου
5 καὶ τῶν ἔξω, διὰ τῆς ἐκείνων παρ᾽ ἀλλήλους
ἐπιμισγόντων, χρήμασί τε δυνατοὶ ἦσαν, ὡς
καὶ τοῖς παλαιοῖς ποιηταῖς δεδήλωται· ἀφνειὸν
γὰρ ἐπωνόμασαν τὸ χωρίον. ἐπειδή τε οἱ
Ἑλληνες μᾶλλον ἔπλῳζον, τὰς ναῦς κτησάμενοι
10 τὸ λῃστικὸν καθῄρουν, καὶ ἐμπόριον παρέχοντες ἀμφότερα δυνατὴν ἔσχον χρημάτων
προσόδῳ τὴν πόλιν. καὶ Ἴωσιν ὕστερον πολὺ 6
γίγνεται ναυτικὸν ἐπὶ Κύρου Περσῶν Strength of the
πρώτου βασιλεύοντος καὶ Καμβύσου Ionians in the
time of Cyrus
15 τοῦ υἱέος αὐτοῦ, τῆς τε καθ᾽ ἑαυτοὺς the Elder.
θαλάσσης Κύρῳ πολεμοῦντες ἐκράτησάν τινα
χρόνον. καὶ Πολυκράτης Σάμου τυραννῶν ἐπὶ
Καμβύσου ναυτικῷ ἰσχύων ἄλλας τε τῶν
νήσων ὑπηκόους ἐποιήσατο καὶ Ῥήνειαν ἑλὼν
20 ἀνέθηκε τῷ Ἀπόλλωνι τῷ Δηλίῳ. Φωκαῆς
τε Μασσαλίαν οἰκίζοντες Καρχηδονίους ἐνίκων
ναυμαχοῦντες· δυνατώτατα γὰρ ταῦτα τῶν 14
ναυτικῶν ἦν. φαίνεται δὲ καὶ ταῦτα πολλαῖς
γενεαῖς ὕστερα γενόμενα τῶν Τρωικῶν τριήρεσι
25 μὲν ὀλίγαις χρώμενα, πεντηκοντόροις δ᾽ ἔτι
καὶ πλοίοις μακροῖς ἐξηρτυμένα ὥσπερ ἐκεῖνα.
ὀλίγον τε πρὸ τῶν Μηδικῶν καὶ τοῦ Δαρείου 2
θανάτου, ὃς μετὰ Καμβύσην Περσῶν ἐβασίλευσε, τριήρεις περί τε Σικελίαν τοῖς τυράννοις
30 ἐς πλῆθος ἐγένοντο καὶ Κερκυραίοις· ταῦτα γὰρ

I   C

14 ΘΟΥΚΥΔΙΔΟΥ

τελευταῖα πρὸ τῆς Ξέρξου στρατείας ναυτικὰ
3 ἀξιόλογα ἐν τῇ Ἑλλάδι κατέστη. Αἰγινῆται
Late origin of
the Athenian
sea power.
γὰρ καὶ Ἀθηναῖοι, καὶ εἴ τινες
ἄλλοι, βραχέα ἐκέκτηντο, καὶ τούτων
τὰ πολλὰ πεντηκοντόρους· ὀψέ τε ἀφ' οὗ 5
Ἀθηναίους Θεμιστοκλῆς ἔπεισεν Αἰγινήταις
πολεμοῦντας, καὶ ἅμα τοῦ βαρβάρου προσ-
δοκίμου ὄντος, τὰς ναῦς ποιήσασθαι αἷσπερ
καὶ ἐναυμάχησαν· καὶ αὗται οὔπω εἶχον διὰ
πάσης καταστρώματα. 10
15 Τὰ μὲν οὖν ναυτικὰ τῶν Ἑλλήνων τοιαῦτα
The wars
inconsiderable.
ἦν, τά τε παλαιὰ καὶ τὰ ὕστερον
γενόμενα. ἰσχὺν δὲ περιεποιήσαντο
ὅμως οὐκ ἐλαχίστην οἱ προσσχόντες αὐτοῖς χρημάτων τε προσόδῳ καὶ ἄλλων ἀρχῇ· ἐπιπλέοντες 15
γὰρ τὰς νήσους κατεστρέφοντο, καὶ μάλιστα ὅσοι
2 μὴ διαρκῆ εἶχον χώραν. κατὰ γῆν δὲ πόλεμος,
ὅθεν τις καὶ δύναμις παρεγένετο, οὐδεὶς ξυνέστη·
πάντες δὲ ἦσαν, ὅσοι καὶ ἐγένοντο, πρὸς ὁμόρους
τοὺς σφετέρους ἑκάστοις, καὶ ἐκδήμους στρατείας 20
πολὺ ἀπὸ τῆς ἑαυτῶν ἐπ' ἄλλων καταστροφῇ
οὐκ ἐξῆσαν οἱ Ἕλληνες. οὐ γὰρ ξυνειστήκεσαν
πρὸς τὰς μεγίστας πόλεις ὑπήκοοι, οὐδ' αὖ
αὐτοὶ ἀπὸ τῆς ἴσης κοινὰς στρατείας ἐποιοῦντο,
κατ' ἀλλήλους δὲ μᾶλλον ὡς ἕκαστοι οἱ 25
3 ἀστυγείτονες ἐπολέμουν. μάλιστα δὲ ἐς τὸν
πάλαι ποτὲ γενόμενον πόλεμον Χαλκιδέων καὶ

3. εἴ τινες] οἵτινες cf[G]   13. γενόμενα cfg: γιγνόμενα
codd.   14. προσσχόντες A: προσέχοντες E: προσχόντες
cett.   23. αὖ om. ABEGM

Ἐρετριῶν καὶ τὸ ἄλλο Ἑλληνικὸν ἐς ξυμμαχίαν ἑκατέρων διέστη. ἐπεγένετο δὲ ἄλλοις 16
τε ἄλλοθι κωλύματα μὴ αὐξηθῆναι, Growth of
καὶ Ἴωσι προχωρησάντων ἐπὶ Persian power.
5 μέγα τῶν πραγμάτων Κῦρος καὶ ἡ Περσικὴ
βασιλεία Κροῖσον καθελοῦσα καὶ ὅσα ἐντὸς
Ἅλυος ποταμοῦ πρὸς θάλασσαν ἐπεστράτευσε
καὶ τὰς ἐν τῇ ἠπείρῳ πόλεις ἐδούλωσε, Δαρεῖός
τε ὕστερον τῷ Φοινίκων ναυτικῷ κρατῶν καὶ
10 τὰς νήσους. τύραννοί τε ὅσοι ἦσαν ἐν ταῖς 17
Ἑλληνικαῖς πόλεσι, τὸ ἐφ᾽ ἑαυτῶν The Greek
μόνον προορώμενοι ἔς τε τὸ σῶμα despots did
nothing con-
καὶ ἐς τὸ τὸν ἴδιον οἶκον αὔξειν siderable.
δι᾽ ἀσφαλείας ὅσον ἐδύναντο μάλιστα τὰς
15 πόλεις ᾤκουν, ἐπράχθη δὲ οὐδὲν ἀπ᾽ αὐτῶν
ἔργον ἀξιόλογον, εἰ μὴ εἴ τι πρὸς περιοίκους
τοὺς αὐτῶν ἑκάστοις· οἱ γὰρ ἐν Σικελίᾳ ἐπὶ
πλεῖστον ἐχώρησαν δυνάμεως. οὕτω πανταχόθεν ἡ Ἑλλὰς ἐπὶ πολὺν χρόνον κατείχετο
20 μήτε κοινῇ φανερὸν μηδὲν κατεργάζεσθαι, κατὰ
πόλεις τε ἀτολμοτέρα εἶναι.
Ἐπειδὴ δὲ οἵ τε Ἀθηναίων τύραννοι καὶ 18
οἱ ἐκ τῆς ἄλλης Ἑλλάδος ἐπὶ πολὺ Beginning of the
καὶ πρὶν τυραννευθείσης οἱ πλεῖστοι Persian wars.
25 καὶ τελευταῖοι πλὴν τῶν ἐν Σικελίᾳ ὑπὸ
Λακεδαιμονίων κατελύθησαν (ἡ γὰρ Λακε-
δαίμων μετὰ τὴν κτίσιν τῶν νῦν ἐνοικούντων

6. βασιλεία] ἐξουσία f   9. τε] δὲ ABGM   10. τε]
δὲ ABEGM   15. δὲ] τε ABEGM ‖ ἀπ᾽ αὐτῶν οὐδὲν ABEGM
16. εἴ om. ABEGM   27. κτῆσιν ABcfGM

αὐτὴν Δωριῶν ἐπὶ πλεῖστον ὧν ἴσμεν χρόνον
στασιάσασα ὅμως ἐκ παλαιτάτου καὶ ηὐνομήθη
καὶ αἰεὶ ἀτυράννευτος ἦν· ἔτη γάρ ἐστι
μάλιστα τετρακόσια καὶ ὀλίγῳ πλείω ἐς τὴν
τελευτὴν τοῦδε τοῦ πολέμου ἀφ' οὗ Λακε- 5
δαιμόνιοι τῇ αὐτῇ πολιτείᾳ χρῶνται, καὶ δι'
αὐτὸ δυνάμενοι καὶ τὰ ἐν ταῖς ἄλλαις πόλεσι
καθίστασαν), μετὰ δὲ τὴν τῶν τυράννων
κατάλυσιν ἐκ τῆς Ἑλλάδος οὐ πολλοῖς ἔτεσιν
ὕστερον καὶ ἡ ἐν Μαραθῶνι μάχη Μήδων 10
2 πρὸς Ἀθηναίους ἐγένετο. δεκάτῳ δὲ ἔτει μετ'
αὐτὴν αὖθις ὁ βάρβαρος τῷ μεγάλῳ στόλῳ

The invasion of   ἐπὶ τὴν Ἑλλάδα δουλωσόμενος
Xerxes. The
Greeks make   ἦλθεν. καὶ μεγάλου κινδύνου ἐπι-
common cause.
κρεμασθέντος οἵ τε Λακεδαιμόνιοι 15
τῶν ξυμπολεμησάντων Ἑλλήνων ἡγήσαντο
δυνάμει προύχοντες, καὶ οἱ Ἀθηναῖοι ἐπιόντων
τῶν Μήδων διανοηθέντες ἐκλιπεῖν τὴν πόλιν
καὶ ἀνασκευασάμενοι ἐς τὰς ναῦς ἐσβάντες
ναυτικοὶ ἐγένοντο. κοινῇ τε ἀπωσάμενοι τὸν 20
βάρβαρον, ὕστερον οὐ πολλῷ διεκρίθησαν πρός
τε Ἀθηναίους καὶ Λακεδαιμονίους οἵ τε ἀποστάντες βασιλέως Ἕλληνες καὶ οἱ ξυμπολε-
μήσαντες. δυνάμει γὰρ ταῦτα μέγιστα διεφάνη·
ἴσχυον γὰρ οἱ μὲν κατὰ γῆν, οἱ δὲ ναυσίν. 25
3 καὶ ὀλίγον μὲν χρόνον ξυνέμεινεν ἡ ὁμαιχμία,
ἔπειτα διενεχθέντες οἱ Λακεδαιμόνιοι καὶ

5. ἀφ' οὗ] ἃ M Hermogenes : ἃ ἀφ' οὗ AB[G]   19. ἐμ-
βάντες ABEGM   24. δὴ ἐφάνη Stephanus   27. post
ἔπειτα add. δὲ ABEGM ‖ po·t καὶ add. οἱ AEM Suid.

Ἀθηναῖοι ἐπολέμησαν μετὰ τῶν ξυμμάχων πρὸς
ἀλλήλους· καὶ τῶν ἄλλων Ἑλλήνων The unanimity
εἴ τινές που διασταῖεν, πρὸς τούτους was short-lived.
ἤδη ἐχώρουν. ὥστε ἀπὸ τῶν Μηδικῶν ἐς τόνδε
5 αἰεὶ τὸν πόλεμον τὰ μὲν σπενδόμενοι, τὰ δὲ
πολεμοῦντες ἢ ἀλλήλοις ἢ τοῖς ἑαυτῶν ξυμμάχοις ἀφισταμένοις εὖ παρεσκευάσαντο τὰ
πολέμια καὶ ἐμπειρότεροι ἐγένοντο μετὰ κινδύνων
τὰς μελέτας ποιούμενοι. καὶ οἱ μὲν Λακε- 19
10 δαιμόνιοι οὐχ ὑποτελεῖς ἔχοντες φόρου τοὺς
ξυμμάχους ἡγοῦντο, κατ᾽ ὀλιγαρχίαν δὲ σφίσιν
αὐτοῖς μόνον ἐπιτηδείως ὅπως πολιτεύσουσι
θεραπεύοντες, Ἀθηναῖοι δὲ ναῦς τε τῶν πόλεων
τῷ χρόνῳ παραλαβόντες πλὴν Χίων καὶ
15 Λεσβίων, καὶ χρήματα τοῖς πᾶσι τάξαντες
φέρειν. καὶ ἐγένετο αὐτοῖς ἐς τόνδε τὸν
πόλεμον ἡ ἰδία παρασκευὴ μείζων ἢ ὡς τὰ
κράτιστά ποτε μετὰ ἀκραιφνοῦς τῆς ξυμμαχίας
ἤνθησαν.
20   Τὰ μὲν οὖν παλαιὰ τοιαῦτα ηὗρον, χαλεπὰ 20
ὄντα παντὶ ἑξῆς τεκμηρίῳ πιστεῦσαι. General
οἱ γὰρ ἄνθρωποι τὰς ἀκοὰς τῶν character of early Greek
προγεγενημένων, καὶ ἢν ἐπιχώρια history.
σφίσιν ᾖ, ὁμοίως ἀβασανίστως παρ᾽ ἀλλήλων
25 δέχονται. Ἀθηναίων γοῦν τὸ πλῆθος Ἵππαρχον 2
οἴονται ὑφ᾽ Ἁρμοδίου καὶ Ἀριστογείτονος
τύραννον ὄντα ἀποθανεῖν, καὶ οὐκ ἴσασιν ὅτι
Ἱππίας μὲν πρεσβύτατος ὢν ἦρχε τῶν
Πεισιστράτου υἱέων, Ἵππαρχος δὲ καὶ Θεσ-

12. πολιτεύσωσι ABEGM

σαλὸς ἀδελφοὶ ἦσαν αὐτοῦ, ὑποτοπήσαντες δέ
τι ἐκείνῃ τῇ ἡμέρᾳ καὶ παραχρῆμα Ἁρμόδιος
καὶ Ἀριστογείτων ἐκ τῶν ξυνειδότων σφίσιν
Ἱππίᾳ μεμηνῦσθαι τοῦ μὲν ἀπέσχοντο ὡς
προειδότος, βουλόμενοι δὲ πρὶν ξυλληφθῆναι ₅
δράσαντές τι καὶ κινδυνεῦσαι, τῷ Ἱππάρχῳ
περιτυχόντες περὶ τὸ Λεωκόρειον καλούμενον
τὴν Παναθηναϊκὴν πομπὴν διακοσμοῦντι ἀπέ-
3 κτειναν. πολλὰ δὲ καὶ ἄλλα ἔτι καὶ νῦν ὄντα
καὶ οὐ χρόνῳ ἀμνηστούμενα καὶ οἱ ἄλλοι ₁₀
Ἕλληνες οὐκ ὀρθῶς οἴονται, ὥσπερ τούς τε
Λακεδαιμονίων βασιλέας μὴ μιᾷ ψήφῳ προσ-
τίθεσθαι ἑκάτερον, ἀλλὰ δυοῖν, καὶ τὸν
Πιτανάτην λόχον αὐτοῖς εἶναι, ὃς οὐδ' ἐγένετο
πώποτε. οὕτως ἀταλαίπωρος τοῖς πολλοῖς ἡ ₁₅
ζήτησις τῆς ἀληθείας, καὶ ἐπὶ τὰ ἑτοῖμα
21 μᾶλλον τρέπονται. ἐκ δὲ τῶν εἰρημένων
τεκμηρίων ὅμως τοιαῦτα ἄν τις νομίζων
μάλιστα ἃ διῆλθον οὐχ ἁμαρτάνοι, καὶ οὔτε
ὡς ποιηταὶ ὑμνήκασι περὶ αὐτῶν ἐπὶ τὸ ₂₀
μεῖζον κοσμοῦντες μᾶλλον πιστεύων, οὔτε ὡς
λογογράφοι ξυνέθεσαν ἐπὶ τὸ προσαγωγότερον
τῇ ἀκροάσει ἢ ἀληθέστερον, ὄντα ἀνεξέλεγκτα
καὶ τὰ πολλὰ ὑπὸ χρόνου αὐτῶν ἀπίστως ἐπὶ
τὸ μυθῶδες ἐκνενικηκότα, ηὑρῆσθαι δὲ ἡγησά- ₂₅
μενος ἐκ τῶν ἐπιφανεστάτων σημείων ὡς
2 παλαιὰ εἶναι ἀποχρώντως. καὶ ὁ πόλεμος
This war surpasses others. οὗτος, καίπερ τῶν ἀνθρώπων ἐν ᾧ
μὲν ἂν πολεμῶσι τὸν παρόντα αἰεὶ

7. περὶ] παρὰ Arist. Ἀθ. Πολ. 18. 3 (nisi ad vi. 57. 3 spectat)

μέγιστον κρινόντων, παυσαμένων δὲ τὰ ἀρχαῖα
μᾶλλον θαυμαζόντων, ἀπ' αὐτῶν τῶν ἔργων
σκοποῦσι δηλώσει ὅμως μείζων γεγενημένος
αὐτῶν.

ι Καὶ ὅσα μὲν λόγῳ εἶπον ἕκαστοι ἢ **22**
μέλλοντες πολεμήσειν ἢ ἐν αὐτῷ   Character of
                                  this history.
ἤδη ὄντες, χαλεπὸν τὴν ἀκρίβειαν   Difficulty of
                                  obtaining re-
αὐτὴν τῶν λεχθέντων διαμνημονεῦσαι liable evidence.
ἦν ἐμοί τε ὧν αὐτὸς ἤκουσα καὶ τοῖς ἄλλοθέν
10 ποθεν ἐμοὶ ἀπαγγέλλουσιν· ὡς δ' ἂν ἐδόκουν
ἐμοὶ ἕκαστοι περὶ τῶν αἰεὶ παρόντων τὰ δέοντα
μάλιστ' εἰπεῖν, ἐχομένῳ ὅτι ἐγγύτατα τῆς
ξυμπάσης γνώμης τῶν ἀληθῶς λεχθέντων,
οὕτως εἴρηται. τὰ δ' ἔργα τῶν πραχθέντων 2
15 ἐν τῷ πολέμῳ οὐκ ἐκ τοῦ παρατυχόντος
πυνθανόμενος ἠξίωσα γράφειν, οὐδ' ὡς ἐμοὶ
ἐδόκει, ἀλλ' οἷς τε αὐτὸς παρῆν καὶ παρὰ τῶν
ἄλλων ὅσον δυνατὸν ἀκριβείᾳ περὶ ἑκάστου
ἐπεξελθών. ἐπιπόνως δὲ ηὑρίσκετο, διότι οἱ 3
20 παρόντες τοῖς ἔργοις ἑκάστοις οὐ ταὐτὰ περὶ
τῶν αὐτῶν ἔλεγον, ἀλλ' ὡς ἑκατέρων τις
εὐνοίας ἢ μνήμης ἔχοι. καὶ ἐς μὲν   This work may   4
                                     be less pleasing,
ἀκρόασιν ἴσως τὸ μὴ μυθῶδες αὐτῶν   but it will be
                                     more instructive
ἀτερπέστερον φανεῖται· ὅσοι δὲ   than others.
25 βουλήσονται τῶν τε γενομένων τὸ σαφὲς
σκοπεῖν καὶ τῶν μελλόντων ποτὲ αὖθις κατὰ
τὸ ἀνθρώπινον τοιούτων καὶ παραπλησίων

9. μοι CG Dion. Hal.   17. ἐδόκει CG : δοκεῖ cett. Dion.
Hal.   21. ἑκατέρων CGM Dion. Hal. : ἑκατέρῳ cett.   27.
ἀνθρώπειον ABEFM Dion. Hal.

ἔσεσθαι, ὠφέλιμα κρίνειν αὐτὰ ἀρκούντως ἕξει.
κτῆμά τε ἐς αἰεὶ μᾶλλον ἢ ἀγώνισμα ἐς τὸ
παραχρῆμα ἀκούειν ξύγκειται.

23 Τῶν δὲ πρότερον ἔργων μέγιστον ἐπράχθη
τὸ Μηδικόν, καὶ τοῦτο ὅμως δυοῖν ναυμαχίαιν ⸗
καὶ πεζομαχίαιν ταχεῖαν τὴν κρίσιν ἔσχεν.
τούτου δὲ τοῦ πολέμου μῆκός τε μέγα προύβη,
παθήματά τε ξυνηνέχθη γενέσθαι ἐν αὐτῷ τῇ
2 Ἑλλάδι οἷα οὐχ ἕτερα ἐν ἴσῳ χρόνῳ. οὔτε
γὰρ πόλεις τοσαίδε ληφθεῖσαι ἠρημώθησαν, αἱ 10
μὲν ὑπὸ βαρβάρων, αἱ δ' ὑπὸ σφῶν αὐτῶν
ἀντιπολεμούντων (εἰσὶ δ' αἳ καὶ οἰκήτορας
μετέβαλον ἁλισκόμεναι), οὔτε φυγαὶ τοσαίδε
ἀνθρώπων καὶ φόνος, ὁ μὲν κατ' αὐτὸν τὸν
3 πόλεμον, ὁ δὲ διὰ τὸ στασιάζειν. τά τε 15
πρότερον ἀκοῇ μὲν λεγόμενα, ἔργῳ δὲ σπανιώ-
τερον βεβαιούμενα οὐκ ἄπιστα κατέστη, σεισμῶν τε πέρι, οἳ ἐπὶ πλεῖστον ἅμα μέρος γῆς
καὶ ἰσχυρότατοι οἱ αὐτοὶ ἐπέσχον, ἡλίου τε
ἐκλείψεις, αἳ πυκνότεραι παρὰ τὰ ἐκ τοῦ πρὶν 20
χρόνου μνημονευόμενα ξυνέβησαν, αὐχμοί τε
ἔστι παρ' οἷς μεγάλοι καὶ ἀπ' αὐτῶν καὶ
λιμοὶ καὶ ἡ οὐχ ἥκιστα βλάψασα καὶ μέρος
τι φθείρασα ἡ λοιμώδης νόσος· ταῦτα γὰρ
πάντα μετὰ τοῦδε τοῦ πολέμου ἅμα ξυνεπέθετο. 25
4 Origin of this   ἤρξαντο δὲ αὐτοῦ Ἀθηναῖοι καὶ
war.   Πελοποννήσιοι λύσαντες τὰς τριακοντούτεις σπονδὰς αἳ αὐτοῖς ἐγένοντο μετὰ
5 Εὐβοίας ἅλωσιν. διότι δ' ἔλυσαν, τὰς αἰτίας

23. ἢ om. ABEF

προύγραψα πρῶτον καὶ τὰς διαφοράς, τοῦ μή
τινα ζητῆσαί ποτε ἐξ ὅτου τοσοῦτος πόλεμος
τοῖς Ἕλλησι κατέστη. τὴν μὲν γὰρ ἀληθεσ- 6
τάτην πρόφασιν, ἀφανεστάτην δὲ λόγῳ, τοὺς
5 Ἀθηναίους ἡγοῦμαι μεγάλους γιγνομένους καὶ
φόβον παρέχοντας τοῖς Λακεδαιμονίοις ἀναγκάσαι ἐς τὸ πολεμεῖν· αἱ δ' ἐς τὸ φανερὸν
λεγόμεναι αἰτίαι αἵδ' ἦσαν ἑκατέρων, ἀφ' ὧν
λύσαντες τὰς σπονδὰς ἐς τὸν πόλεμον κατέ-
10 στησαν.

Ἐπίδαμνός ἐστι πόλις ἐν δεξιᾷ ἐσπλέοντι 24
ἐς τὸν Ἰόνιον κόλπον· προσοικοῦσι The causes
δ' αὐτὴν Ταυλάντιοι βάρβαροι, openly alleged.
Ἰλλυρικὸν ἔθνος. ταύτην ἀπῴκισαν μὲν Κερκυ- 2
15 ραῖοι, οἰκιστὴς δ' ἐγένετο Φαλίος Ἐρατοκλείδου
Κορίνθιος γένος τῶν ἀφ' Ἡρακλέους, κατὰ δὴ
τὸν παλαιὸν νόμον ἐκ τῆς μητροπόλεως κατα-
κληθείς. ξυνῴκισαν δὲ καὶ Κορινθίων τινὲς
καὶ τοῦ ἄλλου Δωρικοῦ γένους. προελθόντος 3
20 δὲ τοῦ χρόνου ἐγένετο ἡ τῶν Ἐπιδαμνίων
δύναμις μεγάλη καὶ πολυάνθρωπος· στασιά- 4
σαντες δὲ ἐν ἀλλήλοις ἔτη πολλά, ὡς λέγεται,
ἀπὸ πολέμου τινὸς τῶν προσοίκων βαρβάρων
ἐφθάρησαν καὶ τῆς δυνάμεως τῆς πολλῆς
25 ἐστερήθησαν. τὰ δὲ τελευταῖα πρὸ Revolution in   5
τοῦδε τοῦ πολέμου ὁ δῆμος αὐτῶν Epidamnus.

1. ἔγραψα CG   2. τινας CGm Dion. Hal. (altero loco)
12. ἐς add. Demetrius : om. codd.   21. δύναμις CG : δύναμις
πόλις EM : πόλις ABF γρ. c

I   C 2

22   ΘΟΥΚΥΔΙΔΟΥ

ἐξεδίωξε τοὺς δυνατούς, οἱ δὲ ἐπελθόντες
μετὰ τῶν βαρβάρων ἐλήζοντο τοὺς ἐν τῇ πόλει
6 κατά τε γῆν καὶ κατὰ θάλασσαν. οἱ δὲ ἐν

Those in
Epidamnus sent
to Corcyra
asking for help.

τῇ πόλει ὄντες Ἐπιδάμνιοι ἐπειδὴ
ἐπιέζοντο, πέμπουσιν ἐς τὴν Κέρ- 5
κυραν πρέσβεις ὡς μητρόπολιν
οὖσαν, δεόμενοι μὴ σφᾶς περιορᾶν φθειρομένους, ἀλλὰ τούς τε φεύγοντας ξυναλλάξαι
σφίσι καὶ τὸν τῶν βαρβάρων πόλεμον κατα-
7 The request
refused.
λῦσαι. ταῦτα δὲ ἱκέται καθεζόμενοι 10
ἐς τὸ Ἥραιον ἐδέοντο. οἱ δὲ Κερκυραῖοι τὴν ἱκετείαν οὐκ ἐδέξαντο, ἀλλ᾽ ἀπράκτους
ἀπέπεμψαν.

25 Γνόντες δὲ οἱ Ἐπιδάμνιοι οὐδεμίαν σφίσιν

The Epidam-
nians then
appealed to
Corinth.

ἀπὸ Κερκύρας τιμωρίαν οὖσαν ἐν 15
ἀπόρῳ εἴχοντο θέσθαι τὸ παρόν,
καὶ πέμψαντες ἐς Δελφοὺς τὸν
θεὸν ἐπήροντο εἰ παραδοῖεν Κορινθίοις τὴν
πόλιν ὡς οἰκισταῖς καὶ τιμωρίαν τινὰ πειρῶντ᾽
ἀπ᾽ αὐτῶν ποιεῖσθαι. ὁ δ᾽ αὐτοῖς ἀνεῖλε 20
2 παραδοῦναι καὶ ἡγεμόνας ποιεῖσθαι. ἐλθόντες
δὲ οἱ Ἐπιδάμνιοι ἐς τὴν Κόρινθον κατὰ τὸ
μαντεῖον παρέδοσαν τὴν ἀποικίαν, τόν τε
οἰκιστὴν ἀποδεικνύντες σφῶν ἐκ Κορίνθου ὄντα
καὶ τὸ χρηστήριον δηλοῦντες, ἐδέοντό τε μὴ 25
σφᾶς περιορᾶν φθειρομένους, ἀλλ᾽ ἐπαμῦναι.
3 Κορίνθιοι δὲ κατά τε τὸ δίκαιον ὑπεδέξαντο

1. ἐπελθόντες Haase : ἀπελθόντες codd.   18. ἐπηρώτων
C[G]   20. αὐτοῖς] αὐτὴν C γρ. G   26. διαφθειρομένους
ABEF

τὴν τιμωρίαν, νομίζοντες οὐχ ἧσσον ἑαυτῶν
εἶναι τὴν ἀποικίαν ἢ Κερκυραίων, ἅμα The request
δὲ καὶ μίσει τῶν Κερκυραίων, ὅτι granted.
αὐτῶν παρημέλουν ὄντες ἄποικοι· οὔτε γὰρ ἐν 4
5 πανηγύρεσι ταῖς κοιναῖς διδόντες γέρα τὰ
νομιζόμενα οὔτε Κορινθίῳ ἀνδρὶ προκαταρχό-
μενοι τῶν ἱερῶν ὥσπερ αἱ ἄλλαι ἀποικίαι,
περιφρονοῦντες δὲ αὐτοὺς καὶ χρημάτων δυνάμει
ὄντες κατ' ἐκεῖνον τὸν χρόνον ὁμοῖα τοῖς
10 Ἑλλήνων πλουσιωτάτοις καὶ τῇ ἐς πόλεμον
παρασκευῇ δυνατώτεροι, ναυτικῷ δὲ καὶ πολὺ
προύχειν ἔστιν ὅτε ἐπαιρόμενοι καὶ κατὰ τὴν
Φαιάκων προενοίκησιν τῆς Κερκύρας κλέος
ἐχόντων τὰ περὶ τὰς ναῦς (ᾗ καὶ μᾶλλον
15 ἐξηρτύοντο τὸ ναυτικὸν καὶ ἦσαν οὐκ ἀδύνατοι·
τριήρεις γὰρ εἴκοσι καὶ ἑκατὸν ὑπῆρχον αὐτοῖς
ὅτε ἤρχοντο πολεμεῖν), πάντων οὖν τούτων 26
ἐγκλήματα ἔχοντες οἱ Κορίνθιοι ἔπεμπον ἐς
τὴν Ἐπίδαμνον ἄσμενοι τὴν ὠφελίαν, οἰκήτορά
20 τε τὸν βουλόμενον ἰέναι κελεύοντες καὶ Ἀμπρακιωτῶν καὶ Λευκαδίων καὶ ἑαυτῶν φρουρούς.
ἐπορεύθησαν δὲ πεζῇ ἐς Ἀπολλωνίαν, Κορινθίων 2·
οὖσαν ἀποικίαν, δέει τῶν Κερκυραίων μὴ
κωλύωνται ὑπ' αὐτῶν κατὰ θάλασσαν περαιού-
25 μενοι.

Κερκυραῖοι δὲ ἐπειδὴ ᾔσθοντο τούς τε οἰκή- 3
τορας καὶ φρουροὺς ἥκοντας ἐς τὴν Corcyra
Ἐπίδαμνον τήν τε ἀποικίαν Κοριν- intervenes.

4. γὰρ secl. Reiske　　9. ὁμοίᾳ AB (ι om. A, adscr. B)
12. post τὴν add. τῶν ABEFM　　15. τὰ ναυτικὰ EGM

θίοις δεδομένην, ἐχαλέπαινον· καὶ πλεύσαντες
εὐθὺς πέντε καὶ εἴκοσι ναυσὶ καὶ ὕστερον
ἑτέρῳ στόλῳ τούς τε φεύγοντας ἐκέλευον κατ'
ἐπήρειαν δέχεσθαι αὐτούς (ἦλθον γὰρ ἐς τὴν
Κέρκυραν οἱ τῶν Ἐπιδαμνίων φυγάδες, τάφους 5
τε ἀποδεικνύντες καὶ ξυγγένειαν, ἣν προϊσχό-
μενοι ἐδέοντο σφᾶς κατάγειν) τούς τε φρουροὺς
οὓς Κορίνθιοι ἔπεμψαν καὶ τοὺς οἰκήτορας
4 ἀποπέμπειν. οἱ δὲ Ἐπιδάμνιοι οὐδὲν αὐτῶν
ὑπήκουσαν, ἀλλὰ στρατεύουσιν ἐπ' αὐτοὺς οἱ 10
Κερκυραῖοι τεσσαράκοντα ναυσὶ μετὰ τῶν
φυγάδων ὡς κατάξοντες, καὶ τοὺς Ἰλλυριοὺς
5 προσλαβόντες. προσκαθεζόμενοι δὲ τὴν πόλιν
προεῖπον Ἐπιδαμνίων τε τὸν βουλόμενον καὶ
τοὺς ξένους ἀπαθεῖς ἀπιέναι· εἰ δὲ μή, ὡς 15
πολεμίοις χρήσεσθαι. ὡς δ' οὐκ ἐπείθοντο, οἱ
μὲν Κερκυραῖοι (ἔστι δ' ἰσθμὸς τὸ χωρίον)
27 ἐπολιόρκουν τὴν πόλιν, Κορίνθιοι δ', ὡς αὐτοῖς
Corinth prepares ἐκ τῆς Ἐπιδάμνου ἦλθον ἄγγελοι
a large force. ὅτι πολιορκοῦνται, παρεσκευάζοντο 20
στρατείαν, καὶ ἅμα ἀποικίαν ἐς τὴν Ἐπίδαμνον
ἐκήρυσσον ἐπὶ τῇ ἴσῃ καὶ ὁμοίᾳ τὸν βουλόμενον ἰέναι· εἰ δέ τις τὸ παραυτίκα μὲν
μὴ ἐθέλει ξυμπλεῖν, μετέχειν δὲ βούλεται
τῆς ἀποικίας, πεντήκοντα δραχμὰς καταθέντα 25
Κορινθίας μένειν. ἦσαν δὲ καὶ οἱ πλέοντες
2 πολλοὶ καὶ οἱ τἀργύριον καταβάλλοντες. ἐδεή-

---

6. ἐπιδεικνύντες B   7. post ἐδέοντο add. τε ABEFM
16. χρήσεσθαι C: χρήσασθαι cett.   21. στρατιάν ABE   24.
ἐθέλει C: ἐθέλοι cett. Phot.

θησαν δὲ καὶ τῶν Μεγαρέων ναυσὶ σφᾶς
ξυμπροπέμψαι, εἰ ἄρα κωλύοιντο ὑπὸ Κερκυραίων πλεῖν· οἱ δὲ παρεσκευάζοντο αὐτοῖς
ὀκτὼ ναυσὶ ξυμπλεῖν, καὶ Παλῆς Κεφαλλήνων
5 τέσσαρσιν. καὶ Ἐπιδαυρίων ἐδεήθησαν, οἳ παρέσχον πέντε, Ἑρμιονῆς δὲ μίαν καὶ Τροιζήνιοι
δύο, Λευκάδιοι δὲ δέκα καὶ Ἀμπρακιῶται ὀκτώ.
Θηβαίους δὲ χρήματα ᾔτησαν καὶ Φλειασίους,
Ἠλείους δὲ ναῦς τε κενὰς καὶ χρήματα. αὐτῶν
10 δὲ Κορινθίων νῆες παρεσκευάζοντο τριάκοντα
καὶ τρισχίλιοι ὁπλῖται.　　　　　　　　28
　　Ἐπειδὴ δὲ ἐπύθοντο οἱ Κερκυραῖοι τὴν
παρασκευήν, ἐλθόντες ἐς Κόρινθον Dispute between
Corinth and
μετὰ Λακεδαιμονίων καὶ Σικυωνίων Corcyra.
15 πρέσβεων, οὓς παρέλαβον, ἐκέλευον Κορινθίους
τοὺς ἐν Ἐπιδάμνῳ φρουρούς τε καὶ οἰκήτορας
ἀπάγειν, ὡς οὐ μετὸν αὐτοῖς Ἐπιδάμνου. εἰ 2
δέ τι ἀντιποιοῦνται, δίκας ἤθελον δοῦναι ἐν
Πελοποννήσῳ παρὰ πόλεσιν αἷς ἂν ἀμφότεροι
20 ξυμβῶσιν· ὁποτέρων δ᾽ ἂν δικασθῇ εἶναι τὴν
ἀποικίαν, τούτους κρατεῖν. ἤθελον δὲ καὶ τῷ
ἐν Δελφοῖς μαντείῳ ἐπιτρέψαι. πόλεμον δὲ 3
οὐκ εἴων ποιεῖν· εἰ δὲ μή, καὶ αὐτοὶ ἀναγκα-
σθήσεσθαι ἔφασαν, ἐκείνων βιαζομένων, φίλους
25 ποιεῖσθαι οὓς οὐ βούλονται ἑτέρους τῶν νῦν
ὄντων μᾶλλον ὠφελίας ἕνεκα. οἱ δὲ Κορίνθιοι 4
ἀπεκρίναντο αὐτοῖς, ἢν τάς τε ναῦς καὶ τοὺς
βαρβάρους ἀπὸ Ἐπιδάμνου ἀπαγάγωσι, βουλεύ-

---

2. ξυμπροπέμψειν ΑΒΕFΜ　　3. δὲ] τε CG　　12. ἐπεὶ CG
28. ἀπάγωσι ΑΒΕFΜ γρ. G ‖ βουλεύσασθαι CG

σεσθαι· πρότερον δ᾽ οὐ καλῶς ἔχειν τοὺς μὲν
5 πολιορκεῖσθαι, αὐτοὺς δὲ δικάζεσθαι. Κερκυραῖοι δὲ ἀντέλεγον, ἢν καὶ ἐκεῖνοι τοὺς ἐν
Ἐπιδάμνῳ ἀπαγάγωσι, ποιήσειν ταῦτα· ἕτοιμοι
δὲ εἶναι καὶ ὥστε ἀμφοτέρους μένειν κατὰ 5
χώραν, σπονδὰς δὲ ποιήσασθαι ἕως ἂν ἡ δίκη
29 γένηται. Κορίνθιοι δὲ οὐδὲν τούτων ὑπήκουον,
ἀλλ᾽ ἐπειδὴ πλήρεις αὐτοῖς ἦσαν αἱ νῆες καὶ
οἱ ξύμμαχοι παρῆσαν, προπέμψαντες κήρυκα
πρότερον πόλεμον προεροῦντα Κερκυραίοις, 10
ἄραντες ἑβδομήκοντα ναυσὶ καὶ πέντε δισχιλίοις
τε ὁπλίταις ἔπλεον ἐπὶ τὴν Ἐπίδαμνον Κερκυ-
2 ραίοις ἐναντία πολεμήσοντες· ἐστρατήγει δὲ
τῶν μὲν νεῶν Ἀριστεὺς ὁ Πελλίχου καὶ
Καλλικράτης ὁ Καλλίου καὶ Τιμάνωρ ὁ 15
Τιμάνθους, τοῦ δὲ πεζοῦ Ἀρχέτιμός τε ὁ
3 Εὐρυτίμου καὶ Ἰσαρχίδας ὁ Ἰσάρχου. ἐπειδὴ
δ᾽ ἐγένοντο ἐν Ἀκτίῳ τῆς Ἀνακτορίας γῆς,
οὗ τὸ ἱερὸν τοῦ Ἀπόλλωνός ἐστιν, ἐπὶ τῷ
στόματι τοῦ Ἀμπρακικοῦ κόλπου, οἱ Κερκυραῖοι 20
κήρυκά τε προύπεμψαν αὐτοῖς ἐν ἀκατίῳ
ἀπεροῦντα μὴ πλεῖν ἐπὶ σφᾶς καὶ τὰς ναῦς
ἅμα ἐπλήρουν, ζεύξαντές τε τὰς παλαιὰς ὥστε
πλωίμους εἶναι καὶ τὰς ἄλλας ἐπισκευάσαντες.
4 ὡς δὲ ὁ κῆρύξ τε ἀπήγγειλεν οὐδὲν εἰρηναῖον 25
παρὰ τῶν Κορινθίων καὶ αἱ νῆες αὐτοῖς ἐπε-
πλήρωντο οὖσαι ὀγδοήκοντα (τεσσαράκοντα γὰρ
Ἐπίδαμνον ἐπολιόρκουν), ἀνταναγαγόμενοι καὶ

2. ἑαυτοὺς [CG]   4. ἀπάγωσι CG   5. δὲ secl. Poppo
17. ἐπεὶ CG (corr. G¹)   28. ἀνταναγαγόμενοι Classen : ἀντανα-
γόμενοι codd.

παραταξάμενοι ἐναυμάχησαν· καὶ ἐνίκησαν οἱ 5
Κερκυραῖοι παρὰ πολὺ καὶ ναῦς The Corcyreans
πέντε καὶ δέκα διέφθειραν τῶν Corinthians at
Κορινθίων. τῇ δὲ αὐτῇ ἡμέρᾳ sea.
5 αὐτοῖς ξυνέβη καὶ τοὺς τὴν Ἐπίδαμνον πολιορ-
κοῦντας παραστήσασθαι ὁμολογίᾳ ὥστε τοὺς
μὲν ἐπήλυδας ἀποδόσθαι, Κορινθίους δὲ δή-
σαντας ἔχειν ἕως ἂν ἄλλο τι δόξῃ. μετὰ δὲ 30
τὴν ναυμαχίαν οἱ Κερκυραῖοι τροπαῖον στή-
10 σαντες ἐπὶ τῇ Λευκίμμῃ τῆς Κερκυραίας
ἀκρωτηρίῳ τοὺς μὲν ἄλλους οὓς ἔλαβον
αἰχμαλώτους ἀπέκτειναν, Κορινθίους δὲ δήσαντες εἶχον. ὕστερον δέ, ἐπειδὴ οἱ Κορίνθιοι 2
καὶ οἱ ξύμμαχοι ἡσσημένοι ταῖς ναυσὶν ἀνεχώ-
15 ρησαν ἐπ᾽ οἴκου, τῆς θαλάσσης ἁπάσης ἐκράτουν
τῆς κατ᾽ ἐκεῖνα τὰ χωρία οἱ Κερκυραῖοι, καὶ
πλεύσαντες ἐς Λευκάδα τὴν Κορινθίων ἀποικίαν
τῆς γῆς ἔτεμον καὶ Κυλλήνην τὸ Ἠλείων
ἐπίνειον ἐνέπρησαν, ὅτι ναῦς καὶ χρήματα
20 παρέσχον Κορινθίοις. τοῦ τε χρόνου τὸν 3
πλεῖστον μετὰ τὴν ναυμαχίαν ἐπεκράτουν τῆς
θαλάσσης καὶ τοὺς τῶν Κορινθίων ξυμμάχους
ἐπιπλέοντες ἔφθειρον, μέχρι οὗ Κορίνθιοι
περιιόντι τῷ θέρει πέμψαντες ναῦς καὶ
25 στρατιάν, ἐπεὶ σφῶν οἱ ξύμμαχοι ἐπόνουν,
ἐστρατοπεδεύοντο ἐπὶ Ἀκτίῳ καὶ περὶ τὸ
Χειμέριον τῆς Θεσπρωτίδος φυλακῆς ἕνεκα τῆς

2. post ναῦς add. τε CG   10. Λευκίμμῃ CG (et sic semper) ‖
Κερκύρας ABEFM   20. τὸν] τὸ BCM[G]   21. ἐπεκράτουν
C: ἐκράτουν cett. [G]   23. ἔφθειραν C[G]   24. περι-
ιόντι Reiske: περιόντι codd.

τε Λευκάδος καὶ τῶν ἄλλων πόλεων ὅσαι
4 σφίσι φίλιαι ἦσαν. ἀντεστρατοπεδεύοντο δὲ
καὶ οἱ Κερκυραῖοι ἐπὶ τῇ Λευκίμμῃ ναυσί τε
καὶ πεζῷ. ἐπέπλεον δὲ οὐδέτεροι ἀλλήλοις,
ἀλλὰ τὸ θέρος τοῦτο ἀντικαθεζόμενοι χειμῶνος 5
ἤδη ἀνεχώρησαν ἐπ᾽ οἴκου ἑκάτεροι.

31   Τὸν δ᾽ ἐνιαυτὸν πάντα τὸν μετὰ τὴν ναυ-
Fresh prepara-   μαχίαν καὶ τὸν ὕστερον οἱ Κορίνθιοι
tions of Corinth.
Corcyra seeks   ὀργῇ φέροντες τὸν πρὸς Κερκυραίους
alliance with
Athens. Corinth   πόλεμον ἐναυπηγοῦντο καὶ παρε- 10
sends to Athens
to oppose the   σκευάζοντο τὰ κράτιστα νεῶν στόλον,
request.   ἔκ τε αὐτῆς Πελοποννήσου ἀγείροντες
καὶ τῆς ἄλλης Ἑλλάδος ἐρέτας, μισθῷ πεί-
2 θοντες. πυνθανόμενοι δὲ οἱ Κερκυραῖοι τὴν
παρασκευὴν αὐτῶν ἐφοβοῦντο, καὶ (ἦσαν γὰρ 15
οὐδενὸς Ἑλλήνων ἔνσπονδοι οὐδὲ ἐσεγράψαντο
ἑαυτοὺς οὔτε ἐς τὰς Ἀθηναίων σπονδὰς οὔτε
ἐς τὰς Λακεδαιμονίων) ἔδοξεν αὐτοῖς ἐλθοῦσιν
ὡς τοὺς Ἀθηναίους ξυμμάχους γενέσθαι καὶ
ὠφελίαν τινὰ πειρᾶσθαι ἀπ᾽ αὐτῶν εὑρίσκεσθαι. 20
3 οἱ δὲ Κορίνθιοι πυθόμενοι ταῦτα ἦλθον καὶ
αὐτοὶ ἐς τὰς Ἀθήνας πρεσβευσόμενοι, ὅπως
μὴ σφίσι πρὸς τῷ Κερκυραίων ναυτικῷ καὶ
τὸ αὐτῶν προσγενόμενον ἐμπόδιον γένηται
4 θέσθαι τὸν πόλεμον ᾗ βούλονται. καταστάσης 25
δὲ ἐκκλησίας ἐς ἀντιλογίαν ἦλθον, καὶ οἱ μὲν
Κερκυραῖοι ἔλεξαν τοιάδε.

32   "Δίκαιον, ὦ Ἀθηναῖοι, τοὺς μήτε εὐεργεσίας

3. τε ABEFM suprascr. G   23. καὶ τὸ αὐτῶν c (in litura)
G : τὸ Ἀττικὸν cett. γρ. G

μεγάλης μήτε ξυμμαχίας προυφειλομένης ἥκοντας
παρὰ τοὺς πέλας ἐπικουρίας, ὥσπερ Speech of the
καὶ ἡμεῖς νῦν, δεησομένους ἀνα- Corcyrean
envoy. 'Our
διδάξαι πρῶτον, μάλιστα μὲν ὡς principle of
holding aloof
5 καὶ ξύμφορα δέονται, εἰ δὲ μή, ὅτι from alliances
has turned out a
γε οὐκ ἐπιζήμια, ἔπειτα δὲ ὡς καὶ mistake and has
caused our pre-
τὴν χάριν βέβαιον ἕξουσιν· εἰ δὲ sent weakness.'
τούτων μηδὲν σαφὲς καταστήσουσι, μὴ ὀργίζεσθαι ἢν ἀτυχῶσιν. Κερκυραῖοι δὲ μετὰ 2
10 τῆς ξυμμαχίας τῆς αἰτήσεως καὶ ταῦτα πιστεύοντες ἐχυρὰ ὑμῖν παρέξεσθαι ἀπέστειλαν
ἡμᾶς. τετύχηκε δὲ τὸ αὐτὸ ἐπιτήδευμα πρός 3
τε ὑμᾶς ἐς τὴν χρείαν ἡμῖν ἄλογον καὶ ἐς τὰ
ἡμέτερα αὐτῶν ἐν τῷ παρόντι ἀξύμφορον.
15 ξύμμαχοί τε γὰρ οὐδενός πω ἐν τῷ πρὸ τοῦ 4
χρόνῳ ἑκούσιοι γενόμενοι νῦν ἄλλων τοῦτο
δεησόμενοι ἥκομεν, καὶ ἅμα ἐς τὸν παρόντα
πόλεμον Κορινθίων ἐρῆμοι δι᾽ αὐτὸ καθέσταμεν.
καὶ περιέστηκεν ἡ δοκοῦσα ἡμῶν πρότερον
20 σωφροσύνη, τὸ μὴ ἐν ἀλλοτρίᾳ ξυμμαχίᾳ τῇ
τοῦ πέλας γνώμῃ ξυγκινδυνεύειν, νῦν ἀβουλία
καὶ ἀσθένεια φαινομένη. τὴν μὲν οὖν γενο- 5
μένην ναυμαχίαν αὐτοὶ κατὰ μόνας ἀπεωσάμεθα
Κορινθίους· ἐπειδὴ δὲ μείζονι παρασκευῇ ἀπὸ
25 Πελοποννήσου καὶ τῆς ἄλλης Ἑλλάδος ἐφ᾽
ἡμᾶς ὥρμηνται καὶ ἡμεῖς ἀδύνατοι ὁρῶμεν ὄντες
τῇ οἰκείᾳ μόνον δυνάμει περιγενέσθαι, καὶ ἅμα
μέγας ὁ κίνδυνος εἰ ἐσόμεθα ὑπ᾽ αὐτοῖς, ἀνάγκη
καὶ ὑμῶν καὶ ἄλλου παντὸς ἐπικουρίας δεῖσθαι,

16. χρόνῳ C : om. cett.

καὶ ξυγγνώμη εἰ μὴ μετὰ κακίας, δόξης δὲ
μᾶλλον ἁμαρτίᾳ τῇ πρότερον ἀπραγμοσύνῃ
ἐναντία τολμῶμεν.

33 " Γενήσεται δὲ ὑμῖν πειθομένοις καλὴ ἡ

'Your com-
pliance with
our request will
bring you ad-
vantages : (1)
you will be help-
ing the wronged :
(2) you will win
our gratitude :
(3) you will have
our fleet on your
side.'

ξυντυχία κατὰ πολλὰ τῆς ἡμετέρας 5
χρείας, πρῶτον μὲν ὅτι ἀδικουμένοις
καὶ οὐχ ἑτέρους βλάπτουσι τὴν
ἐπικουρίαν ποιήσεσθε, ἔπειτα περὶ
τῶν μεγίστων κινδυνεύοντας δεξάμενοι ὡς ἂν μάλιστα μετ' αἰειμνήστου 10
μαρτυρίου τὴν χάριν καταθήσεσθε·
ναυτικόν τε κεκτήμεθα πλὴν τοῦ παρ' ὑμῖν

2 πλεῖστον. καὶ σκέψασθε τίς εὐπραξία σπανιω-
τέρα ἢ τίς τοῖς πολεμίοις λυπηροτέρα εἰ ἢν
ὑμεῖς ἂν πρὸ πολλῶν χρημάτων καὶ χάριτος 15
ἐτιμήσασθε δύναμιν ὑμῖν προσγενέσθαι, αὕτη
πάρεστιν αὐτεπάγγελτος ἄνευ κινδύνων καὶ
δαπάνης διδοῦσα ἑαυτήν, καὶ προσέτι φέρουσα
ἐς μὲν τοὺς πολλοὺς ἀρετήν, οἷς δὲ ἐπαμυνεῖτε
χάριν, ὑμῖν δ' αὐτοῖς ἰσχύν· ἃ ἐν τῷ παντὶ 20
χρόνῳ ὀλίγοις δὴ ἅμα πάντα ξυνέβη, καὶ
ὀλίγοι ξυμμαχίας δεόμενοι οἷς ἐπικαλοῦνται
ἀσφάλειαν καὶ κόσμον οὐχ ἧσσον διδόντες ἢ

3 ληψόμενοι παραγίγνονται. τὸν δὲ πόλεμον, δι'
ὅνπερ χρήσιμοι ἂν εἶμεν, εἴ τις ὑμῶν μὴ 25
οἴεται ἔσεσθαι, γνώμης ἁμαρτάνει καὶ οὐκ
αἰσθάνεται τοὺς Λακεδαιμονίους φόβῳ τῷ

8. ἔπειτα—c. 37. 2 οὐδένα suppl. m fol. viii
θήσεσθε Krüger : καταθῆσθε vel κατάθησθε codd.
ABEF

11. κατα-
θήσεσθε
24. διόπερ

ὑμετέρῳ πολεμησείοντας καὶ τοὺς Κορινθίους
δυναμένους παρ' αὐτοῖς καὶ ὑμῖν ἐχθροὺς ὄντας
καὶ προκαταλαμβάνοντας ἡμᾶς νῦν ἐς τὴν
ὑμετέραν ἐπιχείρησιν, ἵνα μὴ τῷ κοινῷ ἔχθει
5 κατ' αὐτοὺς μετ' ἀλλήλων στῶμεν μηδὲ δυοῖν
φθάσαι ἁμάρτωσιν, ἢ κακῶσαι ἡμᾶς ἢ σφᾶς
αὐτοὺς βεβαιώσασθαι. ἡμέτερον δέ γ' αὖ ἔργον 4
προτερῆσαι, τῶν μὲν διδόντων, ὑμῶν δὲ δεξα-
μένων τὴν ξυμμαχίαν, καὶ προεπιβουλεύειν
10 αὐτοῖς μᾶλλον ἢ ἀντεπιβουλεύειν.

"Ἢν δὲ λέγωσιν ὡς οὐ δίκαιον τοὺς 34
σφετέρους ἀποίκους ὑμᾶς δέχεσθαι,　'You will not be
μαθόντων ὡς πᾶσα ἀποικία εὖ μὲν　acting unjustly.
πάσχουσα τιμᾷ τὴν μητρόπολιν, ἀδικουμένη
15 δὲ ἀλλοτριοῦται· οὐ γὰρ ἐπὶ τῷ δοῦλοι, ἀλλ'
ἐπὶ τῷ ὁμοῖοι τοῖς λειπομένοις εἶναι ἐκπέμπονται. ὡς δὲ ἠδίκουν σαφές ἐστιν· προκλη- 2
θέντες γὰρ περὶ Ἐπιδάμνου ἐς κρίσιν πολέμῳ
μᾶλλον ἢ τῷ ἴσῳ ἐβουλήθησαν τὰ ἐγκλήματα
20 μετελθεῖν. καὶ ὑμῖν ἔστω τι τεκμήριον ἃ πρὸς 3
ἡμᾶς τοὺς ξυγγενεῖς δρῶσιν, ὥστε ἀπάτῃ τε μὴ
παράγεσθαι ὑπ' αὐτῶν δεομένοις τε ἐκ τοῦ
εὐθέος μὴ ὑπουργεῖν· ὁ γὰρ ἐλαχίστας τὰς
μεταμελείας ἐκ τοῦ χαρίζεσθαι τοῖς ἐναντίοις
25 λαμβάνων ἀσφαλέστατος ἂν διατελοίη. λύσετε 35
δὲ οὐδὲ τὰς Λακεδαιμονίων σπονδὰς δεχόμενοι
ἡμᾶς μηδετέρων ὄντας ξυμμάχους·　'You will not be
εἴρηται γὰρ ἐν αὐταῖς, τῶν Ἑλληνίδων　breaking the
πόλεων ἥτις μηδαμοῦ ξυμμαχεῖ,　thirty years' 2
　　　　　　　　　　　　　　　truce.'

2. αὐτῶν F[G]　　7. γ' om. ABEF

ἐξεῖναι παρ' ὁποτέρους ἂν ἀρέσκηται ἐλθεῖν.
3 καὶ δεινὸν εἰ τοῖσδε μὲν ἀπό τε τῶν ἐνσπόνδων
ἔσται πληροῦν τὰς ναῦς καὶ προσέτι καὶ ἐκ
τῆς ἄλλης Ἑλλάδος καὶ οὐχ ἥκιστα ἀπὸ τῶν
ὑμετέρων ὑπηκόων, ἡμᾶς δὲ ἀπὸ τῆς προκει- 5
μένης τε ξυμμαχίας εἴρξουσι καὶ ἀπὸ τῆς
ἄλλοθέν ποθεν ὠφελίας, εἶτα ἐν ἀδικήματι
4 θήσονται πεισθέντων ὑμῶν ἃ δεόμεθα. πολὺ
δὲ ἐν πλέονι αἰτίᾳ ἡμεῖς μὴ πείσαντες ὑμᾶς
ἕξομεν· ἡμᾶς μὲν γὰρ κινδυνεύοντας καὶ οὐκ 10
ἐχθροὺς ὄντας ἀπώσεσθε, τῶνδε δὲ οὐχ ὅπως
κωλυταὶ ἐχθρῶν ὄντων καὶ ἐπιόντων γενήσεσθε,
ἀλλὰ καὶ ἀπὸ τῆς ὑμετέρας ἀρχῆς δύναμιν
προσλαβεῖν περιόψεσθε· ἣν οὐ δίκαιον, ἀλλ'
ἢ κἀκείνων κωλύειν τοὺς ἐκ τῆς ὑμετέρας 15
μισθοφόρους ἢ καὶ ἡμῖν πέμπειν καθ' ὅτι ἂν
πεισθῆτε ὠφελίαν, μάλιστα δὲ ἀπὸ τοῦ προ-
5 φανοῦς δεξαμένους βοηθεῖν. πολλὰ δέ, ὥσπερ
Recapitulation ἐν ἀρχῇ ὑπείπομεν, τὰ ξυμφέροντα
of the
advantages.   ἀποδείκνυμεν, καὶ μέγιστον ὅτι οἵ 20
τε αὐτοὶ πολέμιοι ἡμῖν ἦσαν, ὅπερ σαφεστάτη
πίστις, καὶ οὗτοι οὐκ ἀσθενεῖς, ἀλλ' ἱκανοὶ
τοὺς μεταστάντας βλάψαι· καὶ ναυτικῆς καὶ
οὐκ ἠπειρώτιδος τῆς ξυμμαχίας διδομένης οὐχ
ὁμοία ἡ ἀλλοτρίωσις, ἀλλὰ μάλιστα μέν, εἰ 25
δύνασθε, μηδένα ἄλλον ἐᾶν κεκτῆσθαι ναῦς, εἰ
δὲ μή, ὅστις ἐχυρώτατος, τοῦτον φίλον ἔχειν.

7. εἶτα] εἴ τε Krüger   9. δὲ] δὴ Krüger   15. τὰς
. . μισθοφορίας G   21. ἦσαν secl. Herwerden   25. post
μὲν add. δεῖ Sitzler

" Καὶ ὅτῳ τάδε ξυμφέροντα μὲν δοκεῖ 36
λέγεσθαι, φοβεῖται δὲ μὴ δι᾿ αὐτὰ 'There is no
need for anxiety.
πειθόμενος τὰς σπονδὰς λύσῃ, γνώτω Corcyra will be
a valuable
τὸ μὲν δεδιὸς αὐτοῦ ἰσχὺν ἔχον τοὺς friend.'
5 ἐναντίους μᾶλλον φοβῆσον, τὸ δὲ θαρσοῦν μὴ
δεξαμένου ἀσθενὲς ὂν πρὸς ἰσχύοντας τοὺς
ἐχθροὺς ἀδεέστερον ἐσόμενον, καὶ ἅμα οὐ περὶ
τῆς Κερκύρας νῦν τὸ πλέον ἢ καὶ τῶν Ἀθηνῶν
βουλευόμενος, καὶ οὐ τὰ κράτιστα αὐταῖς
10 προνοῶν, ὅταν ἐς τὸν μέλλοντα καὶ ὅσον οὐ
παρόντα πόλεμον τὸ αὐτίκα περισκοπῶν
ἐνδοιάζῃ χωρίον προσλαβεῖν ὃ μετὰ μεγίστων
καιρῶν οἰκειοῦταί τε καὶ πολεμοῦται. τῆς τε 2
γὰρ Ἰταλίας καὶ Σικελίας καλῶς παράπλου
15 κεῖται, ὥστε μήτε ἐκεῖθεν ναυτικὸν ἐᾶσαι
Πελοποννησίοις ἐπελθεῖν τό τε ἐνθένδε πρὸς
τἀκεῖ παραπέμψαι, καὶ ἐς τἆλλα ξυμφορώτατόν
ἐστιν. βραχυτάτῳ δ᾿ ἂν κεφαλαίῳ, τοῖς τε 3
ξύμπασι καὶ καθ᾿ ἕκαστον, τῷδ᾿ ἂν μὴ προέσθαι
20 ἡμᾶς μάθοιτε· τρία μὲν ὄντα λόγου ἄξια τοῖς
Ἕλλησι ναυτικά, τὸ παρ᾿ ὑμῖν καὶ τὸ ἡμέτερον
καὶ τὸ Κορινθίων· τούτων δὲ εἰ περιόψεσθε
τὰ δύο ἐς ταὐτὸν ἐλθεῖν καὶ Κορίνθιοι ἡμᾶς
προκαταλήψονται, Κερκυραίοις τε καὶ Πελο-
25 ποννησίοις ἅμα ναυμαχήσετε, δεξάμενοι δὲ
ἡμᾶς ἕξετε πρὸς αὐτοὺς πλείοσι ναυσὶ ταῖς
ἡμετέραις ἀγωνίζεσθαι." τοιαῦτα μὲν οἱ Κερκυ- 4
ραῖοι εἶπον· οἱ δὲ Κορίνθιοι μετ᾿ αὐτοὺς τοιάδε.

16. ἐνθένδε] ἐντεῦθεν CG   22. τὸ] τῶν ABEF   23. τὸ
αὐτὸ CG   27. ὑμετέραις CG (corr. G¹)

37 " Ἀναγκαῖον Κερκυραίων τῶνδε οὐ μόνον

Reply of the
Corinthian
envoy.

περὶ τοῦ δέξασθαι σφᾶς τὸν λόγον
ποιησαμένων, ἀλλ᾽ ὡς καὶ ἡμεῖς τε
ἀδικοῦμεν καὶ αὐτοὶ οὐκ εἰκότως πολεμοῦνται,
μνησθέντας πρῶτον καὶ ἡμᾶς περὶ ἀμφοτέρων 5
οὕτω καὶ ἐπὶ τὸν ἄλλον λόγον ἰέναι, ἵνα τὴν
ἀφ᾽ ἡμῶν τε ἀξίωσιν ἀσφαλέστερον προειδῆτε
καὶ τὴν τῶνδε χρείαν μὴ ἀλογίστως ἀπώσησθε.

2 " Φασὶ δὲ ξυμμαχίαν διὰ τὸ σῶφρον οὐδενός

'Corcyra has
held aloof from
alliances that
she may not
have witnesses
of her misdeeds.'

πω δέξασθαι· τὸ δ᾽ ἐπὶ κακουργίᾳ 10
καὶ οὐκ ἀρετῇ ἐπετήδευσαν, ξύμμαχόν τε οὐδένα βουλόμενοι πρὸς
τἀδικήματα οὐδὲ μάρτυρα ἔχειν

3 οὔτε παρακαλοῦντες αἰσχύνεσθαι. καὶ ἡ
πόλις αὐτῶν ἅμα αὐτάρκη θέσιν κειμένη 15
παρέχει αὐτοὺς δικαστὰς ὧν βλάπτουσί τινα
μᾶλλον ἢ κατὰ ξυνθήκας γίγνεσθαι, διὰ τὸ
ἥκιστα ἐπὶ τοὺς πέλας ἐκπλέοντας μάλιστα
τοὺς ἄλλους ἀνάγκῃ καταίροντας δέχεσθαι.

4 καὶ τοῦτο τὸ εὐπρεπὲς ἄσπονδον οὐχ ἵνα μὴ 20
ξυναδικῶσιν ἑτέροις προβέβληνται, ἀλλ᾽ ὅπως
κατὰ μόνας ἀδικῶσι καὶ ὅπως ἐν ᾧ μὲν ἂν
κρατῶσι βιάζωνται, οὗ δ᾽ ἂν λάθωσι πλέον
ἔχωσιν, ἢν δέ πού τι προσλάβωσιν ἀναισχυν-

5 τῶσιν· καίτοι εἰ ἦσαν ἄνδρες, ὥσπερ φασίν, 25
ἀγαθοί, ὅσῳ ἀληπτότεροι ἦσαν τοῖς πέλας,
τόσῳ δὲ φανερωτέραν ἐξῆν αὐτοῖς τὴν ἀρετὴν

9. δὲ] δὴ Krüger   20. κἂν τούτῳ ABEFM[G]   21. ξυνα-
δικήσωσιν ABEFM   23. κρατηθῶσι C[G] ‖ βιάζονται BEFM[G]
24. ἔχουσιν BEFM ‖ προλάβωσιν C ‖ ἀναισχυντοῦσι(ν) BCEFM
27. τόσῳ δὲ Hertlein : τοσῷδε codd.

διδοῦσι καὶ δεχομένοις τὰ δίκαια δεικνύναι.
ἀλλ' οὔτε πρὸς τοὺς ἄλλους οὔτε   'She has   **38**
ἐς ἡμᾶς τοιοίδε εἰσίν, ἄποικοι δ'   wronged her
mother-city.'
ὄντες ἀφεστᾶσί τε διὰ παντὸς καὶ νῦν
5 πολεμοῦσι, λέγοντες ὡς οὐκ ἐπὶ τῷ κακῶς
πάσχειν ἐκπεμφθεῖεν. ἡμεῖς δὲ οὐδ' αὐτοί 2
φαμεν ἐπὶ τῷ ὑπὸ τούτων ὑβρίζεσθαι, κατοικί-
σαι, ἀλλ' ἐπὶ τῷ ἡγεμόνες τε εἶναι καὶ τὰ
εἰκότα θαυμάζεσθαι. αἱ γοῦν ἄλλαι ἀποικίαι 3
10 τιμῶσιν ἡμᾶς, καὶ μάλιστα ὑπὸ ἀποίκων
στεργόμεθα· καὶ δῆλον ὅτι, εἰ τοῖς πλέοσιν 4
ἀρέσκοντές ἐσμεν, τοῖσδ' ἂν μόνοις οὐκ ὀρθῶς
ἀπαρέσκοιμεν, οὐδ' ἐπιστρατεύομεν ἐκπρεπῶς
μὴ καὶ διαφερόντως τι ἀδικούμενοι. καλὸν δ' 5
15 ἦν, εἰ καὶ ἡμαρτάνομεν, τοῖσδε μὲν εἶξαι τῇ
ἡμετέρᾳ ὀργῇ, ἡμῖν δὲ αἰσχρὸν βιάσασθαι τὴν
τούτων μετριότητα· ὕβρει δὲ καὶ ἐξουσίᾳ
πλούτου πολλὰ ἐς ἡμᾶς ἄλλα τε ἡμαρτήκασι
καὶ Ἐπίδαμνον ἡμετέραν οὖσαν κακουμένην
20 μὲν οὐ προσεποιοῦντο, ἐλθόντων δὲ ἡμῶν ἐπὶ
τιμωρίᾳ ἑλόντες βίᾳ ἔχουσιν.

"Καὶ φασὶ δὴ δίκῃ πρότερον ἐθελῆσαι **39**
κρίνεσθαι, ἥν γε οὐ τὸν προύχοντα   'She claims
that she de-
καὶ ἐκ τοῦ ἀσφαλοῦς προκαλού-   manded arbitration : the
25 μενον λέγειν τι δοκεῖν δεῖ, ἀλλὰ   demand was
not sincerely
τὸν ἐς ἴσον τά τε ἔργα ὁμοίως καὶ   made.'
τοὺς λόγους πρὶν διαγωνίζεσθαι καθιστάντα.
οὗτοι δὲ οὐ πρὶν πολιορκεῖν τὸ χωρίον, ἀλλ' 2

13. ἐπεστρατεύομεν, ut videtur, legit Schol., *bellum intulimus*
Valla

ἐπειδὴ ἡγήσαντο ἡμᾶς οὐ περιόψεσθαι, τότε
καὶ τὸ εὐπρεπὲς τῆς δίκης παρέσχοντο. καὶ
δεῦρο ἥκουσιν οὐ τἀκεῖ μόνον αὐτοὶ ἁμαρ-
τόντες, ἀλλὰ καὶ ὑμᾶς νῦν ἀξιοῦντες οὐ
ξυμμαχεῖν, ἀλλὰ ξυναδικεῖν καὶ διαφόρους 5
3 ὄντας ἡμῖν δέχεσθαι σφᾶς· οὓς χρῆν, ὅτε
ἀσφαλέστατοι ἦσαν, τότε προσιέναι, καὶ μὴ
ἐν ᾧ ἡμεῖς μὲν ἠδικήμεθα, οὗτοι δὲ κινδυνεύ-
ουσι, μηδ᾽ ἐν ᾧ ὑμεῖς τῆς τε δυνάμεως αὐτῶν
τότε οὐ μεταλαβόντες τῆς ὠφελίας νῦν μετα- 10
δώσετε καὶ τῶν ἁμαρτημάτων ἀπογενόμενοι
τῆς ἀφ᾽ ἡμῶν αἰτίας τὸ ἴσον ἕξετε, πάλαι
δὲ κοινώσαντας τὴν δύναμιν κοινὰ καὶ τὰ
ἀποβαίνοντα ἔχειν.

40 "Ὡς μὲν οὖν αὐτοι τε μετα προσηκοντων 15
'You will act   ἐγκλημάτων ἐρχόμεθα καὶ οἵδε
unjustly if you
consent.'   βίαιοι καὶ πλεονέκται εἰσὶ δεδήλω-
ται· ὡς δὲ οὐκ ἂν δικαίως αὐτοὺς δέχοισθε
2 μαθεῖν χρή. εἰ γὰρ εἴρηται ἐν ταῖς σπονδαῖς
ἐξεῖναι παρ᾽ ὁποτέρους τις βούλεται τῶν 20
ἀγράφων πόλεων ἐλθεῖν, οὐ τοῖς ἐπὶ βλάβῃ
ἑτέρων ἰοῦσιν ἡ ξυνθήκη ἐστίν, ἀλλ᾽ ὅστις μή,
ἄλλου ἑαυτὸν ἀποστερῶν, ἀσφαλείας δεῖται καὶ
ὅστις μὴ τοῖς δεξαμένοις, εἰ σωφρονοῦσι,
πόλεμον ἀντ᾽ εἰρήνης ποιήσει· ὃ νῦν ὑμεῖς μὴ 25

11. ἀπο (ο ex ω c) γενόμενοι CE[G]   13. κοινωνήσαντας
ABEF (corr. F¹) [G]   14. post ἔχειν add. ἐγκλημάτων C,
ἐγκλημάτων δὲ μόνον ἀμετόχους οὕτως τῶν μετὰ τὰς πράξεις τούτων
μὴ κοινωνεῖν cG   16. ἐγκλημάτων om. C: τοῦ δικαίου κεφα-
λαίων πρὸς ὑμᾶς vel similia cGm   20. τῶν ἀγράφων πόλεων
βούλεται ABEFM   23. ἄλλων cG ‖ αὐτὸν B : αὐτὸν AEM

πειθόμενοι ἡμῖν πάθοιτε ἄν. οὐ γὰρ τοῖσδε 3
μόνον ἐπίκουροι ἂν γένοισθε, ἀλλὰ καὶ ἡμῖν
ἀντὶ ἐνσπόνδων πολέμιοι· ἀνάγκη γάρ, εἰ ἴτε
μετ' αὐτῶν, καὶ ἀμύνεσθαι μὴ ἄνευ ὑμῶν
5 τούτους. καίτοι δίκαιοί γ' ἐστὲ μάλιστα μὲν 4
ἐκποδὼν στῆναι ἀμφοτέροις, εἰ δὲ μή, τοὐναντίον ἐπὶ τούτους μεθ' ἡμῶν ἰέναι (Κορινθίοις
μέν γε ἔνσπονδοί ἐστε, Κερκυραίοις δὲ οὐδὲ
δι' ἀνοκωχῆς πώποτ' ἐγένεσθε), καὶ τὸν νόμον
10 μὴ καθιστάναι ὥστε τοὺς ἑτέρων ἀφισταμένους
δέχεσθαι. οὐδὲ γὰρ ἡμεῖς Σαμίων ἀποστάντων 5
ψῆφον προσεθέμεθα ἐναντίαν ὑμῖν, τῶν ἄλλων
Πελοποννησίων δίχα ἐψηφισμένων εἰ χρὴ
αὐτοῖς ἀμύνειν, φανερῶς δὲ ἀντείπομεν τοὺς
15 προσήκοντας ξυμμάχους αὐτόν τινα κολάζειν.
εἰ γὰρ τοὺς κακόν τι δρῶντας δεχόμενοι 6
τιμωρήσετε, φανεῖται καὶ ἃ τῶν ὑμετέρων οὐκ
ἐλάσσω ἡμῖν πρόσεισι, καὶ τὸν νόμον ἐφ' ὑμῖν
αὐτοῖς μᾶλλον ἢ ἐφ' ἡμῖν θήσετε.
20   "Δικαιώματα μὲν οὖν τάδε πρὸς ὑμᾶς 41
ἔχομεν ἱκανὰ κατὰ τοὺς Ἑλλήνων   'You are morally
νόμους, παραίνεσιν δὲ καὶ ἀξίωσιν   bound to us: we
χάριτος τοιάνδε, ἣν οὐκ ἐχθροὶ   have claims on
                                                         you.'
ὄντες ὥστε βλάπτειν οὐδ' αὖ φίλοι ὥστ' ἐπι-
25 χρῆσθαι, ἀντιδοθῆναι ἡμῖν ἐν τῷ παρόντι
φαμὲν χρῆναι. νεῶν γὰρ μακρῶν σπανίσαντές 2
ποτε πρὸς τὸν Αἰγινητῶν ὑπὲρ τὰ Μηδικὰ
πόλεμον παρὰ Κορινθίων εἴκοσι ναῦς ἐλάβετε·
καὶ ἡ εὐεργεσία αὕτη τε καὶ ἡ ἐς Σαμίους, τὸ

---

1. πάθοιτε oF¹g: πάθητε cett.   5. γ' om. CG

38   ΘΟΥΚΥΔΙΔΟΥ

δι' ἡμᾶς Πελοποννησίους αὐτοῖς μὴ βοηθῆσαι,
παρέσχεν ὑμῖν Αἰγινητῶν μὲν ἐπικράτησιν,
Σαμίων δὲ κόλασιν, καὶ ἐν καιροῖς τοιούτοις
ἐγένετο οἷς μάλιστα ἄνθρωποι ἐπ' ἐχθροὺς
τοὺς σφετέρους ἰόντες τῶν ἁπάντων ἀπερίοπτοί 5
3 εἰσι παρὰ τὸ νικᾶν· φίλον τε γὰρ ἡγοῦνται
τὸν ὑπουργοῦντα, ἢν καὶ πρότερον ἐχθρὸς ᾖ,
πολέμιόν τε τὸν ἀντιστάντα, ἢν καὶ τύχῃ
φίλος ὤν, ἐπεὶ καὶ τὰ οἰκεῖα χεῖρον τίθενται
φιλονικίας ἕνεκα τῆς αὐτίκα.   10
42   "Ὧν ἐνθυμηθέντες καὶ νεώτερός τις παρὰ
'To refuse will   πρεσβυτέρου αὐτὰ μαθὼν ἀξιούτω
be advantageous
to you. To   τοῖς ὁμοίοις ἡμᾶς ἀμύνεσθαι, καὶ
refrain from
wrong is the   μὴ νομίσῃ δίκαια μὲν τάδε λέγε-
safest policy.'   σθαι, ξύμφορα δέ, εἰ πολεμήσει, 15
2 ἄλλα εἶναι. τό τε γὰρ ξυμφέρον ἐν ᾧ ἄν τις
ἐλάχιστα ἁμαρτάνῃ μάλιστα ἕπεται, καὶ τὸ
μέλλον τοῦ πολέμου ᾧ φοβοῦντες ὑμᾶς
Κερκυραῖοι κελεύουσιν ἀδικεῖν ἐν ἀφανεῖ ἔτι
κεῖται, καὶ οὐκ ἄξιον ἐπαρθέντας αὐτῷ φανερὰν 20
ἔχθραν ἤδη καὶ οὐ μέλλουσαν πρὸς Κορινθίους
κτήσασθαι, τῆς δὲ ὑπαρχούσης πρότερον διὰ
Μεγαρέας ὑποψίας σῶφρον ὑφελεῖν μᾶλλον (ἡ
3 γὰρ τελευταία χάρις καιρὸν ἔχουσα, κἂν
4 ἐλάσσων ᾖ, δύναται μεῖζον ἔγκλημα λῦσαι), 25
μηδ' ὅτι ναυτικοῦ ξυμμαχίαν μεγάλην διδόασι,
τούτῳ ἐφέλκεσθαι· τὸ γὰρ μὴ ἀδικεῖν τοὺς
ὁμοίους ἐχυρωτέρα δύναμις ἢ τῷ αὐτίκα

5. ἁπάντων C Schol. : πάντων cett. [G]   13. ἀμύνεσθαι]
ἀμείβεσθαι γρ. Schol.   27. ἐφέλκεσθε AFM

φανερῷ ἐπαρθέντας διὰ κινδύνων τὸ πλέον
ἔχειν. ἡμεῖς δὲ περιπεπτωκότες οἷς ἐν τῇ 43
Λακεδαίμονι αὐτοὶ προείπομεν, τοὺς σφετέρους
ξυμμάχους αὐτόν τινα κολάζειν, νῦν παρ' ὑμῶν
5 τὸ αὐτὸ ἀξιοῦμεν κομίζεσθαι, καὶ μὴ τῇ
ἡμετέρᾳ ψήφῳ ὠφεληθέντας τῇ ὑμετέρᾳ ἡμᾶς
βλάψαι. τὸ δὲ ἴσον ἀνταπόδοτε, γνόντες 2
τοῦτον ἐκεῖνον εἶναι τὸν καιρὸν ἐν ᾧ ὅ τε
ὑπουργῶν φίλος μάλιστα καὶ ὁ ἀντιστὰς
10 ἐχθρός. καὶ Κερκυραίους τούσδε μήτε ξυμμά- 3
χους δέχεσθε βίᾳ ἡμῶν μήτε ἀμύνετε αὐτοῖς
ἀδικοῦσιν. καὶ τάδε ποιοῦντες τὰ προσήκοντά 4
τε δράσετε καὶ τὰ ἄριστα βουλεύσεσθε ὑμῖν
αὐτοῖς."
15 Τοιαῦτα δὲ καὶ οἱ Κορίνθιοι εἶπον. 44
Ἀθηναῖοι δὲ ἀκούσαντες ἀμφο- After an
τέρων, γενομένης καὶ δὶς ἐκκλησίας, debate, a de-
τῇ μὲν προτέρᾳ οὐχ ἧσσον τῶν fensive alliance
Κορινθίων ἀπεδέξαντο τοὺς λόγους, Corcyra.
20 ἐν δὲ τῇ ὑστεραίᾳ μετέγνωσαν Κερκυραίοις
ξυμμαχίαν μὲν μὴ ποιήσασθαι ὥστε τοὺς
αὐτοὺς ἐχθροὺς καὶ φίλους νομίζειν (εἰ γὰρ
ἐπὶ Κόρινθον ἐκέλευον σφίσιν οἱ Κερκυραῖοι
ξυμπλεῖν, ἐλύοντ' ἂν αὐτοῖς αἱ πρὸς Πελο-
25 ποννησίους σπονδαί), ἐπιμαχίαν δ' ἐποιήσαντο
τῇ ἀλλήλων βοηθεῖν, ἐάν τις ἐπὶ Κέρκυραν
ἴῃ ἢ Ἀθήνας ἢ τοὺς τούτων ξυμμάχους.
ἐδόκει γὰρ ὁ πρὸς Πελοποννησίους πόλεμος 2

10. post Κερκυραίους add. τε CG : δὲ F : γε Hude   11.
δέχησθε cG ‖ ἀμύνητε cG

καὶ ὡς ἔσεσθαι αὐτοῖς, καὶ τὴν Κέρκυραν
ἐβούλοντο μὴ προέσθαι τοῖς Κορινθίοις
ναυτικὸν ἔχουσαν τοσοῦτον, ξυγκρούειν δὲ ὅτι
μάλιστα αὐτοὺς ἀλλήλοις, ἵνα ἀσθενεστέροις
οὖσιν, ἤν τι δέῃ, Κορινθίοις τε καὶ τοῖς ἄλλοις 5
ναυτικὸν ἔχουσιν ἐς πόλεμον καθιστῶνται.
3 ἅμα δὲ τῆς τε Ἰταλίας καὶ Σικελίας καλῶς
ἐφαίνετο αὐτοῖς ἡ νῆσος ἐν παράπλῳ κεῖσθαι.
45 Τοιαύτῃ μὲν γνώμῃ οἱ Ἀθηναῖοι τοὺς
Athens sends Κερκυραίους προσεδέξαντο, καὶ τῶν 10
ten ships to
Corcyra. Κορινθίων ἀπελθόντων οὐ πολὺ
ὕστερον δέκα ναῦς αὐτοῖς ἀπέστειλαν βοηθούς·
2 ἐστρατήγει δὲ αὐτῶν Λακεδαιμόνιός τε ὁ
Κίμωνος καὶ Διότιμος ὁ Στρομβίχου καὶ
3 Πρωτέας ὁ Ἐπικλέους. προεῖπον δὲ αὐτοῖς 15
μὴ ναυμαχεῖν Κορινθίοις, ἢν μὴ ἐπὶ Κέρκυραν
πλέωσι καὶ μέλλωσιν ἀποβαίνειν ἢ ἐς τῶν
ἐκείνων τι χωρίων· οὕτω δὲ κωλύειν κατὰ
δύναμιν. προεῖπον δὲ ταῦτα τοῦ μὴ λύειν
46 ἕνεκα τὰς σπονδάς. αἱ ἐν δὴ νῆες ἀφικνοῦν- 20
Corinth sends ται ἐς τὴν Κέρκυραν, οἱ δὲ Κορίν-
150 ships against
Corcyra. θιοι, ἐπειδὴ αὐτοῖς παρεσκεύαστο,
ἔπλεον ἐπὶ τὴν Κέρκυραν ναυσὶ πεντήκοντα
καὶ ἑκατόν. ἦσαν δὲ Ἠλείων μὲν δέκα,
Μεγαρέων δὲ δώδεκα καὶ Λευκαδίων δέκα, 25
2 Ἀμπρακιωτῶν δὲ ἑπτὰ καὶ εἴκοσι καὶ Ἀνακ-
τορίων μία, αὐτῶν δὲ Κορινθίων ἐνενήκοντα·
στρατηγοὶ δὲ τούτων ἦσαν μὲν καὶ κατὰ
πόλεις ἑκάστων, Κορινθίων δὲ Ξενοκλείδης ὁ

2. τοῖς om. ABEFM   5. post ἄλλοις add. τοῖς Bekker

Εὐθυκλέους πέμπτος αὐτός. ἐπειδὴ δὲ προσέ- 3
μειξαν τῇ κατὰ Κέρκυραν ἠπείρῳ ἀπὸ Λευκάδος
πλέοντες, ὁρμίζονται ἐς Χειμέριον τῆς Θεσπρωτίδος γῆς. ἔστι δὲ λιμήν, καὶ πόλις ὑπὲρ 4
5 αὐτοῦ κεῖται ἀπὸ θαλάσσης ἐν τῇ Ἐλαιάτιδι
τῆς Θεσπρωτίδος Ἐφύρη. ἐξίησι δὲ παρ'
αὐτὴν Ἀχερουσία λίμνη ἐς θάλασσαν· διὰ δὲ
τῆς Θεσπρωτίδος Ἀχέρων ποταμὸς ῥέων ἐσβάλλει ἐς αὐτήν, ἀφ' οὗ καὶ τὴν ἐπωνυμίαν
10 ἔχει. ῥεῖ δὲ καὶ Θύαμις ποταμός, ὁρίζων τὴν
Θεσπρωτίδα καὶ Κεστρίνην, ὧν ἐντὸς ἡ ἄκρα
ἀνέχει τὸ Χειμέριον. οἱ μὲν οὖν Κορίνθιοι 5
τῆς ἠπείρου ἐνταῦθα ὁρμίζονταί τε καὶ στρατόπεδον ἐποιήσαντο. οἱ δὲ Κερκυραῖοι ὡς **47**
15 ᾔσθοντο αὐτοὺς προσπλέοντας, πλη-   Corcyra mans
ρώσαντες δέκα καὶ ἑκατὸν ναῦς, ὧν   110 ships.
ἦρχε Μικιάδης καὶ Αἰσιμίδης καὶ Εὐρύβατος,
ἐστρατοπεδεύσαντο ἐν μιᾷ τῶν νήσων αἳ
καλοῦνται Σύβοτα· καὶ αἱ Ἀττικαὶ δέκα
20 παρῆσαν. ἐπὶ δὲ τῇ Λευκίμμῃ αὐτοῖς τῷ 2
ἀκρωτηρίῳ ὁ πεζὸς ἦν καὶ Ζακυνθίων χίλιοι
ὁπλῖται βεβοηθηκότες. ἦσαν δὲ καὶ τοῖς Κοριν- 3
θίοις ἐν τῇ ἠπείρῳ πολλοὶ τῶν βαρβάρων
παραβεβοηθηκότες· οἱ γὰρ ταύτῃ ἠπειρῶται
25 αἰεί ποτε αὐτοῖς φίλοι εἰσίν.

Ἐπειδὴ δὲ παρεσκεύαστο τοῖς Κορινθίοις, **48**
λαβόντες τριῶν ἡμερῶν σιτία ἀνή-   Arrangement of
γοντο ὡς ἐπὶ ναυμαχίαν ἀπὸ τοῦ   the squadrons.

4. γῆς secl. Herwerden   6. ἔξεισι ABEFM   25.
φίλοι αὐτοῖς C[G]   28. ναυμαχίᾳ C[G]

2 Χειμερίου νυκτός, καὶ ἅμα ἕῳ πλέοντες
καθορῶσι τὰς τῶν Κερκυραίων ναῦς μετεώρους
3 τε καὶ ἐπὶ σφᾶς πλεούσας. ὡς δὲ κατεῖδον
ἀλλήλους, ἀντιπαρετάσσοντο, ἐπὶ μὲν τὸ δεξιὸν
κέρας Κερκυραίων αἱ ᾿Αττικαὶ νῆες, τὸ δὲ 5
ἄλλο αὐτοὶ ἐπεῖχον τρία τέλη ποιήσαντες
τῶν ν ὦν, ὧν ἦρχε ‹τῶν› τριῶν στρατηγῶν
4 ἑκάστου εἰς. οὕτω μὲν Κερκυραῖοι ἐτάξαντο,
Κορινθίοι; δὲ τὸ μὲν δεξιὸν κέρας αἱ Μεγα-
ρίδες νῆες εἶχον καὶ αἱ ᾿Αμπρακιώτιδες, κατὰ 10
δὲ τὸ μέσον οἱ ἄλλοι ξύμμαχοι ὡς ἕκαστοι·
εὐώνυμον δὲ κέρας αὐτοὶ οἱ Κορίνθιοι ταῖς
ἄριστα τῶν νεῶν πλεούσαις κατὰ τοὺς ᾿Αθη-
ναίους καὶ τὸ δεξιὸν τῶν Κερκυραίωι εἶχον.
49 ξυμμείξαντες δέ, ἐπειδὴ τὰ σημεῖα ἑκατέροις 15

The battle of
Sybota. The
tactics were old-
fashioned

ἤρθη, ἐναυμάχουν, πολλοὺς μὲν
ὁπλίτας ἔχοντες ἀμφότεροι ἐπὶ τῶν
καταστρωμάτων, πολλοὺς δὲ τοξότας
τε καὶ ἀκοντιστάς, τῷ παλαιῷ τρόπῳ ἀπειρό-
2 τερον ἔτι παρεσκευασμένοι. ἦν τε ἡ ναυμαχία 20
καρτερά, τῇ μὲν τέχνῃ οὐχ ὁμοίως, πεζομαχίᾳ
3 δὲ τὸ πλέον προσφερὴς οὖσα. ἐπειδὴ γὰρ
προσβάλλοιεν ἀλλήλοις, οὐ ῥᾳδίως ἀπελύοντο
ὑπό τε τοῦ πλήθους καὶ ὄχλου τῶν νεῶν, καὶ
μᾶλλόν τι πιστεύοντες τοῖς ἐπὶ τοῦ καταστρώ- 25
ματος ὁπλίταις ἐς τὴν νίκην, οἳ καταστάντες
ἐμάχοντο ἡσυχαζουσῶν τῶν νεῶν· διέκπλοι δ'
οὐκ ἦσαν, ἀλλὰ θυμῷ καὶ ῥώμῃ τὸ πλέον

7. τῶν add. Poppo   23. προσβάλοιεν recc. : προσβάλλοιεν
codd.   24. τοῦ om. ABEFM

ἐναυμάχουν ἡ ἐπιστήμη. πανταχῇ μὲν οὖν 4
πολὺς θόρυβος καὶ ταραχώδης ἦν ἡ ναυμαχία,
ἐν ᾗ αἱ Ἀττικαὶ νῆες παραγιγνόμεναι τοῖς
Κερκυραίοις, εἴ πῃ πιέζοιντο, φόβον μὲν
5 παρεῖχον τοῖς ἐναντίοις, μάχης δὲ οὐκ ἦρχον
δεδιότες οἱ στρατηγοὶ τὴν πρόρρησιν τῶν
Ἀθηναίων. μάλιστα δὲ τὸ δεξιὸν κέρας τῶν 5
Κορινθίων ἐπόνει· οἱ γὰρ Κερκυ- The right wing
ραῖοι εἴκοσι ναυσὶν αὐτοὺς τρεψά- of the Corinthians broken and
10 μενοι καὶ καταδιώξαντες σποράδας pursued.
ἐς τὴν ἤπειρον καὶ μέχρι τοῦ στρατοπέδου
πλεύσαντες αὐτῶν καὶ ἐπεκβάντες ἐνέπρησάν
τε τὰς σκηνὰς ἐρήμους καὶ τὰ χρήματα διήρ-
πασαν. ταύτῃ μὲν οὖν οἱ Κορίνθιοι Their left wing 6
15 καὶ οἱ ξύμμαχοι ἡσσῶντό [τε] καὶ is successful.
οἱ Κερκυραῖοι ἐπεκράτουν· ᾗ δὲ αὐτοὶ ἦσαν οἱ
Κορίνθιοι, ἐπὶ τῷ εὐωνύμῳ, πολὺ ἐνίκων, τοῖς
Κερκυραίοις τῶν εἴκοσι νεῶν ἀπὸ ἐλάσσονος
πλήθους ἐκ τῆς διώξεως οὐ παρουσῶν. οἱ δὲ 7
20 Ἀθηναῖοι ὁρῶντες τοὺς Κερκυραίους Intervention of
πιεζομένους μᾶλλον ἤδη ἀπροφα- the Athenian
fleet.
σίστως ἐπεκούρουν, τὸ μὲν πρῶτον ἀπεχόμενοι
ὥστε μὴ ἐμβάλλειν τινί· ἐπειδὴ δὲ ἡ τροπὴ
ἐγίγνετο λαμπρῶς καὶ ἐνέκειντο οἱ Κορίνθιοι,
25 τότε δὴ ἔργου πᾶς εἴχετο ἤδη καὶ διεκέκριτο
οὐδὲν ἔτι, ἀλλὰ ξυνέπεσεν ἐς τοῦτο ἀνάγκης
ὥστε ἐπιχειρῆσαι ἀλλήλοις τοὺς Κορινθίους
καὶ Ἀθηναίους.

1. οὖν om. CEG   10. καὶ om. ABEFM   14. οὖν om.
CG (add. G¹)   15. τε secl. Krüger   23. ἐπειδὴ C: ἐπεὶ
cett. [G]   24. ἐγίγνετο C: ἐγένετο cett. [G] ‖ ἐπέκειντο M

50 Τῆς δὲ τροπῆς γενομένης οἱ Κορίνθιοι τὰ

The Corinthians slaughter the crews.

σκάφη μὲν οὐχ εἷλκον ἀναδούμενοι τῶν νεῶν ἃς καταδύσειαν, πρὸς δὲ τοὺς ἀνθρώπους ἐτράποντο φονεύειν διεκπλέοντες μᾶλλον ἢ ζωγρεῖν, τούς τε αὐτῶν φίλους, οὐκ 5 ᾐσθημένοι ὅτι ἥσσηντο οἱ ἐπὶ τῷ δεξιῷ κέρᾳ, 2 ἀγνοοῦντες ἔκτεινον. πολλῶν γὰρ νεῶν οὐσῶν ἀμφοτέρων καὶ ἐπὶ πολὺ τῆς θαλάσσης ἐπεχουσῶν, ἐπειδὴ ξυνέμειξαν ἀλλήλοις, οὐ ῥᾳδίως τὴν διάγνωσιν ἐποιοῦντο ὁποῖοι ἐκράτουν 10 ἢ ἐκρατοῦντο· ναυμαχία γὰρ αὕτη Ἕλλησι πρὸς Ἕλληνας νεῶν πλήθει μεγίστη δὴ τῶν 3 πρὸ αὐτῆς γεγένηται. ἐπειδὴ δὲ κατεδίωξαν τοὺς Κερκυραίους οἱ Κορίνθιοι ἐς τὴν γῆν, πρὸς τὰ ναυάγια καὶ τοὺς νεκροὺς τοὺς 15 σφετέρους ἐτράποντο, καὶ τῶν πλείστων ἐκράτησαν ὥστε προσκομίσαι πρὸς τὰ Σύβοτα, οἷ αὐτοῖς ὁ κατὰ γῆν στρατὸς τῶν βαρβάρων προσεβεβοηθήκει· ἔστι δὲ τὰ Σύβοτα τῆς Θεσπρωτίδος λιμὴν ἐρῆμος. τοῦτο δὲ ποιή- 20 σαντες αὖθις ἀθροισθέντες ἐπέπλεον τοῖς Κερκυ-

4 They are about to renew the attack when they sight another Athenian fleet approaching.

ραίοις. οἱ δὲ ταῖς πλωίμοις καὶ ὅσαι ἦσαν λοιπαὶ μετὰ τῶν Ἀττικῶν νεῶν καὶ αὐτοὶ ἀντεπέπλεον, δεί- σαντες μὴ ἐς τὴν γῆν σφῶν 25 5 πειρῶσιν ἀποβαίνειν. ἤδη δὲ ἦν ὀψὲ καὶ ἐπεπαιάνιστο αὐτοῖς ὡς ἐς ἐπίπλουν, καὶ οἱ

---

6. αἰσθόμενοι ΑΒΕFΜ   13. αὐτῆς G : ἑαυτῆς cett.
17. οὗ CG   24. ἀντεπέπλεον C : ἀντέπλεον cett.   27. ἐπεπαιάνιστο cf : ἐπεπαιώνιστο codd.

Κορίνθιοι ἐξαπίνης πρύμναν ἐκρούοντο κατι-
δόντες εἴκοσι ναῦς Ἀθηναίων προσπλεούσας,
ἃς ὕστερον τῶν δέκα βοηθοὺς ἐξέπεμψαν οἱ
Ἀθηναῖοι, δείσαντες, ὅπερ ἐγένετο, μὴ νικηθῶσιν
5 οἱ Κερκυραῖοι καὶ αἱ σφέτεραι δέκα νῆες
ὀλίγαι ἀμύνειν ὦσιν. ταύτας οὖν προϊδόντες 51
οἱ Κορίνθιοι καὶ ὑποτοπήσαντες End of the
ἀπ᾽ Ἀθηνῶν εἶναι οὐχ ὅσας ἑώρων fighting.
ἀλλὰ πλείους ὑπανεχώρουν. τοῖς δὲ Κερκυ- 2
10 ραίοις (ἐπέπλεον γὰρ μᾶλλον ἐκ τοῦ ἀφανοῦς)
οὐχ ἑωρῶντο, καὶ ἐθαύμαζον τοὺς Κορινθίους
πρύμναν κρουομένους, πρίν τινες ἰδόντες εἶπον
ὅτι νῆες ἐκεῖναι ἐπιπλέουσιν. τότε δὲ καὶ
αὐτοὶ ἀνεχώρουν (ξυνεσκόταζε γὰρ ἤδη), καὶ
15 οἱ Κορίνθιοι ἀποτραπόμενοι τὴν διάλυσιν
ἐποιήσαντο. οὕτω μὲν ἡ ἀπαλλαγὴ ἐγένετο 3
ἀλλήλων, καὶ ἡ ναυμαχία ἐτελεύτα ἐς νύκτα.
τοῖς δὲ Κερκυραίοις στρατοπεδευομένοις ἐπὶ 4
τῇ Λευκίμμῃ αἱ εἴκοσι νῆες αἱ ἐκ τῶν Ἀθηνῶν
20 αὗται, ὧν ἦρχε Γλαύκων τε ὁ Λεάγρου καὶ
†Ἀνδοκίδης ὁ Λεωγόρου†, διὰ τῶν νεκρῶν καὶ
ναυαγίων προσκομισθεῖσαι κατέπλεον ἐς τὸ
στρατόπεδον οὐ πολλῷ ὕστερον ἢ ὤφθησαν.
οἱ δὲ Κερκυραῖοι (ἦν γὰρ νύξ) ἐφοβήθησαν 5
25 μὴ πολέμιαι ὦσιν, ἔπειτα δὲ ἔγνωσαν· καὶ
ὡρμίσαντο.

Τῇ δὲ ὑστεραίᾳ ἀναγαγόμεναι αἵ τε 52

13. δὴ C[G] ‖ post καὶ [G] add. οἱ ABEFM[G]   15. ἀπο-
τρεπόμενοι ABF[G]   18. Κερκυραίοις δὲ ABEFM[G]   19. αἱ
ἐκ] ἀπὸ ABEFM[G]   21. Ἀνδοκίδης] Δρακοντίδης in titulo
(C.I.A. i. 179) nominatur   27. ἀναγόμεναι ABEFM

I   D

Ἀττικαὶ τριάκοντα νῆες καὶ τῶν Κερκυραίων

Next day the
Corinthians
decline to renew
the fight. ὅσαι πλώιμοι ἦσαν ἐπέπλευσαν ἐπὶ τὸν ἐν τοῖς Συβότοις λιμένα, ἐν ᾧ οἱ Κορίνθιοι ὥρμουν, βουλόμενοι

2 εἰδέναι εἰ ναυμαχήσουσιν. οἱ δὲ τὰς μὲν ναῦς 5 ἄραντες ἀπὸ τῆς γῆς καὶ παραταξάμενοι μετεώρους ἡσύχαζον, ναυμαχίας οὐ διανοούμενοι ἄρχειν ἑκόντες ὁρῶντες προσγεγενημένας τε ναῦς ἐκ τῶν Ἀθηνῶν ἀκραιφνεῖς καὶ σφίσι πολλὰ τὰ ἄπορα ξυμβεβηκότα, αἰχμαλώτων 10 τε περὶ φυλακῆς οὓς ἐν ταῖς ναυσὶν εἶχον, καὶ ἐπισκευὴν οὐκ οὖσαν τῶν νεῶν ἐν χωρίῳ ἐρήμῳ·

3 τοῦ δὲ οἴκαδε πλοῦ μᾶλλον διεσκόπουν ὅπῃ κομισθήσονται, δεδιότες μὴ οἱ Ἀθηναῖοι νομίσαντες λελύσθαι τὰς σπονδάς, διότι ἐς χεῖρας 15

53 ἦλθον, οὐκ ἐῶσι σφᾶς ἀποπλεῖν. ἔδοξεν οὖν

They send a
protest to the
Athenians. αὐτοῖς ἄνδρας ἐς κελήτιον ἐσβιβάσαντας ἄνευ κηρυκείου προσπέμψαι

τοῖς Ἀθηναίοις καὶ πεῖραν ποιήσασθαι.

2 πέμψαντές τε ἔλεγον τοιάδε. " ἀδικεῖτε, ὦ 20 ἄνδρες Ἀθηναῖοι, πολέμου ἄρχοντες καὶ σπονδὰς λύοντες· ἡμῖν γὰρ πολεμίους τοὺς ἡμετέρους τιμωρουμένοις ἐμποδὼν ἵστασθε ὅπλα ἀνταιρόμενοι. εἰ δ' ὑμῖν γνώμη ἐστὶ κωλύειν τε ἡμᾶς ἐπὶ Κέρκυραν ἢ ἄλλοσε εἴ 25 ποι βουλόμεθα πλεῖν καὶ τὰς σπονδὰς λύετε, ἡμᾶς τούσδε πρώτους λαβόντες χρήσασθε ὡς

17. ἐμβιβάσαντας AB (-ες) CG Lex. Vind., Greg. Cor.
18. προπέμψαι CM Greg. Cor.   25. πῃ CG Lex. Vind.
27. λαβόντες πρῶτον ABEFM

πολεμίοις." οἱ μὲν δὴ τοιαῦτα εἶπον· τῶν δὲ 3
Κερκυραίων τὸ μὲν στρατόπεδον ὅσον ἐπήκου-
σεν ἀνεβόησεν εὐθὺς λαβεῖν τε αὐτοὺς καὶ
ἀποκτεῖναι, οἱ δὲ 'Αθηναῖοι τοιάδε ἀπεκρίναντο.
5 " οὔτε ἄρχομεν πολέμου, ὦ ἄνδρες Πελο- 4
ποννήσιοι, οὔτε τὰς σπονδὰς λύομεν, Κερκυραίοις δὲ τοῖσδε ξυμμάχοις οὖσι βοηθοὶ
ἤλθομεν. εἰ μὲν οὖν ἄλλοσέ ποι βούλεσθε
πλεῖν, οὐ κωλύομεν· εἰ δὲ ἐπὶ Κέρκυραν
10 πλευσεῖσθε ἢ ἐς τῶν ἐκείνων τι χωρίων, οὐ
περιοψόμεθα κατὰ τὸ δυνατόν."
Τοιαῦτα τῶν 'Αθηναίων ἀποκριναμένων οἱ 54
μὲν Κορίνθιοι τόν τε πλοῦν τὸν Both sides
ἐπ' οἴκου παρεσκευάζοντο καὶ victory.
15 τροπαῖον ἔστησαν ἐν τοῖς ἐν τῇ ἠπείρῳ
Συβότοις· οἱ δὲ Κερκυραῖοι τά τε ναυάγια καὶ
νεκροὺς ἀνείλοντο τὰ κατὰ σφᾶς ἐξενεχθέντα
ὑπό τε τοῦ ῥοῦ καὶ ἀνέμου, ὃς γενόμενος τῆς
νυκτὸς διεσκέδασεν αὐτὰ πανταχῇ, καὶ
20 τροπαῖον ἀντέστησαν ἐν τοῖς ἐν τῇ νήσῳ
Συβότοις ὡς νενικηκότες. γνώμη δὲ τοιᾷδε 2
ἑκάτεροι τὴν νίκην προσεποιήσαντο· Κορίνθιοι
μὲν κρατήσαντες τῇ ναυμαχίᾳ μέχρι νυκτός,
ὥστε καὶ ναυάγια πλεῖστα καὶ νεκροὺς προσ-
25 κομίσασθαι, καὶ ἄνδρας ἔχοντες αἰχμαλώτους
οὐκ ἐλάσσους χιλίων ναῦς τε καταδύσαντες
περὶ ἑβδομήκοντα ἔστησαν τροπαῖον· Κερκυραῖοι δὲ τριάκοντα ναῦς μάλιστα διαφθεί-

16. post καὶ add. τοὺς Schol.   17. ἐξενεχθέντων C γρ. Schol.
[G]   18. τε om. ABF   22. ἑκάτεροι τοιᾷδε ABEFM

ραντες, καὶ ἐπειδὴ Ἀθηναῖοι ἦλθον, ἀνελόμενοι
τὰ κατὰ σφᾶς αὐτοὺς ναυάγια καὶ νεκρούς,
καὶ ὅτι αὐτοῖς τῇ τε προτεραίᾳ πρύμναν
κρουόμενοι ὑπεχώρησαν οἱ Κορίνθιοι ἰδόντες
τὰς Ἀττικὰς ναῦς, καὶ ἐπειδὴ ἦλθον οἱ 5
Ἀθηναῖοι, οὐκ ἀντεπέπλεον ἐκ τῶν Συβότων,
55 διὰ ταῦτα τροπαῖον ἔστησαν. οὕτω μὲν
ἑκάτεροι νικᾶν ἠξίουν· οἱ δὲ Κορίνθιοι
The Corinthians ἀποπλέοντες ἐπ᾽ οἴκου Ἀνακτόριον,
sail home with
prisoners. ὅ ἐστιν ἐπὶ τῷ στόματι τοῦ Ἀμ- 10
πρακικοῦ κόλπου, εἷλον ἀπάτῃ (ἦν δὲ κοινὸν
Κερκυραίων καὶ ἐκείνων) καὶ καταστήσαντες
ἐν αὐτῷ Κορινθίους οἰκήτορας ἀνεχώρησαν ἐπ᾽
οἴκου, καὶ τῶν Κερκυραίων ὀκτακοσίους μὲν
οἳ ἦσαν δοῦλοι ἀπέδοντο, πεντήκοντα δὲ καὶ 15
διακοσίους δήσαντες ἐφύλασσον καὶ ἐν θεραπείᾳ
εἶχον πολλῇ, ὅπως αὐτοῖς τὴν Κέρκυραν
ἀναχωρήσαντες προσποιήσειαν· ἐτύγχανον δὲ
καὶ δυνάμει αὐτῶν οἱ πλείους πρῶτοι ὄντες
2 τῆς πόλεως. ἡ μὲν οὖν Κέρκυρα οὕτω 20
This was the περιγίγνεται τῷ πολέμῳ τῶν
first ground of
war between Κορινθίων, καὶ αἱ νῆες τῶν Ἀθη-
Corinth and
Athens. ναίων ἀνεχώρησαν ἐξ αὐτῆς· αἰτία
δὲ αὕτη πρώτη ἐγένετο τοῦ πολέμου τοῖς
Κορινθίοις ἐς τοὺς Ἀθηναίους, ὅτι σφίσιν ἐν 25
σπονδαῖς μετὰ Κερκυραίων ἐναυμάχουν.

56 Μετὰ ταῦτα δ᾽ εὐθὺς καὶ τάδε ξυνέβη
γενέσθαι τοῖς Ἀθηναίοις καὶ Πελοποννησίοις
6. οὐκ ἀντέπλεον EG: οὐ κατέπλεον ABFM   28. τοῖς om. ABEFM

διάφορα ἐς τὸ πολεμεῖν. τῶν γὰρ Κορινθίων 2
πρασσόντων ὅπως τιμωρήσονται Immediately
αὐτούς, ὑποτοπήσαντες τὴν ἔχθραν after the battle, a *second* differ-
αὐτῶν οἱ Ἀθηναῖοι Ποτειδεάτας, ence occurred. Potidaea, a
5 οἳ οἰκοῦσιν ἐπὶ τῷ ἰσθμῷ τῆς colony of Corinth and ally
Παλλήνης, Κορινθίων ἀποίκους, of Athens, was ordered to give
ἑαυτῶν δὲ ξυμμάχους φόρου ὑπο- securities of its loyalty to
τελεῖς, ἐκέλευον τὸ ἐς Παλλήνην Athens.
τεῖχος καθελεῖν καὶ ὁμήρους δοῦναι, τούς τε
10 ἐπιδημιουργοὺς ἐκπέμπειν καὶ τὸ λοιπὸν μὴ
δέχεσθαι οὓς κατὰ ἔτος ἕκαστον Κορίνθιοι
ἔπεμπον, δείσαντες μὴ ἀποστῶσιν ὑπό τε
Περδίκκου πειθόμενοι καὶ Κορινθίων, τούς τε
ἄλλους τοὺς ἐπὶ Θρᾴκης ξυναποστήσωσι
15 ξυμμάχους. ταῦτα δὲ περὶ τοὺς K. Perdiccas of 57
Ποτειδεάτας οἱ Ἀθηναῖοι προ- Macedon encourages
παρεσκευάζοντο εὐθὺς μετὰ τὴν ἐν opposition to Athens in the
Κερκύρᾳ ναυμαχίαν· οἵ τε γὰρ north. 2
Κορίνθιοι φανερῶς ἤδη διάφοροι ἦσαν,
20 Περδίκκας τε ὁ Ἀλεξάνδρου Μακεδόνων
βασιλεὺς ἐπεπολέμωτο ξύμμαχος πρότερον καὶ
φίλος ὤν. ἐπολεμώθη δὲ ὅτι Φιλίππῳ τῷ 3
ἑαυτοῦ ἀδελφῷ καὶ Δέρδᾳ κοινῇ πρὸς αὐτὸν
ἐναντιουμένοις οἱ Ἀθηναῖοι ξυμμαχίαν ἐποιή-
25 σαντο. δεδιώς τε ἔπρασσεν ἔς τε τὴν 4
Λακεδαίμονα πέμπων ὅπως πόλεμος γένηται
αὐτοῖς πρὸς Πελοποννησίους, καὶ τοὺς Κοριν-

2. τιμωρήσωνται AEFGM   14. τοὺς om. ABEFM ‖ ξυναπο-
στήσουσι ABEFM[G]   15. περὶ] πρὸς G : παρὰ M   19. ἤδη
om. CG (add. G¹)

θίους προσεποιεῖτο τῆς Ποτειδαίας ἕνεκα
5 ἀποστάσεω;· προσέφερε δὲ λόγους καὶ τοῖς ἐπὶ
Θρᾴκης Χαλκιδεῦσι καὶ Βοττιαίοις ξυναπο-
στῆναι, νομίζων, εἰ ξύμμαχα ταῦτα ἔχοι ὅμορα
ὄντα τὰ χωρία, ῥᾷον ἂν τὸν πόλεμον μετ' 5
6 αὐτῶν ποιεῖσθαι. ὧν οἱ Ἀθηναῖοι αἰσθόμενοι
καὶ βουλόμενοι προκαταλαμβάνειν τῶν πόλεων
τὰς ἀποστάσεις (ἔτυχον γὰρ τριάκοντα ναῦς
ἀποστέλλοντες καὶ χιλίους ὁπλίτας ἐπὶ τὴν
γῆν αὐτοῦ, Ἀρχεστράτου τοῦ Λυκομήδους μετ' 10
ἄλλων †δέκα† στρατηγοῦντος) ἐπιστέλλουσι
τοῖς ἄρχουσι τῶν νεῶν Ποτειδεατῶν τε
ὁμήρους λαβεῖν καὶ τὸ τεῖχος καθελεῖν, τῶν
τε πλησίον πόλεων φυλακὴν ἔχειν ὅπως μὴ
ἀποστήσονται. 15

58 Ποτειδεᾶται δὲ πέμψαντες μὲν καὶ παρ'

Revolt of
Potidaea and
other places;
Olynthus
becomes their
centre.

Ἀθηναίους πρέσβεις, εἴ πως πεί-
σειαν μὴ σφῶν πέρι νεωτερίζειν
μηδέν, ἐλθόντες δὲ καὶ ἐς τὴν Λακεδαίμονα μετὰ Κορινθίων, [ἔπρασσον] 20
ὅπως ἑτοιμάσαιντο τιμωρίαν, ἢν δέῃ, ἐπειδὴ
ἔκ τε Ἀθηνῶν ἐκ πολλοῦ πράσσοντες οὐδὲν
ηὕροντο ἐπιτήδειον, ἀλλ' αἱ νῆες αἱ ἐπὶ
Μακεδονίαν καὶ ἐπὶ σφᾶς ὁμοίως ἔπλεον, καὶ
τὰ τέλη τῶν Λακεδαιμονίων ὑπέσχετο αὐτοῖς, 25
ἢν ἐπὶ Ποτείδαιαν ἴωσιν Ἀθηναῖοι, ἐς τὴν
Ἀττικὴν ἐσβαλεῖν, τότε δὴ κατὰ τὸν καιρὸν

5. τὰ om. ABEFM   11. δέκα] τεσσάρων Krüger   15.
ἀποστήσονται C: ἀποστήσωνται cett.   20. ἔπρασσον secl.
Poppo   22. Ἀθηνῶν C: Ἀθηναίων cett.   25. ὑπέσχοντο
C? (corr. c) G

τοῦτον ἀφίστανται μετὰ Χαλκιδέων καὶ Βοτ-
τιαίων κοινῇ ξυνομόσαντες. καὶ Περδίκκας 2
πείθει Χαλκιδέας τὰς ἐπὶ θαλάσσῃ πόλεις
ἐκλιπόντας καὶ καταβαλόντας ἀνοικίσασθαι ἐς
5 Ὄλυνθον μίαν τε πόλιν ταύτην ἰσχυρὰν
ποιήσασθαι· τοῖς τ᾽ ἐκλιποῦσι τούτοις τῆς
ἑαυτοῦ γῆς τῆς Μυγδονίας περὶ τὴν Βόλβην
λίμνην ἔδωκε νέμεσθαι, ἕως ἂν ὁ πρὸς
Ἀθηναίους πόλεμος ᾖ. καὶ οἱ μὲν ἀνῳκίζοντό
10 τε καθαιροῦντες τὰς πόλεις καὶ ἐς πόλεμον
παρεσκευάζοντο· αἱ δὲ τριάκοντα νῆες τῶν 59
Ἀθηναίων ἀφικνοῦνται ἐς τὰ ἐπὶ Θρᾴκης, καὶ
καταλαμβάνουσι τήν τε Ποτείδαιαν καὶ τἆλλα
ἀφεστηκότα. νομίσαντες δὲ οἱ στρατηγοὶ 2
15 ἀδύνατα εἶναι πρός τε Περδίκκαν πολεμεῖν τῇ
παρούσῃ δυνάμει καὶ τὰ ξυναφεστῶτα χωρία
τρέπονται ἐπὶ τὴν Μακεδονίαν, ἐφ᾽ ὅπερ καὶ
τὸ πρῶτον ἐξεπέμποντο, καὶ καταστάντες
ἐπολέμουν μετὰ Φιλίππου καὶ τῶν Δέρδου
20 ἀδελφῶν ἄνωθεν στρατιᾷ ἐσβεβληκότων. καὶ 60
ἐν τούτῳ οἱ Κορίνθιοι, τῆς Ποτειδαίας ἀφε-
στηκυίας καὶ τῶν Ἀττικῶν νεῶν Corinth sends
περὶ Μακεδονίαν οὐσῶν, δεδιότες help to
Potidaea.
περὶ τῷ χωρίῳ καὶ οἰκεῖον τὸν κίνδυνον
25 ἡγούμενοι πέμπουσιν ἑαυτῶν τε ἐθελοντὰς καὶ
τῶν ἄλλων Πελοποννησίων μισθῷ πείσαντες
ἑξακοσίους καὶ χιλίους τοὺς πάντας ὁπλίτας
καὶ ψιλοὺς τετρακοσίους. ἐστρατήγει δὲ αὐτῶν 2
Ἀριστεὺς ὁ Ἀδειμάντου, κατὰ φιλίαν τε αὐτοῦ

13. τε om. ABEFM   18. πρῶτον] πρότερον ABEFM Suid.

οὐχ ἥκιστα οἱ πλεῖστοι ἐκ Κορίνθου στρατιῶ-
ται ἐθελονταὶ ξυνέσποντο· ἦν γὰρ τοῖς
3 Ποτειδεάταις αἰεί ποτε ἐπιτήδειος. καὶ ἀφικνοῦνται τεσσαρακοστῇ ἡμέρᾳ ὕστερον ἐπὶ
Θράκης ἢ Ποτείδαια ἀπέστη.   5

61 Ἦλθε δὲ καὶ τοῖς Ἀθηναίοις εὐθὺς ἡ
Reinforcements   ἀγγελία τῶν πόλεων ὅτι ἀφεστᾶσι,
sent from
Athens. After   καὶ πέμπουσιν, ὡς ᾔσθοντο καὶ
patching up a   τοὺς μετ᾽ Ἀριστέως ἐπιπαριόντας,
peace with
Perdiccas, they δισχιλίους ἑαυτῶν ὁπλίτας καὶ 10
advance on
Potidaea.   τεσσαράκοντα ναῦς πρὸς τὰ ἀφε-
στῶτα, καὶ Καλλίαν τὸν Καλλιάδου πέμπτον
2 αὐτὸν στρατηγόν, οἳ ἀφικόμενοι ἐς Μακεδονίαν
πρῶτον καταλαμβάνουσι τοὺς προτέρους χιλίους
Θέρμην ἄρτι ᾑρηκότας καὶ Πύδναν πολιορ- 15
3 κοῦντας. προσκαθεζόμενοι δὲ καὶ αὐτοὶ τὴν
Πύδναν ἐπολιόρκησαν μέν, ἔπειτα δὲ ξύμβασιν
ποιησάμενοι καὶ ξυμμαχίαν ἀναγκαίαν πρὸς
τὸν Περδίκκαν, ὡς αὐτοὺς κατήπειγεν ἡ
Ποτείδαια καὶ ὁ Ἀριστεὺς παρεληλυθώς, 20
4 ἀπανίστανται ἐκ τῆς Μακεδονίας, καὶ ἀφικόμενοι ἐς Βέροιαν κἀκεῖθεν ἐπὶ Στρέψαν καὶ
πειράσαντες πρῶτον τοῦ χωρίου καὶ οὐχ
ἑλόντες ἐπορεύοντο κατὰ γῆν πρὸς τὴν
Ποτείδαιαν, τρισχιλίοις μὲν ὁπλίταις ἑαυτῶν, 25
χωρὶς δὲ τῶν ξυμμάχων πολλοῖς, ἱππεῦσι δὲ
ἑξακοσίοις Μακεδόνων τοῖς μετὰ Φιλίππου καὶ

5. ἢ f: ᾗ cett. : ἢ ᾗ Herwerden   9. ἐπιπαριόντας
Ullrich : ἐπιπαρόντας codd.   22. ἐπὶ Στρέψαν Pluygers :
ἐπιστρέψαντες codd.

Παυσανίου· ἅμα δὲ νῆες παρέπλεον ἑβδομήκοντα. κατ᾽ ὀλίγον δὲ προϊόντες τριταῖοι 5
ἀφίκοντο ἐς Γίγωνον καὶ ἐστρατοπεδεύσαντο.

Ποτειδεᾶται δὲ καὶ οἱ μετὰ Ἀριστέως **62**
5 Πελοποννήσιοι προσδεχόμενοι τοὺς Battle before
Ἀθηναίους ἐστρατοπεδεύοντο πρὸς Potidaea. The
Athenians drive
Ὀλύνθου ἐν τῷ ἰσθμῷ, καὶ ἀγορὰν the Potidaeans
and Pel. into
ἔξω τῆς πόλεως ἐπεποίηντο. στρα- the city.　2
τηγὸν μὲν οὖν τοῦ πεζοῦ παντὸς οἱ ξύμμαχοι
10 ᾕρηντο Ἀριστέα, τῆς δὲ ἵππου Περδίκκαν·
ἀπέστη γὰρ εὐθὺς πάλιν τῶν Ἀθηναίων καὶ
ξυνεμάχει τοῖς Ποτειδεάταις, Ἰόλαον ἀνθ᾽
αὑτοῦ καταστήσας ἄρχοντα. ἦν δὲ ἡ γνώμη 3
τοῦ Ἀριστέως τὸ μὲν μεθ᾽ ἑαυτοῦ στρατόπεδον
15 ἔχοντι ἐν τῷ ἰσθμῷ ἐπιτηρεῖν τοὺς Ἀθηναίους,
ἢν ἐπίωσι, Χαλκιδέας δὲ καὶ τοὺς ἔξω ἰσθμοῦ
ξυμμάχους καὶ τὴν παρὰ Περδίκκου διακοσίαν
ἵππον ἐν Ὀλύνθῳ μένειν, καὶ ὅταν Ἀθηναῖοι
ἐπὶ σφᾶς χωρῶσι, κατὰ νώτου βοηθοῦντας ἐν
20 μέσῳ ποιεῖν αὐτῶν τοὺς πολεμίους. Καλλίας 4
δ᾽ αὖ ὁ τῶν Ἀθηναίων στρατηγὸς καὶ οἱ
ξυνάρχοντες τοὺς μὲν Μακεδόνας ἱππέας καὶ
τῶν ξυμμάχων ὀλίγους ἐπὶ Ὀλύνθου ἀπο-
πέμπουσιν, ὅπως εἴργωσι τοὺς ἐκεῖθεν ἐπι-
25 βοηθεῖν, αὐτοὶ δὲ ἀναστήσαντες τὸ στρατόπεδον
ἐχώρουν ἐπὶ τὴν Ποτείδαιαν, καὶ ἐπειδὴ πρὸς 5
τῷ ἰσθμῷ ἐγένοντο καὶ εἶδον τοὺς ἐναντίους
παρασκευαζομένους ὡς ἐς μάχην, ἀντικαθίσταντο

6. πρὸ G　　7. Ὀλύνθῳ ABEF　　9. οὖν cG : om. cett.
15. ἔχοντα EG　　20. αὐτῶν g : αὑτῶν codd.

I　　　　　　　　　　　　　　　　　　　D 2

6 καὶ αὐτοί, καὶ οὐ πολὺ ὕστερον ξυνέμισγον.
καὶ αὐτὸ μὲν τὸ τοῦ Ἀριστέως κέρας καὶ ὅσοι
περὶ ἐκεῖνον ἦσαν Κορινθίων τε καὶ τῶν
ἄλλων λογάδες ἔτρεψαν τὸ καθ᾽ ἑαυτοὺς καὶ
ἐπεξῆλθον διώκοντες ἐπὶ πολύ· τὸ δὲ ἄλλο 5
στρατόπεδον Ποτειδεατῶν καὶ Πελοποννησίων
ἡσσᾶτο ὑπὸ τῶν Ἀθηναίων καὶ ἐς τὸ τεῖχος
κατέφυγεν.

63 Ἐπαναχωρῶν δὲ ὁ Ἀριστεὺς ἀπὸ τῆς

The Corinthians διώξεως, ὡς ὁρᾷ τὸ ἄλλο στράτευμα 10
enter the city
with difficulty. ἡσσημένον, ἠπόρησε μὲν ὁποτέρωσε
The Athenians
victorious. διακινδυνεύσῃ χωρήσας, ἢ ἐπὶ τῆς
Ὀλύνθου ἢ ἐς τὴν Ποτείδαιαν· ἔδοξε δ᾽ οὖν
ξυναγαγόντι τοὺς μεθ᾽ αὑτοῦ ὡς ἐς ἐλάχιστον
χωρίον δρόμῳ βιάσασθαι ἐς τὴν Ποτείδαιαν, καὶ 15
παρῆλθε παρὰ τὴν χηλὴν διὰ τῆς θαλάσσης
βαλλόμενός τε καὶ χαλεπῶς, ὀλίγους μέν τινας
2 ἀποβαλών, τοὺς δὲ πλείους σώσας. οἱ δ᾽ ἀπὸ
τῆς Ὀλύνθου τοῖς Ποτειδεάταις βοηθοί (ἀπέχει
δὲ ἑξήκοντα μάλιστα σταδίους καὶ ἔστι 20
καταφανές), ὡς ἡ μάχη ἐγίγνετο καὶ τὰ
σημεῖα ἤρθη, βραχὺ μέν τι προῆλθον ὡς
βοηθήσοντες, καὶ οἱ Μακεδόνες ἱππῆς ἀντι-
παρετάξαντο ὡς κωλύσοντες· ἐπειδὴ δὲ διὰ
τάχους ἡ νίκη τῶν Ἀθηναίων ἐγίγνετο καὶ τὰ 25
σημεῖα κατεσπάσθη, πάλιν ἐπανεχώρουν ἐς τὸ
τεῖχος καὶ οἱ Μακεδόνες παρὰ τοὺς Ἀθηναίους·

6. post στρατόπεδον add. τῶν τε ABEF, τῶν M   7. post
καὶ add. τῶν ABEFM   10. ἑώρα cG   13. δ᾽ οὖν Poppo:
γοῦν codd.[G]   14. ἑαυτοῦ ABEFM[G]   15. εἰς (sic)
afM : om. cett.[G]   19. ἀπεῖχε ABEFM[G]

ἱππῆς δ᾽ οὐδετέροις παρεγένοντο. μετὰ δὲ τὴν 3
μάχην τροπαῖον ἔστησαν οἱ Ἀθηναῖοι καὶ
τοὺς νεκροὺς ὑποσπόνδους ἀπέδοσαν τοῖς
Ποτειδεάταις· ἀπέθανον δὲ Ποτειδεατῶν μὲν
5 καὶ τῶν ξυμμάχων ὀλίγῳ ἐλάσσους τριακοσίων,
Ἀθηναίων δὲ αὐτῶν πεντήκοντα καὶ ἑκατὸν
καὶ Καλλίας ὁ στρατηγός. τὸ δὲ ἐκ τοῦ 64
ἰσθμοῦ [τεῖχος] εὐθὺς οἱ Ἀθηναῖοι ἀποτειχί-
σαντες ἐφρούρουν· τὸ δ᾽ ἐς τὴν   Potidaea block-
10 Παλλήνην ἀτείχιστον ἦν· οὐ γὰρ aded, at first from the north,
ἱκανοὶ ἐνόμιζον εἶναι ἔν τε τῷ and presently from the south
ἰσθμῷ φρουρεῖν καὶ ἐς τὴν Παλλήνην also.
διαβάντες τειχίζειν, δεδιότες μὴ σφίσιν οἱ
Ποτειδεᾶται καὶ οἱ ξύμμαχοι γενομένοις δίχα
15 ἐπίθωνται. καὶ πυνθανόμενοι οἱ ἐν τῇ πόλει 2
Ἀθηναῖοι τὴν Παλλήνην ἀτείχιστον οὖσαν,
χρόνῳ ὕστερον πέμπουσιν ἑξακοσίους καὶ
χιλίους ὁπλίτας ἑαυτῶν καὶ Φορμίωνα τὸν
Ἀσωπίου στρατηγόν· ὃς ἀφικόμενος ἐς τὴν
20 Παλλήνην καὶ ἐξ Ἀφύτιος ὁρμώμενος προσή-
γαγε τῇ Ποτειδαίᾳ τὸν στρατὸν κατὰ βραχὺ
προϊὼν καὶ κείρων ἅμα τὴν γῆν, ὡς δὲ οὐδεὶς
ἐπεξῄει ἐς μάχην, ἀπετείχισε τὸ ἐκ τῆς
Παλλήνης [τεῖχος]. καὶ οὕτως ἤδη κατὰ 3
25 κράτος ἡ Ποτείδαια ἀμφοτέρωθεν ἐπολιορκεῖτο
καὶ ἐκ θαλάσσης ναυσὶν ἅμα ἐφορμούσαις.
Ἀριστεὺς δὲ ἀποτειχισθείσης αὐτῆς καὶ ἐλπίδα 65
οὐδεμίαν ἔχων σωτηρίας, ἢν μή τι ἀπὸ Πελο-

---

8. τεῖχος secl. Classen   14. γενομένοις G : γιγνομένοις cett.
24. τεῖχος secl. Herwerden

πονννήσου ἢ ἄλλο παρὰ λόγον γίγνηται, ξυνεβούλευε μὲν πλὴν πεντακοσίων
ἄνεμον τηρήσασι τοῖς ἄλλοις ἐκ-
πλεῦσαι, ὅπως ἐπὶ πλέον ὁ σῖτος
ἀντίσχῃ, καὶ αὐτὸς ἤθελε τῶν μενόν- 5
των εἶναι· ὡς δ' οὐκ ἔπειθε, βουλόμενος τὰ ἐπὶ
τούτοις παρασκευάζειν καὶ ὅπως τὰ ἔξωθεν ἕξει
ὡς ἄριστα, ἔκπλουν ποιεῖται λαθὼν τὴν φυλακὴν
2 τῶν Ἀθηναίων. καὶ παραμένων ἐν Χαλκιδεῦσι
τά τε ἄλλα ξυνεπολέμει καὶ Σερμυλιῶν λοχήσας 10
πρὸς τῇ πόλει πολλοὺς διέφθειρεν, ἔς τε τὴν
Πελοπόννησον ἔπρασσεν ὅπῃ ὠφελία τις
γενήσεται. μετὰ δὲ τῆς Ποτειδαίας τὴν
ἀποτείχισιν Φορμίων μὲν ἔχων τοὺς ἑξακοσίους
καὶ χιλίους τὴν Χαλκιδικὴν καὶ Βοττικὴν ἐδῄου 15
καὶ ἔστιν ἃ καὶ πολίσματα εἷλεν.

66 Τοῖς δ' Ἀθηναίοις καὶ Πελοποννησίοις

Aristeus, the
Corinthian
general, escapes
but remains in
Chalcidice to
encourage war
against Athens.

Thus ill-feeling
between Corinth
and Athens was
increased.

αἰτίαι μὲν αὗται προυγεγένηντο ἐς
ἀλλήλους, τοῖς μὲν Κορινθίοις ὅτι
τὴν Ποτείδαιαν ἑαυτῶν οὖσαν 20
ἀποικίαν καὶ ἄνδρας Κορινθίων τε καὶ
Πελοποννησίων ἐν αὐτῇ ὄντας ἐπολιόρκουν,
τοῖς δὲ Ἀθηναίοις ἐς τοὺς Πελοποννησίους ὅτι
ἑαυτῶν τε πόλιν ξυμμαχίδα καὶ φόρου ὑποτελῆ
ἀπέστησαν, καὶ ἐλθόντες σφίσιν ἀπὸ τοῦ 25
προφανοῦς ἐμάχοντο μετὰ Ποτειδεατῶν. οὐ
μέντοι ὅ γε πόλεμός πω ξυνερρώγει, ἀλλ' ἔτι
ἀνοκωχὴ ἦν· ἰδίᾳ γὰρ ταῦτα οἱ Κορίνθιοι

---

1. παρὰ λόγον Krüger : παράλογον codd.   10. ἐπολέμει
CG ‖ Ἑρμυλίων ΑΒ

ἔπραξαν. πολιορκουμένης δὲ τῆς Ποτειδαίας **67**
οὐχ ἡσύχαζον, ἀνδρῶν τε σφίσιν
ἐνόντων καὶ ἅμα περὶ τῷ χωρίῳ
δεδιότες· παρεκάλουν τε εὐθὺς ἐς
5 τὴν Λακεδαίμονα τοὺς ξυμμάχους
καὶ κατεβόων ἐλθόντες τῶν Ἀθηναίων ὅτι σπονδάς τε λελυκότες εἶεν καὶ
ἀδικοῖεν τὴν Πελοπόννησον. Αἰγινῆταί τε 2
φανερῶς μὲν οὐ πρεσβευόμενοι, δεδιότες τοὺς
10 Ἀθηναίους, κρύφα δὲ οὐχ ἥκιστα μετ' αὐτῶν
ἐνῆγον τὸν πόλεμον, λέγοντες οὐκ εἶναι
αὐτόνομοι κατὰ τὰς σπονδάς. οἱ δὲ Λακε- 3
δαιμόνιοι προσπαρακαλέσαντες τῶν ξυμμάχων
τε καὶ εἴ τίς τι ἄλλο ἔφη ἠδικῆσθαι ὑπὸ
15 Ἀθηναίων, ξύλλογον σφῶν αὐτῶν ποιήσαντες
τὸν εἰωθότα λέγειν ἐκέλευον. καὶ ἄλλοι τε 4
παριόντες ἐγκλήματα ἐποιοῦντο ὡς ἕκαστοι
καὶ Μεγαρῆς, δηλοῦντες μὲν καὶ ἕτερα οὐκ
ὀλίγα διάφορα, μάλιστα δὲ λιμένων τε
20 εἴργεσθαι τῶν ἐν τῇ Ἀθηναίων ἀρχῇ καὶ τῆς
Ἀττικῆς ἀγορᾶς παρὰ τὰς σπονδάς. παρελ- 5
θόντες δὲ τελευταῖοι Κορίνθιοι καὶ τοὺς ἄλλους
ἐάσαντες πρῶτον παροξῦναι τοὺς Λακεδαιμονίους
ἐπεῖπον τοιάδε.

25   "Τὸ πιστὸν ὑμᾶς, ὦ Λακεδαιμόνιοι, τῆς **68**
καθ' ὑμᾶς αὐτοὺς πολιτείας καὶ ὁμι-
λίας ἀπιστοτέρους ἐς τοὺς ἄλλους,
ἤν τι λέγωμεν, καθίστησιν· καὶ ἀπ'
αὐτοῦ σωφροσύνην μὲν ἔχετε, ἀμα-

The Corinthians bring about a congress at Sparta of allies and others having complaints against Athens.

Speech of the Corinthian envoy. 'You have been indifferent to our warnings and complaints.

14. τε om. ABEFM ‖ ἄλλος Reiske   16. ἄλλα τε CG : ἄλλοτε ABF

θίᾳ δὲ πλέονι πρὸς τὰ ἔξω πράγματα χρῆσθε.
2 πολλάκις γὰρ προαγορευόντων ἡμῶν ἃ ἐμέλλο-
μεν ὑπὸ Ἀθηναίων βλάπτεσθαι, οὐ περὶ ὧν
ἐδιδάσκομεν ἑκάστοτε τὴν μάθησιν ἐποιεῖσθε,
ἀλλὰ τῶν λεγόντων μᾶλλον ὑπενοεῖτε ὡς ἕνεκα 5
τῶν αὑτοῖς ἰδίᾳ διαφόρων λέγουσιν· καὶ δι'
αὐτὸ οὐ πρὶν πάσχειν, ἀλλ' ἐπειδὴ ἐν τῷ
ἔργῳ ἐσμέν, τοὺς ξυμμάχους τούσδε παρεκαλέ-
σατε, ἐν οἷς προσήκει ἡμᾶς οὐχ ἥκιστα εἰπεῖν,
ὅσῳ καὶ μέγιστα ἐγκλήματα ἔχομεν ὑπὸ μὲν 10
Ἀθηναίων ὑβριζόμενοι, ὑπὸ δὲ ὑμῶν ἀμελού-
μενοι.
3   "Καὶ εἰ μὲν ἀφανεῖς που ὄντες ἠδίκουν τὴν
'Yet the ambition of Athens is plain enough. Ἑλλάδα, διδασκαλίας ἂν ὡς οὐκ
εἰδόσι προσέδει· νῦν δὲ τί δεῖ 15
μακρηγορεῖν, ὧν τοὺς μὲν δεδουλωμένους ὁρᾶτε,
τοῖς δὲ ἐπιβουλεύοντας αὐτούς, καὶ οὐχ ἥκιστα
τοῖς ἡμετέροις ξυμμάχοις, καὶ ἐκ πολλοῦ
προπαρεσκευασμένους, εἴ ποτε ἄρα πολεμή-
4 σονται ; οὐ γὰρ ἂν Κέρκυράν τε ὑπολαβόντες 20
βίᾳ ἡμῶν εἶχον καὶ Ποτείδαιαν ἐπολιόρκουν,
ὧν τὸ μὲν ἐπικαιρότατον χωρίον πρὸς τὰ ἐπὶ
Θρᾴκης ἀποχρῆσθαι, ἡ δὲ ναυτικὸν ἂν μέγιστον
69 παρέσχε Πελοποννησίοις. καὶ τῶνδε ὑμεῖς
'You have allowed Athens to grow in power and to encroach on the rights of others. αἴτιοι, τό τε πρῶτον ἐάσαντες 25
αὐτοὺς τὴν πόλιν μετὰ τὰ Μηδικὰ
κρατῦναι καὶ ὕστερον τὰ μακρὰ
στῆσαι τείχη, ἐς τόδε τε αἰεὶ

19. ἄρα fM Schol. : om. cett.   23. ἐπιχρῆσθαι M Schol.
24. post παρέσχε add. τοῖς BCG

ἀποστεροῦντες οὐ μόνον τοὺς ὑπ' ἐκείνων
δεδουλωμένους ἐλευθερίας, ἀλλὰ καὶ τοὺς
ὑμετέρους ἤδη ξυμμάχους· οὐ γὰρ ὁ δουλωσά-
μενος, ἀλλ' ὁ δυνάμενος μὲν παῦσαι περιορῶν
5 δὲ ἀληθέστερον αὐτὸ δρᾷ, εἴπερ καὶ τὴν
ἀξίωσιν τῆς ἀρετῆς ὡς ἐλευθερῶν τὴν Ἑλλάδα
φέρεται. μόλις δὲ νῦν γε ξυνήλθομεν καὶ 2
οὐδὲ νῦν ἐπὶ φανεροῖς. χρῆν γὰρ οὐκ εἰ
ἀδικούμεθα ἔτι σκοπεῖν, ἀλλὰ καθ' ὅ τι
10 ἀμυνούμεθα· οἱ γὰρ δρῶντες βεβουλευμένοι
πρὸς οὐ διεγνωκότας ἤδη καὶ οὐ μέλλοντες
ἐπέρχονται. καὶ ἐπιστάμεθα οἵᾳ 'Your supineness 3
ὁδῷ οἱ Ἀθηναῖοι καὶ ὅτι κατ' encourages them.
ὀλίγον χωροῦσιν ἐπὶ τοὺς πέλας. καὶ
15 λανθάνειν μὲν οἰόμενοι διὰ τὸ ἀναίσθητον
ὑμῶν ἧσσον θαρσοῦσι, γνόντες δὲ εἰδότας
περιορᾶν ἰσχυρῶς ἐγκείσονται. ἡσυχάζετε γὰρ 4
μόνοι Ἑλλήνων, ὦ Λακεδαιμόνιοι, οὐ τῇ
δυνάμει τινά, ἀλλὰ τῇ μελλήσει ἀμυνόμενοι,
20 καὶ μόνοι οὐκ ἀρχομένην τὴν αὔξησιν τῶν
ἐχθρῶν διπλασιουμένην δὲ καταλύοντες. καίτοι 5
ἐλέγεσθε ἀσφαλεῖς εἶναι, ὧν ἄρα ὁ λόγος τοῦ
ἔργου ἐκράτει. τόν τε γὰρ Μῆδον αὐτοὶ ἴσμεν
ἐκ περάτων γῆς πρότερον ἐπὶ τὴν Πελοπόν-
25 νησον ἐλθόντα ἢ τὰ παρ' ὑμῶν ἀξίως
προαπαντῆσαι, καὶ νῦν τοὺς Ἀθηναίους οὐχ
ἑκάς, ὥσπερ ἐκεῖνον, ἀλλ' ἐγγὺς ὄντας περιο-
ρᾶτε, καὶ ἀντὶ τοῦ ἐπελθεῖν αὐτοὶ ἀμύνεσθαι

3. ἡμετέρους CG   7. φέρεται] φαίνεται ABEF γρ. M ‖ γε
Stephanus : τε codd.   20. αὔξησιν] δύναμιν CG

βούλεσθε μᾶλλον ἐπιόντας, καὶ ἐς τύχας πρὸς
πολλῷ δυνατωτέρους ἀγωνιζόμενοι καταστῆναι,
ἐπιστάμενοι καὶ τὸν βάρβαρον αὐτὸν περὶ
αὑτῷ τὰ πλείω σφαλέντα, καὶ πρὸς αὐτοὺς
τοὺς Ἀθηναίους πολλὰ ἡμᾶς ἤδη τοῖς ἁμαρτή- 5
μασιν αὐτῶν μᾶλλον ἢ τῇ ἀφ' ὑμῶν τιμωρίᾳ
περιγεγενημένους, ἐπεὶ αἵ γε ὑμέτεραι ἐλπίδες
ἤδη τινάς που καὶ ἀπαρασκεύους διὰ τὸ

6 'We speak as   πιστεῦσαι ἔφθειραν. καὶ μηδεὶς
friends re-
proaching   ὑμῶν ἐπ' ἔχθρᾳ τὸ πλέον ἢ αἰτίᾳ 10
friends.
νομίσῃ τάδε λέγεσθαι· αἰτία μὲν
γὰρ φίλων ἀνδρῶν ἐστιν ἁμαρτανόντων, κατηγορία δὲ ἐχθρῶν ἀδικησάντων.

70   "Καὶ ἅμα, εἴπερ τινὲς καὶ ἄλλοι, ἄξιοι
'Consider the   νομίζομεν εἶναι τοῖς πέλας ψόγον 15
contrast
between your   ἐπενεγκεῖν, ἄλλως τε καὶ μεγάλων
character and
theirs.   τῶν διαφερόντων καθεστώτων, περὶ
ὧν οὐκ αἰσθάνεσθαι ἡμῖν γε δοκεῖτε, οὐδ'
ἐκλογίσασθαι πώποτε πρὸς οἵους ὑμῖν Ἀθηναίους ὄντας καὶ ὅσον ὑμῶν καὶ ὡς πᾶν 20
2 διαφέροντας ὁ ἀγὼν ἔσται. οἱ μέν γε νεωτε-
ροποιοὶ καὶ ἐπινοῆσαι ὀξεῖς καὶ ἐπιτελέσαι
ἔργῳ ἃ ἂν γνῶσιν· ὑμεῖς δὲ τὰ ὑπάρχοντά τε
σῴζειν καὶ ἐπιγνῶναι μηδὲν καὶ ἔργῳ οὐδὲ
3 τἀναγκαῖα ἐξικέσθαι. αὖθις δὲ οἱ μὲν καὶ 25
'They are   παρὰ δύναμιν τολμηταὶ καὶ παρὰ
ingenious,
energetic,   γνώμην κινδυνευταὶ καὶ ἐν τοῖς
daring, sanguine.
You are   δεινοῖς εὐέλπιδες· τὸ δὲ ὑμέτερον

7. γε] τε ABEFM[G]   15. νομίζομεν ἄξιοι CG   23. ἃ
Anon. ad Hermogenem : δ codd.   27. ἐν] ἐπὶ ABF

τῆς τε δυνάμεως ἐνδεᾶ πρᾶξαι τῆς conservative,
slow to move,
τε γνώμης μηδὲ τοῖς βεβαίοις hesitating.
πιστεῦσαι τῶν τε δεινῶν μηδέποτε οἴεσθαι
ἀπολυθήσεσθαι. καὶ μὴν καὶ ἄοκνοι πρὸς 4
5 ὑμᾶς μελλητὰς καὶ ἀποδημηταὶ πρὸς ἐνδημο-
τάτους· οἴονται γὰρ οἱ μὲν τῇ ἀπουσίᾳ ἄν τι
κτᾶσθαι, ὑμεῖς δὲ τῷ ἐπελθεῖν καὶ τὰ ἕτοιμα
ἂν βλάψαι. κρατοῦντές τε τῶν ἐχθρῶν ἐπὶ 5
πλεῖστον ἐξέρχονται καὶ νικώμενοι ἐπ᾽ ἐλά-
10 χιστον ἀναπίπτουσιν. ἔτι δὲ τοῖς μὲν σώμασιν 6
ἀλλοτριωτάτοις ὑπὲρ τῆς πόλεως χρῶνται, τῇ
δὲ γνώμῃ οἰκειοτάτῃ ἐς τὸ πράσσειν τι ὑπὲρ
αὐτῆς. καὶ ἃ μὲν ἂν ἐπινοήσαντες μὴ ἐπεξ- 7
έλθωσιν, οἰκείων στέρεσθαι ἡγοῦνται, ἃ δ᾽ ἂν
15 ἐπελθόντες κτήσωνται, ὀλίγα πρὸς τὰ μέλλοντα
τυχεῖν πράξαντες. ἢν δ᾽ ἄρα του καὶ πείρᾳ
σφαλῶσιν, ἀντελπίσαντες ἄλλα ἐπλήρωσαν
τὴν χρείαν· μόνοι γὰρ ἔχουσί τε ὁμοίως καὶ
ἐλπίζουσιν ἃ ἂν ἐπινοήσωσι διὰ τὸ ταχεῖαν
20 τὴν ἐπιχείρησιν ποιεῖσθαι ὧν ἂν γνῶσιν. καὶ 8
ταῦτα μετὰ πόνων πάντα καὶ κινδύνων δι᾽
ὅλου τοῦ αἰῶνος μοχθοῦσι, καὶ ἀπολαύουσιν
ἐλάχιστα τῶν ὑπαρχόντων διὰ τὸ αἰεὶ κτᾶσθαι
καὶ μήτε ἑορτὴν ἄλλο τι ἡγεῖσθαι ἢ τὸ τὰ
25 δέοντα πρᾶξαι ξυμφοράν τε οὐχ ἧσσον
ἡσυχίαν ἀπράγμονα ἢ ἀσχολίαν ἐπίπονον·
ὥστε εἴ τις αὐτοὺς ξυνελὼν φαίη πεφυκέναι 9
ἐπὶ τῷ μήτε αὐτοὺς ἔχειν ἡσυχίαν μήτε

7. ἐξελθεῖν Ullrich   12. γνώμῃ δὲ ABEFM   13. ἐξελ-
θωσιν ABF   14. οἰκεῖα ABEF

τοὺς ἄλλους ἀνθρώπους ἐᾶν, ὀρθῶς ἂν
εἴποι.

71 "Ταύτης μέντοι τοιαύτης ἀντικαθεστηκυίας
'It is high time πόλεως, ὦ Λακεδαιμόνιοι, διαμέλλετε
to awake and be
doing. καὶ οἴεσθε τὴν ἡσυχίαν οὐ τούτοις 5
τῶν ἀνθρώπων ἐπὶ πλεῖστον ἀρκεῖν οἳ ἂν τῇ
μὲν παρασκευῇ δίκαια πράσσωσι, τῇ δὲ γνώμῃ,
ἢν ἀδικῶνται, δῆλοι ὦσι μὴ ἐπιτρέψοντες,
ἀλλ' ἐπὶ τῷ μὴ λυπεῖν τε τοὺς ἄλλους καὶ
αὐτοὶ ἀμυνόμενοι μὴ βλάπτεσθαι τὸ ἴσον 10
2 νέμετε. μόλις δ' ἂν πόλει ὁμοίᾳ παροικοῦντες
ἐτυγχάνετε τούτου· νῦν δ', ὅπερ καὶ ἄρτι
ἐδηλώσαμεν, ἀρχαιότροπα ὑμῶν τὰ ἐπιτηδεύ-
3 ματα πρὸς αὐτούς ἐστιν. ἀνάγκη δὲ ὥσπερ
τέχνης αἰεὶ τὰ ἐπιγιγνόμενα κρατεῖν· καὶ 15
ἡσυχαζούσῃ μὲν πόλει τὰ ἀκίνητα νόμιμα
ἄριστα, πρὸς πολλὰ δὲ ἀναγκαζομένοις ἰέναι
πολλῆς καὶ τῆς ἐπιτεχνήσεως δεῖ. δι' ὅπερ
καὶ τὰ τῶν Ἀθηναίων ἀπὸ τῆς πολυπειρίας
4 ἐπὶ πλέον ὑμῶν κεκαίνωται. μέχρι μὲν οὖν 20
τοῦδε ὡρίσθω ὑμῶν ἡ βραδυτής· νῦν δὲ τοῖς
τε ἄλλοις καὶ Ποτειδεάταις, ὥσπερ ὑπεδέξασθε,
βοηθήσατε κατὰ τάχος ἐσβαλόντες ἐς τὴν
Ἀττικήν, ἵνα μὴ ἄνδρας τε φίλους καὶ
ξυγγενεῖς τοῖς ἐχθίστοις προῆσθε καὶ ἡμᾶς 25
τοὺς ἄλλους ἀθυμίᾳ πρὸς ἑτέραν τινὰ ξυμ-
5 μαχίαν τρέψητε. δρῶμεν δ' ἂν ἄδικον οὐδὲν
οὔτε πρὸς θεῶν τῶν ὁρκίων οὔτε πρὸς ἀνθρώπων τῶν αἰσθανομένων· λύουσι γὰρ σπονδὰς

9. τοὺς om. ABEFM   18. τῆς om. ABEFM

οὐχ οἱ δι᾽ ἐρημίαν ἄλλοις προσιόντες, ἀλλ᾽ οἱ
μὴ βοηθοῦντες οἷς ἂν ξυνομόσωσιν. βουλο- 6
μένων δὲ ὑμῶν προθύμων εἶναι μενοῦμεν· οὔτε
γὰρ ὅσια ἂν ποιοῖμεν μεταβαλλό- 'If you do not
5 μενοι οὔτε ξυνηθεστέρους ἂν ἄλλους act, we must
seek friends
εὕροιμεν. πρὸς τάδε βουλεύεσθε elsewhere.'   7
εὖ καὶ τὴν Πελοπόννησον πειρᾶσθε μὴ ἐλάσσω
ἐξηγεῖσθαι ἢ οἱ πατέρες ὑμῖν παρέδοσαν."

Τοιαῦτα μὲν οἱ Κορίνθιοι εἶπον. τῶν δὲ 72
10 Ἀθηναίων ἔτυχε γὰρ πρεσβεία Athenian envoys
πρότερον ἐν τῇ Λακεδαίμονι περὶ happened to be
present, and
ἄλλων παροῦσα, καὶ ὡς ᾔσθοντο they wished to
justify the
τῶν λόγων, ἔδοξεν αὐτοῖς παριτητέα conduct of
Athens.
ἐς τοὺς Λακεδαιμονίους εἶναι, τῶν μὲν ἐγκλη-
15 μάτων πέρι μηδὲν ἀπολογησομένους ὧν αἱ
πόλεις ἐνεκάλουν, δηλῶσαι δὲ περὶ τοῦ παντὸς
ὡς οὐ ταχέως αὐτοῖς βουλευτέον εἴη, ἀλλ᾽ ἐν
πλέονι σκεπτέον. καὶ ἅμα τὴν σφετέραν
πόλιν ἐβούλοντο σημῆναι ὅση εἴη δύναμιν, καὶ
20 ὑπόμνησιν ποιήσασθαι τοῖς τε πρεσβυτέροις
ὧν ᾔδεσαν καὶ τοῖς νεωτέροις ἐξήγησιν ὧν
ἄπειροι ἦσαν, νομίζοντες μᾶλλον ἂν αὐτοὺς ἐκ
τῶν λόγων πρὸς τὸ ἡσυχάζειν τραπέσθαι ἢ
πρὸς τὸ πολεμεῖν. προσελθόντες οὖν τοῖς 2
25 Λακεδαιμονίοις ἔφασαν βούλεσθαι καὶ αὐτοὶ
ἐς τὸ πλῆθος αὐτῶν εἰπεῖν, εἴ τι μὴ ἀποκωλύοι. οἱ δὲ ἐκέλευόν τε παριέναι, καὶ
παρελθόντες οἱ Ἀθηναῖοι ἔλεγον τοιάδε.

12. καὶ secl. Krüger   20. ποιήσασθαι Cg: ποιήσεσθαι
cett. (-σθε Μ)   26. ἀποκωλύει F: ἀποκωλύῃ ABEM[G]
27 ἐπιέναι ABEFM γρ. G

73 "Ἡ μὲν πρέσβευσις ἡμῶν οὐκ ἐς ἀντιλογίαν

Speech of an Athenian envoy. 'Do not be misled: Athens has not acted unreasonably.

τοῖς ὑμετέροις ξυμμάχοις ἐγένετο,
ἀλλὰ περὶ ὧν ἡ πόλις ἔπεμψεν·
αἰσθανόμενοι δὲ καταβοὴν οὐκ ὀλί-
γην οὖσαν ἡμῶν παρήλθομεν οὐ 5
τοῖς ἐγκλήμασι τῶν πόλεων ἀντεροῦντες (οὐ
γὰρ παρὰ δικασταῖς ὑμῖν οὔτε ἡμῶν οὔτε
τούτων οἱ λόγοι ἂν γίγνοιντο), ἀλλ' ὅπως μὴ
ῥᾳδίως περὶ μεγάλων πραγμάτων τοῖς ξυμμάχοις
πειθόμενοι χεῖρον βουλεύσησθε, καὶ ἅμα 10
βουλόμενοι περὶ τοῦ παντὸς λόγου τοῦ ἐς
ἡμᾶς καθεστῶτος δηλῶσαι ὡς οὔτε ἀπεικότως
ἔχομεν ἃ κεκτήμεθα, ἥ τε πόλις ἡμῶν ἀξία
λόγου ἐστίν.

2 "Καὶ τὰ μὲν πάνυ παλαιὰ τί δεῖ λέγειν, 15

'Remember the services she has rendered to you in the Persian wars.

ὧν ἀκοαὶ μᾶλλον λόγων μάρτυρες
ἢ ὄψις τῶν ἀκουσομένων ; τὰ δὲ
Μηδικὰ καὶ ὅσα αὐτοὶ ξύνιστε, εἰ
καὶ δι' ὄχλου μᾶλλον ἔσται αἰεὶ προβαλλομένοις, ἀνάγκη λέγειν· καὶ γὰρ ὅτε ἐδρῶμεν, 20
ἐπ' ὠφελίᾳ ἐκινδυνεύετο, ἧς τοῦ μὲν ἔργου
μέρος μετέσχετε, τοῦ δὲ λόγου μὴ παντός, εἴ

3 τι ὠφελεῖ, στερισκώμεθα. ῥηθήσεται δὲ οὐ
παραιτήσεως μᾶλλον ἕνεκα ἢ μαρτυρίου καὶ
δηλώσεως πρὸς οἵαν ὑμῖν πόλιν μὴ εὖ 25

4 βουλευομένοις ὁ ἀγὼν καταστήσεται. φαμὲν
γὰρ Μαραθῶνί τε μόνοι προκινδυνεῦσαι τῷ
βαρβάρῳ καὶ ὅτε τὸ ὕστερον ἦλθεν, οὐχ
ἱκανοὶ ὄντες κατὰ γῆν ἀμύνεσθαι, ἐσβάντες ἐς

4. αἰσθόμενοι ABEFM   23. ὠφέλει E

τὰς ναῦς πανδημεὶ ἐν Σαλαμῖνι ξυνναυμαχῆσαι,
ὅπερ ἔσχε μὴ κατὰ πόλεις αὐτὸν ἐπιπλέοντα
τὴν Πελοπόννησον πορθεῖν, ἀδυνάτων ἂν ὄντων
πρὸς ναῦς πολλὰς ἀλλήλοις ἐπιβοηθεῖν.
5 τεκμήριον δὲ μέγιστον αὐτὸς ἐποίησεν· νικηθεὶς 5
γὰρ ταῖς ναυσὶν ὡς οὐκέτι αὐτῷ ὁμοίας οὔσης
τῆς δυνάμεως κατὰ τάχος τῷ πλέονι τοῦ
στρατοῦ ἀνεχώρησεν. τοιούτου μέντοι τούτου 74
ξυμβάντος, καὶ σαφῶς δηλωθέντος ὅτι ἐν ταῖς
10 ναυσὶ τῶν Ἑλλήνων τὰ πράγματα ἐγένετο,
τρία τὰ ὠφελιμώτατα ἐς αὐτὸ παρεσχόμεθα,
ἀριθμόν τε νεῶν πλεῖστον καὶ ἄνδρα στρατηγὸν
ξυνετώτατον καὶ προθυμίαν ἀοκνοτάτην· ναῦς
μέν γε ἐς τὰς τετρακοσίας ὀλίγῳ ἐλάσσους
15 τῶν δύο μοιρῶν, Θεμιστοκλέα δὲ ἄρχοντα, ὃς
αἰτιώτατος ἐν τῷ στενῷ ναυμαχῆσαι ἐγένετο,
ὅπερ σαφέστατα ἔσωσε τὰ πράγματα καὶ αὐτὸν
διὰ τοῦτο ὑμεῖς ἐτιμήσατε μάλιστα δὴ ἄνδρα
ξένον τῶν ὡς ὑμᾶς ἐλθόντων· προθυμίαν 2
20 δὲ καὶ πολὺ τολμηροτάτην ἐδείξαμεν, οἵ γε,
ἐπειδὴ ἡμῖν κατὰ γῆν οὐδεὶς ἐβοήθει, τῶν
ἄλλων ἤδη μέχρι ἡμῶν δουλευόντων ἠξιώσαμεν
ἐκλιπόντες τὴν πόλιν καὶ τὰ οἰκεῖα διαφθεί-
ραντες μηδ' ὣς τὸ τῶν περιλοίπων ξυμμάχων
25 κοινὸν προλιπεῖν μηδὲ σκεδασθέντες ἀχρεῖοι
αὐτοῖς γενέσθαι, ἀλλ' ἐσβάντες ἐς τὰς ναῦς
κινδυνεῦσαι καὶ μὴ ὀργισθῆναι ὅτι ἡμῖν οὐ

8. ξυμβάντος τούτου ABEFM   15. τῶν G : om. cett.
17. αὐτοὶ ABEFM   18. ὑμεῖς om. ABEFM[G] ‖ δὴ μάλιστα
ἐτιμήσατε ABEFM[G]

3 προυτιμωρήσατε. ὥστε φαμὲν οὐχ ἧσσον αὐτοὶ ὠφελῆσαι ὑμᾶς ἢ τυχεῖν τούτου. ὑμεῖς μὲν γὰρ ἀπό τε οἰκουμένων τῶν πόλεων καὶ ἐπὶ τῷ τὸ λοιπὸν νέμεσθαι, ἐπειδὴ ἐδείσατε ὑπὲρ ὑμῶν καὶ οὐχ ἡμῶν τὸ πλέον, ἐβοηθήσατε 5 (ὅτε γοῦν ἦμεν ἔτι σῶοι, οὐ παρεγένεσθε)· ἡμεῖς δὲ ἀπό τε τῆς οὐκ οὔσης ἔτι ὁρμώμενοι καὶ ὑπὲρ τῆς ἐν βραχείᾳ ἐλπίδι οὔσης κινδυ- νεύοντες ξυνεσώσαμεν ὑμᾶς τε τὸ μέρος καὶ 4 ἡμᾶς αὐτούς. εἰ δὲ προσεχωρήσαμεν πρότερον 10 τῷ Μήδῳ δείσαντες, ὥσπερ καὶ ἄλλοι, περὶ τῇ χώρᾳ, ἢ μὴ ἐτολμήσαμεν ὕστερον ἐσβῆναι ἐς τὰς ναῦς ὡς διεφθαρμένοι, οὐδὲν ἂν ἔδει ἔτι ὑμᾶς μὴ ἔχοντας ναῦς ἱκανὰς ναυμαχεῖν, ἀλλὰ καθ᾽ ἡσυχίαν ἂν αὐτῷ προυχώρησε τὰ 15 πράγματα ᾗ ἐβούλετο.

75 "Ἆρ᾽ ἄξιοί ἐσμεν, ὦ Λακεδαιμόνιοι, καὶ

'Her power was fairly gained; and when gained she was bound to maintain it.

προθυμίας ἕνεκα τῆς τότε καὶ γνώ- μης ξυνέσεως ἀρχῆς γε ἧς ἔχομεν τοῖς Ἕλλησι μὴ οὕτως ἄγαν ἐπι- 20 2 φθόνως διακεῖσθαι; καὶ γὰρ αὐτὴν τήνδε ἐλάβομεν οὐ βιασάμενοι, ἀλλ᾽ ὑμῶν μὲν οὐκ ἐθελησάντων παραμεῖναι πρὸς τὰ ὑπόλοιπα τοῦ βαρβάρου, ἡμῖν δὲ προσελθόντων τῶν ξυμμάχων καὶ αὐτῶν δεηθέντων ἡγεμόνας 25 3 καταστῆναι· ἐξ αὐτοῦ δὲ τοῦ ἔργου κατηναγκά- σθημεν τὸ πρῶτον προαγαγεῖν αὐτὴν ἐς τόδε, μάλιστα μὲν ὑπὸ δέους, ἔπειτα καὶ τιμῆς,

ὕστερον καὶ ὠφελίας. καὶ οὐκ ἀσφαλὲς ἔτι 4
ἐδόκει εἶναι τοῖς πολλοῖς ἀπηχθημένους, καί
τινων καὶ ἤδη ἀποστάντων κατεστραμμένων,
ὑμῶν τε ἡμῖν οὐκέτι ὁμοίως φίλων, ἀλλ᾽
5 ὑπόπτων καὶ διαφόρων ὄντων, ἀνέντας κινδυ-
νεύειν· καὶ γὰρ ἂν αἱ ἀποστάσεις πρὸς ὑμᾶς
ἐγίγνοντο. πᾶσι δὲ ἀνεπίφθονον τὰ ξυμφέροντα 5
τῶν μεγίστων πέρι κινδύνων εὖ τίθεσθαι.
ὑμεῖς γοῦν, ὦ Λακεδαιμόνιοι, τὰς 'Had Sparta **76**
10 ἐν τῇ Πελοποννήσῳ πόλεις ἐπὶ τὸ retained the
hegemony, she
ὑμῖν ὠφέλιμον καταστησάμενοι would have
found it
ἐξηγεῖσθε· καὶ εἰ τότε ὑπομείναντες necessary to
adopt similar
διὰ παντὸς ἀπήχθησθε ἐν τῇ measures.
ἡγεμονίᾳ, ὥσπερ ἡμεῖς, εὖ ἴσμεν μὴ ἂν ἧσσον
15 ὑμᾶς λυπηροὺς γενομένους τοῖς ξυμμάχοις καὶ
ἀναγκασθέντας ἂν ἢ ἄρχειν ἐγκρατῶς ἢ αὐτοὺς
κινδυνεύειν. οὕτως οὐδ᾽ ἡμεῖς θαυμαστὸν οὐδὲν 2
πεποιήκαμεν οὐδ᾽ ἀπὸ τοῦ ἀνθρω- 'We have done
nothing unusual,
πείου τρόπου, εἰ ἀρχήν τε διδομένην and we have
been moderate
20 ἐδεξάμεθα καὶ ταύτην μὴ ἀνεῖμεν in the use of our
power.
ὑπὸ ⟨τριῶν⟩ τῶν μεγίστων νικη-
θέντες, τιμῆς καὶ δέους καὶ ὠφελίας, οὐδ᾽ αὖ
πρῶτοι τοῦ τοιούτου ὑπάρξαντες, ἀλλ᾽ αἰεὶ
καθεστῶτος τὸν ἥσσω ὑπὸ τοῦ δυνατωτέρου
25 κατείργεσθαι, ἄξιοί τε ἅμα νομίζοντες εἶναι
καὶ ὑμῖν δοκοῦντες μέχρι οὗ τὰ ξυμφέροντα
λογιζόμενοι τῷ δικαίῳ λόγῳ νῦν χρῆσθε, ὃν

11. ὑμῶν C[G]   13. ἀπήχθεσθε C Schol. : ἀπήχθησθε
cett. [G]   19. διαδιδομένην fortasse legit Schol.   21.
τριῶν add. Herwerden

οὐδείς πω παρατυχὸν ἰσχύι τι κτήσασθαι
προθεὶς τοῦ μὴ πλέον ἔχειν ἀπετράπετο.
3 ἐπαινεῖσθαί τε ἄξιοι οἵτινες χρησάμενοι τῇ
ἀνθρωπείᾳ φύσει ὥστε ἑτέρων ἄρχειν δικαιότεροι ἢ κατὰ τὴν ὑπάρχουσαν δύναμιν 5
4 γένωνται. ἄλλους γ' ἂν οὖν οἰόμεθα τὰ
ἡμέτερα λαβόντας δεῖξαι ἂν μάλιστα εἴ τι
μετριάζομεν· ἡμῖν δὲ καὶ ἐκ τοῦ ἐπιεικοῦς
ἀδοξία τὸ πλέον ἢ ἔπαινος οὐκ εἰκότως
περιέστη.   10

77   " Καὶ ἐλασσούμενοι γὰρ ἐν ταῖς ξυμβολαίαις

πρὸς τοὺς ξυμμάχους δίκαις καὶ
παρ' ἡμῖν αὐτοῖς ἐν τοῖς ὁμοίοις
νόμοις ποιήσαντες τὰς κρίσεις φιλο-
δικεῖν δοκοῦμεν. καὶ οὐδεὶς σκοπεῖ 15
αὐτῶν τοῖς καὶ ἄλλοθί που ἀρχὴν ἔχουσι καὶ
ἧσσον ἡμῶν πρὸς τοὺς ὑπηκόους μετρίοις οὖσι
διότι τοῦτο οὐκ ὀνειδίζεται· βιάζεσθαι γὰρ
3 οἷς ἂν ἐξῇ, δικάζεσθαι οὐδὲν προσδέονται. οἱ
δὲ εἰθισμένοι πρὸς ἡμᾶς ἀπὸ τοῦ ἴσου ὁμιλεῖν, 20
ἤν τι παρὰ τὸ μὴ οἴεσθαι χρῆναι ἢ γνώμῃ
ἢ δυνάμει τῇ διὰ τὴν ἀρχὴν καὶ ὁπωσοῦν
ἐλασσωθῶσιν, οὐ τοῦ πλέονος μὴ στερισκόμενοι
χάριν ἔχουσιν, ἀλλὰ τοῦ ἐνδεοῦς χαλεπώτερον
φέρουσιν ἢ εἰ ἀπὸ πρώτης ἀποθέμενοι τὸν 25
νόμον φανερῶς ἐπλεονεκτοῦμεν. ἐκείνως δὲ
οὐδ' ἂν αὐτοὶ ἀντέλεγον ὡς οὐ χρεὼν τὸν

6. γένωνται CG γρ. ABF : γεγένηνται cett. γρ. G   11. ξυμ-
βολιιμαίαις Hesych.   16. post που add. τὴν M ‖ χουσιν ἀρχὴν
CG

ἥσσω τῷ κρατοῦντι ὑποχωρεῖν. ἀδικούμενοί 4
τε, ὡς ἔοικεν, οἱ ἄνθρωποι μᾶλλον ὀργίζονται
ἢ βιαζόμενοι· τὸ μὲν γὰρ ἀπὸ τοῦ ἴσου δοκεῖ
πλεονεκτεῖσθαι, τὸ δ' ἀπὸ τοῦ κρείσσονος
5 καταναγκάζεσθαι. ὑπὸ γοῦν τοῦ Μήδου δεινό- 5
τερα τούτων πάσχοντες ἠνείχοντο, 'But they
ἡ δὲ ἡμετέρα ἀρχὴ χαλεπὴ δοκεῖ suffered worse
at the hands of
εἶναι, εἰκότως· τὸ παρὸν γὰρ αἰεὶ Persia.
βαρὺ τοῖς ὑπηκόοις. ὑμεῖς γ' ἂν οὖν εἰ 6
10 καθελόντες ἡμᾶς ἄρξαιτε, τάχα ἂν 'If you replaced
τὴν εὔνοιαν ἣν διὰ τὸ ἡμέτερον δέος us, you would
soon excite
εἰλήφατε μεταβάλοιτε, εἴπερ οἷα ill-feeling.
καὶ τότε πρὸς τὸν Μῆδον δι' ὀλίγου ἡγησάμενοι ὑπεδείξατε, ὅμοια καὶ νῦν γνώσεσθε.
15 ἄμεικτα γὰρ τά τε καθ' ὑμᾶς αὐτοὺς νόμιμα
τοῖς ἄλλοις ἔχετε καὶ προσέτι εἷς ἕκαστος
ἐξιὼν οὔτε τούτοις χρῆται οὔθ' οἷς ἡ ἄλλη
Ἑλλὰς νομίζει.

"Βουλεύεσθε οὖν βραδέως ὡς οὐ περὶ 78
20 βραχέων, καὶ μὴ ἀλλοτρίαις γνώμαις 'Think well and
long before you
καὶ ἐγκλήμασι πεισθέντες οἰκεῖον decide to
embark on a
πόνον πρόσθησθε. τοῦ δὲ πολέμου hazardous war.'
τὸν παράλογον, ὅσος ἐστί, πρὶν ἐν αὐτῷ
γενέσθαι προδιάγνωτε· μηκυνόμενος γὰρ φιλεῖ 2
25 ἐς τύχας τὰ πολλὰ περιίστασθαι, ὧν ἴσον τε
ἀπέχομεν καὶ ὁποτέρως ἔσται ἐν ἀδήλῳ κινδυνεύεται. ἰόντες τε οἱ ἄνθρωποι ἐς τοὺς 3
πολέμους τῶν ἔργων πρότερον ἔχονται, ἃ χρῆν
ὕστερον δρᾶν, κακοπαθοῦντες δὲ ἤδη τῶν

10. ἄρξετε CG   28. ὃ Classen

4 λόγων ἅπτονται. ἡμεῖς δὲ ἐν οὐδεμιᾷ πω
τοιαύτῃ ἁμαρτίᾳ ὄντες οὔτ' αὐτοὶ οὔθ' ὑμᾶς
ὁρῶντες λέγομεν ὑμῖν, ἕως ἔτι αὐθαίρετος
ἀμφοτέροις ἡ εὐβουλία, σπονδὰς μὴ λύειν
μηδὲ παραβαίνειν τοὺς ὅρκους, τὰ δὲ διάφορα 5
δίκῃ λύεσθαι κατὰ τὴν ξυνθήκην. εἰ δὲ μή,
θεοὺς τοὺς ὁρκίους μάρτυρας ποιούμενοι πειρασόμεθα ἀμύνεσθαι πολέμου ἄρχοντας ταύτῃ ᾗ
ἂν ὑφηγῆσθε."

79   Τοιαῦτα δὲ οἱ 'Αθηναῖοι εἶπον. ἐπειδὴ δὲ 10

The Spartans
now debated
among them-
selves, all
strangers having
withdrawn.
Speech of King
Archidamus.

τῶν τε ξυμμάχων ἤκουσαν οἱ
Λακεδαιμόνιοι τὰ ἐγκλήματα τὰ ἐς
τοὺς 'Αθηναίους καὶ τῶν 'Αθηναίων
ἃ ἔλεξαν, μεταστησάμενοι πάντας
ἐβουλεύοντο κατὰ σφᾶς αὐτοὺς περὶ 15

2 τῶν παρόντων. καὶ τῶν μὲν πλεόνων ἐπὶ τὸ
αὐτὸ αἱ γνῶμαι ἔφερον, ἀδικεῖν τε τοὺς
'Αθηναίους ἤδη καὶ πολεμητέα εἶναι ἐν᾿ τάχει·
παρελθὼν δὲ 'Αρχίδαμος ὁ βασιλεὺς αὐτῶν,
ἀνὴρ καὶ ξυνετὸς δοκῶν εἶναι καὶ σώφρων, 20
ἔλεξε τοιάδε.

80   "Καὶ αὐτὸς πολλῶν ἤδη πολέμων ἔμπειρός

'War with
Athens will be a
serious under-
taking.

εἰμι, ὦ Λακεδαιμόνιοι, καὶ ὑμῶν
τοὺς ἐν τῇ αὐτῇ ἡλικίᾳ ὁρῶ, ὥστε
μήτε ἀπειρίᾳ ἐπιθυμῆσαί τινα τοῦ 25
ἔργου, ὅπερ ἂν οἱ πολλοὶ πάθοιεν, μήτε

2 ἀγαθὸν καὶ ἀσφαλὲς νομίσαντα. εὕροιτε δ' ἂν
τόνδε περὶ οὗ νῦν βουλεύεσθε οὐκ ἂν ἐλάχιστον

6. εἰ δὲ μή om. C : ἢ cG   10. prius δὲ] μὲν cGM
28. post τόνδε add. τὸν πόλεμον CG

γενόμενον, εἰ σωφρόνως τις αὐτὸν ἐκλογίζοιτο.
πρὸς μὲν γὰρ Πελοποννησίους καὶ   'We are ill pre- 3
τοὺς ἀστυγείτονας παρόμοιος ἡμῶν   pared to face an
                                   enemy who lives
ἡ ἀλκή, καὶ διὰ ταχέων οἷόν τε   at a distance, is
                                   the greatest
5 ἐφ' ἕκαστα ἐλθεῖν· πρὸς δὲ ἄνδρας naval power,
                                   and is in all
οἳ γῆν τε ἑκὰς ἔχουσι καὶ προσέτι   respects better
                                   equipped than
θαλάσσης ἐμπειρότατοί εἰσι καὶ τοῖς we.
ἄλλοις ἅπασιν ἄριστα ἐξήρτυνται, πλούτῳ τε
ἰδίῳ καὶ δημοσίῳ καὶ ναυσὶ καὶ ἵπποις καὶ
10 ὅπλοις καὶ ὄχλῳ ὅσος οὐκ ἐν ἄλλῳ ἑνί γε
χωρίῳ Ἑλληνικῷ ἐστιν, ἔτι δὲ καὶ ξυμμάχους
πολλοὺς φόρου ὑποτελεῖς ἔχουσι, πῶς χρὴ
πρὸς τούτους ῥᾳδίως πόλεμον ἄρασθαι καὶ τίνι
πιστεύσαντας ἀπαρασκεύους ἐπειχθῆναι ; πό-
15 τερον ταῖς ναυσίν ; ἀλλ' ἥσσους ἐσμέν· εἰ δὲ 4
μελετήσομεν καὶ ἀντιπαρασκευασόμεθα, χρόνος
ἐνέσται. ἀλλὰ τοῖς χρήμασιν ; ἀλλὰ πολλῷ
πλέον ἔτι τούτου ἐλλείπομεν καὶ οὔτε ἐν
κοινῷ ἔχομεν οὔτε ἑτοίμως ἐκ τῶν ἰδίων
20 φέρομεν. τάχ' ἄν τις θαρσοίη ὅτι τοῖς ὅπλοις 81
αὐτῶν καὶ τῷ πλήθει ὑπερφέρομεν, ὥστε τὴν
γῆν δῃοῦν ἐπιφοιτῶντες. τοῖς δὲ ἄλλη γῆ 2
ἐστι πολλὴ ἧς ἄρχουσι, καὶ ἐκ θαλάσσης ὧν
δέονται ἐπάξονται. εἰ δ' αὖ τοὺς ξυμμάχους 3
25 ἀφιστάναι πειρασόμεθα, δεήσει καὶ τούτοις
ναυσὶ βοηθεῖν τὸ πλέον οὖσι νησιώταις. τίς 4
οὖν ἔσται ἡμῶν ὁ πόλεμος ; εἰ   'We shall suffer
μὴ γὰρ ἢ ναυσὶ κρατήσομεν ἢ τὰς   much, and the
                                 war will last
προσόδους ἀφαιρήσομεν ἀφ' ὧν τὸ   long.

2. post γὰρ add. τοὺς ABEFGM   18. ἔτι πλέον ABEFM[G]

5 ναυτικὸν τρέφουσι, βλαψόμεθα τὰ πλείω. κἂν
τούτῳ οὐδὲ καταλύεσθαι ἔτι καλόν, ἄλλως τε
καὶ εἰ δόξομεν ἄρξαι μᾶλλον τῆς διαφορᾶς.
6 μὴ γὰρ δὴ ἐκείνῃ γε τῇ ἐλπίδι ἐπαιρώμεθα
ὡς ταχὺ παυσθήσεται ὁ πόλεμος, ἢν τὴν γῆν 5
αὐτῶν τέμωμεν. δέδοικα δὲ μᾶλλον μὴ καὶ
τοῖς παισὶν αὐτὸν ὑπολίπωμεν· οὕτως εἰκὸς
Ἀθηναίους φρονήματι μήτε τῇ γῇ δουλεῦσαι
μήτε ὥσπερ ἀπείρους καταπλαγῆναι τῷ
πολέμῳ.   10

82   "Οὐ μὴν οὐδὲ ἀναισθήτως αὐτοὺς κελεύω
τούς τε ξυμμάχους ἡμῶν ἐᾶν
βλάπτειν καὶ ἐπιβουλεύοντας μὴ
καταφωρᾶν, ἀλλὰ ὅπλα μὲν μήπω
κινεῖν, πέμπειν δὲ καὶ αἰτιᾶσθαι 15
μήτε πόλεμον ἄγαν δηλοῦντας μήθ' ὡς ἐπιτρέψομεν, κἂν τούτῳ καὶ τὰ ἡμέτερ' αὐτῶν
ἐξαρτύεσθαι ξυμμάχων τε προσαγωγῇ καὶ
Ἑλλήνων καὶ βαρβάρων, εἴ ποθέν τινα ἢ
ναυτικοῦ ἢ χρημάτων δύναμιν προσληψόμεθα 20
(ἀνεπίφθονον δέ, ὅσοι ὥσπερ καὶ ἡμεῖς ὑπ'
Ἀθηναίων ἐπιβουλευόμεθα, μὴ Ἕλληνας μόνον,
ἀλλὰ καὶ βαρβάρους προσλαβόντας διασω-
2 θῆναι), καὶ τὰ αὐτῶν ἅμα ἐκποριζώμεθα. καὶ
ἢν μὲν ἐσακούσωσί τι πρεσβευομένων ἡμῶν, 2ɩ
ταῦτα ἄριστα· ἢν δὲ μή, διελθόντων ἐτῶν δύο
καὶ τριῶν ἄμεινον ἤδη, ἢν δοκῇ, πεφραγμένοι

'My advice is to negotiate with Athens, and in the meantime to add to our resources and seek allies.

6. τέμωμεν Cobet : τάμωμεν codd.   24. αὐτῶν F ?: αὑτῶν
cett.   25. ἐσακούσωσί AE : ἐπακούωσί G   26. post ἐτῶν
add. καὶ ABEM

ἴμεν ἐπ' αὐτούς. καὶ ἴσως ὁρῶντες ἡμῶν ἤδη 3
τήν τε παρασκευὴν καὶ τοὺς λόγους αὐτῇ
ὁμοῖα ὑποσημαίνοντας μᾶλλον ἂν εἴκοιεν, καὶ
γῆν ἔτι ἄτμητον ἔχοντες καὶ περὶ παρόντων
5 ἀγαθῶν καὶ οὔπω ἐφθαρμένων βουλευόμενοι.
μὴ γὰρ ἄλλο τι νομίσητε τὴν γῆν αὐτῶν ἢ 4
ὅμηρον ἔχειν καὶ οὐχ ἧσσον ὅσῳ ἄμεινον
ἐξείργασται· ἧς φείδεσθαι χρὴ ὡς ἐπὶ
πλεῖστον, καὶ μὴ ἐς ἀπόνοιαν καταστήσαντας
10 αὐτοὺς ἀληπτοτέρους ἔχειν. εἰ γὰρ ἀ- 5
παράσκευοι τοῖς τῶν ξυμμάχων ἐγκλήμασιν
ἐπειχθέντες τεμοῦμεν αὐτήν, ὁρᾶτε ὅπως μὴ
αἴσχιον καὶ ἀπορώτερον τῇ Πελοποννήσῳ
πράξομεν. ἐγκλήματα μὲν γὰρ καὶ πόλεων 6
15 καὶ ἰδιωτῶν οἷόν τε καταλῦσαι· πόλεμον δὲ
ξύμπαντας ἀραμένους ἕνεκα τῶν ἰδίων, ὃν οὐχ
ὑπάρχει εἰδέναι καθ' ὅ τι χωρήσει, οὐ ῥᾴδιον
εὐπρεπῶς θέσθαι.

"Καὶ ἀνανδρία μηδενὶ πολλοὺς μιᾷ πόλει 83
20 μὴ ταχὺ ἐπελθεῖν δοκείτω εἶναι. 'It is not coward-
εἰσὶ γὰρ καὶ ἐκείνοις οὐκ ἐλάσσους ice to shrink
from attacking 2
χρήματα φέροντες ξύμμαχοι, καὶ a state so well
equipped as
ἔστιν ὁ πόλεμος οὐχ ὅπλων τὸ Athens.
πλέον ἀλλὰ δαπάνης, δι' ἣν τὰ ὅπλα ὠφελεῖ,
25 ἄλλως τε καὶ ἠπειρώταις πρὸς θαλασσίους.
πορισώμεθα οὖν πρῶτον αὐτήν, καὶ μὴ τοῖς 3
τῶν ξυμμάχων λόγοις πρότερον ἐπαιρώμεθα,
οἵπερ δὲ καὶ τῶν ἀποβαινόντων τὸ πλέον ἐπ'
ἀμφότερα τῆς αἰτίας ἕξομεν, οὗτοι καὶ καθ'

14. πράξομεν CE suprascr. M An. Bekk. : πράξωμεν cett. [G]

84 ἡσυχίαν τι αὐτῶν προΐδωμεν. καὶ τὸ βραδὺ
καὶ μέλλον, ὃ μέμφονται μάλιστα ἡμῶν, μὴ
αἰσχύνεσθε. σπεύδοντές τε γὰρ
σχολαίτερον ἂν παύσαισθε διὰ τὸ
ἀπαράσκευοι ἐγχειρεῖν, καὶ ἅμα 5
ἐλευθέραν καὶ εὐδοξοτάτην πόλιν διὰ παντὸς
2 νεμόμεθα. καὶ δύναται μάλιστα σωφροσύνη
ἔμφρων τοῦτ' εἶναι· μόνοι γὰρ δι' αὐτὸ
εὐπραγίαις τε οὐκ ἐξυβρίζομεν καὶ ξυμφοραῖς
ἧσσον ἑτέρων εἴκομεν· τῶν τε ξὺν ἐπαίνῳ 10
ἐξοτρυνόντων ἡμᾶς ἐπὶ τὰ δεινὰ παρὰ τὸ
δοκοῦν ἡμῖν οὐκ ἐπαιρόμεθα ἡδονῇ, καὶ ἤν τις
ἄρα ξὺν κατηγορίᾳ παροξύνῃ, οὐδὲν δὴ μᾶλλον
3 ἀχθεσθέντες ἀνεπείσθημεν. πολεμικοί τε καὶ
εὔβουλοι διὰ τὸ εὔκοσμον γιγνόμεθα, τὸ μὲν 15
ὅτι αἰδὼς σωφροσύνης πλεῖστον μετέχει,
αἰσχύνης δὲ εὐψυχία, εὔβουλοι δὲ ἀμαθέστερον
τῶν νόμων τῆς ὑπεροψίας παιδευόμενοι καὶ
ξὺν χαλεπότητι σωφρονέστερον ἢ ὥστε αὐτῶν
ἀνηκουστεῖν, καὶ μὴ τὰ ἀχρεῖα ξυνετοὶ ἄγαν 20
ὄντες τὰς τῶν πολεμίων παρασκευὰς λόγῳ
καλῶς μεμφόμενοι ἀνομοίως ἔργῳ ἐπεξιέναι,
νομίζειν δὲ τάς τε διανοίας τῶν πέλας παραπλησίους εἶναι καὶ τὰς προσπιπτούσας τύχας
4 οὐ λόγῳ διαιρετάς. αἰεὶ δὲ ὡς πρὸς εὖ 25
βουλευομένους τοὺς ἐναντίους ἔργῳ παρα-
σκευαζόμεθα· καὶ οὐκ ἐξ ἐκείνων ὡς ἁμαρτησο-

'To our characteristic caution we owe our glory.

---

4. παύσαισθε cGM : παύσησθε cett.　　11. ἐποτρυνόντων
GM　　13. δὴ cG : δὲ C : om. cett.　　17. ἀμαθέστεροι CG
26. παρασκευαζώμεθα ABEFM

μένων ἔχειν δεῖ τὰς ἐλπίδας, ἀλλ᾽ ὡς ἡμῶν
αὐτῶν ἀσφαλῶς πϝονοουμένων. πολύ τε
διαφέρειν οὐ δεῖ νομίζειν ἄνθρωπον ἀνθρώπου,
κράτιστον δὲ εἶναι ὅστις ἐν τοῖς ἀναγκαιοτάτοις
5 παιδεύεται.

"Ταύτας οὖν ἃς οἱ πατέρες τε ἡμῖν παρέ- 85
δοσαν μελέτας καὶ αὐτοὶ διὰ ʼLet us not now
παντὸς ὠφελούμενοι ἔχομεν μὴ break away
from our
παρῶμεν, μηδὲ ἐπειχθέντες ἐν tradition. Send
to Athens and
10 βραχεῖ μορίῳ ἡμέρας περὶ πολλῶν prepare for war.ʼ
σωμάτων καὶ χρημάτων καὶ πόλεων καὶ δόξης
βουλεύσωμεν, ἀλλὰ καθ᾽ ἡσυχίαν. ἔξεστι δ᾽
ἡμῖν μᾶλλον ἑτέρων διὰ ἰσχύν. καὶ πρὸς 2
τοὺς Ἀθηναίους πέμπετε μὲν περὶ τῆς
15 Ποτειδαίας, πέμπετε δὲ περὶ ὧν οἱ ξύμμαχοί
φασιν ἀδικεῖσθαι, ἄλλως τε καὶ ἑτοίμων ὄντων
αὐτῶν δίκας δοῦναι· ἐπὶ δὲ τὸν διδόντα οὐ
πρότερον νόμιμον ὡς ἐπ᾽ ἀδικοῦντα ἰέναι.
παρασκευάζεσθε δὲ τὸν πόλεμον ἅμα. ταῦτα
20 γὰρ καὶ κράτιστα βουλεύσεσθε καὶ τοῖς
ἐναντίοις φοβερώτατα." καὶ ὁ μὲν Ἀρχίδαμος 3
τοιαῦτα εἶπεν· παρελθὼν δὲ Σθενελαΐδας
τελευταῖος, εἷς τῶν ἐφόρων τότε ὤν, ἔλεξεν
[τοῖς Λακεδαιμονίοις] ὧδε.

25 "Τοὺς μὲν λόγους τοὺς πολλοὺς τῶν 86
Ἀθηναίων οὐ γιγνώσκω· ἐπαινέ- Speech of
Sthenelaidas.
σαντες γὰρ πολλὰ ἑαυτοὺς οὐδαμοῦ ʼWe must not
stand by and
ἀντεῖπον ὡς οὐκ ἀδικοῦσι τοὺς see our allies

20. prius καὶ om. ABEFM[G]　　23. post ἔλεξεν add. ἐν
ABEFM　　24. τοῖς Λακεδαιμονίοις secl. Krüger

injured : our strength is in them. ἡμετέρους ξυμμάχους καὶ τὴν Πελοπόννησον· καίτοι εἰ πρὸς τοὺς Μήδους ἐγένοντο ἀγαθοὶ τότε, πρὸς δ᾽ ἡμᾶς κακοὶ νῦν, διπλασίας ζημίας ἄξιοί εἰσιν, ὅτι 2 ἀντ᾽ ἀγαθῶν κακοὶ γεγένηνται. ἡμεῖς δὲ 5 ὁμοῖοι καὶ τότε καὶ νῦν ἐσμεν, καὶ τοὺς ξυμμάχους, ἢν σωφρονῶμεν, οὐ περιοψόμεθα ἀδικουμένους οὐδὲ μελλήσομεν τιμωρεῖν. οἱ δ᾽ 3 οὐκέτι μέλλουσι κακῶς πάσχειν. ἄλλοις μὲν γὰρ χρήματά ἐστι πολλὰ καὶ νῆες καὶ ἵπποι, 10 ἡμῖν δὲ ξύμμαχοι ἀγαθοί, οὓς οὐ παραδοτέα τοῖς Ἀθηναίοις ἐστίν, οὐδὲ δίκαις καὶ λόγοις διακριτέα μὴ λόγῳ καὶ αὐτοὺς βλαπτομένους, ἀλλὰ τιμωρητέα ἐν τάχει καὶ παντὶ σθένει. 4 καὶ ὡς ἡμᾶς πρέπει βουλεύεσθαι ἀδικουμένους 15 μηδεὶς διδασκέτω, ἀλλὰ τοὺς μέλλοντας ἀδικεῖν μᾶλλον πρέπει πολὺν χρόνον βουλεύεσθαι. 5 ψηφίζεσθε οὖν, ὦ Λακεδαιμόνιοι, ἀξίως τῆς

'Let us promptly check Athenian power.' Σπάρτης τὸν πόλεμον, καὶ μήτε τοὺς Ἀθηναίους ἐᾶτε μείζους γίγνε- 20 σθαι μήτε τοὺς ξυμμάχους καταπροδιδῶμεν, ἀλλὰ ξὺν τοῖς θεοῖς ἐπίωμεν ἐπὶ τοὺς ἀδικοῦντας."

87 Τοιαῦτα λέξας ἐπεψήφιζεν αὐτὸς ἔφορος

A division was then taken, and the majority were for war. ὢν ἐς τὴν ἐκκλησίαν τῶν Λακεδαι- 25 μονίων. ὁ δὲ (κρίνουσι γὰρ βοῇ καὶ οὐ ψήφῳ) οὐκ ἔφη διαγιγνώ- σκειν τὴν βοὴν ὁποτέρα μείζων, ἀλλὰ

10. πολλὰ om. CG   22. ἐπὶ] πρὸς ABEFM   24. post
τοιαῦτα add. δὲ ABEFM   28. ποτέρα CG

βουλόμενος αὐτοὺς φανερῶς ἀποδεικνυμένους
τὴν γνώμην ἐς τὸ πολεμεῖν μᾶλλον ὁρμῆσαι
ἔλεξεν "ὅτῳ μὲν ὑμῶν, ὦ Λακεδαιμόνιοι,
δοκοῦσι λελύσθαι αἱ σπονδαὶ καὶ οἱ Ἀθηναῖοι
5 ἀδικεῖν, ἀναστήτω ἐς ἐκεῖνο τὸ χωρίον," δείξας
τι χωρίον αὐτοῖς, "ὅτῳ δὲ μὴ δοκοῦσιν, ἐς
τὰ ἐπὶ θάτερα." ἀναστάντες δὲ διέστησαν, 3
καὶ πολλῷ πλείους ἐγένοντο οἷς ἐδόκουν αἱ
σπονδαὶ λελύσθαι. προσκαλέσαντές τε τοὺς 4
10 ξυμμάχους εἶπον ὅτι σφίσι μὲν δοκοῖεν ἀδικεῖν
οἱ Ἀθηναῖοι, βούλεσθαι δὲ καὶ τοὺς πάντας
ξυμμάχους παρακαλέσαντες ψῆφον ἐπαγαγεῖν,
ὅπως κοινῇ βουλευσάμενοι τὸν πόλεμον
ποιῶνται, ἢν δοκῇ. καὶ οἱ μὲν ἀπεχώρησαν 5
15 ἐπ' οἴκου διαπραξάμενοι ταῦτα, καὶ οἱ Ἀθηναίων πρέσβεις ὕστερον ἐφ' ἅπερ ἦλθον
χρηματίσαντες· ἡ δὲ διαγνώμη αὕτη τῆς 6
ἐκκλησίας, τοῦ τὰς σπονδὰς λελύσθαι, ἐγένετο
ἐν τῷ τετάρτῳ καὶ δεκάτῳ ἔτει τῶν τρια-
20 κοντουτίδων σπονδῶν προκεχωρηκυιῶν, αἳ
ἐγένοντο μετὰ τὰ Εὐβοϊκά. ἐψηφίσαντο δὲ 88
οἱ Λακεδαιμόνιοι τὰς σπονδὰς It was not so much the request of the allies as the fear of Athenian power that influenced Sparta.
λελύσθαι καὶ πολεμητέα εἶναι οὐ
τοσοῦτον τῶν ξυμμάχων πεισθέντες
25 τοῖς λόγοις ὅσον φοβούμενοι τοὺς
Ἀθηναίους μὴ ἐπὶ μεῖζον δυνηθῶσιν,
ὁρῶντες αὐτοῖς τὰ πολλὰ τῆς Ἑλλάδος
ὑποχείρια ἤδη ὄντα.

19. τῷ om. C[G]

I   E

89 Οἱ γὰρ Ἀθηναῖοι τρόπῳ τοιῷδε ἦλθον ἐπὶ

cc. 89-118, the
2 *πεντηκονταετία*,
a sketch of the
origin and
progress of
Athenian power
between the
Persian retreat
and the Pel.
war.

τὰ πράγματα ἐν οἷς ηὐξήθησαν.
ἐπειδὴ Μῆδοι ἀνεχώρησαν ἐκ τῆς
Εὐρώπης νικηθέντες καὶ ναυσὶ καὶ
πεζῷ ὑπὸ Ἑλλήνων καὶ οἱ κατα- 5
φυγόντες αὐτῶν ταῖς ναυσὶν ἐς
Μυκάλην διεφθάρησαν, Λεωτυχίδης
μὲν ὁ βασιλεὺς τῶν Λακεδαιμονίων, ὅσπερ
ἡγεῖτο τῶν ἐν Μυκάλῃ Ἑλλήνων, ἀπεχώρησεν
ἐπ᾽ οἴκου ἔχων τοὺς ἀπὸ Πελοποννήσου 10
ξυμμάχους, οἱ δὲ Ἀθηναῖοι καὶ οἱ ἀπὸ Ἰωνίας
καὶ Ἑλλησπόντου ξύμμαχοι ἤδη ἀφεστηκότες
ἀπὸ βασιλέως ὑπομείναντες Σηστὸν ἐπολιόρκουν
Μήδων ἐχόντων, καὶ ἐπιχειμάσαντες εἷλον
αὐτὴν ἐκλιπόντων τῶν βαρβάρων, καὶ μετὰ 15
τοῦτο ἀπέπλευσαν ἐξ Ἑλλησπόντου ὡς ἕκαστοι
3 κατὰ πόλεις. Ἀθηναίων δὲ τὸ κοινόν, ἐπειδὴ

The Athenians
after the defeat
of Mardonius
rebuilt their
walls and
enlarged the
city, despite the
objections of
Sparta. This
was done under
the advice of
Themistocles,
who outwitted
the Spartans.

αὐτοῖς οἱ βάρβαροι ἐκ τῆς χώρας
ἀπῆλθον, διεκομίζοντο εὐθὺς ὅθεν
ὑπεξέθεντο παῖδας καὶ γυναῖκας 20
καὶ τὴν περιοῦσαν κατασκευήν, καὶ
τὴν πόλιν ἀνοικοδομεῖν παρεσκευάζοντο καὶ τὰ τείχη· τοῦ τε γὰρ
περιβόλου βραχέα εἱστήκει καὶ
οἰκίαι αἱ μὲν πολλαὶ ἐπεπτώκεσαν, 25
ὀλίγαι δὲ περιῆσαν, ἐν αἷς αὐτοὶ ἐσκήνωσαν
οἱ δυνατοὶ τῶν Περσῶν.

90 Λακεδαιμόνιοι δὲ αἰσθόμενοι τὸ μέλλον

26. *ἐσκήνωσαν* C : *ἐσκήνουν* GM : *ἐσκήνησαν* ABEF

ἦλθον πρεσβείᾳ, τὰ μὲν καὶ αὐτοὶ ἥδιον ἂν
ὁρῶντες μήτ᾽ ἐκείνους μήτ᾽ ἄλλον μηδένα
τεῖχος ἔχοντα, τὸ δὲ πλέον τῶν ξυμμάχων
ἐξοτρυνόντων καὶ φοβουμένων τοῦ τε ναυτικοῦ
5 αὐτῶν τὸ πλῆθος, ὃ πρὶν οὐχ ὑπῆρχε, καὶ
τὴν ἐς τὸν Μηδικὸν πόλεμον τόλμαν γενομένην.
ἠξίουν τε αὐτοὺς μὴ τειχίζειν, ἀλλὰ καὶ τῶν 2
ἔξω Πελοποννήσου μᾶλλον ὅσοις εἱστήκει
ξυγκαθελεῖν μετὰ σφῶν τοὺς περιβόλους, τὸ
10 μὲν βουλόμενον καὶ ὕποπτον τῆς γνώμης οὐ
δηλοῦντες ἐς τοὺς Ἀθηναίους, ὡς δὲ τοῦ
βαρβάρου, εἰ αὖθις ἐπέλθοι, οὐκ ἂν ἔχοντος
ἀπὸ ἐχυροῦ ποθεν, ὥσπερ νῦν ἐκ τῶν Θηβῶν,
ὁρμᾶσθαι· τήν τε Πελοπόννησον πᾶσιν ἔφασαν
15 ἀναχώρησίν τε καὶ ἀφορμὴν ἱκανὴν εἶναι. οἱ 3
δ᾽ Ἀθηναῖοι Θεμιστοκλέους γνώμῃ τοὺς μὲν
Λακεδαιμονίους ταῦτ᾽ εἰπόντας ἀποκρινάμενοι
ὅτι πέμψουσιν ὡς αὐτοὺς πρέσβεις περὶ ὧν
λέγουσιν εὐθὺς ἀπήλλαξαν· ἑαυτὸν δ᾽ ἐκέλευεν
20 ἀποστέλλειν ὡς τάχιστα ὁ Θεμιστοκλῆς ἐς
τὴν Λακεδαίμονα, ἄλλους δὲ πρὸς ἑαυτῷ
ἑλομένους πρέσβεις μὴ εὐθὺς ἐκπέμπειν, ἀλλ᾽
ἐπισχεῖν μέχρι τοσούτου ἕως ἂν τὸ τεῖχος
ἱκανὸν ἄρωσιν ὥστε ἀπομάχεσθαι ἐκ τοῦ
25 ἀναγκαιοτάτου ὕψους· τειχίζειν δὲ πάντας
πανδημεὶ τοὺς ἐν τῇ πόλει [καὶ αὐτοὺς καὶ
γυναῖκας καὶ παῖδας], φειδομένους μήτε ἰδίου

---

1. πρεσβείαν AC : ἐς πρεσβείαν cG Schol.   8. εἱστήκει
C : ξυν-(συν-)ειστήκει c rtt.   14. post ἔφασαν habent ἱκανὴν
εἶναι ABEF : εἶναι ἱκανὴν M [G]   24. ἄρωσιν Bekker : αἴρωσιν
codd.   26. καὶ αὐτοὺς καὶ γυναῖκας καὶ παῖδας non legit Schol.

μήτε δημοσίου οἰκοδομήματος ὅθεν τις ὠφελία
ἔσται ἐς τὸ ἔργον, ἀλλὰ καθαιροῦντας πάντα.
4 καὶ ὁ μὲν ταῦτα διδάξας καὶ ὑπειπὼν τἆλλα
5 ὅτι αὐτὸς τἀκεῖ πράξοι ᾤχετο. καὶ ἐς τὴν
Λακεδαίμονα ἐλθὼν οὐ προσῄει πρὸς τὰς 5
ἀρχάς, ἀλλὰ διῆγε καὶ προυφασίζετο. καὶ
ὁπότε τις αὐτὸν ἔροιτο τῶν ἐν τέλει ὄντων
ὅτι οὐκ ἐπέρχεται ἐπὶ τὸ κοινόν, ἔφη τοὺς
ξυμπρέσβεις ἀναμένειν, ἀσχολίας δέ τινος
οὔσης αὐτοὺς ὑπολειφθῆναι, προσδέχεσθαι 10
μέντοι ἐν τάχει ἥξειν καὶ θαυμάζειν ὡς οὔπω
91 πάρεισιν. οἱ δὲ ἀκούοντες τῷ μὲν Θεμιστοκλεῖ
ἐπείθοντο διὰ φιλίαν αὐτοῦ, τῶν δὲ ἄλλων
ἀφικνουμένων καὶ σαφῶς κατηγορούντων ὅτι
τειχίζεταί τε καὶ ἤδη ὕψος λαμβάνει, οὐκ 15
2 εἶχον ὅπως χρὴ ἀπιστῆσαι. γνοὺς δὲ ἐκεῖνος
κελεύει αὐτοὺς μὴ λόγοις μᾶλλον παράγεσθαι ἢ
πέμψαι σφῶν αὐτῶν ἄνδρας οἵτινες χρηστοὶ καὶ
3 πιστῶς ἀναγγελοῦσι σκεψάμενοι. ἀποστέλ-
λουσιν οὖν, καὶ περὶ αὐτῶν ὁ Θεμιστοκλῆς 20
τοῖς Ἀθηναίοις κρύφα πέμπει κελεύων ὡς
ἥκιστα ἐπιφανῶς κατασχεῖν καὶ μὴ ἀφεῖναι
πρὶν ἂν αὐτοὶ πάλιν κομισθῶσιν (ἤδη γὰρ
καὶ ἧκον αὐτῷ οἱ ξυμπρέσβεις, Ἀβρώνιχός τε
ὁ Λυσικλέους καὶ Ἀριστείδης ὁ Λυσιμάχου, 25
ἀγγέλλοντες ἔχειν ἱκανῶς τὸ τεῖχος), ἐφοβεῖτο
γὰρ μὴ οἱ Λακεδαιμόνιοι σφᾶς, ὁπότε σαφῶς
4 ἀκούσειαν, οὐκέτι ἀφῶσιν. οἵ τε οὖν Ἀθηναῖοι
τοὺς πρέσβεις, ὥσπερ ἐπεστάλη, κατεῖχον, καὶ

19. ἀπαγγελοῦσι ABEFM Suid.

ὁ Θεμιστοκλῆς ἐπελθὼν τοῖς Λακεδαιμονίοις
ἐνταῦθα δὴ φανερῶς εἶπεν ὅτι ἡ μὲν πόλις
σφῶν τετείχισται ἤδη ὥστε ἱκανὴ εἶναι σῴζειν
τοὺς ἐνοικοῦντας, εἰ δέ τι βούλονται Λακεδαι-
5 μόνιοι ἢ οἱ ξύμμαχοι πρεσβεύεσθαι παρὰ
σφᾶς, ὡς πρὸς διαγιγνώσκοντας τὸ λοιπὸν
ἰέναι τά τε σφίσιν αὐτοῖς ξύμφορα καὶ τὰ
κοινά. τήν τε γὰρ πόλιν ὅτε ἐδόκει ἐκλιπεῖν 5
ἄμεινον εἶναι καὶ ἐς τὰς ναῦς ἐσβῆναι, ἄνευ
10 ἐκείνων ἔφασαν γνόντες τολμῆσαι, καὶ ὅσα αὖ
μετ᾽ ἐκείνων βουλεύεσθαι, οὐδενὸς ὕστεροι
γνώμῃ φανῆναι. δοκεῖν οὖν σφίσι καὶ νῦν 6
ἄμεινον εἶναι τὴν ἑαυτῶν πόλιν τεῖχος ἔχειν,
καὶ ἰδίᾳ τοῖς πολίταις καὶ ἐς τοὺς πάντας
15 ξυμμάχους ὠφελιμώτερον ἔσεσθαι· οὐ γὰρ 7
οἷόν τ᾽ εἶναι μὴ ἀπὸ ἀντιπάλου παρασκευῆς
ὁμοῖόν τι ἢ ἴσον ἐς τὸ κοινὸν βουλεύεσθαι. ἢ
πάντας οὖν ἀτειχίστους ἔφη χρῆναι ξυμμαχεῖν
ἢ καὶ τάδε νομίζειν ὀρθῶς ἔχειν. οἱ δὲ 92
20 Λακεδαιμόνιοι ἀκούσαντες ὀργὴν μὲν φανερὰν
οὐκ ἐποιοῦντο τοῖς Ἀθηναίοις (οὐδὲ γὰρ ἐπὶ
κωλύμῃ, ἀλλὰ γνώμης παραινέσει δῆθεν τῷ
κοινῷ ἐπρεσβεύσαντο, ἅμα δὲ καὶ προσφιλεῖς
ὄντες ἐν τῷ τότε διὰ τὴν ἐς τὸν Μῆδον
25 προθυμίαν τὰ μάλιστ᾽ αὐτοῖς ἐτύγχανον), τῆς
μέντοι βουλήσεως ἁμαρτάνοντες ἀδήλως ἤχθοντο. οἵ τε πρέσβεις ἑκατέρων ἀπῆλθον ἐπ᾽
οἴκου ἀνεπικλήτως.

1. ὁ om. ABEFM   3. σφῶν] αὐτῶν CG   4. post
ἐνοικοῦντας add. ἐν αὐτῇ CG   6. προδιαγι(γ)νώσκοντας BGM
11. ὕστεροι fg : ὕστερον codd.

93 Τούτῳ τῷ τρόπῳ οἱ Ἀθηναῖοι τὴν πόλιν
2 ἐτείχισαν ἐν ὀλίγῳ χρόνῳ. καὶ δήλη ἡ οἰκο-
δομία ἔτι καὶ νῦν ἐστιν ὅτι κατὰ σπουδὴν
ἐγένετο· οἱ γὰρ θεμέλιοι παντοίων λίθων ὑπό-
κεινται καὶ οὐ ξυνειργασμένων ἔστιν ᾗ, ἀλλ' 5
ὡς ἕκαστόν ποτε προσέφερον, πολλαί τε στῆλαι
ἀπὸ σημάτων καὶ λίθοι εἰργασμένοι ἐγκατε-
λέγησαν· μείζων γὰρ ὁ περίβολος πανταχῇ
ἐξήχθη τῆς πόλεως, καὶ διὰ τοῦτο πάντα
3 ὁμοίως κινοῦντες ἠπείγοντο. ἔπεισε δὲ καὶ τοῦ 10

He also per-
suaded the A. to
fortify the
Piraeus, and
insisted on the
paramount
importance of
the harbours
and the fleet.
Πειραιῶς τὰ λοιπὰ ὁ Θεμιστοκλῆς
οἰκοδομεῖν (ὑπῆρκτο δ' αὐτοῦ πρότερον ἐπὶ τῆς ἐκείνου ἀρχῆς ἧς κατ'
ἐνιαυτὸν Ἀθηναίοις ἦρξε) νομίζων
τό τε χωρίον καλὸν εἶναι, λιμένας 15
ἔχον τρεῖς αὐτοφυεῖς, καὶ αὐτοὺς ναυτικοὺς
γεγενημένους μέγα προφέρειν ἐς τὸ κτήσασθαι
4 δύναμιν (τῆς γὰρ δὴ θαλάσσης πρῶτος ἐτόλ-
μησεν εἰπεῖν ὡς ἀνθεκτέα ἐστί), καὶ τὴν ἀρχὴν
5 εὐθὺς ξυγκατεσκεύαζεν. καὶ ᾠκοδόμησαν τῇ 20
ἐκείνου γνώμῃ τὸ πάχος τοῦ τείχους ὅπερ νῦν
ἔτι δῆλόν ἐστι περὶ τὸν Πειραιᾶ· δύο γὰρ
ἄμαξαι ἐναντίαι ἀλλήλαις τοὺς λίθους ἐπῆγον.
ἐντὸς δὲ οὔτε χάλιξ οὔτε πηλὸς ἦν, ἀλλὰ
ξυνῳκοδομημένοι μεγάλοι λίθοι καὶ ἐντομῇ 25
ἐγγώνιοι, σιδήρῳ πρὸς ἀλλήλους τὰ ἔξωθεν
καὶ μολύβδῳ δεδεμένοι. τὸ δὲ ὕψος ἥμισυ
6 μάλιστα ἐτελέσθη οὗ διενοεῖτο. ἐβούλετο · γὰρ
τῷ μεγέθει καὶ τῷ πάχει ἀφιστάναι τὰς τῶν

6. ἕκαστον C : ἕκαστοι cett.   25. ἐν τομῇ AFGM

πολεμίων ἐπιβουλάς, ἀνθρώπων τε ἐνόμιζεν
ὀλίγων καὶ τῶν ἀχρειοτάτων ἀρκέσειν τὴν
φυλακήν, τοὺς δ' ἄλλους ἐς τὰς ναῦς ἐσβήσε-
σθαι. ταῖς γὰρ ναυσὶ μάλιστα προσέκειτο, ἰδών, 7
5 ὡς ἐμοὶ δοκεῖ, τῆς βασιλέως στρατιᾶς τὴν
κατὰ θάλασσαν ἔφοδον εὐπορωτέραν τῆς κατὰ
γῆν οὖσαν· τόν τε Πειραιᾶ ὠφελιμώτερον
ἐνόμιζε τῆς ἄνω πόλεως, καὶ πολλάκις τοῖς
Ἀθηναίοις παρῄνει, ἢν ἄρα ποτὲ κατὰ · γῆν
10 βιασθῶσι, καταβάντας ἐς αὐτὸν ταῖς ναυσὶ
πρὸς ἅπαντας ἀνθίστασθαι. Ἀθηναῖοι μὲν οὖν 8
οὕτως ἐτειχίσθησαν καὶ τἆλλα κατεσκευάζοντο
εὐθὺς μετὰ τὴν Μήδων ἀναχώρησιν.

Παυσανίας δὲ ὁ Κλεομβρότου ἐκ Λακε- **94**
15 δαίμονος στρατηγὸς τῶν Ἑλλήνων ἐξεπέμφθη
μετὰ εἴκοσι νεῶν ἀπὸ Πελοποννήσου· ξυνέπλεον
δὲ καὶ Ἀθηναῖοι τριάκοντα ναυσὶ καὶ τῶν
ἄλλων ξυμμάχων πλῆθος. καὶ ἐστράτευσαν ἐς 2
Κύπρον καὶ αὐτῆς τὰ πολλὰ κατεστρέψαντο,
20 καὶ ὕστερον ἐς Βυζάντιον Μήδων ἐχόντων, καὶ
ἐξεπολιόρκησαν ἐν τῇδε τῇ ἡγεμονίᾳ. ἤδη δὲ **95**
βιαίου ὄντος αὐτοῦ οἵ τε ἄλλοι
Ἕλληνες ἤχθοντο καὶ οὐχ ἥκιστα   The unpopular-
ity of Pausanias
οἱ Ἴωνες καὶ ὅσοι ἀπὸ βασιλέως   causes the
Greeks, who had
thrown off the
25 νεωστὶ ἠλευθέρωντο· φοιτῶντές τε   Persian yoke, to
choose the
πρὸς τοὺς Ἀθηναίους ἠξίουν αὐτοὺς   Athenians as
leaders of the
ἡγεμόνας σφῶν γίγνεσθαι κατὰ τὸ   confederacy.

1. ἐπιβολὰς Herwerden (ἐπιθέσεις interpretatur Schol.)
21. verba ἐν τῇδε τῇ ἡγεμονίᾳ cum sequentibus coniungit
Stephanus, qui δὲ seclusit ‖ δὲ post τῇδε transp. Hude (tentavit
Poppo)   27. γενέσθαι ABEFM;G]

ξυγγενὲς καὶ Παυσανίᾳ μὴ ἐπιτρέπειν, ἤν που
2 βιάζηται. οἱ δὲ Ἀθηναῖοι ἐδέξαντό τε τοὺς
λόγους καὶ προσεῖχον τὴν γνώμην ὡς οὐ περι-
οψόμενοι τἆλλά τε καταστησόμενοι ᾗ φαίνοιτο
3 ἄριστα αὐτοῖς. ἐν τούτῳ δὲ οἱ Λακεδαιμόνιοι 5
μετεπέμποντο Παυσανίαν ἀνακρινοῦντες ὧν πέρι
ἐπυνθάνοντο· καὶ γὰρ ἀδικία πολλὴ κατηγορεῖτο αὐτοῦ ὑπὸ τῶν Ἑλλήνων τῶν ἀφικνουμένων, καὶ τυραννίδος μᾶλλον ἐφαίνετο μίμησις
4 ἢ στρατηγία. ξυνέβη τε αὐτῷ καλεῖσθαί τε 10
ἅμα καὶ τοὺς ξυμμάχους τῷ ἐκείνου ἔχθει
παρ᾽ Ἀθηναίους μετατάξασθαι πλὴν τῶν ἀπὸ
5 Πελοποννήσου στρατιωτῶν. ἐλθὼν δὲ ἐς Λακεδαίμονα τῶν μὲν ἰδίᾳ πρός τινα ἀδικημάτων
ηὐθύνθη, τὰ δὲ μέγιστα ἀπολύεται μὴ ἀδικεῖν· 15
κατηγορεῖτο δὲ αὐτοῦ οὐχ ἥκιστα μηδισμὸς καὶ
3 ἐδόκει σαφέστατον εἶναι. καὶ ἐκεῖνον μὲν οὐκέτι
ἐκπέμπουσιν ἄρχοντα, Δόρκιν δὲ καὶ ἄλλους
τινὰς μετ᾽ αὐτοῦ στρατιὰν ἔχοντας οὐ πολλήν·
οἷς οὐκέτι ἐφίεσαν οἱ ξύμμαχοι τὴν ἡγεμονίαν. 20
7 οἱ δὲ αἰσθόμενοι ἀπῆλθον, καὶ ἄλλους οὐκέτι
ὕστερον ἐξέπεμψαν οἱ Λακεδαιμόνιοι, φοβούμενοι μὴ σφίσιν οἱ ἐξιόντες χείρους γίγνωνται,
ὅπερ καὶ ἐν τῷ Παυσανίᾳ ἐνεῖδον, ἀπαλλα-
ξείοντες δὲ καὶ τοῦ Μηδικοῦ ˙πολέμου καὶ τοὺς 25
Ἀθηναίους νομίζοντες ἱκανοὺς ἐξηγεῖσθαι καὶ
σφίσιν ἐν τῷ τότε παρόντι ἐπιτηδείους.
96 Παραλαβόντες δὲ οἱ Ἀθηναῖοι τὴν ἡγεμονίαν

---

4. καταστησόμενοι Stephani codices : καταστησάμενοι codd.
[G]   14. τινας Classen

τούτῳ τῷ τρόπῳ ἑκόντων τῶν ξυμμάχων διὰ
τὸ Παυσανίου μῖσος, ἔταξαν ἃς Organisation
of the Delian
τε ἔδει παρέχειν τῶν πόλεων χρή- League.
ματα πρὸς τὸν βάρβαρον καὶ ἃς ναῦς· πρόσ-
5 χημα γὰρ ἦν ἀμύνεσθαι ὧν ἔπαθον δῃοῦντας
τὴν βασιλέως χώραν. καὶ Ἑλληνοταμίαι τότε 2
πρῶτον Ἀθηναίοις κατέστη ἀρχή, οἳ ἐδέχοντο
τὸν φόρον· οὕτω γὰρ ὠνομάσθη τῶν χρημάτων
ἡ φορά. ἦν δ' ὁ πρῶτος φόρος ταχθεὶς τετρα-
10 κόσια τάλαντα καὶ ἑξήκοντα. ταμιεῖόν τε
Δῆλος ἦν αὐτοῖς, καὶ αἱ ξύνοδοι ἐς τὸ ἱερὸν
ἐγίγνοντο. ἡγούμενοι δὲ αὐτονόμων τὸ πρῶτον 97
τῶν ξυμμάχων καὶ ἀπὸ κοινῶν What ensued
has been
ξυνόδων βουλευόντων τοσάδε ἐπῆλθον neglected by
previous
15 πολέμῳ τε καὶ διαχειρίσει πρα- historians: so
there is need
γμάτων μεταξὺ τοῦδε τοῦ πολέμου to sketch the
events by which
καὶ τοῦ Μηδικοῦ, ἃ ἐγένετο πρός the hegemony
was transformed
τε τὸν βάρβαρον αὐτοῖς καὶ πρὸς into an empire.
τοὺς σφετέρους ξυμμάχους νεωτερίζοντας καὶ
20 Πελοποννησίων τοὺς αἰεὶ προστυγχάνοντας ἐν
ἑκάστῳ. ἔγραψα δὲ αὐτὰ καὶ τὴν ἐκβολὴν 2
τοῦ λόγου ἐποιησάμην διὰ τόδε, ὅτι τοῖς πρὸ
ἐμοῦ ἅπασιν ἐκλιπὲς τοῦτο ἦν τὸ χωρίον καὶ
ἢ τὰ πρὸ τῶν Μηδικῶν Ἑλληνικὰ ξυνετίθεσαν
25 ἢ αὐτὰ τὰ Μηδικά· τούτων δὲ ὅσπερ καὶ
ἥψατο ἐν τῇ Ἀττικῇ ξυγγραφῇ Ἑλλάνικος,
βραχέως τε καὶ τοῖς χρόνοις οὐκ ἀκριβῶς
ἐπεμνήσθη. ἅμα δὲ καὶ τῆς ἀρχῆς ἀπόδειξιν
ἔχει τῆς τῶν Ἀθηναίων ἐν οἵῳ τρόπῳ κατέστη.

5. ἀμύνασθαι ABEFM   11. αἱ om. CGM

I   E 2

98 Πρῶτον μὲν Ἡιόνα τὴν ἐπὶ Στρυμόνι Μήδων

Capture of Eion on the Strymon, reduction of Scyrus and
2 Carystus.

ἐχόντων πολιορκίᾳ εἷλον καὶ ἠνδρα-
πόδισαν, Κίμωνος τοῦ Μιλτιάδου
στρατηγοῦντος. ἔπειτα Σκῦρον τὴν
ἐν τῷ Αἰγαίῳ νῆσον, ἣν ᾤκουν Δόλοπες, ἠνδρα- 5
3 πόδισαν καὶ ᾤκισαν αὐτοί. πρὸς δὲ Καρυ-
στίους αὐτοῖς ἄνευ τῶν ἄλλων Εὐβοέων πόλεμος
ἐγένετο, καὶ χρόνῳ ξυνέβησαν καθ᾽ ὁμολογίαν.

4 Revolt and subjugation of Naxos, which receives harsh treatment.

Ναξίοις δὲ ἀποστᾶσι μετὰ ταῦτα
ἐπολέμησαν καὶ πολιορκίᾳ παρεστή- 10
σαντο, πρώτη τε αὕτη πόλις ξυμ-
μαχὶς παρὰ τὸ καθεστηκὸς ἐδουλώθη, ἔπειτα

99 δὲ καὶ τῶν ἄλλων ὡς ἑκάστῃ ξυνέβη. αἰτίαι

Athens became oppressive and unpopular among her allies, who were allowed to compound for personal service by money; and this enabled Athens to keep them in subjection.

δὲ ἄλλαι τε ἦσαν τῶν ἀποστάσεων
καὶ μέγισται αἱ τῶν φόρων καὶ 15
νεῶν ἔκδειαι καὶ λιποστράτιον εἴ
τῳ ἐγένετο· οἱ γὰρ Ἀθηναῖοι ἀκριβῶς ἔπρασσον καὶ λυπηροὶ ἦσαν
οὐκ εἰωθόσιν οὐδὲ βουλομένοις
ταλαιπωρεῖν προσάγοντες τὰς ἀνά- 20
2 γκας. ἦσαν δέ πως καὶ ἄλλως οἱ Ἀθηναῖοι
οὐκέτι ὁμοίως ἐν ἡδονῇ ἄρχοντες, καὶ οὔτε
ξυνεστράτευον ἀπὸ τοῦ ἴσου ῥᾴδιόν τε προσ-
άγεσθαι ἦν αὐταῖς τοὺς ἀφισταμένους. ὧν
3 αὐτοὶ αἴτιοι ἐγένοντο οἱ ξύμμαχοι· διὰ γὰρ 25
τὴν ἀπόκνησιν ταύτην τῶν στρατειῶν οἱ πλείους
αὐτῶν, ἵνα μὴ ἀπ᾽ οἴκου ὦσι, χρήματα ἐτάξαντο ἀντὶ τῶν νεῶν τὸ ἰκνούμενον ἀνάλωμα

13. ἑκάστηι Α : ἑκάστη cett. [G] ‖ ξυνέβη secl. Krüger
20. προσαγαγόντες ABEF[G]

φέρειν, καὶ τοῖς μὲν Ἀθηναίοις ηὔξετο τὸ
ναυτικὸν ἀπὸ τῆς δαπάνης ἣν ἐκεῖνοι ξυμ-
φέροιεν, αὐτοὶ δέ, ὁπότε ἀποσταῖεν, ἀπαράσκευοι καὶ ἄπειροι ἐς τὸν πόλεμον καθί-
5 σταντο.

Ἐγένετο δὲ μετὰ ταῦτα καὶ ἡ ἐπ᾽ Εὐρυ- **100**
μέδοντι ποταμῷ ἐν Παμφυλίᾳ   Battles of the
πεζομαχία καὶ ναυμαχία Ἀθηναίων   Eurymedon.
καὶ τῶν ξυμμάχων πρὸς Μήδους, καὶ ἐνίκων
10 τῇ αὐτῇ ἡμέρᾳ ἀμφότερα Ἀθηναῖοι Κίμωνος
τοῦ Μιλτιάδου στρατηγοῦντος, καὶ εἷλον
τριήρεις Φοινίκων καὶ διέφθειραν τὰς πάσας
ἐς διακοσίας. χρόνῳ δὲ ὕστερον ξυνέβη 2
Θασίους αὐτῶν ἀποστῆναι, διενεχθέντας περὶ
15 τῶν ἐν τῇ ἀντιπέρας Θρᾴκῃ ἐμπορίων καὶ τοῦ
μετάλλου ἃ ἐνέμοντο. καὶ ναυσὶ μὲν ἐπὶ
Θάσον πλεύσαντες οἱ Ἀθηναῖοι ναυμαχίᾳ
ἐκράτησαν καὶ ἐς τὴν γῆν ἀπέβησαν, ἐπὶ δὲ 3
Στρυμόνα πέμψαντες μυρίους οἰκήτορας αὑτῶν
20 καὶ τῶν ξυμμάχων ὑπὸ τοὺς αὐτοὺς   Revolt of
χρόνους ὡς οἰκιοῦντες τὰς τότε   Thasos. Athen-
καλουμένας Ἐννέα ὁδούς, νῦν δὲ   Drabescus.
Ἀμφίπολιν, τῶν μὲν Ἐννέα ὁδῶν αὐτοὶ
ἐκράτησαν, ἃς εἶχον Ἠδωνοί, προελθόντες δὲ
25 τῆς Θρᾴκης ἐς μεσόγειαν διεφθάρησαν ἐν
Δραβησκῷ τῇ Ἠδωνικῇ ὑπὸ τῶν Θρακῶν
ξυμπάντων, οἷς πολέμιον ἦν τὸ χωρίον [αἱ

---

7. ἐν Παμφυλίᾳ om. M, secl. Stahl   13. τε ABEFM
suprascr. G   27. ξυμπάντων] omnes Valla: ξύμπαντες
Poppo ‖ αἱ Ἐννέα ὁδοί secl. Cobet

101 Ἐννέα ὁδοὶ] κτιζόμενον. Θάσιοι δὲ νικηθέντες

Thasos seeks help from Sparta; but an earthquake and the revolt of the helots prevented

2 S. from intervening. The Messenian war.

μάχῃ καὶ πολιορκούμενοι Λακεδαιμονίους ἐπεκαλοῦντο καὶ ἐπαμύνειν
ἐκέλευον ἐσβαλόντας ἐς τὴν Ἀττικήν.
οἱ δὲ ὑπέσχοντο μὲν κρύφα τῶν 5
Ἀθηναίων καὶ ἔμελλον, διεκω-
λύθησαν δὲ ὑπὸ τοῦ γενομένου σεισμοῦ, ἐν ᾧ
καὶ οἱ Εἵλωτες αὐτοῖς καὶ τῶν περιοίκων
Θουριᾶταί τε καὶ Αἰθαιῆς ἐς Ἰθώμην ἀπέστησαν.
πλεῖστοι δὲ τῶν Εἱλώτων ἐγένοντο οἱ τῶν 10
παλαιῶν Μεσσηνίων τότε δουλωθέντων ἀπό-
γονοι· ᾗ καὶ Μεσσήνιοι ἐκλήθησαν οἱ πάντες.

3 πρὸς μὲν οὖν τοὺς ἐν Ἰθώμῃ πόλεμος

Surrender of Thasos.

καθειστήκει Λακεδαιμονίοις, Θάσιοι
δὲ τρίτῳ ἔτει πολιορκούμενοι ὡμο- 15
λόγησαν Ἀθηναίοις τεῖχός τε καθελόντες καὶ
ναῦς παραδόντες, χρήματά τε ὅσα ἔδει
ἀποδοῦναι αὐτίκα ταξάμενοι καὶ τὸ λοιπὸν
φέρειν, τήν τε ἤπειρον καὶ τὸ μέταλλον
ἀφέντες. 20

102 Λακεδαιμόνιοι δέ, ὡς αὐτοῖς πρὸς τοὺς ἐν

Sparta seeks help from Athens against the helots; but becoming suspicious, sends back the force.

Ἰθώμῃ ἐμηκύνετο ὁ πόλεμος, ἄλλους
τε ἐπεκαλέσαντο ξυμμάχους καὶ
Ἀθηναίους· οἱ δ' ἦλθον Κίμωνος
στρατηγοῦντος πλήθει οὐκ ὀλίγῳ. 25

2 μάλιστα δ' αὐτοὺς ἐπεκαλέσαντο ὅτι τειχομαχεῖν ἐδόκουν δυνατοὶ εἶναι, τοῖς δὲ πολιορκίας

2. μάχαις ABEFM   3. ἐπαμῦναι ABEFM γρ. G
9. Αἰθαιεῖς Steph. Byz. : Αἰθνεεῖς vel Αἰθνεεῖς codd.   13.
οὖν C : om. cett. (add. G¹)   27. τοῖς] τῆς recc. et Schol.

μακρᾶς καθεστηκυίας τούτου ἐνδεᾶ ἐφαίνετο·
βίᾳ γὰρ ἂν εἷλον τὸ χωρίον. καὶ διαφορὰ ἐκ 3
ταύτης τῆς στρατείας πρῶτον Λακεδαιμονίοις
καὶ Ἀθηναίοις φανερὰ ἐγένετο. οἱ γὰρ
5 Λακεδαιμόνιοι, ἐπειδὴ τὸ χωρίον βίᾳ οὐχ ἡλί-
σκετο, δείσαντες τῶν Ἀθηναίων τὸ τολμηρὸν
καὶ τὴν νεωτεροποιίαν, καὶ ἀλλοφύλους ἅμα
ἡγησάμενοι, μή τι, ἢν παραμείνωσιν, ὑπὸ τῶν
ἐν Ἰθώμῃ πεισθέντες νεωτερίσωσι, μόνους τῶν
10 ξυμμάχων ἀπέπεμψαν, τὴν μὲν ὑποψίαν οὐ
δηλοῦντες, εἰπόντες δὲ ὅτι οὐδὲν προσδέονται
αὐτῶν ἔτι. οἱ δ' Ἀθηναῖοι ἔγνωσαν οὐκ ἐπὶ 4
τῷ βελτίονι λόγῳ ἀποπεμπόμενοι, This conduct so
ἀλλά τινος ὑπόπτου γενομένου, καὶ greatly incensed
the Athenians
15 δεινὸν ποιησάμενοι καὶ οὐκ ἀξιώ- that they
abandoned the
σαντες ὑπὸ Λακεδαιμονίων τοῦτο alliance with
Sparta, and
παθεῖν, εὐθὺς ἐπειδὴ ἀνεχώρησαν, formed one with
Argos and
ἀφέντες τὴν γενομένην ἐπὶ τῷ Thessaly.
Μήδῳ ξυμμαχίαν πρὸς αὐτοὺς Ἀργείοις τοῖς
20 ἐκείνων πολεμίοις ξύμμαχοι ἐγένοντο, καὶ πρὸς
Θεσσαλοὺς ἅμα ἀμφοτέροις οἱ αὐτοὶ ὅρκοι καὶ
ξυμμαχία κατέστη.
    Οἱ δ' ἐν Ἰθώμῃ δεκάτῳ ἔτει, ὡς οὐκέτι 103
ἐδύναντο ἀντέχειν, ξυνέβησαν πρὸς End of the
Messenian war.
25 τοὺς Λακεδαιμονίους ἐφ' ᾧ ἐξίασιν The helots
ἐκ Πελοποννήσου ὑπόσπονδοι καὶ settled at
Naupactus by
μηδέποτε ἐπιβήσονται αὐτῆς· ἢν δέ Athens.
τις ἁλίσκηται, τοῦ λαβόντος εἶναι δοῦλον. ἢν 2

9. νεωτεροποιήσωσι CG   23. δεκάτῳ] τετάρτῳ Krüger
25. post ᾧ add. τε ABEFM

δέ τι καὶ χρηστήριον τοῖς Λακεδαιμονίοις
Πυθικὸν πρὸ τοῦ, τὸν ἱκέτην τοῦ Διὸς τοῦ
3 Ἰθωμήτα ἀφιέναι. ἐξῆλθον δὲ αὐτοὶ καὶ
παῖδες καὶ γυναῖκες, καὶ αὐτοὺς οἱ Ἀθηναῖοι
δεξάμενοι κατ' ἔχθος ἤδη τὸ Λακεδαιμονίων ἐς 5
Ναύπακτον κατῴκισαν, ἣν ἔτυχον ᾑρηκότες
4 νεωστὶ Λοκρῶν τῶν Ὀζολῶν ἐχόντων. προσε-
χώρησαν δὲ καὶ Μεγαρῆς Ἀθηναίοις ἐς
Megara revolts ξυμμαχίαν Λακεδαιμονίων ἀπο-
to Athens.
Occupation of στάντες, ὅτι αὐτοὺς Κορίνθιοι περὶ 10
Pegae and
Nisaea. γῆς ὅρων πολέμῳ κατεῖχον· καὶ
ἔσχον Ἀθηναῖοι Μέγαρα καὶ Πηγάς, καὶ τὰ
μακρὰ τείχη ᾠκοδόμησαν Μεγαρεῦσι τὰ ἀπὸ
τῆς πόλεως ἐς Νίσαιαν καὶ ἐφρούρουν αὐτοί.
καὶ Κορινθίοις μὲν οὐχ ἥκιστα ἀπὸ τοῦδε τὸ 15
σφοδρὸν μῖσος ἤρξατο πρῶτον ἐς Ἀθηναίους
γενέσθαι.

104 Ἰνάρως δὲ ὁ Ψαμμητίχου, Λίβυς, βασιλεὺς
Egypt revolts Λιβύων τῶν πρὸς Αἰγύπτῳ, ὁρμώ-
from Persia;
Athens sends μενος ἐκ Μαρείας τῆς ὑπὲρ Φάρου 20
aid to Egypt.
πόλεως ἀπέστησεν Αἰγύπτου τὰ
πλείω ἀπὸ βασιλέως Ἀρταξέρξου, καὶ αὐτὸς
2 ἄρχων γενόμενος Ἀθηναίους ἐπηγάγετο. οἱ δὲ
(ἔτυχον γὰρ ἐς Κύπρον στρατευόμενοι ναυσὶ
διακοσίαις αὐτῶν τε καὶ τῶν ξυμμάχων) ἦλθον 25
ἀπολιπόντες τὴν Κύπρον, καὶ ἀναπλεύσαντες
ἀπὸ θαλάσσης ἐς τὸν Νεῖλον τοῦ τε ποταμοῦ
κρατοῦντες καὶ τῆς Μέμφιδος τῶν δύο μερῶν
πρὸς τὸ τρίτον μέρος ὃ καλεῖται Λευκὸν

4. οἱ C : om. cett.

τεῖχος ἐπολέμουν· ἐνῆσαν δὲ αὐτόθι Περσῶν
καὶ Μήδων οἱ καταφυγόντες καὶ Αἰγυπτίων οἱ
μὴ ξυναποστάντες.

Ἀθηναίοις δὲ ναυσὶν ἀποβᾶσιν ἐς Ἁλιᾶς **105**
5 πρὸς Κορινθίους καὶ Ἐπιδαυρίους   Athens at war
μάχη ἐγένετο, καὶ ἐνίκων Κορίνθιοι.   with Peloponnesians.
καὶ ὕστερον Ἀθηναῖοι ἐναυμάχησαν ἐπὶ Κεκρυ-
φαλείᾳ Πελοποννησίων ναυσί, καὶ ἐνίκων
Ἀθηναῖοι. πολέμου δὲ καταστάν-   War between   2
10 τος πρὸς Αἰγινήτας Ἀθηναίοις μετὰ   Athens and
Aegina. The
ταῦτα ναυμαχία γίγνεται ἐπ᾽ Αἰγίνῃ   Corinthians
enter the
μεγάλη Ἀθηναίων καὶ Αἰγινητῶν,   Megarid.
καὶ οἱ ξύμμαχοι ἑκατέροις παρῆσαν, καὶ ἐνίκων
Ἀθηναῖοι καὶ ναῦς ἑβδομήκοντα λαβόντες
15 αὐτῶν ἐς τὴν γῆν ἀπέβησαν καὶ ἐπολιόρκουν,
Λεωκράτους τοῦ Στροίβου στρατηγοῦντος.
ἔπειτα Πελοποννήσιοι ἀμύνειν βουλόμενοι 3
Αἰγινήταις ἐς μὲν τὴν Αἴγιναν τριακοσίους
ὁπλίτας πρότερον Κορινθίων καὶ Ἐπιδαυρίων
20 ἐπικούρους διεβίβασαν, τὰ δὲ ἄκρα τῆς
Γερανείας κατέλαβον καὶ ἐς τὴν Μεγαρίδα
κατέβησαν Κορίνθιοι μετὰ· τῶν ξυμμάχων,
νομίζοντες ἀδυνάτους ἔσεσθαι Ἀθηναίους βοηθεῖν
τοῖς Μεγαρεῦσιν ἔν τε Αἰγίνῃ ἀπούσης στρα-
25 τιᾶς πολλῆς καὶ ἐν Αἰγύπτῳ· ἢν δὲ καὶ
βοηθῶσιν, ἀπ᾽ Αἰγίνης ἀναστήσεσθαι αὐτούς.
οἱ δὲ Ἀθηναῖοι τὸ μὲν πρὸς Αἰγίνῃ στράτευμα 4
οὐκ ἐκίνησαν, τῶν δ᾽ ἐκ τῆς πόλεως ὑπο-
λοίπων οἵ τε πρεσβύτατοι καὶ οἱ νεώτατοι
ἀφικνοῦνται ἐς τὰ Μέγαρα Μυρωνίδου στρα-

5 τηγοῦντος. καὶ μάχης γενομένης ἰσορρόπου
πρὸς Κορινθίους διεκρίθησαν ἀπ᾽ ἀλλήλων,
καὶ ἐνόμισαν αὐτοὶ ἑκάτεροι οὐκ ἔλασσον ἔχειν
6 ἐν τῷ ἔργῳ. καὶ οἱ μὲν Ἀθηναῖοι (ἐκράτησαν
γὰρ ὅμως μᾶλλον) ἀπελθόντων τῶν Κορινθίων 5
τροπαῖον ἔστησαν· οἱ δὲ Κορίνθιοι κακιζόμενοι
ὑπὸ τῶν ἐν τῇ πόλει πρεσβυτέρων καὶ παρασκευασάμενοι, ἡμέραις ὕστερον δώδεκα μάλιστα
ἐλθόντες ἀνθίστασαν τροπαῖον καὶ αὐτοὶ ὡς
νικήσαντες. καὶ οἱ Ἀθηναῖοι ἐκβοηθήσαντες 10
ἐκ τῶν Μεγάρων τούς τε τὸ τροπαῖον ἱστάν-
τας διαφθείρουσι καὶ τοῖς ἄλλοις ξυμβαλόντες

106 Defeat of the
Corinthians by
Myronides.

ἐκράτησαν. οἱ δὲ νικώμενοι ὑπε-
χώρουν, καί τι αὐτῶν μέρος οὐκ
ὀλίγον προσβιασθὲν καὶ διαμαρτὸν τῆς ὁδοῦ 15
ἐσέπεσεν ἔς του χωρίον ἰδιώτου, ᾧ ἔτυχεν
ὄρυγμα μέγα περιεῖργον καὶ οὐκ ἦν ἔξοδος.
2 οἱ δὲ Ἀθηναῖοι γνόντες κατὰ πρόσωπόν τε
εἶργον τοῖς ὁπλίταις καὶ περιστήσαντες κύκλῳ
τοὺς ψιλοὺς κατέλευσαν πάντας τοὺς ἐσελθόν- 20
τας, καὶ πάθος μέγα τοῦτο Κορινθίοις ἐγένετο.
τὸ δὲ πλῆθος ἀπεχώρησεν αὐτοῖς τῆς στρατιᾶς
ἐπ᾽ οἴκου.

107 Ἤρξαντο δὲ κατὰ τοὺς χρόνους τούτους καὶ

The Long Walls
begun at
Athens.

τὰ μακρὰ τείχη Ἀθηναῖοι ἐς 25
θάλασσαν οἰκοδομεῖν, τό τε Φαλη-
2 ρόνδε καὶ τὸ ἐς Πειραιᾶ. καὶ Φωκέων στρα-
τευσάντων ἐς Δωριᾶς τὴν Λακεδαιμονίων μη-

8. ἡμέραις f: ἡμέρας codd.   10. ἐκβοήσαντες CG Schol.
25. ἐς θάλασσαν Ἀθηναῖοι ABEFM

τρόπολιν, Βοιὸν καὶ Κυτίνιον καὶ Ἐρινεόν, καὶ
ἑλόντων ἓν τῶν πολισμάτων τούτων, οἱ Λακεδαιμόνιοι Νικομήδους τοῦ Κλεομβρότου ὑπὲρ
Πλειστοάνακτος τοῦ Παυσανίου βασιλέως νέου
5 ὄντος ἔτι ἡγουμένου ἐβοήθησαν τοῖς Δωριεῦσιν
ἑαυτῶν τε πεντακοσίοις καὶ χιλίοις ὁπλίταις
καὶ τῶν ξυμμάχων μυρίοις, καὶ τοὺς Φωκέας
ὁμολογίᾳ ἀναγκάσαντες ἀποδοῦναι τὴν πόλιν
ἀπεχώρουν πάλιν. καὶ κατὰ θάλασσαν μὲν 3
10 αὐτούς, διὰ τοῦ Κρισαίου κόλπου   The Spartans
εἰ βούλοιντο περαιοῦσθαι, Ἀθηναῖοι   help the Dorians against the
ναυσὶ περιπλεύσαντες ἔμελλον κωλύ- Phocians.
σειν· διὰ δὲ τῆς Γερανείας οὐκ ἀσφαλὲς αὐτοῖς
ἐφαίνετο Ἀθηναίων ἐχόντων Μέγαρα καὶ Πηγὰς
15 πορεύεσθαι. δύσοδός τε γὰρ ἡ Γερανεία καὶ
ἐφρουρεῖτο αἰεὶ ὑπὸ Ἀθηναίων, καὶ τότε ἠσθά-
νοντο αὐτοὺς μέλλοντας καὶ ταύτῃ κωλύσειν.
ἔδοξε δ' αὐτοῖς ἐν Βοιωτοῖς περι-   The Athenians 4
μείνασι σκέψασθαι ὅτῳ τρόπῳ   having occupied the pass of
20 ἀσφαλέστατα διαπορεύσονται.   τὸ   Geranea, the Spartans wait
δέ τι καὶ ἄνδρες τῶν Ἀθηναίων   in Boeotia considering how to
ἐπῆγον αὐτοὺς κρύφα, ἐλπίσαντες   return, and intrigue against
δῆμόν τε καταπαύσειν καὶ τὰ μακρὰ   the democracy.
τείχη οἰκοδομούμενα. ἐβοήθησαν δὲ ἐπ' αὐτοὺς 5
25 οἱ Ἀθηναῖοι πανδημεὶ καὶ Ἀργείων   A strong
χίλιοι καὶ τῶν ἄλλων ξυμμάχων   Athenian force marches out to
ὡς ἕκαστοι· ξύμπαντες δὲ ἐγένοντο   oppose them.
τετρακισχίλιοι καὶ μύριοι. νομίσαντες δὲ ἀπο- 6

12. κωλύειν ABEFM   14. ἐφαίνετο αὐτοῖς ABEFM[G]
15. πορεύεσθαι, ut videtur, non legit Schol., secl. Hude   22
ἐπῆγον αὐτοὺς τῶν Ἀθηναίων C

ρεῖν ὅπῃ διέλθωσιν ἐπεστράτευσαν αὐτοῖς, καί
7 τι καὶ τοῦ δήμου καταλύσεως ὑποψίᾳ. ἦλθον
δὲ καὶ Θεσσαλῶν ἱππῆς τοῖς Ἀθηναίοις κατὰ
τὸ ξυμμαχικόν, οἳ μετέστησαν ἐν τῷ ἔργῳ
108 παρὰ τοὺς Λακεδαιμονίους. γενομένης δὲ μάχης 5
ἐν Τανάγρᾳ τῆς Βοιωτίας ἐνίκων
Λακεδαιμόνιοι καὶ οἱ ξύμμαχοι, καὶ
φόνος ἐγένετο ἀμφοτέρων πολύς.
καὶ Λακεδαιμόνιοι μὲν ἐς τὴν Μεγαρίδα ἐλθόντες καὶ δενδροτομήσαντες 10
πάλιν ἀπῆλθον ἐπ᾽ οἴκου διὰ Γερανείας καὶ
Ἰσθμοῦ· Ἀθηναῖοι δὲ δευτέρᾳ καὶ ἑξηκοστῇ
ἡμέρᾳ μετὰ τὴν μάχην ἐστράτευσαν ἐς Βοιω-
3 τοὺς Μυρωνίδου στρατηγοῦντος, καὶ μάχῃ ἐν
Οἰνοφύτοις τοὺς Βοιωτοὺς νικήσαν- 15
τες τῆς τε χώρας ἐκράτησαν τῆς
Βοιωτίας καὶ Φωκίδος καὶ Τανα-
γραίων τὸ τεῖχος περιεῖλον καὶ Λοκρῶν
τῶν Ὀπουντίων ἑκατὸν ἄνδρας ὁμήρους τοὺς
πλουσιωτάτους ἔλαβον, τά τε τείχη ἑαυτῶν 20
4 τὰ μακρὰ ἀπετέλεσαν. ὡμολόγησαν δὲ καὶ οἱ
Αἰγινῆται μετὰ ταῦτα τοῖς Ἀθηναίοις, τείχη
τε περιελόντες καὶ ναῦς παραδόντες φόρον τε
5 ταξάμενοι ἐς τὸν ἔπειτα χρόνον. καὶ Πελοπόννησον περιέπλευσαν Ἀθηναῖοι Τολμίδου τοῦ 25
Τολμαίου στρατηγοῦντος, καὶ τὸ νεώριον τῶν
Λακεδαιμονίων ἐνέπρησαν καὶ Χαλκίδα Κοριν-

Battle of Tanagra: the Athenians defeated. Two months later the Athenians invade Boeotia and conquer it.

Surrender of Aegina. Naval successes of Tolmides.

5. post δὲ add. τῆς C   15. τοὺς om. CG   20. post
τείχη add. τὰ ABEF   21. ἐπετέλεσαν ABEFM ‖ οἱ om.
ABEFM   26. τῶν] τὸ ABEFM

θίων πόλιν εἷλον καὶ Σικυωνίους ἐν ἀποβάσει
τῆς γῆς μάχῃ ἐκράτησαν.

Οἱ δ' ἐν τῇ Αἰγύπτῳ Ἀθηναῖοι καὶ οἱ ξύμ- **109**
μαχοι ἐπέμενον, καὶ αὐτοῖς πολλαὶ End of the
5 ἰδέαι πολέμων κατέστησαν. τὸ μὲν Egyptian war. 2
γὰρ πρῶτον ἐκράτουν τῆς Αἰγύπτου The Athenian force destroyed.
οἱ Ἀθηναῖοι, καὶ βασιλεὺς πέμπει ἐς Λακε-
δαίμονα Μεγάβαζον ἄνδρα Πέρσην χρήματα
ἔχοντα, ὅπως ἐς τὴν Ἀττικὴν ἐσβαλεῖν πει-
10 σθέντων τῶν Πελοποννησίων ἀπ' Αἰγύπτου
ἀπαγάγοι Ἀθηναίους. ὡς δὲ αὐτῷ οὐ πρου- 3
χώρει καὶ τὰ χρήματα ἄλλως ἀνηλοῦτο, ὁ μὲν
Μεγάβαζος καὶ τὰ λοιπὰ τῶν χρημάτων πάλιν
ἐς τὴν Ἀσίαν ἀνεκομίσθη, Μεγάβυζον δὲ τὸν
15 Ζωπύρου πέμπει ἄνδρα Πέρσην μετὰ στρατιᾶς
πολλῆς· ὃς ἀφικόμενος κατὰ γῆν τούς τε 4
Αἰγυπτίους καὶ τοὺς ξυμμάχους μάχῃ ἐκράτησε
καὶ ἐκ τῆς Μέμφιδος ἐξήλασε τοὺς Ἕλληνας
καὶ τέλος ἐς Προσωπίτιδα τὴν νῆσον κατέ-
20 κλῃσε καὶ ἐπολιόρκει ἐν αὐτῇ ἐνιαυτὸν καὶ ἓξ
μῆνας, μέχρι οὗ ξηράνας τὴν διώρυχα καὶ
παρατρέψας ἄλλῃ τὸ ὕδωρ τάς τε ναῦς ἐπὶ
τοῦ ξηροῦ ἐποίησε καὶ τῆς νήσου τὰ πολλὰ
ἤπειρον, καὶ διαβὰς εἷλε τὴν Egypt again subject to
25 νῆσον πεζῇ. οὕτω μὲν τὰ τῶν Persia. A **110**
Ἑλλήνων πράγματα ἐφθάρη ἓξ ἔτη second Athenian force destroyed.
πολεμήσαντα· καὶ ὀλίγοι ἀπὸ πολλῶν πορευό-

1. πόλιν om. C   4. ἔτι ἔμενον C: ἔτι ἐπέμενον G
7. οἱ C: om. cett.   10. τῶν om. C[G]   14. ἐκομίσθη
ABEFM   16. τε om. ABEFM[G]   24. ἠπείρου C
suprascr. G

μενοι διὰ τῆς Λιβύης ἐς Κυρήνην ἐσώθησαν, οἱ
2 δὲ πλεῖστοι ἀπώλοντο. Αἴγυπτος δὲ πάλιν
ὑπὸ βασιλέα ἐγένετο πλὴν Ἀμυρταίου τοῦ ἐν
τοῖς ἕλεσι βασιλέως· τοῦτον δὲ διὰ μέγεθός
τε τοῦ ἕλους οὐκ ἐδύναντο ἑλεῖν, καὶ ἅμα 5
μαχιμώτατοί εἰσι τῶν Αἰγυπτίων οἱ ἕλειοι.
3 Ἰνάρως δὲ ὁ Λιβύων βασιλεύς, ὃς τὰ πάντα
ἔπραξε περὶ τῆς Αἰγύπτου, προδοσίᾳ ληφθεὶς
4 ἀνεσταυρώθη. ἐκ δὲ τῶν Ἀθηνῶν καὶ τῆς
ἄλλης ξυμμαχίδος πεντήκοντα τριήρεις διάδοχοι 10
πλέουσαι ἐς Αἴγυπτον ἔσχον κατὰ τὸ Μενδήσιον κέρας, οὐκ εἰδότες τῶν γ γονότων οὐδέν·
καὶ αὐτοῖς ἔκ τε γῆς ἐπιπεσόντες πεζοὶ καὶ
ἐκ θαλάσσης Φοινίκων ναυτικὸν διέφθειραν τὰς
πολλὰς τῶν νεῶν, αἱ δ' ἐλάσσους διέφυγον 15
πάλιν. τὰ μὲν κατὰ τὴν μεγάλην στρατείαν
Ἀθηναίων καὶ τῶν ξυμμάχων ἐς Αἴγυπτον
οὕτως ἐτελεύτησεν.

111 Ἐκ δὲ Θεσσαλίας Ὀρέστης ὁ Ἐχεκρατίδου
Unsuccessful υἱὸς τοῦ Θεσσαλῶν βασιλέως φεύ- 20
invasion of
Thessaly. γων ἔπεισεν Ἀθηναίους ἑαυτὸν
κατάγειν· καὶ παραλαβόντες Βοιωτοὺς καὶ
Φωκέας ὄντας ξυμμάχους οἱ Ἀθηναῖοι ἐστράτευσαν τῆς Θεσσαλίας ἐπὶ Φάρσαλον. καὶ
τῆς μὲν γῆς ἐκράτουν ὅσα μὴ προϊόντες πολὺ 25
ἐκ τῶν ὅπλων (οἱ γὰρ ἱππῆς τῶν Θεσσαλῶν
εἶργον), τὴν δὲ πόλιν οὐχ εἷλον, οὐδ' ἄλλο
προυχώρει αὐτοῖς οὐδὲν ὧν ἕνεκα ἐστράτευ-

σαν, ἀλλ' ἀπεχώρησαν πάλιν Ὀρέστην ἔχοντες
ἄπρακτοι. μετὰ δὲ ταῦτα οὐ πολλῷ ὕστερον 2
χίλιοι Ἀθηναίων ἐπὶ τὰς ναῦς τὰς ἐν Πηγαῖς
ἐπιβάντες (εἶχον δ' αὐτοὶ τὰς Πηγάς) παρέ-
5 πλευσαν ἐς Σικυῶνα Περικλέους τοῦ Ξανθίππου
στρατηγοῦντος, καὶ ἀποβάντες Σικυωνίων τοὺς
προσμείξαντας μάχῃ ἐκράτησαν. καὶ εὐθὺς 3
παραλαβόντες Ἀχαιοὺς καὶ δια- Pericles gains a
πλεύσαντες πέραν τῆς Ἀκαρνανίας victory over Sicyon.
10 ἐς Οἰνιάδας ἐστράτευσαν καὶ ἐπολιόρκουν, οὐ
μέντοι εἷλόν γε, ἀλλ' ἀπεχώρησαν ἐπ' οἴκου.

Ὕστερον δὲ διαλιπόντων ἐτῶν τριῶν σπον- 112
δαὶ γίγνονται Πελοποννησίοις καὶ Expedition
against Cyprus:
Ἀθηναίοις πεντέτεις. καὶ Ἑλληνι- death of Cimon. 2
15 κοῦ μὲν πολέμου ἔσχον οἱ Ἀθηναῖοι, ἐς δὲ
Κύπρον ἐστρατεύοντο ναυσὶ διακοσίαις αὐτῶν
τε καὶ τῶν ξυμμάχων Κίμωνος στρατηγοῦντος.
καὶ ἑξήκοντα μὲν νῆες ἐς Αἴγυπτον ἀπ' αὐτῶν 3
ἔπλευσαν, Ἀμυρταίου μεταπέμποντος τοῦ ἐν
20 τοῖς ἕλεσι βασιλέως, αἱ δὲ ἄλλαι Κίτιον
ἐπολιόρκουν. Κίμωνος δὲ ἀποθανόντος καὶ 4
λιμοῦ γενομένου ἀπεχώρησαν ἀπὸ Κιτίου, καὶ
πλεύσαντες ὑπὲρ Σαλαμῖνος τῆς ἐν Κύπρῳ
Φοίνιξι καὶ Κυπρίοις καὶ Κίλιξιν ἐναυμάχησαν
25 καὶ ἐπεζομάχησαν ἅμα, καὶ νικήσαντες ἀμφότερα ἀπεχώρησαν ἐπ' οἴκου καὶ αἱ ἐξ
Αἰγύπτου νῆες πάλιν [αἱ] ἐλθοῦσαι The Sacred
War.
μετ' αὐτῶν. Λακεδαιμόνιοι δὲ μετὰ 5
ταῦτα τὸν ἱερὸν καλούμενον πόλεμον ἐστρά-

24. καὶ Κυπρίοις om. ABEFM   27. αἱ secl. Classen

τευσαν, καὶ κρατήσαντες τοῦ ἐν Δελφοῖς
ἱεροῦ παρέδοσαν Δελφοῖς· καὶ αὖθις ὕστερον
'Αθηναῖοι ἀποχωρησάντων αὐτῶν στρατεύσαντες
καὶ κρατήσαντες παρέδοσαν Φωκεῦσιν.

113 Καὶ χρόνου ἐγγενομένου μετὰ ταῦτα 'Αθη- 5

Boeotia revolts.
The Athenians
defeated at
Coronea.
Boeotia in-
dependent.

ναῖοι, Βοιωτῶν τῶν φευγόντων ἐχόντων 'Ορχομενὸν καὶ Χαιρώνειαν καὶ
ἄλλ' ἄττα χωρία τῆς Βοιωτίας,
ἐστράτευσαν ἑαυτῶν μὲν χιλίοις
ὁπλίταις, τῶν δὲ ξυμμάχων ὡς ἑκάστοις ἐπὶ 10
τὰ χωρία ταῦτα πολέμια ὄντα, Τολμίδου τοῦ
Τολμαίου στρατηγοῦντος. καὶ Χαιρώνειαν
ἑλόντες καὶ ἀνδραποδίσαντες ἀπεχώρουν φυλα-
2 κὴν καταστήσαντες. πορευομένοις δ' αὐτοῖς ἐν
Κορωνείᾳ ἐπιτίθενται οἵ τε ἐκ τῆς 'Ορχομενοῦ 15
φυγάδες Βοιωτῶν καὶ Λοκροὶ μετ' αὐτῶν καὶ
Εὐβοέων φυγάδες καὶ ὅσοι τῆς αὐτῆς γνώμης
ἦσαν, καὶ μάχῃ κρατήσαντες τοὺς μὲν διέφθειραν
3 τῶν 'Αθηναίων, τοὺς δὲ ζῶντας ἔλαβον. καὶ
τὴν Βοιωτίαν ἐξέλιπον 'Αθηναῖοι πᾶσαν, σπον- 20
δὰς ποιησάμενοι ἐφ' ᾧ τοὺς ἄνδρας κομιοῦνται.
4 καὶ οἱ φεύγοντες Βοιωτῶν κατελθόντες καὶ οἱ
ἄλλοι πάντες αὐτόνομοι πάλιν ἐγένοντο.

114 Μετὰ δὲ ταῦτα οὐ πολλῷ ὕστερον Εὔβοια
ἀπέστη ἀπὸ 'Αθηναίων, καὶ ἐς αὐ- 25

Euboea and
Megara revolt.
The Spartans
invade Attica,
but soon with-
draw.

τὴν διαβεβηκότος ἤδη Περικλέους
στρατιᾷ 'Αθηναίων ἠγγέλθη αὐτῷ
ὅτι Μέγαρα ἀφέστηκε καὶ Πελο-

13. καὶ ἀνδραποδίσαντες om. ABEFM   14. ἐγκαταστήσαντες
Herwerden

ποννήσιοι μέλλουσιν ἐσβαλεῖν ἐς τὴν Ἀττικὴν
καὶ οἱ φρουροὶ Ἀθηναίων διεφθαρμένοι εἰσὶν
ὑπὸ Μεγαρέων, πλὴν ὅσοι ἐς Νίσαιαν ἀπέ-
φυγον· ἐπαγαγόμενοι δὲ Κορινθίους καὶ Σικυω-
5 νίους καὶ Ἐπιδαυρίους ἀπέστησαν οἱ Μεγαρῆς.
ὁ δὲ Περικλῆς πάλιν κατὰ τάχος ἐκόμιζε τὴν
στρατιὰν ἐκ τῆς Εὐβοίας. καὶ μετὰ τοῦτο οἱ 2
Πελοποννήσιοι τῆς Ἀττικῆς ἐς Ἐλευσῖνα καὶ
Θριῶζε ἐσβαλόντες ἐδήωσαν Πλειστοάνακτος
10 τοῦ Παυσανίου βασιλέως Λακεδαιμονίων ἡγουμένου, καὶ τὸ πλέον οὐκέτι προελθόντες ἀπεχώρησαν ἐπ᾽ οἴκου. καὶ Ἀθηναῖοι πάλιν ἐς 3
Εὔβοιαν διαβάντες Περικλέους στρα- Pericles
conquers
τηγοῦντος κατεστρέψαντο πᾶσαν, Euboea.
15 καὶ τὴν μὲν ἄλλην ὁμολογίᾳ κατεστήσαντο,
Ἑστιαιᾶς δὲ ἐξοικίσαντες αὐτοὶ τὴν γῆν ἔσχον.
ἀναχωρήσαντες δὲ ἀπ᾽ Εὐβοίας οὐ πολλῷ 115
ὕστερον σπονδὰς ἐποιήσαντο πρὸς The Thirty
Λακεδαιμονίους καὶ τοὺς ξυμμάχους Years' Peace.
20 τριακοντούτεις, ἀποδόντες Νίσαιαν καὶ Πηγὰς
καὶ Τροιζῆνα καὶ Ἀχαίαν· ταῦτα γὰρ εἶχον
Ἀθηναῖοι Πελοποννησίων.

Ἕκτῳ δὲ ἔτει Σαμίοις καὶ Μιλησίοις πόλε- 2
μος ἐγένετο περὶ Πριήνης, καὶ οἱ Revolt of
Samos, and of
25 Μιλήσιοι ἐλασσούμενοι τῷ πολέμῳ Byzantium.
παρ᾽ Ἀθηναίους ἐλθόντες κατεβόων τῶν Σαμίων.
ξυνεπελάβοντο δὲ καὶ ἐξ αὐτῆς τῆς Σάμου
ἄνδρες ἰδιῶται νεωτερίσαι βουλόμενοι τὴν πολι-

1. ἐσβάλλειν CG   4. ἐπαγόμενοι CG   27. ξυνεπε-
λαμβάνοντο ABEFM γρ. G

3 τείαν. πλεύσαντες οὖν Ἀθηναῖοι ἐς Σάμον
ναυσὶ τεσσαράκοντα δημοκρατίαν κατέστησαν,
καὶ ὁμήρους ἔλαβον τῶν Σαμίων πεντήκοντα
μὲν παῖδας, ἴσους δὲ ἄνδρας, καὶ κατέθεντο
ἐς Λῆμνον, καὶ φρουρὰν ἐγκαταλιπόντες ἀνε- 5
4 χώρησαν. τῶν δὲ Σαμίων ἦσαν γάρ τινες οἳ
οὐχ ὑπέμειναν, ἀλλ' ἔφυγον ἐς τὴν ἤπειρον,
ξυνθέμενοι τῶν ἐν τῇ πόλει τοῖς δυνατωτάτοις
καὶ Πισσούθνῃ τῷ Ὑστάσπου ξυμμαχίαν, ὃς
εἶχε Σάρδεις τότε, ἐπικούρους τε ξυλλέξαντες 10
ἐς ἑπτακοσίους διέβησαν ὑπὸ νύκτα ἐς τὴν
5 Σάμον, καὶ πρῶτον μὲν τῷ δήμῳ ἐπανέστησαν
καὶ ἐκράτησαν τῶν πλείστων, ἔπειτα τοὺς
ὁμήρους ἐκκλέψαντες ἐκ Λήμνου τοὺς αὐτῶν
ἀπέστησαν, καὶ τοὺς φρουροὺς τοὺς Ἀθηναίων 15
καὶ τοὺς ἄρχοντας οἳ ἦσαν παρὰ σφίσιν
ἐξέδοσαν Πισσούθνῃ, ἐπί τε Μίλητον εὐθὺς
παρεσκευάζοντο στρατεύειν. ξυναπέστησαν δ'
αὐτοῖς καὶ Βυζάντιοι.

116   Ἀθηναῖοι δὲ ὡς ᾔσθοντο, πλεύσαντες ναυσὶν 20

Pericles sent   ἑξήκοντα ἐπὶ Σάμου ταῖς μὲν ἑκ-
to Samos.   καίδεκα τῶν νεῶν οὐκ ἐχρήσαντο
(ἔτυχον γὰρ αἱ μὲν ἐπὶ Καρίας ἐς προσκοπὴν
τῶν Φοινισσῶν νεῶν οἰχόμεναι, αἱ δὲ ἐπὶ Χίου
καὶ Λέσβου περιαγγέλλουσαι βοηθεῖν), τεσ- 25
σαράκοντα δὲ ναυσὶ καὶ τέσσαρσι Περικλέους
δεκάτου αὐτοῦ στρατηγοῦντος ἐναυμάχησαν πρὸς
Τραγίᾳ τῇ νήσῳ Σαμίων ναυσὶν ἑβδομήκοντα,

7. ὑπέμενον ΑΒΕΦΜ   14. κλέψαντες ΑΒΕΦΜ   18. post
παρεσκευάζοντο add. μετ' αὐτοὺς C, μετ' αὐτοῦ G

ὧν ἦσαν αἱ εἴκοσι στρατιώτιδες (ἔτυχον δὲ αἱ
πᾶσαι ἀπὸ Μιλήτου πλέουσαι), καὶ ἐνίκων
Ἀθηναῖοι. ὕστερον δὲ αὐτοῖς ἐβοήθησαν ἐκ 2
τῶν Ἀθηνῶν νῆες τεσσαράκοντα καὶ Χίων καὶ
5 Λεσβίων πέντε καὶ εἴκοσι, καὶ ἀποβάντες καὶ
κρατοῦντες τῷ πεζῷ ἐπολιόρκουν τρισὶ τείχεσι
τὴν πόλιν καὶ ἐκ θαλάσσης ἅμα. Περικλῆς 3
δὲ λαβὼν ἑξήκοντα ναῦς ἀπὸ τῶν ἐφορμουσῶν
ᾤχετο κατὰ τάχος ἐπὶ Καύνου καὶ Καρίας,
10 ἐσαγγελθέντων ὅτι Φοίνισσαι νῆες ἐπ᾽ αὐτοὺς
πλέουσιν· ᾤχετο γὰρ καὶ ἐκ τῆς Σάμου πέντε
ναυσὶ Στησαγόρας καὶ ἄλλοι ἐπὶ τὰς Φοινίσσας.
ἐν τούτῳ δὲ οἱ Σάμιοι ἐξαπιναίως ἔκπλουν 117
ποιησάμενοι ἀφάρκτῳ τῷ στρα- Submission of
15 τοπέδῳ ἐπιπεσόντες τάς τε προ- Samos and
Byzantium.
φυλακίδας ναῦς διέφθειραν καὶ ναυμαχοῦντες
τὰς ἀνταναγομένας ἐνίκησαν, καὶ τῆς θαλάσσης
τῆς καθ᾽ ἑαυτοὺς ἐκράτησαν ἡμέρας περὶ
τέσσαρας καὶ δέκα, καὶ ἐσεκομίσαντο καὶ ἐξε-
20 κομίσαντο ἃ ἐβούλοντο. ἐλθόντος δὲ Περι- 2
κλέους πάλιν ταῖς ναυσὶ κατεκλῄσθησαν. καὶ ἐκ
τῶν Ἀθηνῶν ὕστερον προσεβοήθησαν τεσσαράκοντα μὲν αἱ μετὰ Θουκυδίδου καὶ Ἅγνωνος καὶ
Φορμίωνος νῆες, εἴκοσι δὲ αἱ μετὰ Τληπολέμου
25 καὶ Ἀντικλέους, ἐκ δὲ Χίου καὶ Λέσβου τριάκοντα. καὶ ναυμαχίαν μέν τινα βραχεῖαν 3
ἐποιήσαντο οἱ Σάμιοι, ἀδύνατοι δὲ ὄντες ἀντίσχειν ἐξεπολιορκήθησαν ἐνάτῳ μηνὶ καὶ προσε-

5. post ἀποβάντες add. ἐς τὴν γῆν CG (del. G¹)   24. αἱ
om. ACG   27. ἀντίσχειν Krüger : ἀντισχεῖν codd.

χώρησαν ὁμολογίᾳ, τεῖχός τε καθελόντες καὶ
ὁμήρους δόντες καὶ ναῦς παραδόντες καὶ χρήματα τὰ ἀναλωθέντα ταξάμενοι κατὰ χρόνους
ἀποδοῦναι. ξυνέβησαν δὲ καὶ Βυζάντιοι ὥσπερ
καὶ πρότερον ὑπήκοοι εἶναι. 5

118 Μετὰ ταῦτα δὲ ἤδη γίγνεται οὐ πολλοῖς
Resumption of ἔτεσιν ὕστερον τὰ προειρημένα, τά
the main
subject (c. 88). τε Κερκυραϊκὰ καὶ τὰ Ποτειδεατικὰ
The Spartans
receive en- καὶ ὅσα πρόφασις τοῦδε τοῦ πολέ-
couragement
2 from Delphi. μου κατέστη. ταῦτα δὲ ξύμπαντα 10
ὅσα ἔπραξαν οἱ Ἕλληνες πρός τε ἀλλήλους
καὶ τὸν βάρβαρον ἐγένετο ἐν ἔτεσι πεντήκοντα
μάλιστα μεταξὺ τῆς τε Ξέρξου ἀναχωρήσεως
καὶ τῆς ἀρχῆς τοῦδε τοῦ πολέμου· ἐν οἷς οἱ
Ἀθηναῖοι τήν τε ἀρχὴν ἐγκρατεστέραν κατε- 15
στήσαντο καὶ αὐτοὶ ἐπὶ μέγα ἐχώρησαν δυνάμεως, οἱ δὲ Λακεδαιμόνιοι αἰσθόμενοι οὔτε
ἐκώλυον εἰ μὴ ἐπὶ βραχύ, ἡσύχαζόν τε τὸ
πλέον τοῦ χρόνου, ὄντες μὲν καὶ πρὸ τοῦ μὴ
ταχεῖς ἰέναι ἐς τοὺς πολέμους, ἢν μὴ ἀναγκά- 20
ζωνται, τὸ δέ τι καὶ πολέμοις οἰκείοις ἐξειργό-
μενοι, πρὶν δὴ ἡ δύναμις τῶν Ἀθηναίων σαφῶς
ἤρετο καὶ τῆς ξυμμαχίας αὐτῶν ἥπτοντο.
τότε δὲ οὐκέτι ἀνασχετὸν ἐποιοῦντο, ἀλλ᾽ ἐπι-
χειρητέα ἐδόκει εἶναι πάσῃ προθυμίᾳ καὶ 25
καθαιρετέα ἡ ἰσχύς, ἢν δύνωνται, ἀραμένοις

3. κατὰ χρόνοις ταξάμενοι ABEFM 13. τε om. ABEFM
14. οἱ om. ABEFM 20. ἢν μὴ ἀναγκάζωνται C Dion. Hal.:
εἰ μὴ ἀναγκάζωνται G: εἰ μὴ ἀναγκάζοιντο cett. 21. τὸ δέ τι]
τότε δέ τι Dion. Hal. : τότε δ᾽ ἔτι Reiske

τόνδε τὸν πόλεμον. αὐτοῖς μὲν οὖν τοῖς 3
Λακεδαιμονίοις διέγνωστο λελύσθαι τε τὰς
σπονδὰς καὶ τοὺς Ἀθηναίους ἀδικεῖν, πέμψαντες δὲ ἐς Δελφοὺς ἐπηρώτων τὸν θεὸν
5 εἰ πολεμοῦσιν ἄμεινον ἔσται· ὁ δὲ ἀνεῖλεν
αὐτοῖς, ὡς λέγεται, κατὰ κράτος πολεμοῦσι
νίκην ἔσεσθαι, καὶ αὐτὸς ἔφη ξυλλήψεσθαι
καὶ παρακαλούμενος καὶ ἄκλητος. αὖθις δὲ τοὺς **119**
ξυμμάχους παρακαλέσαντες ψῆφον Assembly of
10 ἐβούλοντο ἐπαγαγεῖν εἰ χρὴ πολε- allies at Sparta to decide the
μεῖν. καὶ ἐλθόντων τῶν πρέσβεων question of war.
ἀπὸ τῆς ξυμμαχίας καὶ ξυνόδου γ. νομένης οἵ
τε ἄλλοι εἶπον ἃ ἐβούλοντο, κατηγοροῦντες
οἱ πλείους τῶν Ἀθηναίων καὶ τὸν πόλεμον
15 ἀξιοῦντες γίγνεσθαι, καὶ οἱ Κορίνθιοι δεηθέντες
μὲν καὶ κατὰ πόλεις πρότερον ἑκάστων ἰδίᾳ
ὥστε ψηφίσασθαι τὸν πόλεμον, δεδιότες περὶ
τῇ Ποτειδαίᾳ μὴ προδιαφθαρῇ, παρόντες δὲ καὶ
τότε καὶ τελευταῖοι ἐπελθόντες ἔλεγον τοιάδε.
20 "Τοὺς μὲν Λακεδαιμονίους, ὦ ἄνδρες ξύμ-**120**
μαχοι, οὐκ ἂν ἔτι αἰτιασαίμεθα ὡς Speech of the Corinthian
οὐ καὶ αὐτοὶ ἐψηφισμένοι τὸν envoy, 'Athens is a menace to
πόλεμόν εἰσι καὶ ἡμᾶς ἐς τοῦτο all states alike.
νῦν ξυνήγαγον. χρὴ γὰρ τοὺς Let us not shrink from fighting her
25 ἡγεμόνας τὰ ἴδια ἐξ ἴσου νέμοντας now.
τὰ κοινὰ προσκοπεῖν, ὥσπερ καὶ ἐν ἄλλοις
ἐκ πάντων προτιμῶνται. ἡμῶν δὲ ὅσοι μὲν 2
Ἀθηναίοις ἤδη ἐνηλλάγησαν οὐχὶ διδαχῆς

15. γενέσθαι ABEFM   23. ὑμᾶς CG   28. συνηλλάγησαν
(sic) Dion. Hal.

δέονται ὥστε φυλάξασθαι αὐτούς· τοὺς δὲ
τὴν μεσόγειαν μᾶλλον καὶ μὴ ἐν πόρῳ κατῳκημένους εἰδέναι χρὴ ὅτι, τοῖς κάτω ἦν μὴ
ἀμύνωσι, χαλεπωτέραν ἕξουσι τὴν κατακομιδὴν
τῶν ὡραίων καὶ πάλιν ἀντίληψιν ὧν ἡ 5
θάλασσα τῇ ἠπείρῳ δίδωσι, καὶ τῶν νῦν
λεγομένων μὴ κακοὺς κριτὰς ὡς μὴ προση-
κόντων εἶναι, προσδέχεσθαι δέ ποτε, εἰ τὰ
κάτω πρόοιντο, κἂν μέχρι σφῶν τὸ δεινὸν
προελθεῖν, καὶ περὶ αὐτῶν οὐχ ἧσσον νῦν 10
3 βουλεύεσθαι. δι' ὅπερ καὶ μὴ ὀκνεῖν δεῖ
αὐτοὺς τὸν πόλεμον ἀντ' εἰρήνης μεταλαμ-
βάνειν. ἀνδρῶν γὰρ σωφρόνων μέν ἐστιν, εἰ
μὴ ἀδικοῖντο, ἡσυχάζειν, ἀγαθῶν δὲ ἀδικουμένους ἐκ μὲν εἰρήνης πολεμεῖν, εὖ δὲ παρα- 5
σχὸν ἐκ πολέμου πάλιν ξυμβῆναι, καὶ μήτε τῇ
κατὰ πόλεμον εὐτυχίᾳ ἐπαίρεσθαι μήτε τῷ
4 ἡσύχῳ τῆς εἰρήνης ἡδόμενον ἀδικεῖσθαι. ὅ
τε γὰρ διὰ τὴν ἡδονὴν ὀκνῶν τάχιστ' ἂν
ἀφαιρεθείη τῆς ῥᾳστώνης τὸ τερπνὸν δι' ὅπερ 20
ὀκνεῖ, εἰ ἡσυχάζοι, ὅ τε ἐν πολέμῳ εὐτυχίᾳ
πλεονάζων οὐκ ἐντεθύμηται θράσει ἀπίστῳ
5 ἐπαιρόμενος. πολλὰ γὰρ κακῶς γνωσθέντα
ἀβουλοτέρων τῶν ἐναντίων τυχόντα κατωρθώθη,
καὶ ἔτι πλείω καλῶς δοκοῦντα βουλευθῆναι ἐς 25
τοὐναντίον αἰσχρῶς περιέστη· ἐνθυμεῖται γὰρ
οὐδεὶς ὁμοῖα τῇ πίστει καὶ ἔργῳ ἐπεξέρχεται,

10. αὐτῶν F : αὐτῶν cett.   18. ἡσύχῳ C Stobaeus : ἡσυχίῳ
cett.   24. τυχόντα CG Stobaeus : τυχόντων cett.   25. post
πλείω add. ἃ ABEFM γρ. G, τὰ Stobaeus

ἀλλὰ μετ᾽ ἀσφαλείας μὲν δοξάζομεν, μετὰ δέους
δὲ ἐν τῷ ἔργῳ ἐλλείπομεν.

"Ἡμεῖς δὲ νῦν καὶ ἀδικούμενοι τὸν πόλε- **121**
μον ἐγείρομεν καὶ ἱκανὰ ἔχοντες ‘Our prospects
are good. Only
5 ἐγκλήματα, καὶ ὅταν ἀμυνώμεθα a fleet is wanting, and we can
Ἀθηναίους, καταθησόμεθα αὐτὸν ἐν provide one.

καιρῷ. κατὰ πολλὰ δὲ ἡμᾶς εἰκὸς ἐπικρα- 2
τῆσαι, πρῶτον μὲν πλήθει προύχοντας καὶ
ἐμπειρίᾳ πολεμικῇ, ἔπειτα ὁμοίως πάντας ἐς
10 τὰ παραγγελλόμενα ἰόντας, ναυτικόν τε, ᾧ 3
ἰσχύουσιν, ἀπὸ τῆς ὑπαρχούσης τε ἑκάστοις
οὐσίας ἐξαρτυσόμεθα καὶ ἀπὸ τῶν ἐν Δελφοῖς
καὶ Ὀλυμπίᾳ χρημάτων· δάνεισμα γὰρ ποιησάμενοι ὑπολαβεῖν οἷοί τ᾽ ἐσμὲν μισθῷ μείζονι
15 τοὺς ξένους αὐτῶν ναυβάτας. ὠνητὴ γὰρ ἡ
Ἀθηναίων δύναμις μᾶλλον ἢ οἰκεία· ἡ δὲ
ἡμετέρα ἧσσον ἂν τοῦτο πάθοι, τοῖς σώμασι
τὸ πλέον ἰσχύουσα ἢ τοῖς χρήμασιν. μιᾷ τε 4
νίκῃ ναυμαχίας κατὰ τὸ εἰκὸς ἁλίσκονται· εἰ
20 δ᾽ ἀντίσχοιεν, μελετήσομεν καὶ ἡμεῖς ἐν πλέονι
χρόνῳ τὰ ναυτικά, καὶ ὅταν τὴν ἐπιστήμην
ἐς τὸ ἴσον καταστήσωμεν, τῇ γε εὐψυχίᾳ
δήπου περιεσόμεθα. ὃ γὰρ ἡμεῖς ἔχομεν φύσει
ἀγαθόν, ἐκείνοις οὐκ ἂν γένοιτο διδαχῇ· ὃ δ᾽
25 ἐκεῖνοι ἐπιστήμῃ προύχουσι, καθαιρετὸν ἡμῖν
ἐστι μελέτῃ. χρήματα δὲ ὥστε ἔχειν ἐς αὐτά, 5
οἴσομεν· ἢ δεινὸν ἂν εἴη εἰ οἱ μὲν ‘We will find
money for the
ἐκείνων ξύμμαχοι ἐπὶ δουλείᾳ τῇ war.

12. ἐξαρτυσώμεθα ABEFM[G]   16. Ἀθηναίων ἢ ABEFM
25. καθαιρετὸν C : καθαιρετέον cett. (corr. G¹)

αὐτῶν φέροντες οὐκ ἀπεροῦσιν, ἡμεῖς δ' ἐπὶ
τῷ τιμωρούμενοι τοὺς ἐχθροὺς καὶ αὐτοὶ ἅμα
σῴζεσθαι οὐκ ἄρα δαπανήσομεν καὶ ἐπὶ τῷ
μὴ ὑπ' ἐκείνων αὐτὰ ἀφαιρεθέντες αὐτοῖς
122 τούτοις κακῶς πάσχειν. ὑπάρχουσι δὲ καὶ ꜱ

'We can induce
their allies to
revolt; and
establish a
hostile post in
their country.

ἄλλαι ὁδοὶ τοῦ πολέμου ἡμῖν, ξυμ
μάχων τε ἀπόστασις, μάλιστα
παραίρεσις οὖσα τῶν προσόδων
αἷς ἰσχύουσι, καὶ ἐπιτειχισμὸς τῇ
χώρᾳ, ἄλλα τε ὅσα οὐκ ἄν τις νῦν προΐδοι. 10
ἥκιστα γὰρ πόλεμος ἐπὶ ῥητοῖς χωρεῖ, αὐτὸς
δὲ ἀφ' αὑτοῦ τὰ πολλὰ τεχνᾶται πρὸς τὸ
παρατυγχάνον· ἐν ᾧ ὁ μὲν εὐοργήτως αὐτῷ
προσομιλήσας βεβαιότερος, ὁ δ' ὀργισθεὶς περὶ
αὐτὸν οὐκ ἐλάσσω πταίει. 15

2 " Ἐνθυμώμεθα δὲ καὶ ὅτι εἰ μὲν ἡμῶν ἦσαν

'We must unite
and work
together to pull
down the tyrant.

ἑκάστοις πρὸς ἀντιπάλους περὶ γῆς
ὅρων αἱ διαφοραί, οἰστὸν* ἂν ἦν·
νῦν δὲ πρὸς ξύμπαντάς τε ἡμᾶς
Ἀθηναῖοι ἱκανοὶ καὶ κατὰ πόλιν ἔτι δυνα- 20
τώτεροι, ὥστε εἰ μὴ καὶ ἀθρόοι καὶ κατὰ
ἔθνη καὶ ἕκαστον ἄστυ μιᾷ γνώμῃ ἀμυνούμεθα
αὐτούς, δίχα γε ὄντας ἡμᾶς ἀπόνως χειρώσον-
ται. καὶ τὴν ἧσσαν, εἰ καὶ δεινόν τῳ ἀκοῦσαι,
ἴστω οὐκ ἄλλο τι φέρουσαν ἢ ἄντικρυς 25
3 δουλείαν· ὃ καὶ λόγῳ ἐνδοιασθῆναι αἰσχρὸν

'We have been
remiss and
foolish in not
interfering.

τῇ Πελοποννήσῳ καὶ πόλεις τοσάσδε
ὑπὸ μιᾶς κακοπαθεῖν. ἐν ᾧ ἢ
δικαίως δοκοῖμεν ἂν πάσχειν ἢ διὰ

16. καὶ om. CG ‖ ἦσαν ἡμῶν ΑΒΕFM   18. αἱ om. ΑΒΕFM

δειλίαν ἀνέχεσθαι καὶ τῶν πατέρων χείρους
φαίνεσθαι, οἳ τὴν Ἑλλάδα ἠλευθέρωσαν· ἡμεῖς
δὲ οὐδ' ἡμῖν αὐτοῖς βεβαιοῦμεν αὐτό, τύραννον
δὲ ἐῶμεν ἐγκαθεστάναι πόλιν, τοὺς δ' ἐν μιᾷ
5 μονάρχους ἀξιοῦμεν καταλύειν. καὶ οὐκ ἴσμεν 4
ὅπως τάδε τριῶν τῶν μεγίστων ξυμφορῶν
ἀπήλλακται, ἀξυνεσίας ἢ μαλακίας ἢ ἀμελείας.
οὐ γὰρ δὴ πεφευγότες αὐτὰ ἐπὶ τὴν πλείστους
δὴ βλάψασαν καταφρόνησιν κεχωρήκατε, ἢ ἐκ
10 τοῦ πολλοὺς σφάλλειν τὸ ἐναντίον ὄνομα
ἀφροσύνη μετωνόμασται. τὰ μὲν οὖν προ- 123
γεγενημένα τί δεῖ μακρότερον ἢ ἐς 'But now with
ὅσον τοῖς νῦν ξυμφέρει αἰτιᾶσθαι ; encouragement
on all sides, let
περὶ δὲ τῶν ἔπειτα μελλόντων us enter on a
just war.
15 τοῖς παροῦσι βοηθοῦντας χρὴ ἐπιταλαιπωρεῖν
(πάτριον γὰρ ὑμῖν ἐκ τῶν πόνων τὰς ἀρετὰς
κτᾶσθαι), καὶ μὴ μεταβάλλειν τὸ ἔθος, εἰ ἄρα
πλούτῳ τε νῦν καὶ ἐξουσίᾳ ὀλίγον προφέρετε
(οὐ γὰρ δίκαιον ἃ τῇ ἀπορίᾳ ἐκτήθη τῇ
20 περιουσίᾳ ἀπολέσθαι), ἀλλὰ θαρσοῦντας ἰέναι
κατὰ πολλὰ ἐς τὸν πόλεμον, τοῦ τε θεοῦ
χρήσαντος καὶ αὐτοῦ ὑποσχομένου ξυλλήψεσθαι καὶ τῆς ἄλλης Ἑλλάδος ἁπάσης ξυν-
αγωνιουμένης, τὰ μὲν φόβῳ, τὰ δὲ ὠφελίᾳ.
25 σπονδάς τε οὐ λύσετε πρότεροι, ἅς γε καὶ ὁ 2
θεὸς κελεύων πολεμεῖν νομίζει παραβεβάσθαι,
ἠδικημέναις δὲ μᾶλλον βοηθήσετε· λύουσι γὰρ
οὐχ οἱ ἀμυνόμενοι, ἀλλ' οἱ πρότεροι ἐπιόντες.

8. ταῦτα ABEFM[G]   16. ἡμῖν C[G]   20. θαρσοῦντας
fGM : θαρσοῦντες cett.   23. πάσης ABEFM

108 ΘΟΥΚΥΔΙΔΟΥ

124 "Ὥστε πανταχόθεν καλῶς ὑπάρχον ὑμῖν
'Let us then in
the common
interest help
Potidaea, and
through war find
peace and liberty
for all.'

πολεμεῖν καὶ ἡμῶν κοινῇ τάδε
παραινούντων, εἴπερ βεβαιότατον τὸ
ταῦτα ξυμφέροντα καὶ πόλεσι καὶ
ἰδιώταις εἶναι, μὴ μέλλετε Ποτει- 5
δεάταις τε ποιεῖσθαι τιμωρίαν οὖσι Δωριεῦσι
καὶ ὑπὸ Ἰώνων πολιορκουμένοις, οὗ πρότερον
ἦν τοὐναντίον, καὶ τῶν ἄλλων μετελθεῖν τὴν
ἐλευθερίαν, ὡς οὐκέτι ἐνδέχεται περιμένον-
τας τοὺς μὲν ἤδη βλάπτεσθαι, τοὺς δ᾽, εἰ 10
γνωσθησόμεθα ξυνελθόντες μέν, ἀμύνεσθαι δὲ
οὐ τολμῶντες, μὴ πολὺ ὕστερον τὸ αὐτὸ
2 πάσχειν· ἀλλὰ νομίσαντες ἐς ἀνάγκην ἀφῖχθαι,
ὦ ἄνδρες ξύμμαχοι, καὶ ἅμα τάδε ἄριστα
λέγεσθαι, ψηφίσασθε τὸν πόλεμον μὴ φοβη- 15
θέντες τὸ αὐτίκα δεινόν, τῆς δ᾽ ἀπ᾽ αὐτοῦ
διὰ πλείονος εἰρήνης ἐπιθυμήσαντες· ἐκ πολέμου μὲν γὰρ εἰρήνη μᾶλλον βεβαιοῦται, ἀφ᾽
ἡσυχίας δὲ μὴ πολεμῆσαι οὐχ ὁμοίως ἀκίν-
3 δυνον. καὶ τὴν καθεστηκυῖαν ἐν τῇ Ἑλλάδι 20
πόλιν τύραννον ἡγησάμενοι ἐπὶ πᾶσιν ὁμοίως
καθεστάναι, ὥστε τῶν μὲν ἤδη ἄρχειν, τῶν δὲ
διανοεῖσθαι, παραστησώμεθα ἐπελθόντες, καὶ
αὐτοί τε ἀκινδύνως τὸ λοιπὸν οἰκῶμεν καὶ
τοὺς νῦν δεδουλωμένους Ἕλληνας ἐλευθερώσω- 25
μεν." τοιαῦτα μὲν οἱ Κορίνθιοι εἶπον.

125 Οἱ δὲ Λακεδαιμόνιοι ἐπειδὴ ἀφ᾽ ἁπάντων

2. τάδε κοινῇ ABEFM   12. οὐ τολμῶντες] ἀτολμῶντες
CEG : ἀτολμοῦντες suprascr. F γρ. G   13. ἐπ᾽ CG   23.
παραστησόμεθα BCG   24. τε om. ABEFM   26. μὲν
om. ABEFM

ἤκουσαν γνώμην, ψῆφον ἐπήγαγον τοῖς ξυμ-
μάχοις ἅπασιν ὅσοι παρῆσαν ἑξῆς, The majority is
for war. Pre-
καὶ μείζονι καὶ ἐλάσσονι πόλει· καὶ parations were
begun, but took
τὸ πλῆθος ἐψηφίσαντο πολεμεῖν. nearly a year.
5 δεδογμένον δὲ αὐτοῖς εὐθὺς μὲν ἀδύνατα ἦν 2
ἐπιχειρεῖν ἀπαρασκεύοις οὖσιν, ἐκπορίζεσθαι δὲ
ἐδόκει ἑκάστοις ἃ πρόσφορα ἦν καὶ μὴ εἶναι
μέλλησιν. ὅμως δὲ καθισταμένοις ὧν ἔδει
ἐνιαυτὸς μὲν οὐ διετρίβη, ἔλασσον δέ, πρὶν
10 ἐσβαλεῖν ἐς τὴν Ἀττικὴν καὶ τὸν An embassy
πόλεμον ἄρασθαι φανερῶς. ἐν τούτῳ sent to Athens **126**
δὲ ἐπρεσβεύοντο τῷ χρόνῳ πρὸς to demand the
expulsion of
'the accursed.'
τοὺς Ἀθηναίους ἐγκλήματα ποιού- Origin of this
affair : the story
μενοι, ὅπως σφίσιν ὅτι μεγίστη of Cylon.
15 πρόφασις εἴη τοῦ πολεμεῖν, ἢν μή τι ἐσα-
κούσωσιν.

Καὶ πρῶτον μὲν πρέσβεις πέμψαντες οἱ 2
Λακεδαιμόνιοι ἐκέλευον τοὺς Ἀθηναίους τὸ
ἄγος ἐλαύνειν τῆς θεοῦ· τὸ δὲ ἄγος ἦν
20 τοιόνδε. Κύλων ἦν Ἀθηναῖος ἀνὴρ Ὀλυμ- 3
πιονίκης τῶν πάλαι εὐγενής τε καὶ δυνατός,
ἐγεγαμήκει δὲ θυγατέρα Θεαγένους Μεγαρέως
ἀνδρός, ὃς κατ' ἐκεῖνον τὸν χρόνον ἐτυράννει
Μεγάρων. χρωμένῳ δὲ τῷ Κύλωνι ἐν Δελφοῖς 4
25 ἀνεῖλεν ὁ θεὸς ἐν τοῦ Διὸς τῇ μεγίστῃ ἑορτῇ
καταλαβεῖν τὴν Ἀθηναίων ἀκρόπολιν. ὁ δὲ 5
παρά τε τοῦ Θεαγένους δύναμιν λαβὼν καὶ τοὺς

---

7. ἑκάστους Nattmann	15. ἐσακούσωσι F (vel f) GM
20. Ὀλυμπιονίκης ἀνὴρ Ἀθηναῖος ABEFM	25. post ἐν add.
τῇ ABEFM

I	F

φίλους ἀναπείσας, ἐπειδὴ ἐπῆλθεν Ὀλύμπια
τὰ ἐν Πελοποννήσῳ, κατέλαβε τὴν ἀκρόπολιν
ὡς ἐπὶ τυραννίδι, νομίσας ἑορτήν τε τοῦ
Διὸς μεγίστην εἶναι καὶ ἑαυτῷ τι προσήκειν
6 Ὀλύμπια νενικηκότι. εἰ δὲ ἐν τῇ Ἀττικῇ ἢ 5
ἄλλοθί που ἡ μεγίστη ἑορτὴ εἴρητο, οὔτε
ἐκεῖνος ἔτι κατενόησε τό τε μαντεῖον οὐκ
ἐδήλου (ἔστι γὰρ καὶ Ἀθηναίοις Διάσια ἃ
καλεῖται Διὸς ἑορτὴ Μειλιχίου μεγίστη ἔξω
τῆς πόλεως, ἐν ᾗ πανδημεὶ θύουσι πολλὰ οὐχ 10
ἱερεῖα, ἀλλ᾽ ⟨ἁγνὰ⟩ θύματα ἐπιχώρια), δοκῶν
7 δὲ ὀρθῶς γιγνώσκειν ἐπεχείρησε τῷ ἔργῳ. οἱ
δὲ Ἀθηναῖοι αἰσθόμενοι ἐβοήθησάν τε πανδημεὶ ἐκ τῶν ἀγρῶν ἐπ᾽ αὐτοὺς καὶ προσκαθ-
8 εζόμενοι ἐπολιόρκουν. χρόνου δὲ ἐγγιγνομένου 15
οἱ Ἀθηναῖοι τρυχόμενοι τῇ προσεδρίᾳ ἀπῆλθον
οἱ πολλοί, ἐπιτρέψαντες τοῖς ἐννέα ἄρχουσι
τήν τε φυλακὴν καὶ τὸ πᾶν αὐτοκράτορσι
διαθεῖναι ᾗ ἂν ἄριστα διαγιγνώσκωσιν· τότε
δὲ τὰ πολλὰ τῶν πολιτικῶν οἱ ἐννέα ἄρχοντες 20
9 ἔπρασσον. οἱ δὲ μετὰ τοῦ Κύλωνος πολιορκούμενοι φλαύρως εἶχον σίτου τε καὶ ὕδατος
10 ἀπορίᾳ. ὁ μὲν οὖν Κύλων καὶ ὁ ἀδελφὸς
αὐτοῦ ἐκδιδράσκουσιν· οἱ δ᾽ ἄλλοι ὡς ἐπιέζοντο
καί τινες καὶ ἀπέθνῃσκον ὑπὸ τοῦ λιμοῦ, 25
καθίζουσιν ἐπὶ τὸν βωμὸν ἱκέται τὸν ἐν τῇ

1. ἐπῆλθον ABFM   10. πολλὰ C. F. Hermann : πολλοὶ
codd.   11. ἁγνὰ ex Polluce add. Hemsterhuis   12. τῷ
ἔργῳ . . ii. 13. 7 τείχους suppl. m foll. xxv-xxxiii   15. ἐπι-
γιγνομένου ABEF γρ. G   18. τε om. ABEF   24. αὐτοῦ
om. CG

ἀκροπόλει. ἀναστήσαντες δὲ αὐτοὺς οἱ τῶν 11
Ἀθηναίων ἐπιτετραμμένοι τὴν φυλακήν, ὡς
ἑώρων ἀποθνήσκοντας ἐν τῷ ἱερῷ, ἐφ᾽ ᾧ
μηδὲν κακὸν ποιήσουσιν, ἀπαγαγόντες ἀπέ-
5 κτειναν· καθεζομέιους δέ τινας καὶ ἐπὶ τῶν
σεμνῶν θεῶν τοῖς βωμοῖς ἐν τῇ παρόδῳ ἀπεχρήσαντο. καὶ ἀπὸ τούτου ἐναγεῖς καὶ ἀλιτήριοι
τῆς θεοῦ ἐκεῖνοί τε ἐκαλοῦντο καὶ τὸ γένος τὸ
ἀπ᾽ ἐκείνων. ἤλασαν μὲν οὖν καὶ οἱ Ἀθηναῖοι 12
10 τοὺς ἐναγεῖς τούτους, ἤλασε δὲ καὶ Κλεομένης
ὁ Λακεδαιμόνιος ὕστερον μετὰ Ἀθηναίων
στασιαζόντων, τούς τε ζῶντας ἐλαύνοντες καὶ
τῶν τεθνεώτων τὰ ὀστᾶ ἀνελόντες ἐξέβαλον·
κατῆλθον μέντοι ὕστερον, καὶ τὸ γένος αὐτῶν
15 ἔστιν ἔτι ἐν τῇ πόλει. τοῦτο δὴ τὸ ἄγος 127
οἱ Λακεδαιμόνιοι ἐκέλευον ἐλαύνειν The true object
δῆθεν τοῖς θεοῖς πρῶτον τιμωροῦντες, was to make
εἰδότες δὲ Περικλέα τὸν Ξανθίππου Pericles unpopular.
προσεχόμενον αὐτῷ κατὰ τὴν μητέρα καὶ
20 νομίζοντες ἐκπεσόντος αὐτοῦ ῥᾶον ⟨ἂν⟩ σφίσι
προχωρεῖν τὰ ἀπὸ τῶν Ἀθηναίων. οὐ μέντοι 2
τοσοῦτον ἤλπιζον παθεῖν ἂν αὐτὸν τοῦτο ὅσον
διαβολὴν οἴσειν αὐτῷ πρὸς τὴν πόλιν ὡς καὶ
διὰ τὴν ἐκείνου ξυμφορὰν τὸ μέρος ἔσται ὁ
25 πόλεμος. ὢν γὰρ δυνατώτατος τῶν καθ᾽ 3
ἑαυτὸν καὶ ἄγων τὴν πολιτείαν ἠναντιοῦτο πάντα τοῖς Λακεδαιμονίοις, καὶ οὐκ εἴα ὑπείκειν,
ἀλλ᾽ ἐς τὸν πόλεμον ὥρμα τοὺς Ἀθηναίους.

6. post θεῶν add. ἐν ABEF ‖ ἀπεχρήσαντο C: διεχρήσαντο
cett. : ἀνεχρήσαντο Lexx.   15. ἔτι ἔστιν C[G]   20. ἂν
add. Stahl

128 Ἀντεκέλευον δὲ καὶ οἱ Ἀθηναῖοι τοὺς

The Athenians retort by demanding the expulsion of two 'curses.' This demand gives occasion for an account of the treason and death of Pausanias.

Λακεδαιμονίους τὸ ἀπὸ Ταινάρου ἄγος ἐλαύνειν· οἱ γὰρ Λακεδαιμόνιοι ἀναστήσαντές ποτε ἐκ τοῦ ἱεροῦ τοῦ Ποσειδῶνος [ἀπὸ Ταινάρου] ι τῶν Εἱλώτων ἱκέτας ἀπαγαγόντες διέφθειραν, δι' ὃ δὴ καὶ σφίσιν αὐτοῖς νομίζουσι τὸν μέγαν σεισμὸν γενέσθαι 2 ἐν Σπάρτῃ. ἐκέλευον δὲ καὶ τὸ τῆς Χαλκιοίκου ἄγος ἐλαύνειν αὐτούς· ἐγένετο δὲ τοιόνδε. 10 3 ἐπειδὴ Παυσανίας ὁ Λακεδαιμόνιος τὸ πρῶτον μεταπεμφθεὶς ὑπὸ Σπαρτιατῶν ἀπὸ τῆς ἀρχῆς τῆς ἐν Ἑλλησπόντῳ καὶ κριθεὶς ὑπ' αὐτῶν ἀπελύθη μὴ ἀδικεῖν, δημοσίᾳ μὲν οὐκέτι ἐξεπέμφθη, ἰδίᾳ δὲ αὐτὸς τριήρη λαβὼν Ἑρμιονίδα 15 ἄνευ Λακεδαιμονίων ἀφικνεῖται ἐς Ἑλλήσποντον, τῷ μὲν λόγῳ ἐπὶ τὸν Ἑλληνικὸν πόλεμον, τῷ δὲ ἔργῳ τὰ πρὸς βασιλέα πράγματα πράσσειν, ὥσπερ καὶ τὸ πρῶτον ἐπεχείρησεν, 4 ἐφιέμενος τῆς Ἑλληνικῆς ἀρχῆς. εὐεργεσίαν 20 δὲ ἀπὸ τοῦδε πρῶτον ἐς βασιλέα κατέθετο καὶ τοῦ παντὸς πράγματος ἀρχὴν ἐποιήσατο· 5 Βυζάντιον γὰρ ἑλὼν τῇ προτέρᾳ παρουσίᾳ μετὰ τὴν ἐκ Κύπρου ἀναχώρησιν (εἶχον δὲ Μῆδοι αὐτὸ καὶ βασιλέως προσήκοντές τινες 25 καὶ ξυγγενεῖς οἳ ἑάλωσαν ἐν αὐτῷ) τότε τούτους οὓς ἔλαβεν ἀποπέμπει βασιλεῖ κρύφα

5. ἀπὸ Ταινάρου secl. Herwerden   17. Ἑλληνικὸν] Μηδικὸν Gebhardt   18. post ἔργῳ add. βουλόμενος CG   19. ἐνεχείρησεν ABEF

τῶν ἄλλων ξυμμάχων, τῷ δὲ λόγῳ ἀπέδρασαν
αὐτόν. ἔπρασσε δὲ ταῦτα μετὰ Γογγύλου τοῦ 6
Ἐρετριῶς, ᾧπερ ἐπέτρεψε τό τε Βυζάντιον καὶ
τοὺς αἰχμαλώτους. ἔπεμψε δὲ καὶ ἐπιστολὴν
5 τὸν Γόγγυλον φέροντα αὐτῷ· ἐνεγέγραπτο δὲ
τάδε ἐν αὐτῇ, ὡς ὕστερον ἀνηυρέθη· "Παυ- 7
σανίας ὁ ἡγεμὼν τῆς Σπάρτης τούσδε Pausanias writes
τέ σοι χαρίζεσθαι βουλόμενος ἀπο- to Xerxes.
πέμπει δορὶ ἑλών, καὶ γνώμην ποιοῦμαι, εἰ
10 καὶ σοὶ δοκεῖ, θυγατέρα τε τὴν σὴν γῆμαι
καί σοι Σπάρτην τε καὶ τὴν ἄλλην Ἑλλάδα
ὑποχείριον ποιῆσαι. δυνατὸς δὲ δοκῶ εἶναι
ταῦτα πρᾶξαι μετὰ σοῦ βουλευόμενος. εἰ οὖν
τί σε τούτων ἀρέσκει, πέμπε ἄνδρα πιστὸν
15 ἐπὶ θάλασσαν δι' οὗ τὸ λοιπὸν τοὺς λόγους
ποιησόμεθα." τοσαῦτα μὲν ἡ γραφὴ ἐδήλου, 129
Ξέρξης δὲ ἥσθη τε τῇ ἐπιστολῇ Xerxes accepted
καὶ ἀποστέλλει Ἀρτάβαζον τὸν his proposals.
Φαρνάκου ἐπὶ θάλασσαν καὶ κελεύει αὐτὸν
20 τήν τε Δασκυλῖτιν σατραπείαν παραλαβεῖν
Μεγαβάτην ἀπαλλάξαντα, ὃς πρότερον ἦρχε,
καὶ παρὰ Παυσανίαν ἐς Βυζάντιον ἐπιστολὴν
ἀντεπετίθει αὐτῷ ὡς τάχιστα διαπέμψαι καὶ
τὴν σφραγῖδα ἀποδεῖξαι, καὶ ἤν τι αὐτῷ
25 Παυσανίας παραγγέλλῃ περὶ τῶν ἑαυτοῦ
πραγμάτων, πράσσειν ὡς ἄριστα καὶ πιστό-
τατα. ὁ δὲ ἀφικόμενος τά τε ἄλλα ἐποίησεν 2
ὥσπερ εἴρητο καὶ τὴν ἐπιστολὴν διέπεμψεν·

3. ᾧπερ] ᾧ ABEF   10. τὴν om. CG   11. τε
om. CG

3 ἀντενεγέγραπτο δὲ τάδε· "ὧδε λέγει βασιλεὺς
Ξέρξης Παυσανίᾳ. καὶ τῶν ἀνδρῶν οὕς μοι
πέραν θαλάσσης ἐκ Βυζαντίου ἔσωσας κείσεταί
σοι εὐεργεσία ἐν τῷ ἡμετέρῳ οἴκῳ ἐς αἰεὶ
ἀνάγραπτος, καὶ τοῖς λόγοις τοῖς ἀπὸ σοῦ 5
ἀρέσκομαι. καί σε μήτε νὺξ μήθ᾽ ἡμέρα
ἐπισχέτω ὥστε ἀνεῖναι πράσσειν τι ὧν ἐμοὶ
ὑπισχνῇ, μηδὲ χρυσοῦ καὶ ἀργύρου δαπάνῃ
κεκωλύσθω μηδὲ στρατιᾶς πλήθει, εἴ ποι δεῖ
παραγίγνεσθαι, ἀλλὰ μετ᾽ Ἀρταβάζου ἀνδρὸς 10
ἀγαθοῦ, ὅν σοι ἔπεμψα, πρᾶσσε θαρσῶν καὶ
τὰ ἐμὰ καὶ τὰ σὰ ὅπῃ κάλλιστα καὶ ἄριστα
130 ἕξει ἀμφοτέροις." ταῦτα λαβὼν ὁ Παυσανίας

This greatly
encouraged
Pausanias in his
arrogance and
Persian ways,
and led to the
allies going over
to Athens.

τὰ γράμματα, ὧν καὶ πρότερον ἐν
μεγάλῳ ἀξιώματι ὑπὸ τῶν Ἑλλήνων 15
διὰ τὴν Πλαταιᾶσιν ἡγεμονίαν,
πολλῷ τότε μᾶλλον ἦρτο καὶ
οὐκέτι ἐδύνατο ἐν τῷ καθεστῶτι
τρόπῳ βιοτεύειν, ἀλλὰ σκευάς τε Μηδικὰς
ἐνδυόμενος ἐκ τοῦ Βυζαντίου ἐξῄει καὶ διὰ τῆς 20
Θρᾴκης πορευόμενον αὐτὸν Μῆδοι καὶ Αἰγύπτιοι
ἐδορυφόρουν, τράπεζάν τε Περσικὴν παρετίθετο
καὶ κατέχειν τὴν διάνοιαν οὐκ ἐδύνατο, ἀλλ᾽
ἔργοις βραχέσι προυδήλου ἃ τῇ γνώμῃ μειζόνως
2 ἐς ἔπειτα ἔμελλε πράξειν. δυσπρόσοδόν τε 25
αὐτὸν παρεῖχε καὶ τῇ ὀργῇ οὕτω χαλεπῇ
ἐχρῆτο ἐς πάντας ὁμοίως ὥστε μηδένα δύνασθαι

1. ἀντενεγέγραπτο Herwerden : ἀντεπεγέγραπτο CG : ἀντε-
γέγραπτο cett. 3. κεῖται AB 14. πρότερον] πρῶτον CG
18. καθεστηκότι ABEF

προσιέναι· δι' ὅπερ καὶ πρὸς τοὺς Ἀθηναίους
οὐχ ἥκιστα ἡ ξυμμαχία μετέστη.

Οἱ δὲ Λακεδαιμόνιοι αἰσθόμενοι τό τε **131**
πρῶτον δι' αὐτὰ ταῦτα ἀνεκάλεσαν   Pausanias
                                     recalled. He
5 αὐτόν, καὶ ἐπειδὴ τῇ Ἑρμιονίδι   went out again,
                                     but was sent for
νηὶ τὸ δεύτερον ἐκπλεύσας οὐ κελευ- and arrested.
σάντων αὐτῶν τοιαῦτα ἐφαίνετο ποιῶν, καὶ ἐκ
τοῦ Βυζαντίου βίᾳ ὑπ' Ἀθηναίων ἐκπολιορκη-
θεὶς ἐς μὲν τὴν Σπάρτην οὐκ ἐπανεχώρει, ἐς
10 δὲ Κολωνὰς τὰς Τρῳάδας ἱδρυθεὶς πράσσων
τε ἐσηγγέλλετο αὐτοῖς ἐς τοὺς βαρβάρους καὶ
οὐκ ἐπ' ἀγαθῷ τὴν μονὴν ποιούμενος, οὕτω δὴ
οὐκέτι ἐπέσχον, ἀλλὰ πέμψαντες κήρυκα οἱ
ἔφοροι καὶ σκυτάλην εἶπον τοῦ κήρυκος μὴ
15 λείπεσθαι, εἰ δὲ μή, πόλεμον αὐτῷ Σπαρτιάτας
προαγορεύειν. ὁ δὲ βουλόμενος ὡς ἥκιστα 2
ὕποπτος εἶναι καὶ πιστεύων χρήμασι διαλύσειν
τὴν διαβολὴν ἀνεχώρει τὸ δεύτερον ἐς Σπάρτην.
καὶ ἐς μὲν τὴν εἱρκτὴν ἐσπίπτει τὸ πρῶτον
20 ὑπὸ τῶν ἐφόρων (ἔξεστι δὲ τοῖς ἐφόροις τὸν
βασιλέα δρᾶσαι τοῦτο), ἔπειτα διαπραξάμενος
ὕστερον ἐξῆλθε καὶ καθίστησιν ἑαυτὸν ἐς
κρίσιν τοῖς βουλομένοις περὶ αὐτῶν ἐλέγχειν.
καὶ φανερὸν μὲν εἶχον οὐδὲν οἱ   **132**
25 Σπαρτιᾶται σημεῖον, οὔτε οἱ ἐχθροὶ   The evidence
                                        against him was
οὔτε ἡ πᾶσα πόλις, ὅτῳ ἂν πιστεύ-   not thought
                                        conclusive until
σαντες βεβαίως ἐτιμωροῦντο ἄνδρα   a messenger
                                        entrusted with
γένους τε τοῦ βασιλείου ὄντα καὶ   a letter to the
                                        Persian king
ἐν τῷ παρόντι τιμὴν ἔχοντα (Πλεί-   informed the
                                        ephors.

11. ἐς] πρὸς ABEF   23. αὐτῶν C Schol. : αὐτὸν cett. [G]

σταρχον γὰρ τὸν Λεωνίδου ὄντα βασιλέα καὶ
2 νέον ἔτι ἀνεψιὸς ὢν ἐπετρόπευεν), ὑποψίας δὲ
πολλὰς παρεῖχε τῇ τε παρανομίᾳ καὶ ζηλώσει
τῶν βαρβάρων μὴ ἴσος βούλεσθαι εἶναι τοῖς
παροῦσι, τά τε ἄλλα αὐτοῦ ἀνεσκόπουν, εἴ τί 5
που ἐξεδεδιῄτητο τῶν καθεστώτων νομίμων,
καὶ ὅτι ἐπὶ τὸν τρίποδά ποτε τὸν ἐν Δελφοῖς,
ὃν ἀνέθεσαν οἱ Ἕλληνες ἀπὸ τῶν Μήδων
ἀκροθίνιον, ἠξίωσεν ἐπιγράψασθαι αὐτὸς ἰδίᾳ
τὸ ἐλεγεῖον τόδε·   10

　　Ἑλλήνων ἀρχηγὸς ἐπεὶ στρατὸν ὤλεσε Μήδων
　　Παυσανίας Φοίβῳ μνῆμ᾿ ἀνέθηκε τόδε.

3 τὸ μὲν οὖν ἐλεγεῖον οἱ Λακεδαιμόνιοι ἐξεκό-
λαψαν εὐθὺς τότε ἀπὸ τοῦ τρίποδος τοῦτο
καὶ ἐπέγραψαν ὀνομαστὶ τὰς πόλεις ὅσαι 15
ξυγκαθελοῦσαι τὸν βάρβαρον ἔστησαν τὸ ἀνά-
θημα· τοῦ μέντοι Παυσανίου ἀδίκημα καὶ τότ᾿
ἐδόκει εἶναι, καὶ ἐπεί γε δὴ ἐν τούτῳ καθειστήκει, πολλῷ μᾶλλον παρόμοιον πραχθῆναι
4 ἐφαίνετο τῇ παρούσῃ διανοίᾳ. ἐπυνθάνοντο δὲ 20
καὶ ἐς τοὺς Εἵλωτας πράσσειν τι αὐτόν, καὶ
ἦν δὲ οὕτως· ἐλευθέρωσίν τε γὰρ ὑπισχνεῖτο
αὐτοῖς καὶ πολιτείαν, ἢν ξυνεπαναστῶσι καὶ
5 τὸ πᾶν ξυγκατεργάσωνται. ἀλλ᾿ οὐδ᾿ ὡς
οὐδὲ τῶν Εἱλώτων μηνυταῖς τισι πιστεύσαντες 25
ἠξίωσαν νεώτερόν τι ποιεῖν ἐς αὐτόν, χρώμενοι
τῷ τρόπῳ ᾧπερ εἰώθασιν ἐς σφᾶς αὐτούς, μὴ
ταχεῖς εἶναι περὶ ἀνδρὸς Σπαρτιάτου ἄνευ

17. τότ᾿ Struve: τοῦτ᾿ codd.　　18. ἐπεί γε δὴ C: ἐπειδὴ cett.

ἀναμφισβητήτων τεκμηρίων βουλεῦσαί τι ἀνή-
κεστον, πρίν γε δὴ αὐτοῖς, ὡς λέγεται, ὁ
μέλλων τὰς τελευταίας βασιλεῖ ἐπιστολὰς πρὸς
Ἀρτάβαζον κομιεῖν, ἀνὴρ Ἀργίλιος, παιδικά
5 ποτε ὢν αὐτοῦ καὶ πιστότατος ἐκείνῳ, μηνυτὴς
γίγνεται, δείσας κατὰ ἐνθύμησίν τινα ὅτι οὐδείς
πω τῶν πρὸ ἑαυτοῦ ἀγγέλων πάλιν ἀφίκετο,
καὶ παρασημηνάμενος σφραγῖδα, ἵνα, ἢν ψευσθῇ
τῆς δόξης ἢ καὶ ἐκεῖνός τι μεταγράψαι αἰτήσῃ,
10 μὴ ἐπιγνῷ, λύει τὰς ἐπιστολάς, ἐν αἷς ὑπο-
νοήσας τι τοιοῦτον προσεπεστάλθαι καὶ αὐτὸν
ηὗρεν ἐγγεγραμμένον κτείνειν.   τότε δὴ οἱ ἔφοροι **133**
δείξαντος αὐτοῦ τὰ γράμματα μᾶλλον   The ephors
μὲν ἐπίστευσαν, αὐτήκοοι δὲ βουλη-   contrived to
                                      overhear a
15 θέντες ἔτι γενέσθαι αὐτοῦ Παυσανίου   treasonable
τι λέγοντος, ἀπὸ παρασκευῆς τοῦ   conversation
                                      between
ἀνθρώπου ἐπὶ Ταίναρον ἱκέτου οἰχο-   Pausanias and
                                      the messenger.
μένου καὶ σκηνησαμένου διπλῆν διαφράγματι
καλύβην, ἐς ἣν τῶν [τε] ἐφόρων ἐντός τινας
20 ἔκρυψε, καὶ Παυσανίου ὡς αὐτὸν ἐλθόντος
καὶ ἐρωτῶντος τὴν πρόφασιν τῆς ἱκετείας
ᾔσθοντο πάντα σαφῶς, αἰτιωμένου τοῦ ἀνθρώπου τά τε περὶ αὐτοῦ γραφέντα καὶ τἄλλ'
ἀποφαίνοντος καθ' ἕκαστον, ὡς οὐδὲν πώποτε
25 αὐτὸν ἐν ταῖς πρὸς βασιλέα διακονίαις παραβάλοιτο, προτιμηθείη δ' ἐν ἴσῳ τοῖς πολλοῖς
τῶν διακόνων ἀποθανεῖν, κἀκείνου αὐτά τε

---

8. παρασημηνάμενος Pollux : παραποιησάμενος codd.   11.
αὐτὸν Stephanus : αὐτὸν codd.   12. δὲ AEF   19. τε
secl. Poppo   27. τε om. ABEF

I   F 2

ταῦτα ξυνομολογοῦντος καὶ περὶ τοῦ παρόντος
οὐκ ἐῶντος ὀργίζεσθαι, ἀλλὰ πίστιν ἐκ τοῦ
ἱεροῦ διδόντος τῆς ἀναστάσεως καὶ ἀξιοῦντος
ὡς τάχιστα πορεύεσθαι καὶ μὴ τὰ πρασσόμενα
134 διακωλύειν. ἀκούσαντες δὲ ἀκριβῶς τότε μὲν 5

Pausanias took
refuge in sacred
place, and was
starved to
death.

ἀπῆλθον οἱ ἔφοροι, βεβαίως δὲ ἤδη
εἰδότες ἐν τῇ πόλει τὴν ξύλληψιν
ἐποιοῦντο. λέγεται δ᾽ αὐτὸν μέλλοντα
ξυλληφθήσεσθαι ἐν τῇ ὁδῷ, ἑνὸς μὲν τῶν
ἐφόρων τὸ πρόσωπον προσιόντος ὡς εἶδε, γνῶναι 10
ἐφ᾽ ᾧ ἐχώρει, ἄλλου δὲ νεύματι ἀφανεῖ χρη-
σαμένου καὶ δηλώσαντος εὐνοίᾳ πρὸς τὸ ἱερὸν
τῆς Χαλκιοίκου χωρῆσαι δρόμῳ καὶ προκατα-
φυγεῖν· ἦν δ᾽ ἐγγὺς τὸ τέμενος. καὶ ἐς οἴκημα
οὐ μέγα ὃ ἦν τοῦ ἱεροῦ ἐσελθών, ἵνα μὴ 15
2 ὑπαίθριος ταλαιπωροίη, ἡσύχαζεν. οἱ δὲ τὸ
παραυτίκα μὲν ὑστέρησαν τῇ διώξει, μετὰ δὲ
τοῦτο τοῦ τε οἰκήματος τὸν ὄροφον ἀφεῖλον
καὶ τὰς θύρας ἔνδον ὄντα τηρήσαντες αὐτὸν
καὶ ἀπολαβόντες εἴσω ἀπῳκοδόμησαν, προσ- 20
3 καθεζόμενοί τε ἐξεπολιόρκησαν λιμῷ. καὶ
μέλλοντος αὐτοῦ ἀποψύχειν ὥσπερ εἶχεν ἐν
τῷ οἰκήματι, αἰσθόμενοι ἐξάγουσιν ἐκ τοῦ
ἱεροῦ ἔτι ἔμπνουν ὄντα, καὶ ἐξαχθεὶς ἀπέθανε
4 παραχρῆμα. καὶ αὐτὸν ἐμέλλησαν μὲν ἐς τὸν 25
Καιάδαν, [οὗπερ τοὺς κακούργους,] ἐσβάλλειν·
ἔπειτα ἔδοξε πλησίον που κατορύξαι. ὁ δὲ

4. τὰ om. CG   23. post αἰσθόμενοι add. τε ABEF
26. [οὗπερ τοὺς κακούργους] ut videtur, non legit Schol., seclusi ∥
εἰώθασιν (C) vel εἰώθεσαν (-εισαν) vel ante vel post ἐσβάλλειν
add. CFG suprascr. AB: ἐμβάλλειν ABF: ἐμβαλεῖν E

θεὸς ὁ ἐν Δελφοῖς τόν τε τάφον ὕστερον
ἔχρησε τοῖς Λακεδαιμονίοις μετενεγκεῖν οὗπερ
ἀπέθανε (καὶ νῦν κεῖται ἐν τῷ προτεμενίσματι,
ὃ γραφῇ στῆλαι δηλοῦσι) καὶ ὡς ἄγος αὐτοῖς
5 ὃν τὸ πεπραγμένον δύο σώματα ἀνθ᾽ ἑνὸς τῇ
Χαλκιοίκῳ ἀποδοῦναι.   οἱ δὲ ποιησάμενοι
χαλκοῦς ἀνδριάντας δύο ὡς ἀντὶ Παυσανίου
ἀνέθεσαν. οἱ δὲ Ἀθηναῖοι, ὡς καὶ τοῦ θεοῦ 135
ἄγος κρίναντος, ἀντεπέταξαν τοῖς It was
10 Λακεδαιμονίοις ἐλαύνειν αὐτό.

Τοῦ δὲ μηδισμοῦ τοῦ Παυσανίου οἱ   2
Λακεδαιμόνιοι πρέσβεις πέμψαντες
παρὰ τοὺς Ἀθηναίους ξυνεπῃτιῶντο καὶ τὸν
Θεμιστοκλέα, ὡς ηὕρισκον ἐκ τῶν περὶ Παυ-
15 σανίαν ἐλέγχων, ἠξίουν τε τοῖς αὐτοῖς κολάζε-
σθαι αὐτόν.   οἱ δὲ πεισθέντες (ἔτυχε γὰρ 3
ὠστρακισμένος καὶ ἔχων δίαιταν μὲν ἐν Ἄργει,
ἐπιφοιτῶν δὲ καὶ ἐς τὴν ἄλλην Πελοπόννησον)
πέμπουσι μετὰ τῶν Λακεδαιμονίων ἑτοίμων
20 ὄντων ξυνδιώκειν ἄνδρας οἷς εἴρητο ἄγειν ὅπου
ἂν περιτύχωσιν. ὁ δὲ Θεμιστοκλῆς προαισθό- 136
μενος φεύγει ἐκ Πελοποννήσου ἐς He now fled to
Κέρκυραν, ὢν αὐτῶν εὐεργέτης. δε- Corcyra, and
διέναι δὲ φασκόντων Κερκυραίων
25 ἔχειν αὐτὸν ὥστε Λακεδαιμονίοις καὶ Ἀθηναίοις
ἀπεχθέσθαι, διακομίζεται ὑπ᾽ αὐτῶν ἐς τὴν
ἤπειρον τὴν καταντικρύ. καὶ διωκόμενος ὑπὸ 2
τῶν προστεταγμένων κατὰ πύστιν ᾗ χωροίη,

It was
found that
Themistocles
was involved.
He had been
ostracised.

He now fled to
Corcyra, and
thence to
Admetus, king
of the Molossi.

11. οἱ om. ABEF   14. περὶ Παυσανίαν] Παυσανίου C
26. ἀπεχθέσθαι fort. legit Schol. : ἀπέχθεσθαι codd.

ἀναγκάζεται κατά τι ἄπορον παρὰ Ἄδμητον
τὸν Μολοσσῶν βασιλέα ὄντα αὐτῷ οὐ φίλον
3 καταλῦσαι. καὶ ὁ μὲν οὐκ ἔτυχεν ἐπιδημῶν,
ὁ δὲ τῆς γυναικὸς ἱκέτης γενόμενος διδάσκεται
ὑπ᾽ αὐτῆς τὸν παῖδα σφῶν λαβὼν καθέζεσθαι 5
4 ἐπὶ τὴν ἑστίαν. καὶ ἐλθόντος οὐ πολὺ ὕστερον
τοῦ Ἀδμήτου δηλοῖ τε ὅς ἐστι καὶ οὐκ ἀξιοῖ,
εἴ τι ἄρα αὐτὸς ἀντεῖπεν αὐτῷ Ἀθηναίων
δεομένῳ, φεύγοντα τιμωρεῖσθαι· καὶ γὰρ ἂν
ὑπ᾽ ἐκείνου πολλῷ ἀσθενεστέρου ἐν τῷ παρόντι 10
κακῶς πάσχειν, γενναῖον δὲ εἶναι τοὺς ὁμοίους
ἀπὸ τοῦ ἴσου τιμωρεῖσθαι. καὶ ἅμα αὐτὸς
μὲν ἐκείνῳ χρείας τινὸς καὶ οὐκ ἐς τὸ σῶμα
σῴζεσθαι ἐναντιωθῆναι, ἐκεῖνον δ᾽ ἄν, εἰ ἐκδοίη
αὐτόν (εἰπὼν ὑφ᾽ ὧν καὶ ἐφ᾽ ᾧ διώκεται), 15
137 σωτηρίας ἂν τῆς ψυχῆς ἀποστερῆσαι. ὁ δὲ
ἀκούσας ἀνίστησί τε αὐτὸν μετὰ τοῦ ἑαυτοῦ
From him he   υἱέος, ὥσπερ καὶ ἔχων αὐτὸν ἐκαθέ-
got means to
escape to Asia.   ζετο, καὶ μέγιστον ἦν ἱκέτευμα
τοῦτο, καὶ ὕστερον οὐ πολλῷ τοῖς τε Λακε- 20
δαιμονίοις καὶ Ἀθηναίοις ἐλθοῦσι καὶ πολλὰ
εἰποῦσιν οὐκ ἐκδίδωσιν, ἀλλ᾽ ἀποστέλλει βουλόμενον ὡς βασιλέα πορευθῆναι ἐπὶ τὴν ἑτέραν
θάλασσαν πεζῇ ἐς Πύδναν τὴν Ἀλεξάνδρου.
2 ἐν ᾗ ὁλκάδος τυχὼν ἀναγομένης ἐπ᾽ Ἰωνίας 25
καὶ ἐπιβὰς καταφέρεται χειμῶνι ἐς τὸ Ἀθηναίων
στρατόπεδον, ὃ ἐπολιόρκει Νάξον. καί (ἦν

5. καθέζεσθαι recc.: καθίζεσθαι codd. 10. ἀσθενέστερος
recc.: se . . multo imbecilliorem ab illo laedi Valla   13.
post καὶ add Θεμιστοκλῆς ABF: ὁ Θεμιστοκλῆς E   20. τε
C: om. cett.

γὰρ ἀγνὼς τοῖς ἐν τῇ νηί) δείσας φράζει τῷ
ναυκλήρῳ ὅστις ἐστὶ καὶ δι᾽ ἃ φεύγει, καὶ εἰ
μὴ σώσει αὐτόν, ἔφη ἐρεῖν ὅτι χρήμασι πεισθεὶς
αὐτὸν ἄγει· τὴν δὲ ἀσφάλειαν εἶναι μηδένα
5 ἐκβῆναι ἐκ τῆς νεὼς μέχρι πλοῦς γένηται·
πειθομένῳ δ᾽ αὐτῷ χάριν ἀπομνήσεσθαι ἀξίαν.
ὁ δὲ ναύκληρος ποιεῖ τε ταῦτα καὶ ἀποσαλεύσας
ἡμέραν καὶ νύκτα ὑπὲρ τοῦ στρατοπέδου ὕστερον ἀφικνεῖται ἐς Ἔφεσον. καὶ ὁ Θεμιστοκλῆς 3
10 ἐκεῖνόν τε ἐθεράπευσε χρημάτων δόσει (ἦλθε
γὰρ αὐτῷ ὕστερον ἔκ τε Ἀθηνῶν παρὰ τῶν
φίλων καὶ ἐξ Ἄργους ἃ ὑπεξέκειτο) καὶ μετὰ
τῶν κάτω Περσῶν τινος πορευθεὶς ἄνω ἐσπέμπει
γράμματα πρὸς βασιλέα Ἀρταξέρξην τὸν Ξέρξου
15 νεωστὶ βασιλεύοντα. ἐδήλου δὲ ἡ γραφὴ ὅτι 4
" Θεμιστοκλῆς ἥκω παρὰ σέ, ὃς κακὰ μὲν
πλεῖστα Ἑλλήνων εἴργασμαι τὸν ὑμέτερον
οἶκον, ὅσον χρόνον τὸν σὸν πατέρα ἐπιόντα
ἐμοὶ ἀνάγκῃ ἠμυνόμην, πολὺ δ᾽ ἔτι πλείω
20 ἀγαθά, ἐπειδὴ ἐν τῷ ἀσφαλεῖ μὲν ἐμοί, ἐκείνῳ
δὲ ἐν ἐπικινδύνῳ πάλιν ἡ ἀποκομιδὴ ἐγίγνετο.
καί μοι εὐεργεσία ὀφείλεται (γράψας τήν τε
ἐκ Σαλαμῖνος προάγγελσιν τῆς ἀναχωρήσεως
καὶ τὴν τῶν γεφυρῶν, ἣν ψευδῶς προσεποιή-
25 σατο, τότε δι᾽ αὐτὸν οὐ διάλυσιν), καὶ νῦν
ἔχων σε μεγάλα ἀγαθὰ δρᾶσαι πάρειμι διωκόμενος ὑπὸ τῶν Ἑλλήνων διὰ τὴν σὴν φιλίαν.

6. ἀπομνησθήσεσθαι L. Dindorf ‖ post ἀπομνήσεσθαι add.
καὶ C, κατ᾽ Hude   14. πρὸς] εἰς ABEF   22. τε om.
ABEF

βούλομαι δ' ἐνιαυτὸν ἐπισχὼν αὐτός σοι περὶ
138 ὧν ἥκω δηλῶσαι." βασιλεὺς δέ, ὡς λέγεται,
ἐθαύμασέ τε αὐτοῦ τὴν διάνοιαν καὶ ἐκέλευε

He was liberally
treated by the
great king, and
died in exile.
ποιεῖν οὕτω. ὁ δ' ἐν τῷ χρόνῳ ὃν
ἐπέσχε τῆς τε Περσίδος γλώσσης 5
ὅσα ἐδύνατο κατενόησε καὶ τῶν
2 ἐπιτηδευμάτων τῆς χώρας· ἀφικόμενος δὲ μετὰ
τὸν ἐνιαυτὸν γίγνεται παρ' αὐτῷ μέγας καὶ
ὅσος οὐδείς πω Ἑλλήνων διά τε τὴν προϋπ-
άρχουσαν ἀξίωσιν καὶ τοῦ Ἑλληνικοῦ ἐλπίδα, 10
ἣν ὑπετίθει αὐτῷ δουλώσειν, μάλιστα δὲ ἀπὸ
τοῦ πεῖραν διδοὺς ξυνετὸς φαίνεσθαι.

3 Ἦν γὰρ ὁ Θεμιστοκλῆς βεβαιότατα δὴ

Character of
Themistocles.
φύσεως ἰσχὺν δηλώσας καὶ διαφερόντως τι ἐς αὐτὸ μᾶλλον ἑτέρου 15
ἄξιος θαυμάσαι· οἰκείᾳ γὰρ ξυνέσει καὶ οὔτε
προμαθὼν ἐς αὐτὴν οὐδὲν οὔτ' ἐπιμαθών, τῶν
τε παραχρῆμα δι' ἐλαχίστης βουλῆς κράτιστος
γνώμων καὶ τῶν μελλόντων ἐπὶ πλεῖστον τοῦ
γενησομένου ἄριστος εἰκαστής· καὶ ἃ μὲν μετὰ 20
χεῖρας ἔχοι, καὶ ἐξηγήσασθαι οἷός τε, ὧν δ'
ἄπειρος εἴη, κρῖναι ἱκανῶς οὐκ ἀπήλλακτο·
τό τε ἄμεινον ἢ χεῖρον ἐν τῷ ἀφανεῖ ἔτι
προεώρα μάλιστα. καὶ τὸ ξύμπαν εἰπεῖν
φύσεως μὲν δυνάμει, μελέτης δὲ βραχύτητι 25
κράτιστος δὴ οὗτος αὐτοσχεδιάζειν τὰ δέοντα
4 ἐγένετο. νοσήσας δὲ τελευτᾷ τὸν βίον· λέγουσι
δέ τινες καὶ ἑκούσιον φαρμάκῳ ἀποθανεῖν αὐτόν,
ἀδύνατον νομίσαντα εἶναι ἐπιτελέσαι βασιλεῖ

5. τε C : om. cett. [G]   9. τε om. C[G]

ἃ ὑπέσχετο. μνημεῖον μὲν οὖν αὐτοῦ ἐν 5
Μαγνησίᾳ ἐστὶ τῇ Ἀσιανῇ ἐν τῇ ἀγορᾷ·
ταύτης γὰρ ἦρχε τῆς χώρας, δόντος βασιλέως
αὐτῷ Μαγνησίαν μὲν ἄρτον, ἣ προσέφερε
5 πεντήκοντα τάλαντα τοῦ ἐνιαυτοῦ, Λάμψακον
δὲ οἶνον (ἐδόκει γὰρ πολυοινότατον τῶν τότε
εἶναι), Μυοῦντα δὲ ὄψον. τὰ δὲ ὀστᾶ φασι
κομισθῆναι αὐτοῦ οἱ προσήκοντες οἴκαδε κελεύ-
σαντος ἐκείνου καὶ τεθῆναι κρύφα Ἀθηναίων
10 ἐν τῇ Ἀττικῇ· οὐ γὰρ ἐξῆν θάπτειν ὡς ἐπὶ
προδοσίᾳ φεύγοντος. τὰ μὲν κατὰ Παυσανίαν 6
τὸν Λακεδαιμόνιον καὶ Θεμιστοκλέα τὸν Ἀθηναῖον,
λαμπροτάτους γενομένους τῶν καθ' ἑαυτοὺς
Ἑλλήνων, οὕτως ἐτελεύτησεν.

15   Λακεδαιμόνιοι δὲ ἐπὶ μὲν τῆς πρώτης 139
πρεσβείας τοιαῦτα ἐπέταξάν τε καὶ   Resumption of
                                     the history.
ἀντεκελεύσθησαν περὶ τῶν ἐναγῶν τῆς   Spartan
                                      ultimatum to
ἐλάσεως· ὕστερον δὲ φοιτῶντες παρ'   Athens.
Ἀθηναίους Ποτειδαίας τε ἀπανίστασθαι ἐκέλευον
20 καὶ Αἴγιναν αὐτόνομον ἀφιέναι, καὶ μάλιστά
γε πάντων καὶ ἐνδηλότατα προύλεγον τὸ περὶ
Μεγαρέων ψήφισμα καθελοῦσι μὴ ἂν γίγνεσθαι
πόλεμον, ἐν ᾧ εἴρητο αὐτοὺς μὴ χρῆσθαι τοῖς
λιμέσι τοῖς ἐν τῇ Ἀθηναίων ἀρχῇ μηδὲ τῇ
25 Ἀττικῇ ἀγορᾷ. οἱ δὲ Ἀθηναῖοι οὔτε τἆλλα 2
ὑπήκουον οὔτε τὸ ψήφισμα καθῄρουν, ἐπικα-
λοῦντες ἐπεργασίαν Μεγαρεῦσι τῆς γῆς τῆς ἱερᾶς
καὶ τῆς ἀορίστου καὶ ἀνδραπόδων ὑποδοχὴν τῶν
ἀφισταμένων. τέλος δὲ ἀφικομένων τῶν τελευ- 3

ταίων πρέσβεων ἐκ Λακεδαίμονος, 'Ραμφίου
τε καὶ Μελησίππου καὶ 'Αγησάνδρου, καὶ
λεγόντων ἄλλο μὲν οὐδὲν ὧν πρότερον εἰώθεσαν,
αὐτὰ δὲ τάδε ὅτι " Λακεδαιμόνιοι βούλονται τὴν
εἰρήνην εἶναι, εἴη δ' ἂν εἰ τοὺς "Ελληνας 5
αὐτονόμους ἀφεῖτε," ποιήσαντες ἐκκλησίαν οἱ
'Αθηναῖοι γνώμας σφίσιν αὐτοῖς προυτίθεσαν,
καὶ ἐδόκει ἅπαξ περὶ ἁπάντων βουλευσαμένους
4 ἀποκρίνασθαι. καὶ παριόντες ἄλλοι τε πολλοὶ
ἔλεγον ἐπ' ἀμφότερα γιγνόμενοι ταῖς γνώμαις 10
καὶ ὡς χρὴ πολεμεῖν καὶ ὡς μὴ ἐμπόδιον
εἶναι τὸ ψήφισμα εἰρήνης, ἀλλὰ καθελεῖν, καὶ
παρελθὼν Περικλῆς ὁ Ξανθίππου, ἀνὴρ κατ'
ἐκεῖνον τὸν χρόνον πρῶτος 'Αθηναίων, λέγειν
τε καὶ πράσσειν δυνατώτατος, παρῄνει τοιάδε. 15

140   " Τῆς μὲν γνώμης, ὦ 'Αθηναῖοι, αἰεὶ τῆς

Pericles spoke   αὐτῆς ἔχομαι, μὴ εἴκειν Πελοπον-
against
compliance.   νησίοις, καίπερ εἰδὼς τοὺς ἀνθρώπους
Exordium.
                 οὐ τῇ αὐτῇ ὀργῇ ἀναπειθομένους
τε πολεμεῖν καὶ ἐν τῷ ἔργῳ πράσσοντας, πρὸς 20
δὲ τὰς ξυμφορὰς καὶ τὰς γνώμας τρεπομένους.
ὁρῶ δὲ καὶ νῦν ὅμοια καὶ παραπλήσια ξυμβου-
λευτέα μοι ὄντα, καὶ τοὺς ἀναπειθομένους ὑμῶν
δικαιῶ τοῖς κοινῇ δόξασιν, ἢν ἄρα τι καὶ
σφαλλώμεθα, βοηθεῖν, ἢ μηδὲ κατορθοῦντας 25
τῆς ξυνέσεως μεταποιεῖσθαι. ἐνδέχεται γὰρ
τὰς ξυμφορὰς τῶν πραγμάτων οὐχ ἧσσον
ἀμαθῶς χωρῆσαι ἢ καὶ τὰς διανοίας τοῦ
ἀνθρώπου· δι' ὅπερ καὶ τὴν τύχην, ὅσα ἂν
παρὰ λόγον ξυμβῇ, εἰώθαμεν αἰτιᾶσθαι. 30

" Λακεδαιμόνιοι δὲ πρότερόν τε δῆλοι ἦσαν 2
ἐπιβουλεύοντες ἡμῖν καὶ νῦν οὐχ   They refuse arbitration.
ἥκιστα. εἰρημένον γὰρ δίκας μὲν   ' If we comply, they will only
τῶν διαφορῶν ἀλλήλοις διδόναι καὶ   press us farther.
5 δέχεσθαι, ἔχειν δὲ ἑκατέρους ἃ ἔχομεν, οὔτε
αὐτοὶ δίκας πω ᾔτησαν οὔτε ἡμῶν διδόντων
δέχονται, βούλονται δὲ πολέμῳ μᾶλλον ἢ λόγοις
τὰ ἐγκλήματα διαλύεσθαι, καὶ ἐπιτάσσοντες
ἤδη καὶ οὐκέτι αἰτιώμενοι πάρεισιν. Ποτει- 3
10 δαίας τε γὰρ ἀπανίστασθαι κελεύουσι καὶ
Αἴγιναν αὐτόνομον ἀφιέναι καὶ τὸ Μεγαρέων
ψήφισμα καθαιρεῖν· οἱ δὲ τελευταῖοι οἵδε
ἥκοντες καὶ τοὺς Ἕλληνας προαγορεύουσιν
αὐτονόμους ἀφιέναι. ὑμῶν δὲ μηδεὶς νομίσῃ 4
15 περὶ βραχέος ἂν πολεμεῖν, εἰ τὸ Μεγαρέων
ψήφισμα μὴ καθέλοιμεν, ὅπερ μάλιστα προύχονται, εἰ καθαιρεθείη, μὴ ἂν γίγνεσθαι τὸν
πόλεμον, μηδὲ ἐν ὑμῖν αὐτοῖς αἰτίαν ὑπολίπησθε
ὡς διὰ μικρὸν ἐπολεμήσατε. τὸ γὰρ βραχύ 5
20 τι τοῦτο πᾶσαν ὑμῶν ἔχει τὴν βεβαίωσιν καὶ
πεῖραν τῆς γνώμης. οἷς εἰ ξυγχωρήσετε, καὶ
ἄλλο τι μεῖζον εὐθὺς ἐπιταχθήσεσθε ὡς φόβῳ
καὶ τοῦτο ὑπακούσαντες· ἀπισχυρισάμενοι δὲ
σαφὲς ἂν καταστήσαιτε αὐτοῖς ἀπὸ τοῦ ἴσου
25 ὑμῖν μᾶλλον προσφέρεσθαι. αὐτόθεν δὴ δια- 141
νοήθητε ἢ ὑπακούειν πρίν τι βλαβῆναι, ἢ εἰ
πολεμήσομεν, ὥσπερ ἔμοιγε ἄμεινον δοκεῖ εἶναι,
καὶ ἐπὶ μεγάλῃ καὶ ἐπὶ βραχείᾳ ὁμοίως

24. καταστήσετε ΑΕF : καταστήσηται C (corr. c) [G]   27.
ὥσπερ] ὡς ΑΒΕF

126 ΘΟΥΚΥΔΙΔΟΥ

προφάσει μὴ εἴξοντες μηδὲ ξὺν φόβῳ ἔξοντες
ἃ κεκτήμεθα· τὴν γὰρ αὐτὴν δύναται δούλωσιν
ἥ τε μεγίστη καὶ ἐλαχίστη δικαίωσις ἀπὸ τῶν
ὁμοίων πρὸ δίκης τοῖς πέλας ἐπιτασσομένη.

2 "Τὰ δὲ τοῦ πολέμου καὶ τῶν ἑκατέροις 5
'The disadvan- ὑπαρχόντων ὡς οὐκ ἀσθενέστερα
tages of the
Peloponnesians ἕξομεν γνῶτε καθ᾽ ἕκαστον ἀκούοντες.
for fighting us
3 are many. αὐτουργοί τε γάρ εἰσι Πελοποννήσιοι
καὶ οὔτε ἰδίᾳ οὔτ᾽ ἐν κοινῷ χρήματά ἐστιν
αὐτοῖς, ἔπειτα χρονίων πολέμων καὶ διαποντίων 10
ἄπειροι διὰ τὸ βραχέως αὐτοὶ ἐπ᾽ ἀλλήλους
4 ὑπὸ πενίας ἐπιφέρειν. καὶ οἱ τοιοῦτοι οὔτε
ναῦς πληροῦντες οὔτε πεζὰς στρατιὰς πολλάκις
ἐκπέμπειν δύνανται, ἀπὸ τῶν ἰδίων τε ἅμα
ἀπόντες καὶ ἀπὸ τῶν αὐτῶν δαπανῶντες καὶ 15
5 προσέτι καὶ θαλάσσης εἰργόμενοι· αἱ δὲ
περιουσίαι τοὺς πολέμους μᾶλλον ἢ αἱ βίαιοι
ἐσφοραὶ ἀνέχουσιν. σώμασί τε ἑτοιμότεροι οἱ
αὐτουργοὶ τῶν ἀνθρώπων ἢ χρήμασι πολεμεῖν,
τὸ μὲν πιστὸν ἔχοντες ἐκ τῶν κινδύνων κἂν 20
περιγενέσθαι, τὸ δὲ οὐ βέβαιον μὴ οὐ προανα-
λώσειν, ἄλλως τε κἂν παρὰ δόξαν, ὅπερ εἰκός,
6 ὁ πόλεμος αὐτοῖς μηκύνηται. μάχῃ μὲν γὰρ
μιᾷ πρὸς ἅπαντας Ἕλληνας δυνατοὶ Πελοποννήσιοι καὶ οἱ ξύμμαχοι ἀντισχεῖν, πολεμεῖν δὲ 25
μὴ πρὸς ὁμοίαν ἀντιπαρασκευὴν ἀδύνατοι, ὅταν
μήτε βουλευτηρίῳ ἑνὶ χρώμενοι παραχρῆμά τι
ὀξέως ἐπιτελῶσι πάντες τε ἰσόψηφοι ὄντες καὶ

3. post καὶ add. ἡ CG   13. πληροῦν Herwerden   15.
αὐτῶν Stephanus : αὐτῶν codd.   25. ἀντίσχειν Krüger

οὐχ ὁμόφυλοι τὸ ἐφ' ἑαυτὸν ἕκαστος σπεύδῃ·
ἐξ ὧν φιλεῖ μηδὲν ἐπιτελὲς γίγνεσθαι. καὶ 7
γὰρ οἱ μὲν ὡς μάλιστα τιμωρήσασθαί τινα
βούλονται, οἱ δὲ ὡς ἥκιστα τὰ οἰκεῖα φθεῖραι.
χρόνιοί τε ξυνιόντες ἐν βραχεῖ μὲν μορίῳ
σκοποῦσί τι τῶν κοινῶν, τῷ δὲ πλέονι τὰ
οἰκεῖα πράσσουσι, καὶ ἕκαστος οὐ παρὰ τὴν
ἑαυτοῦ ἀμέλειαν οἴεται βλάψειν, μέλειν δέ τινι
καὶ ἄλλῳ ὑπὲρ ἑαυτοῦ τι προϊδεῖν, ὥστε τῷ
10 αὐτῷ ὑπὸ ἁπάντων ἰδίᾳ δοξάσματι λανθάνειν
τὸ κοινὸν ἀθρόον φθειρόμενον.

"Μέγιστον δέ, τῇ τῶν χρημάτων σπάνει 142
κωλύσονται, ὅταν σχολῇ αὐτὰ πορι- 'We need not
ζόμενοι διαμέλλωσιν· τοῦ δὲ πολέμου fear a hostile
                                        post in our
15 οἱ καιροὶ οὐ μενετοί. καὶ μὴν οὐδ' territory.   2
ἡ ἐπιτείχισις οὐδὲ τὸ ναυτικὸν αὐτῶν ἄξιον
φοβηθῆναι. τὴν μὲν γὰρ χαλεπὸν καὶ ἐν 3
εἰρήνῃ πόλιν ἀντίπαλον κατασκευάσασθαι, ἢ
που δὴ ἐν πολεμίᾳ τε καὶ οὐχ ἧσσον ἐκείνοις
20 ἡμῶν ἀντεπιτετειχισμένων· φρούριον δ' εἰ 4
ποιήσονται, τῆς μὲν γῆς βλάπτοιεν ἄν τι μέρος
καταδρομαῖς καὶ αὐτομολίαις, οὐ μέντοι ἱκανόν
γε ἔσται ἐπιτειχίζειν τε κωλύειν ἡμᾶς πλεύ-
σαντας ἐς τὴν ἐκείνων καί, ᾗπερ ἰσχύομεν, ταῖς
25 ναυσὶν ἀμύνεσθαι· πλέον γὰρ ἡμεῖς 'In naval skill 5
                                        they cannot
ἔχομεν τοῦ κατὰ γῆν ἐκ τοῦ ναυτικοῦ rival us.
ἐμπειρίας ἢ ἐκεῖνοι ἐκ τοῦ κατ' ἤπειρον ἐς τὰ
ναυτικά. τὸ δὲ τῆς θαλάσσης ἐπιστήμονας 6

18. παρασκευάσασθαι ABEF   24. ἐς τὴν] ἐν τῇ C   25.
post γὰρ add. ὅμως C[G]

128 ΘΟΥΚΥΔΙΔΟΥ

γενέσθαι οὐ ῥᾳδίως αὐτοῖς προσγενήσεται.
7 οὐδὲ γὰρ ὑμεῖς μελετῶντες αὐτὸ εὐθὺς ἀπὸ
τῶν Μηδικῶν ἐξείργασθέ πω· πῶς δὴ ἄνδρες
γεωργοὶ καὶ οὐ θαλάσσιοι, καὶ προσέτι οὐδὲ
μελετῆσαι ἐασόμενοι διὰ τὸ ὑφ' ἡμῶν πολλαῖς 5
ναυσὶν αἰεὶ ἐφορμεῖσθαι, ἄξιον ἄν τι δρῷεν ;
8 πρὸς μὲν γὰρ ὀλίγας ἐφορμούσας κἂν διακιν-
δυνεύσειαν πλήθει τὴν ἀμαθίαν θρασύνοντες,
πολλαῖς δὲ εἰργόμενοι ἡσυχάσουσι καὶ ἐν τῷ
μὴ μελετῶντι ἀξυνετώτεροι ἔσονται καὶ δι' 10
9 αὐτὸ καὶ ὀκνηρότεροι. τὸ δὲ ναυτικὸν τέχνης
ἐστίν, ὥσπερ καὶ ἄλλο τι, καὶ οὐκ ἐνδέχεται,
ὅταν τύχῃ, ἐκ παρέργου μελετᾶσθαι, ἀλλὰ
μᾶλλον μηδὲν ἐκείνῳ πάρεργον ἄλλο γίγνεσθαι.
143 " Εἴ τε καὶ κινήσαντες τῶν Ὀλυμπίασιν ἢ 15
'They will not be able to tempt our sailors away from us. Δελφοῖς χρημάτων μισθῷ μείζονι
πειρῷντο ἡμῶν ὑπολαβεῖν τοὺς
ξένους τῶν ναυτῶν, μὴ ὄντων μὲν
ἡμῶν ἀντιπάλων ἐσβάντων αὐτῶν τε καὶ τῶν
μετοίκων δεινὸν ἂν ἦν· νῦν δὲ τόδε τε ὑπάρχει, 20
καί, ὅπερ κράτιστον, κυβερνήτας ἔχομεν πολίτας
καὶ τὴν ἄλλην ὑπηρεσίαν πλείους καὶ ἀμείνους
2 ἢ ἅπασα ἡ ἄλλη Ἑλλάς. καὶ ἐπὶ τῷ κινδύνῳ
οὐδεὶς ἂν δέξαιτο τῶν ξένων τήν τε αὐτοῦ
φεύγειν καὶ μετὰ τῆς ἥσσονος ἅμα ἐλπίδος 25
ὀλίγων ἡμερῶν ἕνεκα μεγάλου μισθοῦ δόσεως
ἐκείνοις ξυναγωνίζεσθαι.
3 " Καὶ τὰ μὲν Πελοποννησίων ἔμοιγε τοιαῦτα

3. πω om. ABEF[G]   7. post ὀλίγας add. ναῦς CG (del.
G¹)   23. πᾶσα ABEF

καὶ παραπλήσια δοκεῖ εἶναι, τὰ δὲ ἡμέτερα
τούτων τε ὧνπερ ἐκείνοις ἐμεμψάμην ἀπηλλάχθαι καὶ ἄλλα οὐκ ἀπὸ τοῦ ἴσου μεγάλα
ἔχειν. ἤν τε ἐπὶ τὴν χώραν ἡμῶν πεζῇ ἴωσιν, 4
5 ἡμεῖς ἐπὶ τὴν ἐκείνων πλευσούμεθα, 'We can do them
more harm than
καὶ οὐκέτι ἐκ τοῦ ὁμοίου ἔσται they can do us.
Πελοποννήσου τε μέρος τι τμηθῆναι καὶ τὴν
Ἀττικὴν ἅπασαν· οἱ μὲν γὰρ οὐχ ἕξουσιν
ἄλλην ἀντιλαβεῖν ἀμαχεί, ἡμῖν δ' ἐστὶ γῆ
10 πολλὴ καὶ ἐν νήσοις καὶ κατ' ἤπειρον· μέγα Ε
γὰρ τὸ τῆς θαλάσσης κράτος. σκέψασθε δέ·
εἰ γὰρ ἦμεν νησιῶται, τίνες ἂν ἀληπτότεροι
ἦσαν; καὶ νῦν χρὴ ὅτι ἐγγύτατα τούτου
διανοηθέντας τὴν μὲν γῆν καὶ οἰκίας ἀφεῖναι,
15 τῆς δὲ θαλάσσης καὶ πόλεως φυλακὴν ἔχειν,
καὶ Πελοποννησίοις ὑπὲρ αὐτῶν 'We must not
attempt to fight
ὀργισθέντας πολλῷ πλέοσι μὴ διαμά- them in Attica.
χεσθαι (κρατήσαντές τε γὰρ αὖθις οὐκ ἐλάσσοσι
μαχούμεθα καὶ ἢν σφαλῶμεν, τὰ τῶν ξυμμάχων,
20 ὅθεν ἰσχύομεν, προσαπόλλυται· οὐ γὰρ ἡσυχάσουσι μὴ ἱκανῶν ἡμῶν ὄντων ἐπ' αὐτοὺς
στρατεύειν), τήν τε ὀλόφυρσιν μὴ οἰκιῶν καὶ
γῆς ποιεῖσθαι, ἀλλὰ τῶν σωμάτων· οὐ γὰρ
τάδε τοὺς ἄνδρας, ἀλλ' οἱ ἄνδρες ταῦτα
25 κτῶνται. καὶ εἰ ᾤμην πείσειν ὑμᾶς, αὐτοὺς ἂν
ἐξελθόντας ἐκέλευον αὐτὰ δῃῶσαι καὶ δεῖξαι
Πελοποννησίοις ὅτι τούτων γε ἕνεκα οὐχ
ὑπακούσεσθε.

7. τε om. ABEF   16. Πελοπονησίοις (sic) C: Πελοποννησίους cett.

144 " Πολλὰ δὲ καὶ ἄλλα ἔχω ἐς ἐλπίδα τοῦ
περιέσεσθαι, ἢν ἐθέλητε ἀρχήν τε
μὴ ἐπικτᾶσθαι ἅμα πολεμοῦντες καὶ
κινδύνους αὐθαιρέτους μὴ προστί-
θεσθαι· μᾶλλον γὰρ πεφόβημαι τὰς οἰκείας 5
ἡμῶν ἁμαρτίας ἢ τὰς τῶν ἐναντίων διανοίας.
2 ἀλλ᾽ ἐκεῖνα μὲν καὶ ἐν ἄλλῳ λόγῳ ἅμα τοῖς
ἔργοις δηλωθήσεται· νῦν δὲ τούτοις
ἀποκρινάμενοι ἀποπέμψωμεν, Μεγα-
ρέας μὲν ὅτι ἐάσομεν ἀγορᾷ καὶ λιμέσι χρῆσθαι, 10
ἢν καὶ Λακεδαιμόνιοι ξενηλασίας μὴ ποιῶσι
μήτε ἡμῶν μήτε τῶν ἡμετέρων ξυμμάχων (οὔτε
γὰρ ἐκεῖνο κωλύει ἐν ταῖς σπονδαῖς οὔτε τόδε),
τὰς δὲ πόλεις ὅτι αὐτονόμους ἀφήσομεν, εἰ
καὶ αὐτονόμους ἔχοντες ἐσπεισάμεθα, καὶ ὅταν 15
κἀκεῖνοι ταῖς ἑαυτῶν ἀποδῶσι πόλεσι μὴ σφίσι
[τοῖς Λακεδαιμονίοις] ἐπιτηδείως αὐτονομεῖσθαι,
ἀλλ᾽ αὐτοῖς ἑκάστοις ὡς βούλονται· δίκας τε
ὅτι ἐθέλομεν δοῦναι κατὰ τὰς ξυνθήκας, πολέμου
δὲ οὐκ ἄρξομεν, ἀρχομένους δὲ ἀμυνούμεθα. 20
ταῦτα γὰρ δίκαια καὶ πρέποντα ἅμα τῇδε τῇ
3 πόλει ἀποκρίνασθαι. εἰδέναι δὲ χρὴ ὅτι ἀνάγκη
πολεμεῖν (ἢν δὲ ἑκούσιοι μᾶλλον δεχώμεθα,
ἧσσον ἐγκεισομένους τοὺς ἐναντίους ἕξομεν), ἔκ
τε τῶν μεγίστων κινδύνων ὅτι καὶ πόλει καὶ 25
4 ἰδιώτῃ μέγισται τιμαὶ περιγίγνονται. οἱ γοῦν
πατέρες ἡμῶν ὑποστάντες Μήδους καὶ οὐκ ἀπὸ

'Nor must we indulge in schemes of conquest.

'Let us return them a firm answer.'

13. ἐν om. Dion, Hal.   14. τε ABEF   16. αὐτῶν
vel αὐτῶν ABEF   17. τοῖς Λακεδαιμονίοις secl. Schol.
18. τε Hude : δὲ codd.

τοσῶνδε ὁρμώμενοι, ἀλλὰ καὶ τὰ ὑπάρχοντα
ἐκλιπόντες, γνώμῃ τε πλέονι ἢ τύχῃ καὶ τόλμῃ
μείζονι ἢ δυνάμει τόν τε βάρβαρον ἀπεώσαντο
καὶ ἐς τάδε προήγαγον αὐτά. ὧν οὐ χρὴ
5 λείπεσθαι, ἀλλὰ τούς τε ἐχθροὺς παντὶ τρόπῳ
ἀμύνεσθαι καὶ τοῖς ἐπιγιγνομένοις πειρᾶσθαι
αὐτὰ μὴ ἐλάσσω παραδοῦναι."

Ὁ μὲν Περικλῆς τοιαῦτα εἶπεν, οἱ δὲ **145**
Ἀθηναῖοι νομίσαντες ἄριστα σφίσι His advice is
10 παραινεῖν αὐτὸν ἐψηφίσαντο ἃ adopted.
ἐκέλευε, καὶ τοῖς Λακεδαιμονίοις ἀπεκρίναντο
τῇ ἐκείνου γνώμῃ καθ' ἕκαστά τε ὡς ἔφρασε
καὶ τὸ ξύμπαν, οὐδὲν κελευόμενοι ποιήσειν,
δίκῃ δὲ κατὰ τὰς ξυνθήκας ἑτοῖμοι εἶναι δια-
15 λύεσθαι περὶ τῶν ἐγκλημάτων ἐπὶ ἴσῃ καὶ ὁμοίᾳ.
καὶ οἱ μὲν ἀπεχώρησαν ἐπ' οἴκου καὶ οὐκέτι
ὕστερον ἐπρεσβεύοντο· αἰτίαι δὲ αὗται καὶ **146**
διαφοραὶ ἐγένοντο ἀμφοτέροις πρὸ During the
τοῦ πολέμου, ἀρξάμενοι εὐθὺς ἀπὸ events preceding the war
20 τῶν ἐν Ἐπιδάμνῳ καὶ Κερκύρᾳ· there had been
much suspicion,
ἐπεμείγνυντο δὲ ὅμως ἐν αὐταῖς καὶ but communication had been
παρ' ἀλλήλους ἐφοίτων ἀκηρύκτως kept up.
μέν, ἀνυπόπτως δὲ οὔ· σπονδῶν γὰρ ξύγχυσις
τὰ γιγνόμενα ἦν καὶ πρόφασις τοῦ πολεμεῖν.

11. post τοῖς add. τε ABEF

NOTES

1. **Θουκυδίδης κτλ.**—a formal method of opening, after the manner of the gnomic poets, not due, as Bloomfield imagined, to 'the modesty of our author.' Cf. Herod. init. ; Intr. p. xv.

ξυνέγραψε—a characteristic word of Thuc., who is known to the ancient critics as ὁ συγγραφεύς, much as Homer is ὁ ποιητής. It denotes the bringing together in one work of many occurrences—*composing* in its etymological sense. (How some find a reference to the hunting up of materials is not clear.)

3. **ὡς ἐπολέμησαν** — 'namely, how,' i.e. 'showing how they waged war.' Of course different from ὃν ἐ., which would be absurdly tautological. The aorist is called *complexive*.

4. **ἀρξάμενος (τοῦ ξυγγράψαι) κτλ** —we are to understand that as soon as the war broke out Thuc. began to put down what occurred, and kept a sort of diary of the war.

εὐθὺς καθισταμένου—supply τοῦ πολέμου.

5. **ἐλπίσας**—'expecting.' On the relation of the participles here see Intr. p. xli. This first sentence is very characteristic of Thuc., in whose periods form is constantly subordinated to sense. O. Müller well says that Thuc. has two favourite forms of period, (*a*) the main predication, followed by clauses giving the circumstances and reasons, which may in turn be explained in similar clauses ; and (*b*) the reasons, circumstances in participial and other clauses followed by the resulting fact or opinion, as in c. **2**, 2.

ἀξιολογώτατον τῶν π. —the illogical form of comparison, as in c. **10**, 3, cf. 'fairest of her daughters Eve': Tac. *Agric.* 34 *celerorum fugacissimi.* It is frequent in Greek.

133 ·

6. τεκμαιρόμενος—'inferring this,' adding the grounds of the ἐλπίς. These grounds are (1) ὅτι ἀκμάζοντες . ., (2) ὁρῶν . . Thus the clause with ὅτι is co-ordinate with a partic. of *cause*; cf. Xen. *Symp.* 8, 11 τεκμαίρομαι τῇ καλοκἀγαθίᾳ καὶ ὅτι σε ὁρῶ.

7. ἀκμάζοντές . . παρασκευῇ—'at the height of their military power.' That ἦσαν, not ἦσαν, is the true reading there cannot be a doubt; for ἰέναι ἐς in this pregnant use see L. & S.

8. τὸ ἄλλο Ἑλληνικόν—including the Greeks outside Greece proper. Cf. τὸ λῃστικόν, τὸ βαρβαρικόν, τὸ ξενικόν, and many others.

10. καὶ διανοούμενον—sc. ξυνίστασθαι, the ellipse of an infin. with διανοεῖσθαι being common, as in 124, 3. The καί serves to bring διανοούμενον into connexion with ξυνιστάμενον; we should put 'actually' with τὸ μὲν εὐθύς. The Sicilian Greeks are a good example.

γάρ—as 'the movement' meant by κίνησις must be (1) the war itself, and (2) the unrest that preceded it, γάρ cannot introduce the reason of the expectation that the war would be important, but must be epexegetic.

12. μέρει τινί—'a considerable part,' as, for example, Thrace and Macedon. Supply ἐγένετο, 'affected.'

ὡς δὲ εἰπεῖν—qualifying πλεῖστον. Note that ὡς (ἔπος) εἰπεῖν never apologises for a metaphor, but always limits a sweeping or universal statement. Hence '(it extended, ἐγένετο), one might almost say, over the greatest part of mankind'; i.e. it affected perhaps a greater part of mankind than had been affected by any previous commotion. Of course the possible exception is the Persian wars.

(Whatever be the exact construction of μεγίστη δὴ . . ἀνθρώπων—and the words are variously interpreted—Thuc. over-estimates the importance of the war. If we supply μεγίστη δὴ ἐγένετο to μέρει τινί and ἐπὶ πλεῖστον, the exaggeration is extreme. ἐπὶ πλεῖστον is taken by Classen and others to mean 'the greatest part of the (known) world'; but this involves a very great exaggeration of a fact ascertainable; and it is unlikely that Thuc. would make such a sweeping statement. It looks also as if πλεῖστον, 'more than before,' were meant to be parallel to μεγίστη, 'greater than before.' The text has no appearance of being corrupt or interpolated.)

13. τὰ πρὸ αὐτῶν—'the events that preceded this disturbance (κίνησις).' The neut. αὐτά is frequently used by Thuc. with reference to the details of the subject he is dealing with.

(This phrase cannot refer to events that *immediately* preceded the war; for (a) διὰ χρόνου πλῆθος would then be absurd, (b) Thuc. himself gives an account of the fifty years preceding the war as a period well known, (c) the Persian wars could not be included in οὐ μεγάλα νομίζω γενέσθαι κατὰ τοὺς πολέμους (cf. c. 18, 2). Thuc. must be thinking of the period of the Trojan war and of that between the Trojan war and the Persian war, i.e. to the end of the Tyrants. But the words are very inexact; cf. Intr. p. xx).

14. τὰ ἔτι παλαίτερα—events preceding the Trojan war.

15. ἀδύνατα—Thuc. frequently uses the neut. plur. of the *verbal* or of an adj. for the sing. where the subject is an infin. or a sentence. The use is mainly poetical.

τεκμηρίων — these 'evidences' are detailed in cc. 2-17: (1) migrations were frequent ; (2) there was no common name ; (3) weakness by sea ; (4) the expeditions by land were on a small scale and were confined to border-fighting ; (5) the tyrants hampered Greece proper, and Persia hampered Ionia.

PAGE 2.

1. ὧν belongs to πιστεῦσαι, and is probably attracted from ἅ. Chambry quotes Soph. O. T. 646 πίστευσον, Οἰδίπους, τάδε, for the accus. with πιστεύω.

ἐπὶ μακρότατον σκοποῦντι—'by carrying my inquiry to the farthest limit (of the past).' ἐπὶ μακρότατον of *time* also in Herod. i. 171, in a similar connexion.

5. οἰκουμένη — this and the following participles are imperfect.

6. οὖσαι—sc. φαίνονται.

τὰ πρότερα—the adverbial accus. in plur. is common in Thuc., but is seldom found in other prose authors.

8. βιαζόμενοι—the pres. and imperf. of this verb in a passive sense are far less common in other prose authors than in Thuc.

ὑπό τινων αἰεὶ πλειόνων — what is noticeable here is that αἰεί ('from time to time') occurs with τινων, and not with τῶν, which—as the older critics note—is the usual form of expression.

9. τῆς γὰρ ἐμπορίας κτλ.—see note on p. 1 l. 6. The causes to which the readiness to migrate are ascribed are (1) absence of commerce and intercommunication : τῆς γὰρ . .

θαλάσσης : (2) low state of agriculture and absence of capital
sunk in the land : νεμόμενοί τε . . φυτεύοντες : (3) absence of
demand for anything beyond the necessaries of life, which
could be procured anywhere : τῆς τε . . ἐπικρατεῖν.

ἐπιμιγνύντες—the mid. is used in the same sense, e.g. in
c. 146. At a period when the tribes of Greece regarded one
another as enemies, it was impossible that ἐπιμιξία should exist,
ἐπιμιξία being based upon treaties. In later times ἐπιμιξία
terminated as soon as a state of war existed.

10. διά—the sea as the *medium* of intercourse.

11. νεμόμενοι—the word is used of *enjoyment of profits
derived*, which may be combined with *occupation*. The following participles—ἔχοντες, φυτεύοντες—are circumstances explana-
tory of the degree of 'enjoyment' attained. (νέμεσθαι ὡς τὸ πολὺ
τὸ λαμβάνειν πρόσοδον παρὰ Θουκυδίδῃ, Photius.)

τὰ αὑτῶν—what they had acquired by adverse possession.

12. ὅσον—i.e. τοσοῦτον, ὅσον, where ὅσον = ὥστε, and is assimi-
lated to the adverbial accus. τοσοῦτον.

ἀποζῆν—this word occurs nowhere else in Attic, but is
used by late writers (Lucian, Aelian, etc.), some at least of
whom think it means 'to live poorly,' inferring the sense
implied in this passage.

περιουσίαν κτλ. — had they accumulated stores for the
purpose of barter, and had they planted trees, it would have
been less easy to migrate.

13. ἄδηλον ὄν—accus. abs.

14. ἐπελθὼν καὶ ἀτειχίστων ἅμα ὅ.—(1) alternative explanations, seldom desirable, are here clearly called for ; (2) taking
ἀτειχίστων ὄντων first : the sense is, 'as they were without
walls.' The simplest way is to suppose this *masc.* and dependent on ἀφαιρήσεται. This involves making καί . . ἅμα almost
equivalent to ἄλλως τε καί : καί, we are told, does not = 'and,'
but καί . . ἅμα = 'particularly,' as in 102, 3 and elsewhere.
But (3) this makes it impossible to explain why τις . . ἄλλος,
which go together, are separated, because ἐπελθὼν . . ὄντων is
not then *one* expression. (4) This objection *is diminished* if καί
. . ὄντων is taken as a *parenthetical gen. abs.*, either (*a*) *masc.*,
with αὐτῶν supplied, or (*b*) *neut.*, with subj. supplied from context, like πλωιμωτέρων ὄντων c. 7. (5) The objection *disappears*
if καί = 'and,' ἐπελθὼν καὶ ἀ. ἅμα ὄντων giving the two circumstances leading to loss—ἀφαιρήσεται. Though one circumstance

is *modal*—ἐπελθών—the other *causal*, it is like Thuc. to connect them by καί.

15. **ἀναγκαίου**—of what will just suffice, as in *necessarius cibus*. ἀναγκαῖος is frequently *fem.* in Plato. βίαιος and βέβαιος always have two terminations in Thuc.

16. **πανταχοῦ**—'anywhere.' The sense *any* frequently belongs to πᾶς and words from it.

17. **δι' αὐτό**—'accordingly'; Thuc. often uses αὐτό (-ά) in reference to a previous statement.

μεγέθει—of the number of inhabitants, as in c. **10.**

18. **παρασκευῇ**—naval and military resources, as distinct from κατασκευή, the external adornment of a city.

19. **ἡ ἀρίστη**—cf. τῆς γῆς οὐ πολλὴν ἔτεμον vi. 7. The attraction is most common with πολύς, but is fairly frequent with other adjectives.

20. **νῦν . . καλουμένη** belongs to both nouns. In early times the districts had no general name.

22. **'Αρκαδίας**—the exemption was due to the isolated character of Arcadia, the consequence of its mountains. ἄρκτος, 'Bear-land'; cf. ἄρκειος. The Arcadians were unaffected by the Dorian migration. They prided themselves on being autochthones (cf. Xen. *Hell.* vii. i. 23), and on their primeval antiquity (cf. L. & S. under προσέληνος).

κράτιστα—'best,' the regular meaning of κράτιστος when applied to *land*.

23. **ἀρετήν**—'fertility.' When Greece was in the village stage, (1) the inhabitants of some districts grew (comparatively) wealthy, and as a consequence there were disputes between the 'haves' and 'have-nots'; (2) these fertile districts excited the cupidity of other clans.

25. **μᾶλλον**—more than communities whose land was not so fertile.

26. **γοῦν**—'at any rate' the immunity of Attica was due to its barrenness; it is therefore likely that the troubles of other districts were due to their fertility.

τοῦ ἐπὶ πλεῖστον, 'the remotest time.' ἐπὶ πλεῖστον, adverbial ('extending farthest back'), has the art. like τὸ πρίν, etc.

τὸ λεπτόγεων—(1) the constant use of neut. adj. or partic. for a subst. is a feature of Thuc.'s style; (2) the soil of

Attica is in general stony and dry. The Attic Plain is watered by the Ilissus and Cephisus, but in summer the former is almost dry and the latter "*μειοῦται τελέως*" : the land yields a return only to diligent cultivation. Of course in these early times the land was not scientifically dealt with ; and it is noteworthy, as bearing on Thuc.'s point, that it *looks* more barren than it is.

28. **παράδειγμα**—the meaning of this term in Greek rhetoric is not merely 'example,' but 'an example *used to support an argument.*'

τόδε—referring to the sentence that follows, ἐκ γάρ κτλ.

τοῦ λόγου—explained by διά, etc.

29. **διὰ τὰς μετοικίας κτλ.**—'that it was owing to the habit of settling elsewhere (to which I have referred) that *Greece* in other respects (besides *population and security*) had not advanced so fast (as Attica).' μετοικίας is used exactly as in Aesch. *Eum.* 1019, where the Furies refer to their μετοικία to and in Athens. 1. That ἐκ γάρ κτλ. explains τόδε is proved by the usage of Thuc. 2. διὰ . . αὐξηθῆναι is beset with difficulties. With the MS. reading τὰς μετοικίας ἐς τὰ ἄλλα three explanations have been proposed : (*a*) '*Attica* did not grow *in other respects so fast* as in population.' But this does not fall in with the general line of the argument. (*b*) '*Attica* through the presence of μέτοικοι advanced *much more* (μὴ ὁμοίως) in other respects.' But neither is this the argument, nor is there any proof that μὴ ὁμοίως can in such a connexion as this mean ' much more.' (*c*) With regard to the rendering given above, it is denied that *Greece* can be the subject of αὐξηθῆναι. But, if we examine c. 2 as a whole, this does not appear impossible. The chapter deals with the early condition of Greece in general— ἡ νῦν Ἑλλὰς καλουμένη—the smallness of the communities (οὔτε μεγέθει πόλεων ἰσχυον) and their weakness. To these conditions the very fertility of the soil contributed. Attica, which was barren, was an exception in both respects. It did not lose inhabitants by στάσις : it did not excite the cupidity of strangers. On the other hand, strangers settled in Attica because it offered security ; and thus the population of Attica was still further increased, and it was able to colonise. These last facts lend further support to my general argument (ὁ λόγος), viz. that the weakness of the early Greeks in all respects is largely accounted for by the shifting nature of the population. ἡ Ἑλλὰς is in the writer's mind throughout. ἐς τὰ ἄλλα is explained by many ' with reference to its other parts ' ; but it more naturally means 'in other respects than those points to

which I have specifically referred.' A striking example of this
(*ex contrario*) is the colonising energy of Attica, the consequence
of freedom from migration. Some take ἐς τὰ ἄλλα with
μετοικίας—migrations to other parts; but τά is then wrong.
Ullrich's emendation, according to which τὰ ἄλλα, 'other parts
of Greece,' is subject of αὐξηθῆναι—see crit. n.—is generally
accepted ; but it is not absolutely necessary.

PAGE 3.

2. πολέμῳ—referring to ὑπὸ ἀλλοφύλων ἐπεβουλεύοντο.

3. οἱ δυνατώτατοι—limiting apposition to οἱ ἐκπίπτοντες.
This kind of apposition is common in Thuc. — The most
conspicuous instance is that of the Alcmaeonidae from Pylus.

ὡς βέβαιον ὄν—taken as (1) *accus. abs.*, with ἀναχωρεῖν
παρ' Ἀθηναίους implied ; (2) by Classen as governed by παρά,
in a loose apposition to Ἀθηναίους. The second, though loose
in grammar, gives a better sense.

4. πολῖται γιγνόμενοι—the imperf. partic. points to the
many instances in which citizenship was bestowed. Of course
this system of conferring civic rights belongs to a time when
only the Eupatrids had any political power. They admitted
new families freely. In later days, on the contrary, when
Athens had attained power and the demos ruled, the Ecclesia
was very jealous of the citizenship. Yet this welcome of
political exiles remained an honourable tradition, as we see
from the plays of Euripides.

εὐθὺς ἀπὸ παλαιοῦ with ἐποίησαν, but εὐθύς belongs to
ἀπὸ π., being equivalent to ἀρξάμενοι εὐθύς : cf. c. 146 and
142, 7.

7. ἐξέπεμψαν—sc. οἱ Ἀθηναῖοι. The colonising activity of
Attica is supposed to have begun in the eleventh cent. B.C.

9. δηλοῖ — second proof of weakness, viz. lack of communication.

τῶν παλαιῶν — *neut.*, like τὰ πρὸ αὐτῶν καὶ τὰ ἔτι
παλαίτερα in c. 2. Here τὰ παλαιά is explained to mean τὰ
πρὸ τῶν Τρωικῶν. The lit. trans. is 'insignificance in our early
history.'

11. πρότερον—this merely repeats the sense of πρό, as in οὐ
πρότερον . . πρίν κτλ.

12. δοκεῖ δέ μοι — (1) at first parenthetical, afterwards
(2) δοκεῖ ἡ ἐπίκλησις οὐδὲ εἶναι, (3) δοκεῖ ἄλλα (*nom.*) . .

παρέχεσθαι, (4) δοκεῖ "Ελληνας καλεῖσθαι, (5) ? parenthetical, before ἐδύνατο. When a verb can take more than one construction, Thuc. sometimes combines alternative constructions in the same sentence *without repeating the verb*.

13. τὰ πρὸ "Ελληνος—*adv. accus.*, as τὰ πρότερα c. 2, τὰ ἐν τῇ εἰρήνῃ iii. 54, 9. Hellen was son of Deucalion and Pyrrha; and Hellenes from Phthiotis accompanied Achilles to Troy. How the name came to be extended to all the Greeks is unknown.

14. καὶ πάνυ—emphasised by being separated from εἶναι. Cf. Xen. *Anab* i. 5 καὶ μάλα κατὰ πρανοῦς γηλόφου, Demosth. 5, 15 καὶ πάνυ φησί τις αὐτοὺς ἀναισθήτους εἶναι, and so with οὐ (μή) πάνυ not unfrequently. We should rather expect οὐ πάνυ μοι δοκεῖ οὐδ' εἶναι.

εἶναι—this and the infins. that follow are imperfect.

15. κατὰ ἔθνη—distributive. This forms subject to παρέχεσθαι = 'various tribes,' ἄλλα τε καὶ τὸ Π., 'among others the P. tribe,' being in apposition to κ. ἔθνη. Adverbial phrases are frequent in Thuc. as equivalent of a case of a subst. : as in vi. 39 ταῦτα καὶ κατὰ μέρη καὶ ξύμπαντα.

16. τὸ Πελασγικόν—a tribe of aborigines, whom Homer speaks of as dwelling in Asia Minor and Crete as well as in Greece. For the facts and theories about them see Abbott, *Hist. Greece* i. p. 27 fol. "When the Pelasgi became established [in literature] as an ancient tribe, those nations which laid claim to great antiquity, as the Athenians and Arcadians, became Pelasgians." (This is enough to know.)

ἐπὶ πλεῖστον—this belongs to τὸ Πελασγικόν, meaning that the name of the P. was *more widely extended* than that of any other tribe.

17. παρέχεσθαι—sc. 'to the country.'

τῶν παίδων—Aeolus, Dorus, and Xuthus.

18. ἰσχυσάντων—ingressive aor., 'having become mighty.'

19. ἐπαγομένων—sc. τινῶν.

ἐπ' ὠφελίᾳ—'to aid them.' ὠφελία often = βοήθεια ; cf. p. 64 l. 21.

20. καθ' ἑκάστους—subject of καλεῖσθαι : 'the several tribes more and more (ἤδη μᾶλλον) began to be called Hellenes in consequence of their intercourse' (with the Hellenes).

21. πολλοῦ χρόνου—*time within which* (partitive), less commonly found in positive sentences.

22. [ἐδύνατο]—sc. τὸ καλεῖσθαι "Ελληνας. Shil. quotes Eur. *Phoen.* 12 καλοῦσι δ' Ἰοκάστην με, τοῦτο γὰρ πατὴρ | ἔθετο. The ἐδύνατο is probably spurious, because, though the constrn. of δοκεῖ shifts (see on l. 12), the two clauses καθ' ἑκάστους μὲν . . οὐ μέντοι should have the same form, just as τὰ μὲν . κατὰ ἔθνη δέ have. Even if the constrn. were again changed here, we should probably have ἐξενίκησε.

25. ὠνόμασεν—sc. "Ελληνας.

οὐδ' ἄλλους — i.e. Hellas in Homer is Phthiotis, B 684 It has been pointed out that in a 344, δ 726, 816, o 80 'Ελλάς with "Αργος denotes Greece in general. The lines are perhaps spurious.

27. τὰ ἔπη—'the poems.'

28. ἀνακαλεῖ—'distinguishes them as.' ἀνακαλῶ is 'call by a distinctive, official name.'

οὐ μὴν οὐδέ — 'nor even'; οὐ μὴν ἀλλά = 'not but what.'

PAGE 4.

1. βαρβάρους εἴρηκε—'mentioned barbarians, because not yet had the Hellenes either been distinguished under one name in opposition' (to them). There is a difficulty as to the construction of ἀντίπαλον. (1) Eustathius, followed by Stahl and Steup, made it agree with ὄνομα, despite the order; and the adj. is occasionally separated by a prep. from its subst. ; (2) Classen thought it an adverb like τοὐναντίον : the absence of art. is one reason against this ; (3) Böhme made it internal accus. to ἀποκεκρίσθαι, 'to have undergone an opposing separation,' and Krüger favours this ; (4) Mr. Forbes says it is in apposition to "Ελληνας, which means 'the word Greeks.' But should we not even so require ἀντιπάλους or "Ελληνες ?—The edd. note that Thuc. neglects the epithet βαρβαρόφωνοι, of the Carians, in *Il.* ii. 867. But this simply means 'speaking an unknown tongue,' and the statement of Thuc. is substantially correct. The Greeks could not be conscious that they were a *separate* people before they were conscious that they were *one* people.

3. δ' οὖν — resuming after the digression of which § 3 consists.

οἱ . . ὡς ἕκαστοι . . κληθέντες — the main subject is οἱ "Ελληνες κληθέντες, 'those who came to be called H.' This is divided into (a) ὡς ἕκαστοι κατὰ πόλεις τε ὅσοι ἀ. ξυνίεσαν,

I G

referring to καθ' ἑκάστους μὲν ἤδη . . "Ελληνας § 2; (b) καὶ ξύμπαντες ὕστερον, referring to οὐ μέντοι . . ἄπασιν ἐκνικῆσαι. In (a) τε=both is misplaced, the irregularity being explained by the fact that κατὰ . . ξυνιέσαν is added to ὡς ἕκαστοι as an afterthought. Possibly, however, τε=and, but it is hard to see any distinction between ὡς ἕκαστοι and κατὰ π. The sentence is overloaded, since ὕστερον, i.e. long after the Trojan War (cf. § 3), is combined with a statement of what happened πρὸ τῶν Τρωικῶν. Observe also that this apparent recapitulation (οἱ δ' οὖν κτλ.) does not agree entirely with the statements made in § 2, where nothing is said about a common language. Thuc., as others have noticed, does not seem to have a clear view of the matter.

8. The MS. ξυνῆλθον will not do : ἐξέρχομαι, ἔξειμι with accus. are not rare in Attic prose in a military sense ; but ἔρχομαι, εἶμι are not used so.

9. Μίνως γάρ—from this point to c. 8 Thuc. deals with the gradual growth of maritime enterprise, and the 'barbarian character of the early Greeks.' For Minos see Abbott, Hist. Greece i. p. 122.

παλαίτατος — 'was the first to.' This does not belong to τῶν Κυκλάδων . . ἐγένετο, and perhaps not to τῆς νῦν . . ἐκράτησε.

10. τῆς . . θαλάσσης—this may depend on ἐπὶ πλεῖστον, or on ἐκράτησε.

12. ἦρξε—'became ruler.'

13. πρῶτος—later the Athenians colonised the islands, and after that an Athenian would be honoured as οἰκιστής. See c. 12, 4.

15. ἐγκαταστήσας—this partic. is of course not antecedent in time to the main verb ἐγένετο. It is aor. merely because it is the explanation how ἐγένετο οἰκιστής, the partic. being equivalent to καί+aor. ind. (This use of the aor. partic. in Thuc. disposes of the passages discussed by Mr. Forbes, Thuc. i. p. 142.)

ὡς εἰκός—'as was natural' (in one who ruled the sea).

16. καθῆρει—used of destroying, putting an end to a power, as in c. 16, 1.

17. τοῦ . . ἰέναι—purpose, generally with μή. Tac. imitates this in An. ii. 59 Aegyptum proficiscitur cognoscendae antiquitatis, etc.

21. ἐπ'—'to,' not 'against.'

23. οὐ τῶν ἀδυνατωτάτων = τῶν δυνατωτάτων.

κέρδους ἕνεκα — a frequent phrase. Notice the place of ἕνεκα, which is usual when it applies to two nouns, as e.g. Antiphon **6**, 7 διαβολῆς ἕνεκα καὶ ἀπάτης, Lys. **32**, 10 καὶ τῆς ἀδελφῆς ἕνεκα καὶ σφῶν αὐτῶν. But the rule is not absolute.

24. **τοῖς ἀσθενέσι τροφῆς** — cf. Demosth. i. § 22 τὰ τῆς τροφῆς τοῖς ξένοις. ἀσθενεῖς = 'weak.'

25. **πόλεσιν ἀτειχίστοις** — i.e. village communities. We cannot help thinking of the great aphorism in vii. **77**, 7 ἄνδρες γὰρ πόλις καὶ οὐ τείχη.

27. **βίου** — 'livelihood.' **ἐποιοῦντο** = 'would get,' a sense more familiar in the corresponding passive forms, ὁ βίος ἐγίγνετο αὐτοῖς.

ἐποιοῦντο — see L. & S. A. ii. 2.

ἔχοντος — synonymous with **φέροντος**: ii. **37**, 3 (νόμων) ὅσοι αἰσχύνην φέρουσι, ib. **41**, 3 τῷ πολεμίῳ ἀγανάκτησιν ἔχει.

PAGE 5.

2. **δηλοῦσι** — i.e. show the truth of the preceding statements : there is even in the present day evidence for what I have said.

τῶν ἠπειρωτῶν τινες — i.e. those dwelling in the coast towns of the mainland.

3. **καλῶς** — 'cleverly,' as often in καλῶς λέγειν.

τοῦτο δρᾶν — a regular expression for referring to a previous verb.

4. **οἱ παλαιοί** — sc. δηλοῦσι.

τὰς πύστεις . . ἐρωτῶντες — lit. 'everywhere agreeing in putting the stock question to strangers who come by sea, "are you pirates?" thus showing that the persons addressed were not accustomed to disown the occupation, and that those who made it their business to know did not censure it.' Of ' the old poets' Homer is one (*Od.* iii. 71 and ix. 252); and there is the *Hymn to Apollo* l. 452 ; but of course Thuc. knew other passages. The wording of the sentence has been questioned ; but Thuc. seems to have had in mind ἡ πύστις τῶν καταπλεόντων ἐστὶν εἰ λῃσταί εἰσιν. The *poets* are said to ask the question : for the characters are the mouthpiece of the poet.

6. οὔτε . . τε frequently correspond, as in Lat. *neque . . et.*

πυνθάνονται . . ἐπιμελὲς εἴη—the forms of the *recta* and *obliqua* are combined, as frequently in Xen. =ὧν πυνθανόμεθα . . οἷς ἂν ἐπιμελὲς ᾖ. It expresses the thought of the poets. (Others seem to consider πυνθάνονται as *hist. pres.* and εἴη as pure *iterative* opt.)

8. καὶ κατ' ἤπειρον—i.e. they not only carried on piracy at sea, but plundered one another on land as well. κατ' ἤ. =κατὰ γῆν. That Thuc. is thinking here of the towns near the coast is shown by c. **7** § 5 αἱ δὲ παλαιαὶ (πόλεις) διὰ τὴν λῃστείαν ἀπὸ θαλάσσης ᾠκίσθησαν.

10. τῷ παλαιῷ τρόπῳ—i.e. κατὰ κώμας οἰκούμενα καὶ ἁρπαζόμενα.

περί—'in the parts about.' The names of the people are used by Thuc. indifferently with the *place*-names.

12. τε—'and so.'

13. σιδηροφορεῖσθαι—below we have the act. : the mid. means 'to provide one's self with, see that one has.' Such compounds of φορῶ (cf. κανηφορῶ, χρυσοφορῶ) are not ordinarily used in mid. ; but cf. Arist. *Pol.* 1268 b.

16. οἰκήσεις—'settlements,' the πόλεις of c. **5**, 1.

17. (διὰ τὰς) . . ἐφόδους—'their hazardous intercourse.'

ξυνήθη κτλ. =ξυνήθως ἐδιῃτῶντο.

19. ταῦτα . . ἔτι οὕτω νεμόμενα—'the fact that in these parts of Greece men still live in this way.' This predicative use of the partic. is less common in Gk. than in Lat. (see *M. T.* 829 *b*). It is most often found with prepositions, and especially in phrases indicating *time*, with μετά, ἐπί, ἅμά. With certain well-defined exceptions, it does not occur unless the noun and verb yield sense without the partic.; i.e. the partic. was felt to be separate from the noun.

20. ἐς πάντας ὁμοίων—lit. 'extending in similar form to all,' like ἐς ὀλίγους οἰκεῖν in ii. **37**, 1. The substitution of the noun διαιτημάτων for the verb inf. τοῦ . . διαιτᾶσθαι with suitable constrn. is characteristic of the old style.

21. ἐν τοῖς πρῶτοι—the undoubted exx. of this idiom in Thuc. are, besides this place (where Prof. Tucker wrongly says the evidence favours πρώτοις), iii. **82**, 1 (στάσις) ἐν τοῖς πρώτη ἐγένετο : vii. **24**. 3 μέγιστον καὶ ἐν τοῖς πρῶτον : ib. **71**, 3 ἐν τοῖς χαλεπώτατα : viii. **90**, 1 ἐν τοῖς μάλιστα. In vii. **19**, 4 the MSS. give ἐν τοῖς πρώτοις (not πρῶτοι) : ib. **27**, ἐν τοῖς πρώτοις (not πρῶτον or πρώτη) : in viii. **89** ἐν τοῖς πρώτοις (not πρῶτοι). Pre-eminence is not necessarily implied in any example, and Herbst is perhaps right in saying that prominence only is meant. If so, it may be that the *nom.* is due only to attraction to the subject ; the principle being naturally extended to the adverb.

22. ἀνειμένη τῇ διαίτῃ—dat. of manner.

24. αὑτοῖς—ethic dat., very common in Thuc. where the gen. might be used.

25. εὐδαιμόνων—in the popular meaning.

διὰ τὸ ἀβροδίαιτον—with φοροῦντες. For the long linen (Ionian) χιτών worn by Ionians, Carians, Lydians see Gardner and Jevons, *Gk. Ant.* p. 49. Cf. Aesch. *Persae* 41 ἀβροδιαίτων δ' ἕπεται Λυδῶν ὄχλος. After the Persian wars the short (Dorian) χιτών of wool was substituted for it.

οὐ πολὺς χρόνος ἐπειδή—'no long time ago.' ἀφ' οὗ, ἐξ οὗ, ἐπεί, ὡς, ὅτε are all found in such phrases.

27. χρυσῶν τεττίγων seem to be pins with figures of grass-hoppers at the end. Several might be used, apparently, for one κρώβυλος, like hairpins. Helbig, however, thinks that metal spiral ornaments through which the 'tail' of the hair was passed are meant, and Studniczka supports this view ; but it does not seem probable. The κρώβυλος—which doubtless took different forms—is perhaps to be recognised on ancient monuments, since Xen. *Anab.* v. iv. 13 speaks of leather helmets adorned with a κρώβυλος and resembling a tiara (the various forms of which are well known). εἴρω, twist, favours 'coil' ; but, if the pins had a bend in them, we can understand ἔνερσις. (The v.l. ἐν ἔρσει is prob. a false division like ἐν τομῇ for ἐντομῇ, c. **93**, 5.) Cf. Aristoph. *Eq.* 1325, *Nub.* 984.

28. ἀφ' οὗ—'from this circumstance.' It is likely that Thuc. is mistaken in saying that the Athenians carried the fashion to Asia Minor, and that it spread rather from the Ionians (Carians, Lydians) to the Athenians. Cf. Herod. v. 88.

PAGE 6.

1. ἐπὶ πολύ—*temporal.*

μετρίᾳ—this may mean that the Dorians too for a time had worn the 'Ionian' dress ; but more probably Thuc. in μετρίᾳ and ἐς τὸν νῦν τρόπον thought rather of the Athenians, and meant merely that the Spartans originated the 'Dorian' χιτών.

4. **ἰσοδίαιτοι** with πρὸς τοὺς πολλούς. τὰ μείζω, which is unusual for τὰ πλείω, is thought to refer to the fact that *land* was the sole form of wealth in early Sparta.

6. **ἐς τὸ φανερὸν ἀποδύντες**—*ἐς τὸ φ.* is a standing phrase for 'openly,' 'in public,' with verbs of motion, or suggestive of motion. The simplest form of phrase is such as *ἐς τὸ φ. ἐνεγκεῖν* (Hyperid. I. v. 3), but Thuc., as so often, strains the use of the prep.

λίπα—'with oil,' frequent in Homer. It is generally explained as *instrumental* case, but K.W.Krüger calls it *internal accus.*

μετὰ τοῦ—in company with, i.e. 'when they . .,' as iii. 59, 3 βίου κίνδυνος ἐγγὺς μετ᾽ αὐτοῦ (sc. τοῦ τελευτᾶν λόγου).

7. **ἠλείψαντο**—*reflexive* mid. like λούομαι, ὁπλίζομαι, and other words of the toilet.

8. **διαζώματα**—*Il.* 23, 683 ζῶμα δέ οἱ πρῶτον παρακάββαλεν.

10. **πέπαυται**—sc. τὸ διαζώματα ἔχοντας ἀγωνίζεσθαι.

The order is ἔτι δὲ καὶ νῦν ἐν τοῖς β. ἔστιν οἷς (=ἐνίοις), καὶ μάλιστα (ἐν) τοῖς Ἀσιανοῖς. In the *nom.* plur. *always* εἰσὶν οἱ, αἱ ; in *oblique* cases *always* ἔστιν ὧν etc. in Thuc., unless words intervene, as in vii. 25 ἦσαν τῶν σταυρῶν οὕς.

12. **ἆθλα τίθεται καί**=ἆθλων τιθεμένων.

13. **πολλὰ . . ὁμοιότροπα**—internal accus. to διαιτώμενον.

16. **ὅσαι μέν κτλ.** — "This clause (down to ἔκαστοι ἰσχύος) is really subordinate to αἱ δὲ παλαιαί κτλ. 'Whereas the most recent cities,' etc.," Forbes.

17. **πλωιμωτέρων ὄντων**—'when navigation was easier,' *impers. gen. abs.* corresponding to πλωιμώτερα ἐγένετο 8, 2. It is a question whether περιουσίας . . ἔχουσαι goes closely with πλωιμωτέρων ὄντων, so that καί joins νεώτατα to ἔχουσαι, or belongs to ἐκτίζοντο : c. 8 καταστάντος τοῦ Μίνω ναυτικοῦ πλωιμώτερα ἐγένετο (i.e. as early as Minos) favours the former ; but c. 8 § 3 seems to show that Thuc. uses νεώτατα here vaguely of cities founded since Minos purged the seas.

20. **ἀπελάμβανον**—'occupied,' cutting them off from the mainland with walls. The change of subject from the place-names to their inhabitants is common, e.g. vi. 48 ; 74, 1 ; 75, 2 ; 88, 8 ; 94, 1.

21. **ἔκαστοι**—in this place because it goes closely with πρὸς τοὺς προσοίκους. On the order of ἕνεκα see 5, 1.

22. ἐπὶ πολύ—temporal.

23. On ἀντίσχουσαν (= διὰ τὸ τὴν λ. ἀντίσχειν) see **6**, 2 l. 19.

24. καὶ ἐν—the art. not repeated, as often in Thuc. (**6**, 1), even when the two members are contrasted.

25. ἔφερον—sc. οἱ λῃστεύοντες. They plundered not only one another but those who, though not sea-farers, lived on the coasts (= παραθαλάσσιοι ἦσαν).

PAGE 7.

1. οἱ νησιῶται—the island *barbarians* were pirates οὐχ ἧσσον ἢ οἱ Ἕλληνες.

3. ᾤκησαν—previous to the time of Minos.

Δήλου—in 426 B.C. ; iii. **104**. The 'proof' applies only to the Carians, whence it may be inferred that the presence of Phoenicians in the islands was questioned by none.

6. ὑπὲρ ἡμισύ—subject, = πλείους τῶν ἡμίσεων (though of course it might be taken as adverbial).

7. τῇ σκευῇ τῶν ὅπλων—lit. 'their equipment (consisting) of arms,' *not* 'the style of their arms.'

9. Here Thuc. resumes from c. **4**.

πλωιμώτερα ἐγένετο—the neut. plur. as in **7**, 1.

10. ἐκ τῶν νήσων—ἐκ for ἐν by (the regular method of) attraction to the verb.

11. ὅτεπερ—'namely, when,' referring back to c. **4**.

12. οἱ παρὰ θάλασσαν—cf. οἱ παρ' ἔπαλξιν ii. **13**, 5, παρά *with dat.* not being used of *inanimates* except when *persons* are clearly implied.

15. τείχη περιεβάλλοντο—referring to cities already in existence, but hitherto without walls : hence not as in c. **7**.

ὡς πλουσιώτεροι ἑαυτῶν γ.—the omission of αὐτοί in this idiom is rare : 'as was natural, since they were now growing wealthier than they had been hitherto.'

16. γάρ refers to βεβαιότερον ᾤκουν. The double τε presents the same process under two different aspects.

18. δουλείαν—'dependence,' as often ; so with δουλεύειν. The weaker states became tributaries of the stronger.

περιουσίας ἔχοντες—usually rendered 'because they had wealth at their command' and used it to extend their power ;

but more probably, 'having funds in hand' and being anxious to increase them. The more the funds increased, the more eager would they be to increase them still further.

20. ἐν τούτῳ . . ὄντες—'when they had now advanced to this condition,' i.e. navigated the seas and were grown richer.

21. ὕστερον χρόνῳ—'in course of time.'

22. 'Α. τέ μοι δοκεῖ—'and so it seems to me that it was because,' etc.

23. οὐ τοσοῦτον (ὅσον προύχων) with ἄγων, 'not so much because he was leader of . ., they being bound by their oaths to T.' Tyndareus, Helen's supposed father, made her suitors swear to protect the rights of that one whom she should choose.

26. Thuc. supports his view by reference to the origin of the kingship in Atreus' house.

27. Πελοποννησίων—masc., with οἱ, 'those of the Pel. who have received the truest account by tradition.' For the order of the gen. edd. compare c. 48, 4; 126, 11. It is supposed that Thuc. means the Argives, whose legends the Lesbian historian Hellanicus related. A fragment of H. gives the story here referred to.

PAGE 8.

3. τὴν ἐπωνυμίαν . . σχεῖν—lit. 'secured the naming of the country after himself, though a stranger.'

ἐπηλυν—there is no authority for the form ἐπηλύτης in Attic. The passage in Xen. Oec. cited in L. & S. is corrupt.

4. μείζω—neut. plur.; ξυνενεχθῆναι, 'fell to the lot of,' as often in Herod.; after Thuc. not found in Attic.

5. Εὐρυσθέως μέν κτλ.—the relationship of the persons mentioned is as follows:—

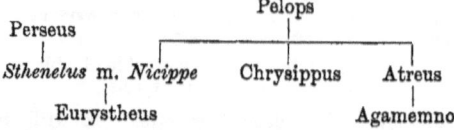

ἐν τῇ 'Αττικῇ—according to the story, Eurystheus was killed in the Megarid (Euripides represents him as taken prisoner) when at war with Demophon, king of Athens, from whom he had demanded the surrender of the Heraclidae. The Megarid was then part of Attica.

7. **καὶ ἐπιτρέψαντος .Εὐ.** — there is parataxis here for ᾽Ατρεῖ δὲ μητρὸς ἀδελφῷ ὄντι ἐπιτρέψαντος.

10. **Χρυσίππου**—Atreus and Thyestes conspired and murdered Ch. their half-brother.

12. **καὶ . . παραλαβεῖν**—co-ordinate with ἔτι μεῖζω ξυνενε-χθῆναι . . ᾽Ατρεῖ.

13. **καὶ ἅμα** —-the καί joins δοκοῦντα to βουλομένων.

δυνατόν—i.e. in point of wealth.

17. **ἅ**—the wealth and power of the two families.

18. **καὶ ναυτικῷ**—the MSS. give καὶ ναυτικῷ τε, and two explanations are suggested : (1) τε=too, Shilleto; and (2) τε=and, while καί emphasises ναυτικῷ. vi. 44 καὶ πρός τε τοὺς ᾽Ρηγίνους, viii. 68, 2 καὶ αὐτός τε, ib. 76, 5 καὶ ἑαυτούς τε give rise to a similar question. The use of τε is supported by examples in Herod. and tragedy ; but the MS. variants and certain examples of corruption in the case of τε are so numerous that it is very doubtful if the passages can be relied on. On the whole καὶ . . δέ = and moreover is more probable.

19. **ἰσχύσας**—ingressive.

20. **οὐ . . τὸ πλέον ἤ** = ἧσσον ἤ.

χάριτι . . φόβῳ — for the contrast cf. Demosth. 20 § 16 μείζων ὁ τοῦ μέλλοντος φόβος τῆς παρούσης χάριτος, but there it is the fear and good-will felt ; here it is the feelings inspired.

21. **φαίνεται γάρ**—the passages referred to are Il. ii. 576 τῶν ἑκατὸν νεῶν ἦρχε κρείων ᾽Αγαμέμνων, and ii. 610 ff. αὐτὸς γάρ σφιν δῶκεν ἄναξ ἀνδρῶν ᾽Αγαμέμνων | νῆας, and so on.

23. **ὡς . . τοῦτο**—Shilleto refers to Plat. Theaet. 193 D ὃ ἐν τοῖς πρόσθεν οὕτως ἔλεγον for a similar redundancy.

τῳ—'in any one's opinion.' Τὸ τεκμηριῶσαι supply τοῦτο : it is only with ref. to the details that Thuc. suggests a doubt.

24. **ἐν τοῦ σκήπτρου τῇ παραδόσει**—in the passage where the sceptre of Agamemnon is said to have been transmitted through his family ; Il. ii. 101 ff. For this method of referring to passages in times before the division into books, etc. was made cf. c. 10, 4 ; St. Mark xii. 26 ἐπὶ τῆς βάτου ; Ep. Rom. xi. 2.

26. **οὐκ ἄν . . ἐκράτει**—'he would not have been ruler' (as

I   G 2 he was). Classen's version, 'he would not be (in the *Iliad*) ruler,' is less likely.

27. οὐκ ἂν εἶεν—*M.T.* § 238.

2. καὶ ταύτῃ τῇ στρατείᾳ—i.e. this expedition itself was not on a very large scale : all the more insignificant must have been those undertakings that preceded it.

4. ὅτι μέν—lit. 'that M. was a small place, or if any of the towns of those days seems now insignificant—(this) could not be considered a valid argument for refusing to believe that,' etc. (1) The clauses introduced by ὅτι and εἰ form the object to χρώμενος. (2) The μέν is not regularly answered, but is resumed in οὐκ οὖν ἀπιστεῖν χρή (§ 3) after a long parenthesis. (3) ἦν may mean 'was before its destruction,' which is said by later writers to have occurred in 468 B.C. (there is no sufficient ground for doubting the statement). This is supported by νῦν δοκεῖ which refers to towns still in existence. Or it may be 'was in heroic times,' and this is supported by τότε. But, which-ever be meant, the argument is not affected. The simple explanation of the insignificance of Mycenae—now of prime importance to the archaeologist—is that the only part that could be called 'city' was the acropolis, and that was occupied by the castle of the chief. The rest of the settlement consisted of the villages of the clans ; and there is no sign that in historic times the villages ever gave way to a city. Thuc. represents the fact correctly.

9. λόγος κατέχει—*fama obtinet* ; 'tradition affirms.'

Λακεδαιμονίων γάρ—there were no signs of magnificence about Sparta until after the triumphs of Lysander. Even then, its appearance, remote from the world and unfortified, must have been comparatively insignificant. It does not seem clear that Thuc. wrote this passage before 404 B.C.

11. κατασκευῆς—κ. includes everything that makes a place habitable and usable. Here 'buildings.'

13. πρός—'in comparison with.'

14. τῶν πέντε τὰς δύο μ.—'two-fifths.' ('Two of the five divisions' is, as Mr. Forbes remarks, wrong.) Of course Messenia is included in Laconia. Notice the way in which fractions are expressed. The gen. is omitted when the *denomi-nator* is one higher than the *numerator*—as τὰ τρία μέρη = ¾.

15. τῆς ξυμπάσης—roughly speaking. In ii. 9 Thuc. ex-

pressly notes that Argos was not under the leadership of Sparta. But the omission here is of no importance, because we do not want an exact statement, but a general account of the power of Sparta.

16. **τῶν ἔξω ξ.**—'their allies beyond P., who are many.'

17. **πόλεως**—for τῆς πόλεως, 'since the city was not compactly built.' For the omission of art. Steup compares iv. **18**, 3 and viii. **95**, 2. (Mr. Forbes's rendering 'when a city is not built continuously' is disproved by the fact that ἡ δύναμις Λακεδαιμονίων—and not *the* power of *any* city—must be supplied to φαίνοιτ' ἄν. Herbst's view that πόλεως is *predicative*—'since it has not been brought together into a compact city '—is inconsistent with Λακεδαιμονίων ἡ πόλις above.)

18. **κατασκευαῖς**—the plur. in concrete sense, as in ii. **65**, 2.

21. **διπλασίαν** . . **ἤ**—these compds. are constructed as comparatives : πολλαπλάσιοι τῶν ἐναντίων iv. **94** ; πολλαπλάσιοι ἢ ἦλθον ib. **127** ; διπλάσια δοῦναι ἢ ἄλλῳ τινί Lysias 19.

22. **εἰκάζεσθαι** depends on οἶμαι.

ἀπὸ τῆς φ. ὄψεως—*not* 'from the notable or striking appearance' (Forbes), but 'from the *mere* (external) appearance.' φανερός is, as usual, what is seen, and ὄψις is the appearance *in contrast with the reality*, as in vi. **31** τῇ ὄψει ἀνεθάρσουν (where my rendering 'by the sight' is also wrong).

26. **μεγίστην μὲν γ.**—'proved, it is true.' **δέ**—'and yet.' For τῶν πρὸ αὐτῆς cf. **1**, 1.

λειπομένην with gen. as vi. **72** οὐδενὸς λειπόμενος.

PAGE 10.

1. **ἦν**—rel. to στρατείαν. According to the regular principle in Greek, the following clause, to which the nom. is supplied from ἦν, is without the rel. In the second clause the rel. is often replaced by the required case of αὐτός or οὗτος—ii. **4**, 5, ὃ ἦν τοῦ τείχους καὶ αἱ θύραι ἀνεῳγμέναι ἔτυχον αὐτοῦ. vii. **29**, 5 ὅπερ μέγιστον ἦν καὶ ἄρτι ἔτυχον οἱ παῖδες εἰσεληλυθότες. It is the repetition of the rel. that is unusual, as in vi. **4**, 3 τὸ χωρίον οὗ νῦν ἡ πόλις ἐστὶ καὶ ὃ πρῶτον ἐτειχίσθη. If, however, the first clause is neg. and the second pos., the rel. must be repeated, as in ii. **43**, 2 οὐκ ἐν ᾧ κεῖται μᾶλλον, ἀλλ' ἐν ᾧ ἡ δόξα καταλείπεται. The same omission or substitution is frequent in Lat., as Liv. xxiii. 8 cum quo steterat nec cum patria majestas sententia deputerat. In Engl. cf. Hooker, Eccles. Pol. ' *Whom* though to know be life, and joy to make mention of *His* name.'

Johnson, *Tour in Heb.* 'we treated her with great respect, *which* she received as customary, and was neither elated *by it,* nor confused.' Macaulay, *Warren Hastings* '*To whom* she seemed to listen, but did not hear *them.*'

ἐπὶ τὸ μεῖζον κοσμῆσαι—'exaggerate by using his fancy.'

3. ἐνδεεστέρα—' comparatively insignificant.'

πεποίηκε γάρ—'out of a fleet of 1200 ships the poet has described those of the B. as carrying 120 men (ἐν δὲ ἑκάστῃ | κοῦροι Βοιωτῶν ἑκατὸν καὶ εἴκοσι βαῖνον *Il.* ii. 510), and those of Ph. as carrying 50 (ἐρέται δ' ἐν ἑκάστῃ πεντήκοντα | ἐμβέβασαν, τόξων εὖ εἰδότες ἶφι μάχεσθαι ib. 719), specifying the largest and the smallest.' ἀνδρῶν is gen. of measure, as in τεῖχος ἑπτὰ σταδίων, almost confined to expressions of magnitude. The absence of a second art. with ἐλαχίστας is interesting : Shilleto rightly compares Aesch. *Ag.* 314 νικᾷ δ' ὁ πρῶτος καὶ τελευταῖος δραμών, where the reference is to a team, of which every member wins ; just as here the two things combined are items of one fleet. As to the numbers, in Thuc.'s time the average complement of a trireme was 200. Therefore a fleet of 1200 would require 240,000 men : but the rationalistic calculation of Thuc. gives about 103,000 for the Trojan War. Of course 103,000 is a far larger number than was sent out by any *one* state in the time of Thuc. The number of men who sailed for Sicily in 415 B.C. may be roughly set down as 36,000. But § 5 shows that Thuc. thinks of the combined forces of all Greek states, and the forces in the field during the Peloponnesian War would exceed his calculation for the Trojan War. (It seems, nevertheless, that Thuc. has not made out a very satisfactory case : τῶν νῦν in § 3 should have been qualified.)

7. ἄλλων depends on μεγέθους.

8. αὐτερέται—the fighting men served also as rowers. This was quite unusual in Thuc.'s day. See *Il.* 719 quoted above.

9. ἐν—as ἐν . . παραδόσει c. 9, 4, and ἐν νεῶν καταλόγῳ above.

11. περίνεως—the only passengers would be the kings and those immediately under them.

13. μέλλοντας . . ἔχοντας—though these agree with περίνεως, they apply in sense equally to all the Greeks. We should expect *gen. abs.*

14. μετὰ σκευῶν—the want of *space* is what Thuc. alludes to. The room not taken up by the rowers would be filled with materials.

15. κατάφαρκτα—i.e. the boats had no gangways projecting along them. These gangways (πάροδοι) were used only in ships with a deep draught, and Thuc. means that, as there were none in 'Homeric' ships, those ships can have had only a small draught, and therefore there was not much room in them. At intervals along the πάροδοι were upright posts, and the open spaces between could be closed with curtains (παραρρύματα) in battle or rough weather, and thus served in a trireme to protect the bodies of the thranitae (top set of rowers). The word is generally explained 'decked'; but so far as one can judge, the only connexion between κατάστρωμα, the deck from end to end, and κατάφαρκτος is that only ships that were κατάφαρκτοι had καταστρώματα. The Homeric ships, it is true, had no καταστρώματα, but this is not the point here.

16. ληστικώτερον—'more like pirate craft' than warships.

17. πρός—'as compared with.' σκοποῦντι is dat. of the person judging, a frequent use of a partic. ; cf. c. **21**, 2

19. ὡς—'considering that.'

21. αἴτιον—this predicate, so often in neut. sing. whatever be gender and number of the subject, is practically a noun.

23. τε—answered by ἐπειδὴ δέ, as e.g. in vi. **83**, 1 ; vii. **81** ; and c. **25**, 3.

24. ὅσον—'only so large as.' αὐτόθεν with βιοτεύσειν, 'support itself in the (enemy's) country.'

25. ἀφικόμενοι—'on their arrival,' i.e. immediately after they landed. (This passage, from this word to the end of § 2, is much disputed.)

26. μάχῃ ἐκράτησαν—the conjecture ἐκρατήθησαν reduces the words τοῖς αἰεί . . ὄντες below to absurdity ; and κρατοῦντες would have to be changed to κρατήσαντες. The Greeks were able to raise a rampart because they had won a victory.

τὸ γάρ—'for otherwise.' This rampart is not that referred to in *Il.* vii. 336 and 433 as built in the tenth year by the counsel of Nestor, but one built immediately after the arrival of the Greeks, though this does not necessitate inserting εὐθύς after ἂν with Dittrich. Similarly the γεωργία τῆς Χερσονήσου below is not heard of in the *Il.* Thuc. doubtless got these details from a poem that related the earlier events of the war. Cf. the Schol. here : ἔρυμα λέγει νῦν οὐχ ὅπερ ἐν τῇ η' λέγει "Ομηρος γενέσθαι, ἀλλὰ πρότερον μικρότερον διὰ τὰς τῶν βαρβάρων ἐπιδρομάς. (Strabo quotes the opinion of Aristotle that the τεῖχος of *Il.* 7, which was so promptly destroyed by Poseidon, was in reality never built. It seems impossible that Thuc. can have had that τεῖχος in mind.)

27. **φαίνονται δέ**—this is δέ *in apodosis*, and it is here apparently suggested by the contrast set up by the parenthesis : *though* they fortified a camp, they did not employ their whole force. This δέ generally follows a parenthesis ; but not in ii. 65, 1 ἐπειδὴ ὁ πόλεμος κατέστη, ὁ δὲ φαίνεται καὶ ἐν τούτῳ προγνοὺς τὴν δύναμιν.

28. **ἐνταῦθα**—before Troy ; and consequently the Trojans held out.

PAGE 11.

2. **αὐτῶν**—'of their own accord.'

τὰ δέκα ἔτη—'those ten years.'

3. **βίᾳ**—'in the field.' They were not penned up in the city.

ὑπολειπομένοις—imperf., 'who at any given time were left behind.'

7. **ῥᾳδίως ἂν μάχῃ . . Τροίαν εἷλον**—does this passage refer to 'the two natural stages of the expedition'— battle followed by siege, or two *alternative* means of taking Troy,—either by pitched battle outside the gates, or by siege ? Those who adopt the first, either (*a*) bracket the first εἷλον with Krüger as spurious, and explain the δ' after πολιορκίᾳ as (a violent) apodotic δέ, or, with Krüger bracket it ; or else (*b*) make the first εἷλον mean, *not* 'capture (Troy),' but, with Herbst, 'defeat (the Trojans).' Those who adopt the second with Bauer, make μάχῃ κρατοῦντες = 'by superiority in the field,' and not 'being as they were superior in the field' ; and πολιορκίᾳ προσκαθεζόμενοι = 'by a regular siege,' instead of 'by persisting in a siege.' But the difficulties involved in this are insuperable ; for—apart from the extraordinary way in which the supposed alternative methods are expressed, and joined by δέ instead of ἤ—the sense obtained, though at first sight attractive, makes περιουσίαν ἔχοντες τροφῆς and ξυνεχῶς τὸν πόλεμον διέφερον pointless in so far as the *first* method— superiority in the field + assault—is concerned ; it necessitates forcing the meaning 'by an immediate assault' (κατὰ κράτος) into μάχῃ κρατοῦντες, and thus making this wholly distinct from μάχῃ ἐκράτησαν in § 1 ; and it strains no less the mean-ing of πολιορκίᾳ προσκαθεζόμενοι. We therefore prefer the

first plan, but slightly modified ; if the first εἶλον is genuine, it is probably a mere anticipation of the second. Trans. 'If they had . . carried on the war persistently, they would easily have continued superior in the field and have taken the city, seeing that . . : if, then, they had persisted in a siege, they would have taken Troy.' προσκαθεζόμενοι governs πολιορκίᾳ.

11. ἀλλά—in contrast with περιουσίαν εἰ ἦλθον ἔχοντες τροφῆς.

τούτων—i.e. τῶν Τρωικῶν.

13. τῶν πρίν—c. 1, 1 ; 10, 3.

γενόμενα—'though it proved.'

15. κατεσχηκότος—attributive. When an attributive partic. is itself further defined—διὰ τοὺς ποιητὰς κατ.—it is frequently placed outside the art. This idiom is by no means confined to Thuc.

16. μετανίστατο — 'Greece (i.e. the Greeks) was still occupied with migration and settlement, so that the country did not quiet down (ingressive) and so increase.' Ἑλλάς here is used as in c. 6, for the Greek nation—ἡ Ἑ. ἐσιδηροφόρει—and this explains (a) the use of μετανίστατο, (b) the accus. ἡσυχάσασαν, for which, as it refers to the subject of the main verb, ἡσυχάσασα would be expected. Ἑλλάς takes a slightly different meaning after the ὥστε. A similar change of meaning may be detected in vii. 34, 6 ναυμαχήσαντες δὲ ἀντίπαλα καὶ ὡς αὐτοὺς ἑκατέρους ἀξιοῦν νικᾶν, where the ὡς-clause is general in sense, ' the way in which both sides lay claim to victory.'

17. ὥστε μὴ ἡ. αὐξηθῆναι—the μή belongs to both partic. and infin., and ὥστε . . αὐξηθῆναι expresses ἀχρηματία.

20. ἐνεόχμωσε = ἐνεωτέρισε. In sense this is pluperf. The verb occurs in Herod., but only here in Attic. Thuc. thought of the fate of Agamemnon, Teucer, and other heroes.

καὶ στάσεις—two things are not clear, (1) whether the disturbances alluded to are intended to be connected with the return from Troy, or merely to be an explanation of ὥστε μὴ ἡσυχάσασαν αὐ.; (2) how Βοιωτοί τε γάρ is connected with what precedes. The passage is commonly referred to as though γάρ introduced an illustration of the στάσεις, but Steup (who thinks γάρ spurious) rightly points out that we hear nothing of στάσις in the matter of the migrations referred to. If γάρ is retained, we must assume that the migrations are introduced as an illustration of the general unrest that continued ; i.e. the γάρ refers rather to § 1 than to the immediately preceding sentence.

21. ὡς ἐπὶ πολύ—'for the most part,' 'in most cases.'

ἀφ' ὧν—'as the result of which,' referring to στάσεις.

22. τὰς πόλεις—prob. the article is distributive=cities in each instance. (Others, 'the well-known cities': but this is rightly objected to by several edd. as a strange assumption of knowledge and as clashing awkwardly with ἐν ταῖς πόλεσιν.)

23. οἱ νῦν—meaning *not* that the Boeotians had changed their name, but the Boeotians 'as we know them now,' i.e. as inhabiting all Boeotia, instead of dwelling partly in Thessaly and partly in Boeotia.

ἑξηκοστῷ ἔτει—the instances seem to be chosen in order to show that disturbances continued *for a long period* after the war.

μετὰ 'Ιλίου ἅλωσιν—the art. replaced by a gen., as in διὰ χρόνου πλῆθος c. 1, 2.

26. ἀποδασμός—i.e. a part that had *voluntarily* separated from the main body, not ἀνάσταντες, like the rest. The word only here in Attic; but cf. Φωκέες ἀποδάσμιοι Herod. i. 146.

27. ἀφ' ὧν—the plur. κατὰ σύνεσιν. The ref. is to *Il.* ii. 494, where the Boeotians, however, possess the chief cities of Boeotia.

PAGE 12.

2. ἔσχον—cf. σχεῖν, c. 9, 2.

3. ἡσυχάσασα βεβαίως—'gaining unbroken rest and no longer subject to violent changes.' Notice the ingressive aor. and imperf. combined.

5. "Ιωνας—the Ionian cities of Asia Minor. νησιωτῶν—the Cyclades; cf. c. 4. Isocr. *Panath.* 43.

6. 'Ιταλίας—i.e. the *modern* Calabria, the peninsula reaching to the Laus on W. and to Metapontum on E. 'The chief Peloponnesian founders of Sicilian and Italian cities were the Corinthians who founded Syracuse, and through Syracuse, Camarina [Acrae and Casmenae], the Megarians who founded the Hyblaean Megara, and through Megara, Selinus: the Achaeans who founded Sybaris and Croton, some Lacedaemonians who founded Tarentum,' (Forbes). But (1) Megara is not part of the Peloponnese (ii. 9), see next note; (2) it is not clear that Tarentum is reckoned in Italy.

8. ἔστιν ἃ χωρία—it is supposed that the colonies of Corinth in the W., Corcyra, Leucas, Ambracia, etc. are referred

NOTES 157

to. If so (1) τὸ πλεῖστον above is an exaggeration ; (2) Ἑλλάς
is here used for all the country ultimately inhabited by
Greeks—as in Thuc.'s time : but Ἑλλάς was not so used above ;
(3) the vagueness of the reference to these colonies is strange.
Steup gets over all these difficulties by taking ἔστιν ἃ χωρία as
nom., so that the Megarian (see last note), Locrian and
Chalcidian colonies would be included. This is tempting,
and for the use of χωρία we might compare vii. **14** τὰ τρέφοντα
ἡμᾶς χωρία τῆς Ἰταλίας, ὁρῶντα ἐν ᾧ ἐσμεν. But it must be
confessed that (1) ἔστιν ἃ looks like an antithesis to τὸ πλεῖστον :
(2) πάντα δὲ ταῦτα appears to refer to ἔστιν ἃ χωρία as well as
to the colonies mentioned before. Perhaps Thuc. writes
somewhat vaguely here.

11. ἔτι . . ἢ πρότερον—referring to c. **8**, 3.

12. τὰ πολλά—'in most cases.'

13. τῶν προσόδων μ. γιγνομένων—this goes closely with
καθίσταντο, 'tyrannies were established where the revenues (of
the government) increased.' But δυνατωτέρας . . ποιουμένης is
a general statement with regard to Greece, and qualifies the
whole sentence down to ἀντείχοντο. Thuc. means that a
tyranny was generally established in a city enjoying a large
revenue, which one man, whether a member of the governing
class or not, succeeded in getting into his hands as the result
of political agitation.

14. πρότερον δέ—not necessarily *immediately* before, for in
most cases oligarchy preceded tyranny, but 'in earlier days'
where one man ruled, his power was limited.

ἐπὶ ῥητοῖς γέρασι—'with' (under the condition of) 'fixed
prerogatives,' viz. as priest, judge and leader (Arist. *Pol.*
iii. 14, 12). The purpose of this parenthesis is to point out
that the rule of a single man, though it was known before the
age of the tyrants, had been of a wholly different character.
The age of the tyrants synchronises with an advance in Greece ;
yet the deeds even of the tyrants were relatively insignificant.
As to tyranny, Aristotle agrees with Thuc. : ἐπεὶ δὲ χείρους
γενόμενοι ἐχρηματίζοντο ἀπὸ τῶν κοινῶν, ἐντεῦθέν ποθεν εὔλογον
γενέσθαι τὰς ὀλιγαρχίας . . ἐκ δὲ τούτων πρῶτον εἰς τυραννίδας
μετέβαλον.

17. ἐγγύτατα—superlative of ἐγγύς. Cf. *prope* and *propius.*

18. μεταχειρίσαι—Thuc., like Herod., uses the act. of this
word, whereas other authors use mid.

19. καὶ . . ναυπηγηθῆναι—καί = 'and in fact,' the building
of a trireme marking a climax in naval affairs (τὰ περὶ τὰς ναῦς).

τῆς Ἑλλάδος goes with πρῶτον : cf. ii. **18** ἀφίκετο τῆς Ἀττικῆς ἐς Οἰνόην πρῶτον.   Herod. i. **163** πρώτῃ δὲ Φωκαίῃ Ἰωνίης ἐπε- χείρησε.—The τετρήρης made its appearance in the second half of the fourth cent., and was the normal type of ship in the hellenistic period.   It is not likely that it had four banks of oars.

22. **ναῦς**—whether these were triremes or not does not appear.

23. **τοῦδε τοῦ πολέμου**—the dates given are circ. 704 and 664 B.C. (or, if the Archidamian War is meant, see Introd. p. xxvi, circ. 721 and 681 B.C.).

24. **ὅτε**—'since.'

Σαμίοις ἦλθε—the dat. after (simple) verbs of motion is common in tragedy, but does not occur in Attic prose outside Thuc. ; cp. c. **27**, 1 ; **61**, 1 ; **107**, 7.

25. **γίγνεται**—'turns out to be.'

26. **καὶ ταύτῃ**—lit. 'this too reckons 260 years.'   The καί brings the battle into relation with the event above.   (Thuc. seems to be maintaining the priority of Corinth against some other claimant.)   The ταύτῃ is *possessive* dat., as Herod. ii. **145** Ἡρακλέϊ ὅσα φασὶ εἶναι ἔτεα ἐς Ἄμασιν.

PAGE 13.

1. **τὴν πόλιν**—'their city.'

2. **αἰεὶ δή ποτε**—as δή ποτε means 'in the past' (frequent in tragedy), so αἰεὶ δή ποτε = always in the past, i.e. 'from the earliest times.'

3. **τῶν Ἑλλήνων . . ἐπιμισγόντων**—two points are made : (1) the early commerce of the Greeks was carried on mainly by land, (2) the Isthmus was on the high-road between οἱ ἐντός and οἱ ἔξω II.   The sentence would be much clearer with a partic. like πορευομένων, as proposed by Steup, after Ἑλλήνων, so that τε would mean 'and.'

7. **ἀφνειόν**—we have only one instance, *Il.* ii. 570.

9. **μᾶλλον ἔπλῳζον**—cf. c. **8**, 2.

τὰς ναῦς—the ships referred to in § 2.   These enabled Greece to extinguish piracy, and thus to further her commerce ; and the outcome of that, it is implied, was the formation of a considerable fleet.

11. **ἀμφότερα** with παρέχοντες, 'in both ways,' i.e. as the

context shows, by sea and land. ἀμφότερα and κατ' ἀμφότερα do not of themselves mean 'on both elements,' but show the same accus. as τοῦτον τὸν τρόπον, and κατὰ πολλοὺς τρόπους. It is the context that gives the special meaning.

ἴσχον—ingressive.

12. "Ἴωσιν—those of Asia Minor, among whom the Phocaeans and Samos are specially mentioned.

13. ἐπὶ Κύρου—556-529 B.C.

16. Κύρῳ πολεμοῦντες—they were ultimately reduced by Harpagus. Cf. c. 16.

17. ἐπὶ Καμβύσου—C. reigned 529-521 B.C. Polycrates ruled 532-521 B.C. According to Herod. iii. 164, Samos was πολίων πασέων πρώτη Ἑλληνίδων καὶ βαρβάρων in the time of Polycrates.

19. 'Ρηνείαν ἑλών—Herod. iii. 39 assigns far more imposing achievements to Polycrates: cf. ib. 122 τῆς δὲ ἀνθρωπίνης (i.e. not 'heroic,' like Minos) λεγομένης γενεῆς Πολυκράτης πρῶτος, ἐλπίδας πολλὰς ἔχων Ἰωνίης τε καὶ νήσων ἄρξειν. This gift was made to the Delian Apollo as the Ionian deity.

21. Μασσαλίαν οἰκίζοντες—'at the time when they founded Massilia.' Herod. i. 166 gives an account of a victory of the Etruscans and Carthaginians about 546 B.C., the time of which Thuc. is here speaking. But Eusebius and others placed the foundation of Marseilles 600 B.C. : there is plainly a discrepancy in the dates given for its foundation. (Classen in the 3rd ed. took ἐνίκων to mean 'gained victories,' and referred them to 600 B.C. ; but Thuc. is plainly referring to circ. 546 B.C. See Steup's appendix.)

22. ταῦτα γάρ—'these, in fact, were the strongest navies,' i.e. the strongest possessed by Ionians (cf. § 6).

23. φαίνεται with χρώμενα and ἐξηρτυμένα : 'though these fleets were built . . we find ' etc.

25. πεντηκοντόροις—Gardner and Jevons, p. 652. It is plain from Herod. i. 163 that penteconters counted as νῆες μακραί, and stand in contrast to νῆες στρογγύλαι, merchant-ships (cf. Thuc. ii. 97, 1). Therefore the πλοῖα μακρά are doubtless long ships of larger and smaller size than penteconters. To their resemblance in size to merchant-ships the word πλοῖα seems to point.

26. ἐκεῖνα—those existing in the time of the Trojan War.

27. τοῦ Δαρείου θανάτου—485 B.C. ἐβασίλευσε, 'reigned,' rather than 'became king.'

29. περί τε Σικελίαν—for the vague use of περί cf. Isocr. v. 111 εἶχε μεγίστην δύναμιν τῶν περὶ τὴν Ἀσίαν. This is the age of the great Sicilian tyrants—Thero, Gelo, Hiero.

30. ἐς πλῆθος ἐγένοντο—'reached a considerable number'; probably the lit. sense is 'came to.'

PAGE 14.

3. εἴ τινες ἄλλοι—sc. ἐκέκτηντο ναυτικά.

4. βραχέα—sc. ναυτικά, 'small fleets.' This sense of βραχύς is frequent in Thuc.

5. τὰ πολλά—'the greater part of these consisted of.'

ὀψέ τε ἀφ' οὗ—sc. ἦν, 'it was late when.' For ἀφ' οὗ we should expect ὅτε: but instead of saying 'already when they started to build, it was so late that they could not get a strong fleet before the invasion of Xerxes,' he says 'from the time that they started' etc. The building of the ships took place in 483-82 B.C., the archonship of Nicodemus, and the invasion in 480 B.C. Herod. vii. 144 does not say that Them. looked forward to a Persian invasion when he advised the building of the ships. It is thought that Herod. wanted to belittle Them.

9. ἐναυμάχησαν—at Salamis.

διὰ πάσης—' throughout,' an adverbial expression like ἀπὸ τῆς ἴσης c. 15 ; ἀπὸ (τῆς) πρώτης, etc. (This is better than supplying νεώς.)

10. καταστρώματα—the Homeric ship was covered only fore and aft, the part in which the men rowed being open. (Cf. on c. 10, 4.)

12. τὰ παλαιά—i.e. the early fleets mentioned in c. 13. τὰ ὕστερον γενόμενα—i.e. those mentioned in c. 14 § 3.

14. οὐκ ἐλαχίστην—'considerable,' in spite of smallness of the fleets.

αὐτοῖς—τοῖς ναυτικοῖς.

χρημάτων προσόδῳ—see c. 13 § 5. The possessi. of a fleet enabled them still further to increase their trade.

16. τὰς νήσους κ.—'began to' or 'endeavoured to reduce the islands.' The enterprise of Athens and Corinth is alluded to, as in (ἐκεῖνοι) ὅσοι μή.

18. ὅθεν τις — 'as the result of which any considerable force was brought together,' or 'from which any considerable power was gained.' This seems to be the meaning, corresponding

to ἰσχὺν δὲ κτλ. above. But παραγίγνομαι in Thuc. of troops regularly means 'be assembled in the field,' and with dat. 'come to the support of.' 'To be added to' is προσγίγνομαι. Hence many edd. render 'in consequence of which any considerable force was collected.' ὅθεν is then strange.

ξυνέστη—frequently used in this connexion from Herod. downwards.

22. οὐ γὰρ ξυνειστήκεσαν—'they were not joined to the strongest states as subjects, nor yet did they of their own accord unite on an equal footing for a campaign.'

25. κατ' ἀλλήλους—inter se.

ὡς ἕκαστοι—cf. c. 3 § 4. Strictly ἐπολέμουν is supplied with ὡς, but the phrase practically becomes a distributive numeral.

27. Χαλκιδέων καὶ Ἐρετριῶν—the date of this war, fought for the possession of the Lelantian plain, is unknown. Herod. says that Samos helped Chalcis and Miletus helped Eretria, and of course both sides must have attracted many other allies. The ultimate cause of the war was commercial rivalry. (Busolt i. p. 313.)

PAGE 15.

1. καὶ τὸ ἄλλο Ἑ —'the rest of the Greeks also took sides as allies of the one or the other.'

2. ἐπεγένετο—often of unfavourable occurrences, especially of anything sudden and unexpected, such as natural phenomena.

3. ἄλλοθι—'in different parts.'

μή—according to the constr. with verbs of hindrance (M.T. 749, 807), though κωλύω generally has the simple infin.

4. καί—'and in particular.'—Ἴωσι is governed both by προχωρησάντων and by ἐπεστράτευσε. There is an anacoluthon at ἐπεστράτευσε, for strictly ἐπεγένετο should govern Ἴωσι with an abstract noun parallel to κωλύματα for its subject.

6. βασιλεία—mss. authority is altogether in favour of this against ἐξουσία, and ἐξουσία does not seem to occur before Aristotle in this sense. Stahl thinks βασιλεία is a gloss on ἐξουσία. But it is possible that ἐξουσία itself is a gloss. The matter is complicated by the fact that both βασιλεία and ἐξουσία have a double sense (ἐξουσία, 'power to do a thing,' a 'power'; cf. βασιλεία τὸ ἀξίωμα καὶ τὸ ἔθνος βασιλευόμενον, Suidas). Of course here the sense is concrete.

Κροῖσον—the destruction of the Lydian monarchy was 546 B.C., Herod. i. 87 etc.

ὅσα—a part. of εἰμί is constantly omitted after ὅσος.

ἐντὸς "Αλυος ποταμοῦ—ἐντός from the Greek point of view. When ποταμός is added the art. is regularly inserted before the name of a river in Attic. But Herod. does not use the art., and Thuc. omits it in six passages. The only other known exx. are Isocr. 7, 80 (al-o ἐντὸς "Αλυος π.) and Xen. Anab. iv. 7, 18.

9. **καὶ τὰς νήσους**—according to Herod. i. 169, when the Ionian cities of the mainland submitted to Harpagus, the islands also gave in; but. no doubt the submission of the islands was incomplete. Otherwise the rise of Polycrates would be unaccountable. Thuc. alludes to their reduction after Lade, 494 B.C.

10. **τύραννοι**—see c. 13 § 1. The course of the argument was there broken by the reference to the fleets, which were first dealt with.

11. **τὸ ἐφ' ἑαυτῶν**—'their own interests.'

12. **τὸ σῶμα**—'with regard to their personal good and the increase of their own estate.' σῶμα includes safety and enjoyment.

14. **δι' ἀσφαλείας . . μάλιστα**=ὅσον ἐδύναντο ἀσφαλέστατα. 'Had the utmost regard for security in the administration of their cities,' i.e. 'pursued a cautious policy' by avoiding great enterprises. δι' ἀσφαλείας is an adverbial phrase, like those with which ἔχειν is usually found, as δι' ἐπιμελείας, δι' ἡσυχίας, διὰ φυλακῆς.

15. **ἀπ' αὐτῶν**—'on their part.'

16. **εἰ μὴ εἴ τι**—εἰ μή εἰ, nisi si, only here in Thuc. (see crit. note). εἰ μή becomes an adverb. M.T. 476, 4.

17. **οἱ γάρ**—for the use of γάρ cf. c. 14, 1. 'The Sicilian tyrants in fact attained to the *greatest* power,' i.e. greater power than any other of the tyrants (and they fought against their neighbours). The sense of πλεῖστον here is that of c. 1 § 2 ἐπὶ πλεῖστον ἀνθρώπων. There is no need for excision.

18. **οὕτω πανταχόθεν**—summing up the whole from c. 13.

19. **κατείχετο**—'was held in check,' 'constrained.' Cf. c. 16; but the second clause, κατὰ πόλεις τε shows that κατείχετο is felt here not as a verb of *prevention*, but of *compulsion*.

22. **'Αθηναίων**—the overthrow of Hippias, 510 B.C.

23. οἱ ἐκ τῆς—the prep. by attraction to κατελύθησαν.

ἐπὶ πολὺ κτλ.—lit. 'which over a large area had been under tyrants even before Athens.' The earliest instance was at Sicyon, where Orthagoras became tyrant circ. 670 B.C.

24. οἱ πλεῖστοι . . Σικελίᾳ — limiting apposition to οἱ τύραννοι, καὶ . . Σικελίᾳ explaining πλεῖστοι, 'most of them, the last in fact except those in Sicily.' In Syracuse the tyrants lasted till 466 B.C., when Thrasybulus was expelled.

25. ὑπὸ Λακεδαιμονίων—the Spartans were called μισοτύραννοι. Cf. Aristotle, Pol. v. 10 Λακ. πλείστας κατέλυσαν τυραννίδας. But their traditional policy of tyrant-breaking was dropped in the fourth cent., when αὐτονομία became their watchword. Thus in 371 B.C. an orator is represented by Xen. as taunting the Spartans with preferring tyranny to free institutions. Alcibiades in his speech at Sparta (vi. 89—winter of 415-4 B.C.) makes a point out of this tradition.

27. τὴν κτίσιν—strictly speaking the Dorians did not found Sparta: it existed before the invasion ; but there is no difficulty in speaking of the second founders thus.

PAGE 16

1. ὧν ἴσμεν = ἐκείνων οὓς ἴσμεν. The στάσις lasted longer at Sparta than elsewhere : cf. Herod. i. 65, the Spartans before Lycurgus κακονομώτατοι ἦσαν σχεδὸν πάντων Ἑλλήνων κατά τε σφέας αὐτοὺς καὶ ξείνοισι ἀπρόσμικτοι. In spite of this, they were the earliest to obtain good laws—μετέβαλον ἐς εὐνομίην (Herod. l.c.) = ηὐνομήθη.

4. τετρακόσια—this gives a later date than 884 B.C. which other authorities assign to Lycurgus.

7. δυνάμενοι = δυνατοὶ ὄντες, see L. & S.

8. μετὰ δέ—the main sentence is resumed after the parenthesis. Cf. the use of δέ (δ' οὖν) in c. 11, 1 ; οὖν in vii. 42, 3 ; δέ is frequent. So autem, sed, igitur.

τὴν κατάλυσιν ἐκ τῆς Ἑλλάδος — the art. is not repeated with a verbal substantive. The words necessary to complete its sense generally follow, but sometimes precede it, as in ii. 18, 3 κατὰ τὴν ἄλλην πορείαν ἡ σχολαιότης. In the latter case, the prepositional phrase is connected with the verb of the sentence (cf. ii. 7, 2 ; 38, 1) as well as with the verbal substantive.

10. καὶ ἡ ἐν Μαραθῶνι μάχη—i.e. now begins the modern period, τὰ Μηδικά.

12. τῷ μ. στόλῳ—'the great armada.'

14. ἐπικρεμασθέντος—'impending,' as ii. 53, 4 ; iii. 40, 7.

16. τῶν ξυμπολεμησάντων—this and ἡγήσαντο are ingressive ; 'assumed the leadership of those who entered on the war as allies.' προύχοντες—causal.

19. καὶ ἀνασκευασάμενοι . . ἐσβάντες . . ἐγένοντο = ἀναλαβόντες τὰ σκεύη ἐσέβησαν καὶ ἐγένοντο. Observe the historical importance of ναυτικοὶ ἐγένοντο, which is emphasised by its connexion with ἡγήσαντο τῶν Ἑλλήνων.

20. ἀπωσάμενοι . . διεκρίθησαν—the subject modified in the course of the sentence from 'the confederates' to the confederates exclusive of Athens and Sparta, and those Asiatic cities and islands that revolted from Persia after Salamis.

24. ταῦτα—Athens and Sparta. διεφάνη—'it had become clear that,' denoting the singling out of these two from among the rest. The aor. in sense of plup. appears in (1) sentences introduced by 'when,' 'since,' 'until' regularly ; (2) in rel. and other subord. sentences often ; (3) in principal sentences occasionally.

26. ὁμαιχμία—used by Herod. and late writers ; the adj. ὅμαιχμος in iii. 58, 4.

27. διενεχθέντες—open war in 457 B.C., dispute in 461 B.C. See c. 102. ἐπολέμησαν—till the thirty years' truce 445 B.C. See c. 107.

PAGE 17.

4. ἤδη ἐχώρουν—'now regularly joined these states'—i.e. entered the alliance of Athens or Sparta. Contrast the earlier state of affairs, c. 15, 2 οὐ γὰρ ξυνειστήκεσαν κτλ.

5. τὰ μὲν σπενδόμενοι—this should mean 'now making truces' ; but we certainly expect 'being now at peace.' In the previous sentences Thuc. has described the state of affairs (a) from the battle of Salamis to 457 B.C., (b) from 457 onwards. Now during period (a) Athens and Sparta were at peace ; but from 466 disputes began between Athens and her allies. During period (b) Athens and Sparta might be said to be 'making truces' (450, 445 B.C.) or making war. The ὥστε therefore seems to refer to what happened from 456 onwards ; but ἀπὸ τῶν Μηδικῶν—the war with Xerxes to the battle of Plataea (or Mycale) does not agree with this. There is a want of precision in the passage.

7. εὖ παρεσκευάσαντο τὰ πολέμια—cf. Arist. *Ath. Pol.* 23 of the Athenians, συνέβη τὰ εἰς τὸν πόλεμον ἀσκῆσαι. τὰ πολέμια in the sense of τὰ πολεμικά is found in Herod. and Hippocrates; Xen. *Anab.* i. 6, 1; Arist. *Ath. Pol.* c. 3 and 23.

11. ἡγοῦντο—sc. αὐτῶν.

κατ' ὀλιγαρχίαν κτλ.—i.e. θεραπεύοντες δὲ ὅπως πολιτεύσουσι κατ'-ὀλιγαρχίαν (κατά of manner), ἐπιτηδείως σφίσιν αὐτοῖς μόνον ('in their, the Lacedaemonian, interests alone'). Cf. Arist. *Pol.* iv. 11 τῶν ἐν ἡγεμονίᾳ γενομένων τῆς Ἑλλάδος . . οἱ μὲν δημοκρατίας καθίστασαν, οἱ δ' ὀλιγαρχίας, οὐ πρὸς τὸ τῶν πόλεων συμφέρον σκοποῦντες ἀλλὰ πρὸς τὸ σφέτερον αὐτῶν.

13. ναῦς τε τῶν πόλεων—having gradually taken over (assumed possession of) the ships of the various cities. Cf. c. **99**, 3.

16. καὶ ἐγένετο αὐτοῖς—two widely different views are taken of this passage according as αὐτοῖς means (a) 'the Athenians' only or (b) 'the Athenians and Lacedaemonians.' Omitting minor differences, we get (a) 'and so her own resources for carrying on this war reached a greater strength than (what she had) when she stood at the height of her prosperity side by side with the undamaged forces of her confederates'; i.e. Athens had appropriated the forces of her confederates, as it were, and thus was stronger than when she was at the head of a body of independent allies. (b) The forces of Athens and Sparta separately were stronger than they had been (both together) during the period of the ὁμαιχμία (Classen) or 'stronger than the strongest power each separately had wielded with its still undamaged συμμαχία' (Herbst). (a) accords with what Thuc. afterwards says of the growth of Athenian power (cf. c. **118**). By τὰ κράτιστα he means the time before the reduction of Naxos (466 B.C.). ξυμμαχία ἀκραιφνής is in contrast with the appropriation of ships and imposition of tribute. (b) with Classen's rendering is too strong; with Herbst, we certainly hardly feel the statement, as far as it refers to Sparta, consistent with the reference to her policy made above.

20. τὰ παλαιά—this, as Herbst and Steup point out, refers only to the time *before the expulsion of the tyrants*—see note on c. 1 § 2 τὰ γὰρ πρὸ αὐτῶν κτλ. The events of the Persian wars were fully known, and in c. **18**, 1 Thuc. comes to them as to *modern* events. Therefore we must suppose cc. **18** and **19** to form a long parenthesis—see the analysis of the προοίμιον, Intr. III. note.

τοιαῦτα—i.e. comparatively insignificant, οὐ μεγάλα.

χαλεπὰ ὄντα — 'though it is difficult to trust every piece of evidence as put forward *in the traditions about them.*' This is the *personal* constrn. for χαλεπὸν ὂν παντὶ ἐξῆς τ. π. The clause is amplified in what follows, and does not refer to what has preceded. πᾶν ἐξῆς = 'every one without exception.'

22. ἀκοάς — 'accounts.'

24. σφίσιν — the indirect reflexive, which, as regularly used in subord. sentences, refers to subject of principal sentence. But later writers generally use ἑαυτούς etc. as both indirect and direct reflex.

ὁμοίως — as events that did not occur in their own place.

25. γοῦν — cf. c. 2 § 5. Here 'for example' (? and there too).

Ἵππαρχον — there is a more detailed account of the matter in vi. 54-59. Herod. v. 55; vi. 123; Arist. *Ath. Pol.* c. 18. There are no discrepancies between this account and the statement of Herod. and Arist. (for the statement in the latter that Thessalus was half - brother of Hipparchus is not necessarily a contradiction of this); but there are several differences between the Aristotelian account and the longer account given in book vi.

PAGE 18.

1. ὑποτοπήσαντές τι — 'feeling some suspicion.' (Some connect τί with μεμηνῦσθαι.) ὑποτοπῆσαι used by Thuc. only in *aor.* inf. or partic.

2. ἐκείνῃ τῇ ἡμέρᾳ καὶ π. with μεμηνῦσθαι, 'on that great day at the very moment,' before they were to take action.

3. ἐκ . . μεμηνῦσθαι — the other places in Thuc. in which ἐκ practically = ὑπό are ii. 49, 1; iii. 69, 1; v. 104; vi. 36, 2. The use is Ionic, not found in Aristoph., and there are only doubtful traces of it in the orators.

5. πρὶν ξυλληφθῆναι . . κινδυνεῦσαι — 'wishing to do something before they were arrested (and) then to take their chance.' πρὶν ξ. goes with δράσαντές τι, and καί = 'on that condition.'

7. περὶ τὸ Λεωκόρειον — ἐν μέσῳ τῷ Κεραμεικῷ (Harpocration), but *inside* the city. Meanwhile Hippias (according to vi. 57) was marshalling the procession outside the gates. The *Ath. Pol.* however says that Hippias was awaiting the procession on the acropolis. The route of the procession was from the (outer) Ceramicus to the temple of Athena Polias. As for the

Leocorion, the story was that the three daughters of King Leos were sacrificed to Pallas to avert famine from Athens. The chapel is connected with the worship of Apollo as god of purification.

9. πολλὰ δὲ καὶ ἄλλα — 'as regards'; or (what comes to the same) οἴονται may be rendered 'conceive.'

10. οὐ χρόνῳ ἀμνηστούμενα—·'le grec renforce souvent une idée positive en la reprenant sous forme négative' (Chambry). Cf. p. 112 l. 16.

11. ὥσπερ κτλ.—Herod. vi. 57, if the kings are not present at a meeting of the Council, (κελεύουσι) τοὺς μάλιστά σφι τῶν γερόντων προσήκοντας ἔχειν τὰ τῶν βασιλέων γέρεα, δύο ψήφους τιθεμένους, τρίτην δὲ τὴν ἑωυτῶν. It may be that Thuc. is referring to that passage, and took it to imply that each king had two votes (though it is doubtful whether Herod. meant that). In ix. 53 Herod. mentions the λόχος Πιτανάτης as present at Plataea. It can hardly be doubted that Thuc. consciously includes Herod. among οἱ ἄλλοι "Ελληνες. See Jebb, *The Speeches of Thuc.*, in *Hellenica*, p. 273.

12. μιᾷ ψήφῳ—we expect the accus., as in Aesch. *Eum.* 738 ψῆφον δ' Ὀρέστῃ τήνδ' ἐγὼ προσθήσομαι, but the sense is 'give their opinion (sc. γνώμην) with one vote.' (*Eum.* l.c. does not support the opinion of Classen and Steup that the use of the dat. is to be explained by the fact that the kings voted last.) The errors noted illustrate the difficulty of getting information about Spartan proceedings.

17. ἐκ . . τεκμηρίων with νομίζων. The object is (ἐκεῖνα) ἃ διῆλθον, the pred. τοιαῦτα μάλιστα (εἶναι). The partic. νομίζων, πιστεύων, ἡγησάμενος are co-ordinate ; but they express *not* condition, but *means* : lit. 'However, it is by considering the proofs I have given and in the light of them thinking that . . that one will escape error, and not by preferring to follow the embellishments and exaggerations of poets or the attractive but untrustworthy compositions of prose writers . . but by coming to the conclusion.' Edd. generally represent the participles as conditional, but μήτε . . μήτε would then be required. See *M. T.* § 835.

20. ἐπὶ τό—'so as to please the ear of the public rather than to arrive at the truth.' The double compar. as regularly where two qualities in the same person or thing are contrasted : ἰὼ στρατηγοὶ πλέονες ἢ βελτίονες.

23. ὄντα—agreeing with the implied object of ξυνέθεσαν. τὰ πολλά is in limiting apposition to this object, and αὐτῶν depends on τὰ πολλά.

24. ἀπίστως—'so as to be incredible.' This pregnant use of an adverb may often be noticed in the phrases with ἔχειν, διακεῖσθαι, διατιθέναι.

ἐπὶ τὸ μυθῶδες ἐκνενικηκότα—generally rendered 'have won their way into the region of the fabulous': but Croiset explains 'in which the fabulous character has ended by prevailing.'

26. ὡς παλαιὰ εἶναι—for the restrictive infin. see M. T. § 781 ; 'sufficiently considering their antiquity.' The 'plainest indications' are the τεκμήρια of § 1.

27. καὶ ὁ πόλεμος—Thuc. having ascertained, as clearly as is possible, the small importance of earlier undertakings, now returns to the Pel. War, which, to all who judge it in the light of the facts, will be found to have proved more important than they (τὰ παλαιά).

28. ἐν ᾧ—'while.'

PAGE 19.

3. δηλώσει—with partic., as in ii. 50 ἐδήλωσε . . ἄλλο τι ὄν. Cf. v. 9 δείξω οὐ παραινέσαι οἷός τε ὤν. Cf. Jebb on Soph. Ant. 20.

5. καὶ ὅσα μέν—after his reference to the importance of the war, Thuc. goes on to explain the manner in which he has dealt with it. ὅσα = 'as regards all that.'

λόγῳ—Steup is probably right in explaining this, not as merely pleonastic, but as a reference to the set speeches, as distinct from 'words' generally : hence = 'in debate.' Note, however, the implied contrast between τὰ ἔργα τῶν λεχθέντων and τὰ ἔργα τῶν πραχθέντων, deeds of speech and of act.

6. ἐν αὐτῷ—i.e. ἐν τῷ πολεμεῖν.

7. χαλεπόν — for the implied sense 'impossible' Steup compares c. 20, 1 ; vii. 87, 4.

9. ὧν—rel. to τῶν λεχθέντων.

ἄλλοθέν ποθεν—'from the various places where they happened to be.'

10. ὡς δ' ἂν ἐδόκουν κτλ.—'I have represented the various speakers as uttering the sentiments that seemed to me appropriate to the particular occasion, while I have kept as closely as possible to the general sense of what was really said' : lit. 'as I believed that they would have best expressed what it

was necessary to say.' ἄν and μάλιστα belong to εἰπεῖν : ἐχομένῳ κτλ. to εἴρηται, to which ἐμοί is supplied. The order is thus awkward, but it is made easier by the preceding ἐμοί. (The sense does not allow us to connect ἐχομένῳ with ἐδόκουν.)

11. **τὰ δέοντα**—i.e. the best arguments that could be found to support the ξύμπασα γνώμη of the speaker. (Jebb, *Hellenica* p. 275, thinks that Thuc. is tacitly contrasting this method with that of Herod., and, as it can scarcely be doubted that he does so in the passage that follows, this is probably true.)

14. **τὰ δ' ἔργα τῶν πραχθέντων** — verbally this is opposed to τὴν ἀκρίβειαν τῶν λεχθέντων rather than to ὅσα λόγῳ εἶπον.

16. **ἠξίωσα**—'thought it my business.'

οὐδ' ὡς ἐμοὶ ἐδόκει—'in accordance with my own whims.'

17. **οἷς τε αὐτὸς παρῆν**—i.e. (ἠξίωσα γράφειν ἐκεῖνα) οἷς: I described 'facts which I myself witnessed and (I described facts) after inquiring about each detail from others,' thus ἐπεξελθών is parallel to οἷς αὐτὸς παρῆν, which, as Mr. Forbes says, is equivalent to αὐτὸς παραγενόμενος. (Another way is to make ἐπεξελθών govern οἷς αὐτὸς παρῆν, but this has the great disadvantage of making οἷς αὐτὸς παρῆν and παρὰ τῶν ἄλλων parallel phrases. See crit. note.)

18. **ὅσον δυνατὸν ἀκριβείᾳ**—for (τοσοῦτον) ὅσον (accus. δυνατὸν (ἦν) ἀ. Notice that ἀκριβείᾳ here is *subjective* in sense, meaning the accuracy of Thuc., *not* the accuracy of the facts, as in § 1.

21. **ἑκατέρων**—'towards either side,' objective gen. to εὐνοίας, as in vii. 57, 10 Ἀθηναίων εὐνοίᾳ. (Croiset connects ἑκατέρων τις, *ex utrisque partibus quisque*.)

ὡς . . εὐνοίας ἢ μνήμης ἔχοι—for the gen., that of the *sphere in which*, depending on ὡς, πῶς, ποῦ, ποῖ, and occasionally other advs. of manner, cf. c. 36, 2. ἔχοι is iterative.

23. **τὸ μὴ μυθῶδες**—'the fact that he hears no legend in my history.' μή is here subjective, referring to what the reader will feel. (The edd., as frequently in Thuc., give various explanations of this μή.)

αὐτῶν—with τὸ μὴ μ. ; cf. c. 1, 2.

24. **ἀτερπέστερον**—'less attractive.'

25. **τῶν γενομένων**—this means 'the past' so far as Thuc. records it, the period with which he deals ; for Thuc. could

not suppose that his work would be useful as a record of *all* past history.

τὸ σαφές—'the truth,' 'the exact nature.'

26. τῶν μελλόντων κτλ.—'of what is likely to be repeated at some future time with more or less exactness.'

PAGE 20.

1. κρίνειν—subject τούτους. αὐτά—'my history,' as αὐτῶν above.

2. τε—concluding, 'and so.'

ἀγώνισμα—the word means 'performance,' 'feat,' 'show piece,' or 'prize'; here of a prize composition.

ἐς τὸ παραχρῆμα ἀκούειν—'for immediate hearing.'

4. τῶν δὲ πρότερον—it is by this time shown that τὰ παλαιά (cc. 2-17) were unimportant as compared with the Pel. War. But there remains the war against Xerxes (τὸ Μηδικόν, see c. 18, 2, the μέγας στόλος); and to that Thuc. now passes.

5. δυοῖν ναυμαχίαιν καὶ πεζομαχίαιν — which battles were these ? The Schol. says Artemisium and Salamis ; Thermopylae and Plataea. But it is difficult to see how Mycale could be left out, and owing to the indecisive character of Artemisium, it is likely that Thuc. did not mean to include it, and reckoned Mycale as a ναυμαχία.

7. τούτου δὲ τοῦ π.—it is not possible to say with certainty whether Thuc. alludes to the Ten Years' War, or the whole of the Pel. War.

μέγα—predicative.

8. ξυνηνέχθη—cf. c. 9, 2. This use also, with an infin., is frequent in Herod.

11. ὑπὸ βαρβάρων—if the Ten Years' War is meant, the only case mentioned by Thuc. is Colophon (iii. 34) ; but if the Twenty-seven Years' War be meant, Mycalessus (vii. 29) may be included, though ἠρημώθησαν is somewhat exaggerated.

ὑπὸ σφῶν αὐτῶν—as Plataea (iii. 68), Mytilene (iii. 50), Thyrea (iv. 57).

12. οἰκήτορας μετέβαλον—as Aegina (ii. 27), Potidaea (ii. 70), Anactorium (iv. 49), Scione (v. 32), Delos (v. 1), Melos (v. 116).

13. **φυγαί**—sc. ἐγένοντο. Instances of exile as the direct consequence of the war are the Plataeans (ii. 5), driven out by the Thebans ; the Lesbians, who fled before the Athenians (iv. 52) ; exile as the result of στάσις occurred at Corcyra (iii. 69), Megara (iv. 74).

15. **τά τε πρότερον κτλ.** — 'moreover what was formerly repeated on hearsay, but seldom confirmed by fact, now became credible,' because men saw it all.

17. **σεισμῶν τε πέρι . . ἡλίου τε ἐκλείψεις**—the construction changes slightly. We might have had σεισμοί or περὶ ἐκλείψεων.

19. **οἱ αὐτοί**—'moreover,' emphasising ἰσχυρότατοι. Cf. the use of *idem*.

20. **πυκνότεραι**—of course Thuc. does not record all the strange things that befell μετὰ τοῦδε τοῦ πολέμου: e.g. he records no instances of αὐχμός or λιμός (for λιμοί evidently does not refer to hunger caused by siege). He records two eclipses of the sun, one in 431 B.C. (ii. 28), the other in 424 B.C. (iv. 52), but if the Ten Years' War be meant, *three* eclipses could have been observed in Greece ; or if the Twenty-seven Years' War is alluded to, *six*. Of course it is not certain that all of the eclipses were actually observed ; Thuc., as Mr. Forbes says, only gives the popular opinion.

παρὰ τά—'as compared with' ; cf. iv. 6 χειμὼν μείζων παρὰ τὴν καθεστηκυῖαν ὥραν.

23. **καὶ ἡ . . ἡ νόσος**—the art. is similarly repeated to throw emphasis on the second part of the phrase—'the disease that . . I mean the pestilence '—in c. 126, 4, and in several other instances. With νόσος most edd. supply ἐγένετο : but Steup rightly says οὐκ ἄπιστος κατέστη, for when Thuc. describes the plague in ii. 47, he expressly says that 'it was said that it had broken out in several other places previously ' to 430 B.C.

μέρος τι—object of φθείρασα, sc. τῆς Ἑλλάδος, 'a great number' of the Greeks.

26. **ἤρξαντο δέ** — the narrative of the war begins at the opening of Bk. ii., the remainder of this book being occupied with the αἰτίαι καὶ διαφοραί. The main emphasis is on λύσαντες κτλ. ; the date of the recovery of Euboea is 445 B.C. (c. 115).

29. **τὰς αἰτίας . . καὶ τὰς διαφοράς** — these are again denoted by ἡ ἀληθεστάτη πρόφασις and αἱ . . αἰτίαι in § 6.

PAGE 21.

3. **τὴν μὲν γὰρ κτλ.**—apparently τὴν . . λόγῳ is attributive predicate to τοὺς Ἀθηναίους . . ἀναγκάσαι, as Classen
explains, lit. 'As for the truest motive . . I think that the
A. . . forced' etc. The assumption of a 'confusion of construction' (Krüger) seems unnecessary. Chambry explains
τὴν ἀ. πρόφασιν τοὺς Ἀθηναίους ἡγοῦμαι . . καὶ (ἡγοῦμαι) . .
ἀναγκάσαι, so that ἡγοῦμαι has two objects differently expressed, but γιγνομένους and παρέχοντας can scarcely be
separated.

4. **πρόφασιν**—of the *actual* motive, as in vi. 6, and now
and then in other authors. When so used it seems to denote
the motive as it appears to the mind of the *writer* as distinct
from the motive as put forward by the doer.

5. **μεγάλους γιγνομένους**—in c. 118 Thuc. says that the
Athenians during the period between the foundation of the
Delian Confederacy and the war (the *Pentecontaetia*) ἐπὶ μέγα
ἐχώρησαν δυνάμεως. We might, therefore, look for μείζους ἀεὶ
in place of μεγάλους, but, as this is the first mention of
Athenian power, the pos. is quite natural. This growing
greatness of A. is described in cc. 88-118; αἱ . . λ. αἰτίαι
occupy cc. 24-87.

11. **Ἐ. ἐστι πόλις**—'there is a city named E.'

ἐσπλέοντι—dat. of the 'person judging,' frequent in Thuc.
The direct accus. instead of ἐς after ἐσπλεῖν is poetical, and
occurs nowhere else in prose.

12. **Ἰόνιον**—the Adriatic.

16. **Κορίνθιος**—when a city that was a colony founded
a colony in turn, it was usual to choose a founder from the
original mother-city.

τῶν ἀφ' Ἡ. depends on Φαλίος, 'of the family of the
Heraclidae.'

21. **δύναμις**—see crit. note. The gloss πόλις is, of course, due
to πολυάνθρωπος. An obvious change would be δύναμις μ. καὶ
⟨πόλις⟩ πολυάνθρωπος, but δύναμις πολυάνθρωπος is surely a
possible phrase, as δύναμις denotes *military* power: cf. 33, 2
αὕτη (ἡ δύναμις) πάρεστιν αὐτεπάγγελτος.

23. **ἀπὸ πολέμου . . ἐφθάρησαν**—'in consequence of a war
with . . they became crippled.'

24. **τῆς δυνάμεως** depends on τῆς πολλῆς, i.e. the idiom ἡ
πολλὴ τῆς δ. is used.

25. τὰ δὲ τελευταῖα .. πολέμου—'in the period immediately preceding this war.'

PAGE 22.

1. ἐπελθόντες—this conjecture seems required, since with ἀπελθόντες ('the departed exiles') we miss a circumstantial partic. to ἐλήξοντο.

7. περιορᾶν φθειρομένους—in c. 35, 4 περιορῶ with infin. With *infin.* περιορῶ occurs only in Herod. and Thuc., and =ἐῶ: with partic. (pres. or aor. with different shade of meaning)='look on' with indifference.

15. ἐν ἀπόρῳ εἴχοντο—ἔχεσθαι ἐν πολλῇ ἀπορίᾳ occurs in Antiphon v. 16, Lys. xiii. 11; εἶναι ἐν ἀπόρῳ Thuc. iii. 22. The ordinary phrase is ἐν (πολλῇ) ἀπορίᾳ εἶναι.

16. θέσθαι τὸ παρόν—'how to arrange the matter.'

18. εἰ παραδοῖεν—oblique for the *delib. subjunct.*

19. τιμωρίαν τινὰ ποιεῖσθαι—cf. c. 5, 1, 'obtain help'; but the words would naturally mean 'to bring help' (the idiom with ποιεῖσθαι). In vi. 60, however, ἄδειαν ποιεῖσθαι means 'to obtain immunity.'

20. αὐτοῖς—'the Corinthians,' depending on παραδοῦναι.

24. σφῶν—here, and frequently in Herod. and Thuc., as direct reflexive, referring to the subject of the *same* clause.

27. κατά τε τὸ δίκαιον—this does not mean 'as was right,' but that τὸ δίκαιον was the motive put forward by the Corinthians; i.e. τὸ δίκαιον has its rhetorical use, and the plea may be illustrated by the saying συγγνώμη ἀδελφῷ βοηθεῖν.

PAGE 23.

2. ἅμα δὲ καί—for the δέ following τε cf. c. 11, 1.

4. οὔτε γάρ—the verb is ἔπεμπον (c. 26, 1), but, owing to the length of the sentence, the construction is changed (*anacoluthon*), and instead of οἱ Κερκυραῖοι being the subject of the verb, a new subject, οἱ Κορίνθιοι, is introduced. The outline of the sentence is as follows: 1. (*a*) οὔτε .. νομιζόμενα, (*b*) οὔτε .. ἀποικίαι: 2. περιφρονοῦντες δέ, (*a*) καί ('both') .. πλουσιωτάτοις, (*b*) καί .. δυνατώτεροι, (*c*) ναυτικῷ δὲ .. ἐπαιρόμενοι, etc.

I   H

4. ἐν πανηγύρεσι ταῖς κοιναῖς—festivals common to Corinth and Corcyra.

5. γέρα—the schol. rather vaguely says τὰς τιμὰς καὶ προεδρίας. The corresponding passage in Diodorus says that the Corcyraeans neglected to send animals for sacrifice.

6. Κορινθίῳ ἀνδρὶ . . ἱερῶν—Herod. vi. 81 (Cleomenes of Sparta at Argos) Xen. Hell. iii. 4 (Agesilaus of Sparta at Aulis) allude to the fact that a ξένος could not offer sacrifice in a strange city without permission. Dittenberger shows that προκατάρχεσθαι is equivalent to προθύειν (cf. Syl. Ins. Gr. 323 and 358): certain ceremonies took place before a victim was killed for sacrifice (Gardner and Jevons, p. 250), and these ceremonies had to be performed by a citizen of the place. The Corcyraeans would not perform them for Corinthians, and thus prevented the latter from sacrificing in Corcyra. Thuc. uses προκατάρχεσθαι here for the usual κατάρχεσθαι.

8. καὶ χρημάτων κτλ. — 'partly because the power that money gave them put them on a level with the richest of the Greeks.' By 'the richest of the Greeks' the Corinthians themselves are meant. There is some exaggeration, no doubt, for the Athenians were actually among the richest; but the wealth of Corinth had become a tradition (see c. 13). ὁμοία ὄντες is not possible (see crit. note), and δυνατοί cannot be supplied with Herbst from δυνατώτεροι. ⟨ἐν⟩ δυνάμει . . ὁμοίᾳ or δυνάμει . . ὁμοῖοι would give the required sense with a proper construction, but no correction is certain.

12. προύχειν—ἐπαίρομαι is found only here with infin. = 'boast.'

ἔστιν ὅτε — with καὶ κατὰ κτλ., 'sometimes even on the ground that the Phaeacians, who were famous for seamanship, had dwelt in Corcyra before them.' The Greeks identified Corcyra with the Scheria of the Odyssey. For the naval reputation of the Phaeacians see Od. vii. 34–39, where they are called ναυσικλυτοί.

14. ᾗ καί—'this circumstance (that they were proud of the reputation of the Phaeacians) led them to.' καί='and in fact.'

15. οὐκ ἀδύνατοι, meiosis for δυνατώτατοι.

18. ἔπεμπον—'sent,' the imperf. being frequently used with πέμπω and other verbs—κελεύω, δέομαι etc.—where we look for aor. Perhaps it is because it takes time to deliver the message.

20. καὶ Ἀμπρακιωτῶν—with φρουρούς.

22. Ἀπολλωνίαν—now the ruins of Pollina, S. of Durazzo.

PAGE 24.

2. **καὶ ὕστερον**—in contrast with εὐθύς. The ἕτερος στόλος seems to anticipate ἀλλὰ στρατεύουσιν κτλ. in § 4; but the edd. explain with Poppo, that this new force consisted of fifteen ships (hence forty below, cf. c. **29**, 4). But στρατεύουσιν ἐπ' αὐτούς should not allude to a hostile move made by the twenty-five ships already *on the spot* (the rendering 'assume the offensive' being inadmissible): they should refer only to the new force sent from home.

3. **κατ' ἐπήρειαν**—'in a threatening manner,' with ἐκέλευον.

6. **ἀποδεικνύντες**—cf. c. **25**, 2, 'calling their attention to graves (of their common ancestors buried at Corcyra) and ties of blood, to which they appealed.' ἦν applies equally to both nouns, but is attracted to the nearer.

9. **αὐτῶν**—neut., with οὐδέν, 'the demands.'

10. **ἀλλὰ στρατεύουσιν**—*parataxis*, the sense being, 'but, *instead of* the E. listening to their demands, the C.'

14. **προεῖπον** combines public 'summons' with 'notice'; Herod. ii. **115**; vii. **149**. Infins. of different kinds are combined also with λέγω and γιγνώσκω.

18. **αὐτοῖς**—see on c. **13**, 3.

22. **ἐπὶ τῇ . . ἰέναι**—epexegesis of ἀποικίαν, and governed by ἐκήρυσσον. For the dat. fem. in adverbial phrase cf. c. **15**, 2. The new colonies were to have equal rights with the old.

24. **ἐθέλει . . βούλεται**—if ἐθέλοι is right, the two moods are combined in *O.O.*; ἐθέλοι represents ἐθέλει of ricta, and there is no change of meaning. It should be noticed that the *Laurentian* gives ἐθέλει: for the change of indic. after εἰ to optat. is rare, but occurs occasionally, as in Lys. vii. 34 προσῆλθον λέγων ὅτι . . ἕτοιμός εἰμι, εἴ τινα βούλοιτο (=βούλει), παραδοῦναι. In Thuc. viii. **89**, 3 εἰ μὴ ἥκοιεν represents εἰ μὴ ἥκουσι.

26. **Κορινθίας**—the Cor. drachma was about two-thirds of the value of the Attic.

μένειν—oblique for μενέτω.

PAGE 25.

4. **Κεφαλλήνων** — partitive; there were four πόλεις in Cephallenia, of which Pale was one.

9. **κενάς**—sc. ἀνδρῶν.

15. παρέλαβον — 'had taken with them,' to support the request. There is no difficulty in supposing that Sparta and Sicyon were ready to lend their voice to a request that Corinth should withdraw the new settlers. These οἰκήτορες must have appropriated the property of the exiled Corcyraean oligarchs ; and the proceeding of Corinth was in this respect high-handed. The sending of the πρέσβεις did not commit Sparta to anything.

18. ἀντιποιοῦνται—sc. Ἐπιδάμνου.

δίκας δοῦναι—'submit the case to arbitration.' δ. διδόναι καὶ δέχεσθαι is a technical phrase for legal arbitration between states as opposed to war : cf. vii. 18 ὅπλα μὴ ἐπιφέρειν ἢν δίκας ἐθέλωσι διδόναι.

19. αἷς ἄν κτλ. =παρ' αἷς ἄν δίκας δοῦναι ἄ. ξ.

21. κρατεῖν—sc. ἤθελον.

ἤθελον δέ—an alternative suggestion to submit the decision to Apollo.

22. πόλεμον δὲ κτλ.—'but they charged them not to cause a war.' Notice the difference between πόλεμον ποιῶ and π. ποιοῦμαι.

23. εἰ δὲ μή—M. T. § 478. καὶ αὐτοί—'they in turn.' The elaborate wording of the allusion to Athens is intended to mark the earnestness and reluctance of the Corcyraeans.

24. ἐκείνων βιαζομένων—'if the Corinthians forced them.'

25. ἑτέρους τῶν νῦν—gen. of comparison ; Xen. Mem. IV. iv. 25 ἄλλα τῶν δικαίων. So Lat. alius occasionally has abl. τῶν νῦν ὄντων means the Peloponnesians whose confederacy Corcyra threatens to leave. μᾶλλον goes with φίλους ποιεῖσθαι, 'sooner' than agree to the demand of Corinth.

26. ὠφελίας ἕνεκα—'in self-defence.'

PAGE 26.

1. πρότερον δ' κτλ. — equivalent to οὐ καλῶς ἔχειν πρότερον αὐτούς (the Corinthians and Corcyraeans) δικάζεσθαι, πολιορκουμένων τῶν Ἐπιδαμνίων, but the logic of the sentence is sacrificed to a verbal antithesis.

4. ταῦτα—i.e. withdraw the ships and the Illyrians.

ἕτοιμοι δὲ εἶναι—Krüger supplies δικάζεσθαι, and ὥστε then ='on the understanding that'; but this is not very satis-factory after ποιήσειν ταῦτα has intervened. Böhme and others make μένειν depend on ἐτοῖμοι εἶναι, with ὥστε pleonastic; and for this ἱκανὸς ὥστε is cited from Plat. *Protag.* 338 c. In either case the sense is the same; they were prepared to agree that besiegers and besieged should stay as they were and make a truce until the arbitration was concluded. ποιήσασθαι is co-ordinate with μένειν. (Mr. Forbes supplies ποιεῖν ταῦτα to ἐτοῖμοι εἶναι: but ποιεῖν ταῦτα cannot = δικάζεσθαι, for in that case the second proposal of the Corcyraeans, ἦν καὶ ἐκεῖνοι κτλ., is a less conciliatory suggestion than their original proposal, § 2.)

9. προπέμψαντες . . πρότερον—pleonasm, as in c. 23, 5.

11. ἑβδομήκοντα καὶ πέντε—the numbers given in c. 27, 2 amount to 68, but to these are to be added the νῆες κεναί from Elis.

δισχιλίοις—the number is puzzling, as in c. 27, 2 the Cor. are said to be preparing to send 3000.

12. ἐπί—'for,' not 'against.' ἐναντία, internal accus. as adv.; cf. c. 6, 6.

19. τὸ ἱερὸν Ἀπόλλωνος—'the celebrated temple' of Ἀπόλλων Ἄκτιος, best known to us from its connexion with the battle of Actium.

21. προύπεμψαν—before taking hostile action.

23. ζεύξαντες—probably this means that they inserted new cross-beams, called ζυγώματα or ζυγά, connecting one side of the ship with the other. (The ζυγώματα, however, may be ribs, σταμῖνες.) This has nothing to do with undergirding, which, as Mr. Forbes says, would be ζώσαντες.

24. ἐπισκευάσαντες—'overhauled' to see if repairs were needed.

27. τεσσαράκοντα—see c. 25, 4.

PAGE 27.

2. παρὰ πολύ—always with a word implying comparison; cf. παρὰ πολὺ ἡσσηθέντες ii. 89, 3.

6. παραστήσασθαι—sc. τὴν Ἐπίδαμνον.

ὥστε = ἐφ' ᾧτε. ἐπήλυδας—the οἰκήτορες of c. 26, 1.

10. Λευκίμμῃ—*Leukimo*, SE. of Corcyra, near which the battle was doubtless fought.

11. ἄλλους—those taken in the sea-fight.

18. τῆς γῆς—partitive.

20. τοῦ τε χρόνου τὸν πλεῖστον—with μέχρι οὗ, 'most of the time' they were controlling the sea and plundering the allies, 'until.' (Classen and Herbst understand by ὁ χρόνος the remainder of the *campaigning season*, but, without any qualification of χρόνος, this is surely impossible.) Of course the time intended must depend on the meaning of περιόντι τῷ θέρει, for which see next note. Thuc. means that the Corcyraeans did not keep their fleet at sea all the time between the departure of the Corinthian fleet and its reappearance.

24. περιόντι τῷ θέρει—περιόντι, being the reading of all MSS., may be accepted. If περιεῖναι is intended, the explanation offered (Ullrich and others) is in 'the remaining part of the summer.' Herbst supports this rendering with ἐν τῷ αὐτῷ θέρει τελευτῶντι etc. (see the passages quoted by Mr. Forbes). But τῷ θέρει τελευτῶντι means 'in the summer when it was ending'; and περιόντι τῷ θέρει = 'in the summer when it was (all) remaining over,' the predicative partic., as Krüger says, modifying the whole sphere covered by the sense of the noun (cf. Bloomfield's note): this cannot yield the sense 'in the remaining part of the summer.' περιόντι must therefore be referred to περιιέναι, Aeolic elision. Examples of this elision of the ι of περί are Aesch. *Ag.* 1145 περέβαλον, *Eum.* 634 περεσκήνωσεν, and περιών is frequently given in MSS. for περιιών. In Xen. *Hell.* III. ii. 25 the best MS. has περιόντι τῷ ἐνιαυτῷ. This means 'during the summer when it was coming round' to autumn, drawing to a close. Steup and others, following the Schol. ἐνισταμένῳ, understand 'when the summer came round' to mean, when the *next* summer came; but this does not square so well with the concluding words of the chapter, which seem to refer to the winter of the year in which the battle was fought. If 'drawing to a close' is the meaning, then the dates would be :

Battle of Leucimme (c. 29, 4), . . Spring 435.
Return of Corinthian fleet (c. 30, 3), Autumn 435.
Corinthian preparations (c. 31, 1) . Summer 435-33.

If, however, the sense is 'when the next summer came,' the first two dates should be altered to summer 435, and spring 434. (Remember that 'summer' in Thuc. includes spring and autumn.) In either case the calculations are based on the date of the battle of Sybota, for which see c. 51.

25. σφῶν—see c. 25, 2.

PAGE 28.

5. τὸ θέρος τοῦτο—i.e. for what was left of the campaigning season of 435. (If περιόντι applies to the next summer, then the whole summer of 434 would be meant.)

9. ὀργῇ φέροντες—'excited by' the war, ὀργή being 'passion, excitement, impulse,' as well as anger. It is the 'war fever' that Thuc. means.

11. τὰ κράτιστα—cf. c. 19, end.

12. ἔκ τε αὐτῆς κτλ.—ἐρέτας is object of ἀγείροντες, to which μισθῷ πείθοντες is subordinate. Steup, however, supplies ναῦς to ἀγείροντες, and makes μ. πείθοντες co-ordinate with ἀγείροντες. He joins τῆς ἄλλης 'Ε. ἐρέτας together ('rowers belonging to other parts of Greece'). With the ordinary construction, supply ἐκ before τῆς.

16. ἔνσπονδοι = ξύμμαχοι. ἐσεγράψαντο—causal mid.

19. γενέσθαι—dependent on πειρᾶσθαι. Under the terms of the treaty the ἄγραφοι πόλεις might seek the alliance of either Athens or Sparta ; but of course the request might be refused.

20. ὠφελίαν = βοήθειαν.

22. πρεσβευσόμενοι—'to negotiate with them.' The mid. seems to express reciprocity, and the word is rather loosely used.

24. προσγενόμενον—trans. 'the addition of their fleet to . . ,' the chief emphasis being on the partic.

25. θέσθαι—as in c. 25, 1.

26. ἐς ἀντιλογίαν ἦλθον—cf. εἰς λόγους ἐλθεῖν τινι.

28. εὐεργεσίας . . προυφειλομένης — 'without having a claim through some great service rendered or through a previously existing alliance.' The meaning is simply 'we cannot urge that we are seeking to renew an old ξυμμαχία or that we have a claim on you for services rendered.' 'We are not εὐεργέται of Athens' : for this see on c. 137, 4 καί μοι εὐεργεσία ὀφείλεται and c. 128, 4.

PAGE 29.

2. τοὺς πέλας—'others.'

4. πρῶτον—answered by ἔπειτα δέ.

5. ξύμφορα—internal accus. = ξύμφορον δέησιν.

7. **βέβαιον**—(cf. c. 2) pred., 'unfailing.'

εἰ . . καταστήσουσι—'if they do not propose to . . .'

9. **μετά**—'while' or 'besides,' a characteristic substitute for μετὰ τοῦ τὴν ξυμμαχίαν αἰτεῖν.

12. **τετύχηκε δὲ κτλ.**—lit. 'it has turned out that the same conduct not only involves us in inconsistency in our dealing with you, as regards the request we make, but is also disadvantageous (to us) in respect of our own position at the present time'; i.e. because we have hitherto abstained from entering your alliance it is inconsistent to be seeking it now, and for the same reason we are now in danger. Τὸ ἄλογον and ἀξύμφορον supply ὄν, which is often omitted with τυγχάνω, φαίνομαι, διατελῶ, and occasionally with other verbs; cf. c. 34 end.

16. **ἑκούσιοι**— 'having deliberately avoided all alliances' (not 'having entered into no alliance, if we could help it'). The strained position of ἑκούσιοι, and other words, throws special emphasis on the different parts of the clause. This statement is referred to by the Corinthian at c. 37, 2 ξυμμαχίαν οὐδενός πω δέξασθαι.

18. **Κορινθίων**—with πόλεμον; cf. θεῶν πόλεμος, θεῶν ὅρκος, 'oath by the gods.'

δι' αὐτό—'on that account,' a favourite use of αὐτό and αὐτά with Thuc.

19. **περιέστηκεν . . φαινομένη**—'what formerly seemed discretion in us . . has now on the contrary proved clearly to be want of foresight and weakness.' The partic. with περιεστάναι as in the construction τυγχάνει οὖσα. But cf. c. **120**, 5.

20. **τῇ . . γνώμῃ**—with ξυγ., 'to share the risks of another's policy.'

22. **τὴν . . ναυμαχίαν**—internal accus.

23. **κατὰ μόνας**—perhaps δυνάμεις is the subst. omitted in this phrase = 'unaided.'

28. **μέγας**—sc. ἔσται ἡμῖν.

PAGE 30.

1. **μὴ μετὰ κακίας κτλ.**—'not maliciously, but because we were mistaken in our policy, we boldly act in a manner inconsistent with our former inactivity.' There is nothing mean in seeking an alliance now for the first time when we are in danger : we were mistaken in not seeking it before.

4. ἡ ξυντυχία . . τῆς ἡ. χρείας—lit. 'the coincidence of our request,' i.e. 'our request, coming at such a moment.'

10. ὡς ἂν μάλιστα . . μαρτυρίου—sc. καταθεῖσθε, lit. 'as you would most with a record never forgotten,' i.e. 'in the manner most certain to be remembered for ever by us.'

11. καταθήσεσθε—necessary correction of καταθῆσθε, 'will confer the favour on us.' The met. is from investment of money. Cf. c. 128, 4.

12. ναυτικόν τε still depends on ὅτι.

15. καὶ (πρὸ πολλῆς) χάριτος—i.e. your gratitude would have been great even if you could only have gained this accession of power for a large sum. Isocr. 13, 11; Dem. pro. 33.

16. δύναμιν—'a power' (powerful state), to be translated as subject of πάρεστιν.

18. φέρουσα ἐς—'producing in the minds of others an impression of generosity, a feeling of gratitude in those whom . . .' Notice the use of ἀρετή here.

23. ἀσφάλειαν—referring to ἰσχύν: κόσμον referring to ἀρετὴν καὶ χάριν.

PAGE 31.

1. ὑμετέρῳ—'of you.'

2. δυναμένους—Stahl takes this and ὄντας in apposition to Κορινθίους, and removes the second καὶ so that only προκαταλαμβάνοντας depends on αἰσθάνεται. It is better with Steup to render the first καὶ 'both,' and to make ὄντας also depend on αἰσθάνεται: 'and are preparing by trying to subdue us for an attack on you.'

5. κατ' αὐτοὺς . . στῶμεν—'confront them.'

δυοῖν φθάσαι ἁμάρτωσιν—(1) 'may not lose two things' means 'may secure one or the other': hence ἢ . . ἢ following. (2) But the construction of φθάσαι and δυοῖν is doubtful. Taking δυοῖν dependent on ἁμάρτωσιν, as in Andoc. i. 20 δυοῖν τοῖν μεγίστοιν κακοῖν οὐκ ἦν αὐτῷ ἁμαρτεῖν, most edd. make φθάσαι epexegetic, 'to gain them before (we make alliance).' The order is against this, and φθάσαι should then = 'to gain one of them.' It has been proposed to remove φθάσαι; but it is best, with Croiset, to take δυοῖν as dat. = 'fail to be beforehand with two things.' Either they will inflict a disastrous defeat on Corcyra, or frighten her into joining themselves.

8. διδόντων—'offering,' as frequently.

I   H 2

9. προεπιβουλεύειν . . ἀντεπιβουλεύειν — the jingle called paronomasia, to which Thuc. is partial; e.g. vi. 76 οὐκ ἀξυνετωτέρου κακοξυνετωτέρου δέ.

16. ἐκπέμπονται—sc. οἱ ἄποικοι, from πᾶσα ἀποικία.

17. προκληθέντες—see c. 28, 2.

19. τῷ ἴσῳ —τῷ νόμῳ καὶ τῷ δικαίῳ, παρ' οἷς ἡ ἰσότης (Schol.). τὰ ἐγκλήματα μετελθεῖν—like δίκην μέτειμι, 'enforce their claims.'

21. ὥστε—for the construction cf. c. 49, 7; 129, 3.

22. ἐκ τοῦ εὐθέος—'in a straightforward way,' with δεομένοις.

25. λαμβάνων—the same use with subst. referring to the feelings, c. 77, 6; cf. ii. 64 τὸ ἐπίφθονον λαμβάνειν.

27. μηδετέρων—on account of the subjective sense given by δεχόμενοι—it is from the Lac. point of view.

28. εἴρηται—'there is a clause' in the thirty years' truce.

PAGE 32.

1. ἀρέσκηται—sc. ἐλθεῖν, mid., not as in c. 129 τοῖς λόγοις ἀρέσκομαι. The use of the mid. is Ionic.

5. προκειμένης—'open to all.'

7. εἶτα—'and actually' as a climax of arrogance an object if you help us.

9. ἐν αἰτίᾳ ἔχειν — a frequent idiom in Thuc. (Kr., followed by Steup, reads ὠφελίας. εἴ τε ἐν . . δεόμεθα, πολὺ δὴ κτλ.)

11. οὐχ ὅπως—'so far from.'

14. περιόψεσθε—in sense = ἐάσετε, hence the infin. With the partic. περιορᾶν = to overlook what actually occurs; p. 22 l. 7.

ἤν—sc. δύναμιν προσλαβεῖν αὐτοὺς περιιδεῖν.

ἀλλ'—sc. δίκαιόν ἐστι.

15. κἀκείνων . . καὶ ἡμῖν—i.e. stop them too from getting help, if you will not help us, or help us too if you let them 'help themselves' from your empire. κωλύω with a pers. object and without infin., 'stop the mercenaries they draw,' is not common; Eur. frag. 1041 Nauck οἰκοφθόρον γὰρ ἄνδρα κωλύει γυνὴ ἐσθλή.

16. πέμπειν ὠφελίαν—means 'send aid' without concluding

a formal alliance: βοηθεῖν ἀπὸ τοῦ π. δεξαμένους = 'openly receive us into alliance and so help us.'

19. **ὑπείπομεν** — 'suggested.' The ref. is to c. **33, 1** γενήσεται καλὴ ἡ ξυντυχία κατὰ πολλά.

20. **μέγιστον**—sc. τὸ ξυμφέρον ἀποδείκνυμεν. *We* have the same powerful enemies as *you* have ; and that is a great advantage to you, because it will bind us to you.

21. **ἦσαν**—'are, as we saw' ; the didactic imperf. : but the word is prob. spurious, because (1) this use of the imperf. is not made out for the speeches of Thuc. : (2) we cannot supply ἦσαν to what follows—οὗτοι . . βλάψαι—but require εἰσίν, since nothing has been said to suggest that.

23. **τοὺς μεταστάντας**—'those who shall have abandoned your alliance.' This seems more probable than the rendering 'those who have abandoned *them* (Corinth),' as the mother-city. Athens may feel that Corcyra would be afraid to abandon the alliance with her.

24. **οὐχ ὁμοία ἡ ἀλλοτρίωσις**—Classen and others understand 'the rejection of it is not the same thing (as if it were a continental alliance),' i.e. is more dangerous to you. Stahl, Steup and others : 'to estrange us is not a matter of indifference to you,' which accounts better for the ἀλλά following : 'but you should make friends with a naval power if you cannot prevent its existence.'

26. **ἐᾶν . . ἔχειν**—infin. in *imperative* sense. (Some think δεῖ is lost before εἰ δὲ μή.)

PAGE 33.

2. **φοβεῖται δέ**—supply ὅστις as subject, but it is usual to omit the second rel. in Greek in such a case.

3. **τὰς σπονδὰς λύσῃ**—i.e. if he has not been convinced by what we have said on this point ; see c. **35, 1.** *Legally,* the speaker has already explained, there will be no breach of the truce ; but the alliance might be *considered by Corinth* as a breach of its spirit.

4. **τὸ δεδιός** — a favourite construction of Thuc.: ii. **59,** 3 τὸ ὀργιζόμενον τῆς γνώμης : below c. **84,** 6 ; τὸ μέλλον **90,** 2 ; **142,** 8. The neut. *partic.* with art. as noun is rarely used by other prose authors : Xen. *Cyr.* IV. v. 39 τὸ ἐλλεῖπον.

ἰσχὺν ἔχον—as the result of alliance with us.

5. **μὴ δεξαμένου**—'if he rejects our request.'

7. ἀδεέστερον — 'less formidable': here in passive sense. Cf. the double meaning of φοβερός, *formidolosus*.

οὐ . . τὸ πλέον = ἧσσον.

10. ἐς τὸν . . ἐνδοιάζῃ κτλ. — 'hesitates to secure for her in view of the war . . a place which becomes friend or enemy with most important consequences to you' (in either case).

13. τῆς . . Σικελίας depends on παράπλου, 'the coasting voyage *to* I. and S.,' Corcyra being the half-way house when the ordinary route to Sicily and Lower (Greek) Italy was taken —viz. round the coast of Peloponnese and to Corcyra and thence across. The gen. παράπλου depends on καλῶς in the phrase καλῶς κεῖται constructed on the analogy of καλῶς ἔχει, ὡς ἔχει (e.g. c. 22, 3) etc.

16. ἐπελθεῖν—generally go to attack, here to help. Sparta hoped for such help from the west.

τό τε ἐνθένδε—a fleet going from Athens to Italy or Sicily. This passage was prob. written by Thuc. later in the war, when Athens *had* sent out such fleets *via* Corcyra.

18. βραχυτάτῳ κτλ. — 'this is the briefest summary, including the whole situation and the details, by which . .' τοῖς τε ξύμπασι καὶ καθ' ἕκαστον is taken by Classen as adverbial = 'on the whole as well as in detail,' but there is no parallel for the phrase in dative. It is awkward, but better, to make it apposition to κεφαλαίῳ (Krüger). It is true that only one general matter is presently referred to (viz. the naval strength of Corcyra), so that τὰ καθ' ἕκαστον seem wanting (Stahl) ; but the speaker means '*if you think out this summary*, you will find it includes all detailed arguments too.' If we look at the ξυμφέροντα to Athens that are brought forward in this speech, we shall notice (1) that the speaker in each case leads up to the fleet of Corcyra as the crowning argument, (2) that he is well aware that this is the argument that will really impress Athens. It is therefore right to insist on it at the end. κεφάλαιον means 'summary' of the points previously raised. Edd. seem to overlook the fact that this passage is *rhetorical*, and not necessarily strictly accurate. (The remedy proposed is to make τοῖς . . ἕκαστον *masc.*, either as dat. commodi depending on β. κεφαλαίῳ (Poppo, Steup) or placed after or before ξυμφορώτατόν ἐστι.)

20. τρία μέν—sc. ἐστί : ὄντα belongs to λόγου ἄξια. (There is no anacoluthon here.)

26. πλείοσι κτλ. — 'with our ships in addition (to yours). For this use of πλείων cf. e.g. Aesch. *Ag.* 755 τὸ δυσσεβὲς γὰρ

ἔργον . . πλείονα τίκτει. (To take ταῖς ἡμετέραις as dat. of *measure* dependent on πλείοσι gives an ugly construction.)

3. ὡς καί for καὶ ὡς, unless καί is due to dittography (ὡς and καί are sometimes confused in MSS.). The parallels quoted, like ii. 44 ὅ τι ἄξιον καὶ εἰπεῖν, are not close. (Steup thinks that after καί a clause is lost in which one of the two topics summed up in ἀμφοτέρων was expressed.)

5. ἀμφοτέρων—strictly τὸ ἡμᾶς ἀδικεῖν and τὸ αὐτοὺς πολεμοῦσθαι are but one topic differently expressed, and the two aspects of the matter are not clearly distinguished in what follows.

6. οὕτω—like *tum demum.*

7. ἀξίωσιν—'claim.'

8. μὴ ἀλογίστως—together as one word.

10. τὸ δέ—'but that,' τό being *demonstrative* in sense.

11. ἀρετῇ—either depending on ἐπί, or perhaps rather causal dat. ἀρετή means τὸ σῶφρον : cf. c. 32, 4.

ξύμμαχόν τε—we have here the only example of τε followed by οὔτε (before παρακαλοῦντες. οὔτε . . τε is common) : 'wishing to have no ally in their nefarious schemes (persecuting their neighbours) or witness (οὐδέ does not mean 'not even' here as Mr. Forbes supposes), and to avoid exposing themselves to shame by asking others to aid them (in such schemes).' The simplest change proposed is to alter οὐδέ to οὔτε (Weil), so that τε would co-ordinate βουλόμενοι to ἐπὶ κακουργίᾳ καὶ οὐκ ἀρετῇ and οὔτε μ. ἔχειν='neither to have any ally as a witness in their schemes nor to . .'

15. αὐτάρκη θέσιν — *internal* accus. : the meaning is presently explained in διὰ τὸ κτλ.

16. παρέχει αὐτοὺς κτλ. —'makes them judges of the wrongs they inflict more than (they would be) if they were hampered by treaties.' With μᾶλλον ἢ κατά, 'more than accords with,' cf. c. 76, 3: ii. 50 χαλεπωτέρως ἢ κατὰ τὴν ἀνθρωπείαν φύσιν. (γίγνεσθαι does not belong to the phrase, but to δικαστάς only.)

δικαστάς—the meaning is that a citizen of another state who went to law with a Corcyrean must proceed as a ξένος in the Corcyrean courts : Corcyra does not experience a similar difficulty, whether real or assumed, because her citizens do not need to have dealings with other states to anything like the same extent. Corcyra was, of course, the port of call for all vessels passing to and from the west by the 'coasting' route ; but the grievance based on this fact is surely exaggerated here.

18. **ἐκπλέοντας** agrees with 'the Corcyreans' : others when at sea ἀνάγκῃ καταίρουσι to Corcyra.

20. **καὶ τοῦτο κτλ.** — the speaker now alludes to disputes between Corcyra and another state (meaning Corinth). ἐν τούτῳ, 'this being their conduct' (see crit. note), is not right, because the argument shifts here to a new point.

τὸ εὐπρεπὲς ἄσπονδον—cf. e.g. vi. 34 τὸ ξυνηθὲς ἥσυχον.

21. **προβέβληνται**—as a shield or cloak to cover their ἀδικία.

22. **καὶ ὅπως**—this explains κατὰ μόνας ἀδικῶσι, and means whether they make unrighteous gains by force or by deceit— these two ways are summed up in ἤν . . προσλάβωσιν—they feel no shame, because there is no witness.

25. **καίτοι**—the sentence that follows refers to *both* the grievances just alleged.

26. **ἀληπτότεροι ἦσαν**—the imperf. by assimilation to the other verbs. ἐξῆν is, of course, potential according to Goodwin, *M. T.* § 415. ἀληπτότεροι because of their αὐτάρκης θέσις.

PAGE 35.

1. **διδοῦσι καὶ δεχομένοις τὰ δ.** — Corcyra had offered δίκας in this case (c. 28, 2) ; but the Corinthian means that they would not enter into an alliance, a condition of which was regularly the settlement of disputes by arbitration.

4. **διὰ παντός**—temporal.

8. **τὰ εἰκότα θαυμάζεσθαι**—'to receive the proper marks of honour,' for which see c. 25, 4.

12. **ἀρέσκοντες**—Soph. *O. T.* 274 ὅσοις τάδ' ἔστ' ἀρέσκοντ'.

13. **ἐπιστρατεύομεν** — 'nor is it our way to attack a colony exceptionally unless we have suffered . .' The partic. must be *conditional* ; but the sense is much improved by ἐπεστρατεύομεν, sc. ἄν, 'nor should we be attacking *them* (Corcyra) in a manner so exceptional ' (as we are doing). Thus μὴ ἀ. would = εἰ μὴ ἠδικούμεθα. If ἐπιστρατεύομεν be right, ἐκπρεπῶς may = 'unreasonably,' being explained by μὴ . . ἀδικούμενοι : but 'exceptionally ' has much more point here.

14. **καλὸν δ' ἦν**—cf. c. 37, 5.

16. αἰσχρόν—slight anacoluthon, adding to the vigour of the sentence.

17. μετριότητα—sc. εἰ μέτριοι ἦσαν.

ὕβρει δὲ κτλ.—solemnity of 'gnomic' style; cf. L. & S. under κόρος.

19. κακουμένην—*temporal*.

20. προσεποιοῦντο—as in c. 8, 3. For the treatment of Epidamnus by Corcyra see c. 24, and for the intervention of Corinth c. 26.

21. ἔχουσι—'now hold it.'

23. ἤν γε κτλ. = ἀλλὰ ταύτην γε οὐκ ἐκεῖνον ὃς προύχων καὶ ἐκ τοῦ ἀσφαλοῦς προκαλεῖται, so that προύχοντα, 'from a position of superiority' (gained by the use of force), is co-ordinate with ἐκ τοῦ ἀσφαλοῦς.

25. λέγειν τι—'talk seriously.'

26. ἐς ἴσον . . καθιστάντα—this clause is in contrast with προύχοντα καὶ ἐκ τοῦ ἀσφαλοῦς, and must mean that in order that a demand for arbitration may be entertained, the party making the demand must first set himself on a level with the other party not merely in free discussion with him, but (what is more important), by giving up any advantage he has gained till a decision is arrived at. Transl. 'but he who, before having recourse to arms, puts himself in deeds as well as in words on a level.' πρὶν διαγωνίζεσθαι may mean 'before any solution,' whether by arms or arbitration ; but πρὶν πολιορκεῖν favours the more confined sense. The meaning of ἐς ἴσον . . καθιστάντα cannot be, according to the old explan., 'whose deeds square with his words.'

28. πρὶν πολιορκεῖν—πρὶν 'before' ; for the infin. after a neg. preceding πρὶν cf. c. 68, 2.

PAGE 36.

5. ξυμμαχεῖν . . ξυναδικεῖν—c. 33, 4.

διαφόρους ὄντας agrees with σφᾶς.

7. προσιέναι—' to have applied to you.'

8. ἐν ᾧ—'under present circumstances, when.'

11. ἀπογενόμενοι = οὐ μεταλαβόντες.

13. κοινώσαντες—'having given you a share in.' The confusion of κοινοῦν and κοινωνεῖν (have a share in) in MSS. is very common. τὰ ἀποβαίνοντα means ὠφελία, the natural result τοῦ πάλαι κοινῶσαι τὴν δύναμιν. (ἐγκλημάτων in C is an

oversight—see the next line. The text of G gives a Scholium on this false reading from πάλαι to ἐγκλημάτων.)

21. ἀγράφων = τῶν μήπω ἐγγεγραμμένων.

οὐ τοῖς κτλ.—'that clause does not apply to those whose application is intended to cause injury to others.'

22. ἀλλ' (ἐκείνῳ) ὅστις—'who does not withdraw from another'; cf. c. 38, 1. For the construction of ἀποστερῶν Croiset quotes Antiphon v. 78 οὐκ ἀποστερῶν γε . . ἑαυτὸν οὐδενός (neut.).

24. τοῖς δεξαμένοις κτλ.—'will not cause war instead of peace for those who have admitted them': εἰ σωφρονοῦσι applies to the whole sentence, and means 'as they—*those to whom they make the application*—know if they are prudent.' The brachylogy is the same as in vi. 11, 7 οὐ περὶ τῶν ἐν Σικελίᾳ . . ὁ ἀγών, εἰ σωφρονοῦμεν, and also in iii. 44, 1. (This is Steup's view, the best explanation that has been given of this awkward sentence. Classen, Stahl, Krüger and others assume that the ref. is to the conduct of the parties *after* the alliance is concluded, and understand 'who will assure peace, not war to those who receive them, if they, οἱ δεξάμενοι, show ordinary discretion.' Croiset seems to refer εἰ σωφρονοῦσιν to those *making the application*, but the two parallel passages tell against this. Weil proposes κεὶ σωφρονοῦσιν.)

25. ποιήσει—'will cause.'

ὅ—i.e. τὸ πόλεμον ἔχειν κτλ.

PAGE 37.

3. ἐνσπόνδων—i.e. you would be wiped out of the thirty years' truce, so far as we are concerned.

ἀνάγκη γάρ—the threat, we shall include you with them in our hostile measures, is vaguely expressed. τούτους is obj. to ἀμύνεσθαι, and μὴ ἄνευ ὑμῶν = μεθ' ὑμῶν.

5. καίτοι—here means 'and surely,' not 'and yet.'

δίκαιοί γ'—the personal construction common with δίκαιος.

6. ἐκποδὼν στῆναι—neutrality is your best plan.

9. δι' ἀνοκωχῆς . . ἐγένεσθε—cf. c. 73, 2 δι' ὄχλου εἶναι. ἀνοκωχή is an armistice.

10. ὥστε . . δέχεσθαι explains τὸν νόμον.

11. Σαμίων ἀποστάντων—in 440 B.C., c. 115. The resemblance between the two cases is more verbal than real.

The Corinthian keeps using ἀποστῆναι of Corcyra ; but Corcyra's ἀπόστασις was really only the estrangement of a colony from the mother-city, whereas Samos really revolted from the Athenian alliance.

13. **δίχα ἐψηφισμένων**—'were divided in their votes.'

14. **ἀντείπομεν**—'made a counter proposal.'

15. **αὐτόν**—*ipsum.* τινά = πάντα τινά.

16. **εἰ γὰρ τοὺς κακόν κτλ.** — an argument from expediency to support the exhortation τὸν νόμον μὴ καθιστάναι . . δέχεσθαι. But the γάρ is strange, and should perhaps be altered to δέ or τε. (Steup proposes to place this sentence at the end of c. **42**, where τῷ αὐτίκα φανερῷ fits in with φανεῖται καὶ ἅ.)

17. **τιμωρήσετε**—supply a dat. ; the case of the common object follows the partic. according to the usual const. ; cf. c. **5**, 1.

φανεῖται καὶ ἅ—perhaps 'a prophecy after the event' due to Thuc. himself. Potidaea, Lesbos and other parts revolted not so long after. ἅ (in place of οἵ) adds to the bitterness of the sentence ; and the unexpected word φανεῖται is sarcastic, φαίνομαι being constantly used in this way of the coming of *deliverers, helpers*, etc. (ὁ λωφήσων γὰρ οὐ πέφηνέ πω, ὧ χρόνῳ φανεῖς and so on). From the point of view of *Corinth* the revolt would be a 'coming' of this kind.

23. **ἥν**—antecedent χάριτος. We are not your enemies, so you cannot refuse on *that* ground ; we are not your friends, so that you cannot object that services on both sides are natural, and that we should not reckon what we did for you as laying you under an obligation. The ἐπι- denotes *reciprocity* : 'to be on terms of intimacy.' This antithesis is somewhat artificial, and, but for the verbal correspondence, we should look for something like ὥστ' εἰκὸς εἶναι προῖκα ἐπιχρῆσθαι ἡμᾶς (you and we) ἀλλήλοις. (The transl. 'so as to use you freely' would be easier ; but there is no authority for ἐπιχρῆσθαι in this sense.)

27. **ποτέ**—in the first war with Aegina, 505-491 B.C. ; hence ὑπὲρ τὰ Μηδικά = πρὸ τῶν Μηδικῶν, see c. **14**, 2.

PAGE 38.

2. **ἐπικράτησιν**—the partiality of Thuc. for nouns in -σις formed from verbs is well known ; some of them, like this and πρέσβευσις (c. **73**), occur nowhere else in classical authors. A

good example of the preference for nouns over verbs occurs at
c. **137**, 4 γράψας . . διάλυσιν: ἐνθύμησις, p. 117, l. 5.

4. οἷς for ἐν οἷς after ἐν καιροῖς, by a common idiom.

9. τὰ οἰκεῖα—'their own interests.'

11. νεώτερός τις—in ref. to the Aeginetan War. The
sing. has attracted the verbs into the sing. in spite of ἐνθυμηθέντες. αὐτά might of course have been omitted, but Thuc. is
fond of putting it into the second member of a rel. sentence.
(To repeat the rel. is exceptional.)

13. τοῖς ὁμοίοις ἀμύνεσθαι—'to requite us with like treatment.' ἀμύνομαι in this sense generally implies the paying
back of *injuries*, and here we should expect ἀμείβεσθαι (see crit.
note, and cf. L. & S. under ἀμείβομαι). Presently we have an
ordinary phrase, τὸ ἴσον ἀνταποδοῦναι: but it may be that, in
opposing the Corinthian "δίκαιον" to the Corcyrean "ξυμφέρον,"
Thuc. purposely makes the speaker use a word that is properly
used of dealings between *enemies*: the speaker means "*They*
say we are your enemies (see c. **33**, 3): you must judge of that
by our actions in the past, and pay us for our so-called enmity
with the same sort of 'enmity.'"

15. εἰ πολεμήσει—'in the event of war.' The Corinthian,
like the Corcyrean, insisted on (1) τὸ δίκαιον, (2) τὸ ξυμφέρον,
but—as Fr. Müller says—he deals vaguely with the latter
topic, since Corinth had clearly less to offer Athens than
Corcyra had.

16. ἐν ᾧ—c. **37**, 4. ἔπεται = 'is found,' 'is there.' It
is a *moral* sentiment—much like 'virtue is its own reward'—
but not much in point here. Grammatically τις is for τινι,
being attracted into the relative clause.

17. τὸ μέλλον τοῦ πολέμου—i.e. it is not certain that war
is coming.

20. ἐπαρθέντας αὐτῷ—'prompted by that expectation';
Eur. *Orest.* 286 ὅστις μ' ἐπάρας ἔργον ἀνοσιώτατον ('to a . . ')
κτλ.

22. ὑπαρχούσης πρότερον—'that existed already.' This is
the Engl. equivalent, though ὑπαρχούσης is really *imperf.* partic.,
past in reference to ὑφείλομεν. ὑφελεῖν μᾶλλον 'is to diminish
rather than to add to,' and the *gen.* is *partitive* (μᾶλλον does
not belong to σῶφρον as Classen took it). For πρότερον ὑπῆρχε
cf. vii. **28** πόλεμον οὐδὲν ἐλάσσω προσανείλοντο τοῦ πρότερον
ὑπάρχοντος. The transl. 'that has existed for some time' is
simple, but scarcely justified.

διὰ Μεγαρέας—what event is alluded to? Edd. are much divided between (1) 'the Megarian decree,' by which Athens excluded Megara from all her ports and markets (c. 67); (2) the revolt of Megara to Athens after a dispute with Corinth (c. 103 for τὸ σφοδρὸν μῖσος that Corinth conceived for Athens on this account) in 465 B.C.; (3) the revolt of Megara with Corinthian support, *from* Athens in 445 B.C. (cc. 114-115). The ὑποψία is that felt *by* Corinth, so that (3) appears unlikely—note ἔγκλημα. As (1) is the only one of these events that had happened since the thirty years' truce, it is the most probable; but the date of the Megarian decree is unfortunately doubtful, and some suppose, on insufficient evidence, that it was not passed so early as 433 B.C.

23. ἡ τελευταία χάρις—the service that Athens will render to Corinth by refusing the Corcyrean request. 'This will be highly opportune, though involving a trifling sacrifice' (Morris).

25. μεῖζον ἔγκλημα—the complaint that we have against you about Megara. (If the first explan. above is right, this ἔγκλημα would be that Athens had violated the thirty years' truce.)

PAGE 39.

1. διὰ κινδύνων—with ἔχειν = ἐπικινδύνως. Classen con-structs τό with πλέον, to which it is objected that πλέον ἔχειν, not τὸ πλέον ἔχειν = πλεονεκτεῖν, 'be grasping'; and hence Cl. proposed τι for τό. But διὰ . . ἔχειν is a combination of two phrases:

(1) διὰ κινδύνων τὴν δύναμιν ἔχειν,
(2) διὰ κινδύνων πλέον ἔχειν.

For (1) cf. vii. 8 τὸ στρατόπεδον διὰ φυλακῆς μᾶλλον ἢ δι' ἑκουσίων κινδύνων ἔχων. The *art.* before πλέον is occasioned by the preceding δύναμις. Stahl constructs τό with ἔχειν, but the position of the *two* members outside the article—τῷ . . ἐπαρθέντας and διὰ κ.—is against this.

2. περιπεπτωκότες οἷς . . κολάζειν—the simplest explan. is 'now that we find ourselves in the condition that we spoke of at Sparta, when we urged . .' Thus οἷς = ἐκείνοις ἅ, προείπομεν does double duty, 'spoke of, and urged that' and τοὺς . . κολάζειν is epexegetic. The only objection is that this is rather artificial. The *condition* alluded to is that of a city whose allies are in ἀπόστασις, as Corinth holds that Corcyra is from her—διὰ παντὸς ἀφεστᾶσι. Stahl followed by Classen and others supplies περιπεπτωκότα after

οἷς, 'now that we find ourselves in the circumstances in which, as we ourselves urged . .' This is doubtful grammar. Dobree bracketed τοὺς . . κολάζειν as spurious and repeated from c. **40**: this gives an easy construction, and σφετέρους instead of ἑαυτοῦ, with sing. αὐτόν τινα, is unusual.

18. τῇ μὲν προτέρᾳ — temporal, like μάχῃ τῇ πρώτῃ vii. **11.** ἐν δὲ τῇ ὑστεραίᾳ (ἐκκλησίᾳ) must mean 'in the assembly held on the following day,' according to the meaning of such adjs. in -αῖος. Cobet read ὑστέρᾳ, 'in the subsequent assembly.' We must assume that the assembly met on the next day when a debate was adjourned (and this seems to be the meaning of καὶ δίς). There is no evidence.

23. σφίσιν = τοῖς Κερκυραίοις. αὐτοῖς = τοῖς 'Αθηναίοις.

ἐκέλευον . . ἐλύοντ' ἄν—the condition expressed from the point of view of Thuc. himself (Forbes).

25. ἐπιμαχίαν—a defensive (ξυμμαχία, an offensive and defensive) alliance.

26. τῇ ἀλλήλων—c. **15**, 2.

PAGE 40.

1. καὶ ὥς—i.e. even if they rejected the Corcyrean request altogether. ὥς = οὕτως often after καί, ἀλλ', οὐδ', μηδ'.

6. ναυτικὸν ἔχουσιν—to be regarded as one word. Hence the insertion of τοῖς before ναυτικὸν is unnecessary.

8. ἐν παράπλῳ—contrast the construction at c. **36**, 2.

14. Κίμωνος — the great statesman. Plutarch says that he had given this name to his son out of compliment to Sparta.

18. ἐκείνων = τῶν Κερκυραίων.

22. παρεσκεύαστο—impers.

PAGE 41.

1. πέμπτος αὐτός—cf. c. **61**, 1; **116**, 1. The form of phrase denotes the chief in command.

2. κατά—'opposite.'

6. ἐξίησι — of water discharging into the sea only in Thuc. and Herod. until Polybius. These geographical details remind us of a similar passage in ii. **102**. Mr. Forbes thinks

that Thuc. mentions the city because there was no town, but
only a roadstead at Chimerium. But in the facts that follow
there is no special significance, and it is more likely that we
have here a trace of the manner of the logographers. Thuc.,
like them, is not averse to imparting information ' by the way.'

8. **ἐσβάλλει** — the ordinary word in Attic in this sense is
ἐμβάλλει.

10. **ἔχει**—sc. ἡ λίμνη.

ῥεῖ—sc. ἐνταῦθα.

13. **τῆς ἠπείρου**—partitive with a verb, as in ἄλλῃ τῆς
πόλεως, etc.

20. **παρῆσαν**—' were there,' *not* 'arrived.'

αὐτοῖς—Thuc. has this curious order several times.

21. **Ζακυνθίων**—allies of Athens. The interest and policy
of Zacynthus coincided with those of Corcyra.

24. **παρα-βεβοηθηκότες** — 'along the coast'; cf. **παρα-
πλεῖν.**

27. **τριῶν ἡμερῶν σιτία** — cf. τριῶν μηνῶν μισθός, ὅσου
εἶχον τὰ ἐπιτήδεια, etc.

28. **ὡς ἐπί**—both dat. and accus. are found in the same
sense with this expression, and with a verb of motion the
dat. occurs iii. 4, 3 ; vi. 34, 5.

PAGE 42.

5. **τὸ δὲ ἄλλο**—the construction shifts.

7. **τῶν**—necessary, because of c. 47, 1. The object of the
peculiar order is to draw ἑκάστου εἶς together.

11. **ὡς ἔκαστοι**—cf. c. 3, 4.

12. **ταῖς ἄριστα τῶν νεῶν πλεούσαις**—notice the order of
the partitive gen. : the rule in Attic is that it is not placed
in attributive position unless the last word is an adj. or partic.,
and even then it is rare except in Thuc. : the most exceptional
instance of this order is iv. 62 τοὺς τῶν Σικελῶν (' among the S.')
ξυμμάχους.

16. **πολλοὺς μὲν ὁπλίτας**—in the Pel. War only ten ἐπι-
βάται were on board ; and it is specially noted (in the case of
what battle ?) in the seventh book as exceptional to have many
fighting men on a trireme. But in the earlier sea-fights the

opposing ships were rowed alongside, and the battle was really 'a land fight on sea.'

19. ἀπειρότερον ἔτι—'still with little experience' of naval tactics.

21. τέχνῃ — dat. of *cause*, 'not so much because of the skill displayed, but for the most part (sc. καρτερά) resembling a land engagement.' The latter clause means 'it was like a stoutly contested land battle.'

25. μᾶλλόν τι — '*considerably* more.' The phrase is common.

26. καταστάντες—καθίστημι means frequently 'put into a (settled) state,' with ἐς: the intrans. 'settle down.' As the ships were motionless, a *regular* pitched battle was fought.

27. διέκπλοι—the famous manœuvre consisted of 'rowing through the intervals of the enemy's line, and thus getting in their rear, . . and before the ship of the adversary could change its position, of striking it either in the stern, or in some weak part' (Grote). It is first heard of in Herod. vi. 12.

PAGE 43.

3. παραγιγνόμεναι—iterative.

5. μάχης . . ἦρχον—'take the aggressive.'

6. πρόρρησιν = ἃ προείρητο.

10. σποράδας—'in confusion.'

13. ἐρήμους—sc. οὔσας: cf. Xen. *Anab.* II. i. 6 πέλται καὶ ἅμαξαι ἦσαν φέρεσθαι ἔρημοι.

15. [τε]—this joins the whole clause οἱ Κορίνθιοι . . ἡσσῶντο to the second. It is scarcely necessary to bracket it.

18. ἀπὸ ἐλάσσονος πλήθους—compare the total numbers, c. 46, 1 ; 47, 1.

24. ἐγίγνετο—'was beginning': better than ἐγένετο—the completion is first alluded to in c. 50, 1.

λαμπρῶς — 'decidedly.' τότε δή introduces the decisive act.

26. ξυνέπεσεν—impers., 'things came to such a pass.'

PAGE 44.

1. τὰ σκάφη μὲν κτλ. —all iterative, the imperfs. referring to the several hulls disabled.

3. ἄς — when a rel. sentence stands for a substantive, no antecedent being expressed, Thuc. regularly attracts the rel., as in c. 37, 3 δικαστὰς ὧν βλάπτουσι. In ii. 61 ἐγκαρτερεῖν ἃ ἔγνωτε is for ἐγκαρτερεῖν ἐκεῖνα (not ἐκείνοις) ἃ ἔ. But when a rel. sentence stands as an adjective, the rel. is not *necessarily* attracted ; cf. e.g. c. 52, 2 αἰχμαλώτων . . οὕς . . εἶχον : vii. 1, 2 etc. See n. on p. 87 l. 16.

καταδύσειαν—not sank, but 'disabled.' The usual way was to tow them away as prizes.

4. φονεύειν . . ζωγρεῖν — depending on ἐτράποντο as in ἐτράποντο τὰ πράγματα ἐνδιδόναι ii. 65. Thus ἐτράποντο has here a double construction. φονεύω is an Ionic word, not found in prose outside Herod. and Thuc.

διεκπλέοντες—the edd. point out that this cannot be the technical διέκπλους—the object of which, indeed, was not to kill, but to disable an enemy's ship (see on c. 49)—but merely alludes to rowing in amongst the enemy's disabled ships.

6. οἱ ἐπὶ τῷ δεξιῷ κέρᾳ—the Ambraciots and Megarians (c. 48, 4) who were defeated and pursued to the mainland (c. 49, 5). It is not possible to see how the conquering Corinthians on the left could have fallen in with any of the flying right wing unless some of those on the right wing had not fled with the rest towards the mainland ; and that some were left behind is suggested by ἐπὶ πολὺ . . ἐπεχουσῶν.

9. ξυνέμειξαν—plup. in sense, and this clause belongs to what follows.

10. ὁποῖοι—not much different from οἵτινες, but denoting, as Stahl points out, that there were no distinguishing marks of dress and appearance to show whether those they fell in with belonged to the winning or losing side. Cf. the common use of ποῖος for τίς in tragedy.

11. ναυμαχία γάρ—cf. c. 1, 2.

22. καὶ ὅσαι — i.e. those that had taken no part in the previous engagement.

26. πειρῶσιν—only Herod. and Thuc. use the active where Attic generally has πειρῶμαι.

PAGE 45.

1. πρύμναν ἐκρούοντο — 'began to back,' so as to retire ; cf. ἀνακρούεσθαι with or without πρύμναν.

196   THUCYDIDES I

6. ὀλίγαι ἀμύνειν — cf. ii. 61 ταπεινὴ ὑμῶν ἡ διάνοια ἐγκαρτερεῖν ; v. 3, 2 τὰ ὑπάρχοντα βραχέα περιγίγνεσθαι.

7. ὑποτοπήσαντες—rare and poetical verb, used by Thuc. several times only in aor. infin. or partic.

9. τοῖς δὲ Κερκυραίοις—dat. of agent, which Thuc. with the poets uses with all parts of the passive.

10. ἐπέπλεον—sc. αἱ Ἀττικαὶ νῆες. With ἐκ τοῦ ἀφανοῦς supply αὐτοῖς, 'from a quarter where they were invisible.'

12. πρίν—'until': here and elsewhere the indic. is used after a positive sentence ; but notice οὐχ ἑωρῶντο, and see M. T. § 635.

13. ἐκεῖναι—'yonder.' Notice the vivid form.

16. ἡ ἀπαλλαγὴ ἐγένετο = ἀπηλλάγησαν.

17. ἐτελεύτα ἐς νύκτα—pregnant construction.

21. Ἀνδοκίδης—there is some doubt about the name, because an inscription relating to the expenses of this fleet is extant, and in it Glaucon is mentioned as στρατηγός, and two other names, both mutilated, are given (see crit. note) ; neither name can have been Andocides. However, if Andocides did hold some sort of command in this fleet, he is the grandfather of the orator Andocides. (My opinion is that the text is right, and that Thuc. has made a mistake here. If Andocides is the wrong name, Leogoras, too, must be due to corruption ; and the double corruption seems very unlikely. If Andocides sen. had held this command, the orator would have alluded to the matter. He mentions that his grandfather had a hand in the thirty years' peace.)

26. ὡρμίσαντο—subject 'the Athenian ships,' the abrupt change being characteristic.

PAGE 46.

4. βουλόμενοι — for this 'sense' construction after νῆες cf. 110, 4.

5. τὰς μὲν ναῦς — poetical construction with αἴρω in this sense ; elsewhere it is absol. or has ταῖς ναυσίν. Croiset compares αἴρειν στόλον in tragedy.

12. ἐπισκευὴν οὐκ οὖσαν—sc. ὁρῶντες, the two examples of τὰ ἄπορα being given in different form.

13. τοῦ . . πλοῦ = περὶ τοῦ πλοῦ, anticipating ὅπῃ κομισθήσον-ται : the gen. placed thus at the head of a sentence with a verb

of speaking or thinking about is common in Plato ; and the constn. comes down from epic. For trag. cf. Soph. *O. T.* 317, *Trach.* 169 τοῦ κασιγνήτου τί φῄς; Plat. *Rep.* 576 D εὐδαιμονίας ὡσαύτως ἢ ἄλλως πως κρίνεις;

18. ἄνευ κηρυκείου—cf. c. 146. Had they sent him with a herald's wand they would have admitted a state of war, and treated the Athenians as enemies.

21. πολέμου ἄρχοντες—'acting as aggressors in war and breaking treaties': in reality the ref. is to the thirty years' treaty, but the vague expression heightens the effect.

26. λύετε—we expect λύειν. εἰ δ' nearly = ἐπεὶ δ'.

PAGE 47.

1. τῶν δὲ Κερκυραίων—this is divided into τὸ μὲν στρατό πεδον and οἱ δὲ Ἀθηναῖοι, possibly because the Athenians and Corcyreans together make up the other, or Corcyrean, side ; possibly by a slight anacoluthon.

2. ὅσον—'as far as they' were within hearing.

16. τά τε ναυάγια καὶ νεκρούς—the τε is answered by καὶ τροπαῖον ἀντέστησαν. The Corcyreans were able to recover their dead without asking permission. Hence, technically, they could support a claim to have won a success.

17. κατὰ σφᾶς—'opposite them,' i.e. 'on their coast.' The τά before κατά makes τοὺς νεκρούς unlikely.

18. (ὑπὸ) ἀνέμου, ὅς—'a wind which.'

20. τοῖς ἐν τῇ νήσῳ Συβότοις—Sybota must be the name of some place on one of the group of islands collectively called Sybota.

28. τριάκοντα ναῦς—c. 49, 5: ἀνελόμενοι c. 54, 1: ὅτι ὑπεχώρησαν c. 51, 1: οὐκ ἀντεπέπλεον c. 52, 2. The claims put forward by the Corcyreans are set out in a formal style ; notice esp. the repetition of ἐπειδὴ Ἀ. ἦλθον.

PAGE 48.

11. κοινόν—'in common.' Corcyra must have had some share in the colonisation of Anactorium.

16. ἐν θεραπείᾳ εἶχον—'treated them with great consideration,' cf. θεραπεύω and θεράπων. These prisoners returned in 427 B.C. and civil war broke out in Corcyra.

19. δυνάμει—'influence.'

21. περιγίγνεται—not 'defeated,' but 'maintained its ground.' Corinth had not secured Epidamnus.

25. ἐς τοὺς 'A.—cf. c. 66, 1.

PAGE 49.

1. διάφορα—'constituting matters of dispute leading to war.'

2. πρασσόντων ὅπως—'forming plans of.'

7. φόρου ὑποτελεῖς—c. 19.

8. τὸ ἐς Παλλήνην—i.e. the southern wall (see map), so that Potidaea would be accessible from the sea.

10. ἐπιδημιουργούς—δημιουργός is known from inscriptions to be the title of magistrates in many Dorian cities. ἐπι- would mean chief magistrates exercising some sort of general supervision.

13. Περδίκκου—Perdiccas II. of Macedon, son of Alexander the Philhellene. His shifty policy gave Athens much trouble in the Pel. War. Before 432 he was in alliance with Athens; but he presently encouraged Potidaea to revolt because Athens was in alliance with his brother Philip and his cousin Derdas. In 431 he was reconciled for a time to Athens.

14. ἐπὶ Θράκης—prop. 'in the direction of Thrace,' the regular way of referring collectively to the Greek cities on the coast of Thrace, esp. Chalcidice.

15. ταῦτα δὲ κτλ.—'the battle . . had only recently been fought when the A. . . .'

19. φανερῶς ἤδη—their *hatred* of Athens is of earlier origin. See p. 38 l. 22 note.

21. ἐπεπολέμωτο—c. 36, 1.

25. ἔς τε πέμπων . . καὶ . . προσεποιεῖτο—the construction passes from the partic. to the finite verb. This form of anacoluthon is by no means confined to Thuc.; but cf. e.g. ii. 47, 3 λεγόμενον μὲν . . οὐ μέντοι . . ἐμνημονεύετο γενέσθαι.

PAGE 50.

1. προσεποιεῖτο—'tried to . . .'

8. ἔτυχον γάρ introduces what follows, as in c. 31, 2.

10. αὐτοῦ—Perdiccas.

11. δέκα—there would thus be *eleven* στρατηγοί, and *five* more belonging to the same year are mentioned in c. **61**. As the number of στρατηγοί was regularly ten, Krüger altered δέκα to τεσσάρων (δ'). But instead of μετ' ἄλλων τεσσάρων we expect πεμπτοῦ αὐτοῦ. Perhaps Thuc. wrote only μετ' ἄλλων, and had no record of the number; cf. c. **51**, 4.

20. [ἔπρασσον]—this spoils the structure of the period, for the principal sentence must begin at τότε δή. There is, for example, a similar intrusion of a verb—μετεῖχον—in ii. **16**; ἔξεστιν in viii. **27**.

22. ἐκ πολλοῦ—'for a long time.'

23. αἱ νῆες αἱ—'the ships that were to operate against M. (c. **57**, 6) were sent just as much against themselves.'

25. τὰ τέλη—c. **10**, 4; cf. παν-τελής, having full τέλος.

27. κατὰ τὸν καιρὸν τοῦτον—this occurs after τότε δή again in ii. **84**.

PAGE 51.

4. ἀνοικίσασθαι—c. **7**.

5. μίαν πόλιν l.—predicate.

6. τῆς ἑαυτοῦ γῆς — partitive, with ἔδωκε. τῆς Μυγδονίας may be in apposition, but perhaps depends on περὶ τὴν λίμνην. The construction would be improved with τά before περί, as νέμομαι περί is unusual. νέμεσθαι depends on ἔδωκε: 'to cultivate and live from ' (Forbes).

14. ἀφεστηκότα—'in a state of revolt.'

16. ξυναφεστῶτα—not 'with Perdiccas,' but 'together.'

18. τὸ πρῶτον—this was their *original* purpose. The orders about Potidaea had been added subsequently.

20. ἄνωθεν—'from the upper country.'

21. ἐν τούτῳ—'hereupon.'

24. περί—common in Thuc. with dat. after verbs of *fear*, and this is usual in Attic. ἐφοβεῖτο περὶ τοῦ πολιτικοῦ in viii. **93** is unusual.

27. τοὺς πάντας—'in all.'

PAGE 52.

4. ὕστερον . . ἤ — cf. τοὐναντίον ἤ. We might have ἐπεί, ἐπειδή, ἀφ' οὗ or ὅτε in place of this. (ἤ, not ᾗ, is probably necessary. The confusion of the two is common.)

7. τῶν πόλεων—objective ; cf. Antig. 11 μῦθος φίλων.

9. ἐπιπαριόντας — technical word of an army advancing on an objective. The force seems to have gone by land (ἐπιπαρόντας of the MSS. is almost certainly a blunder). Cf. Anab. III. iv. 30 κατὰ τὸ ὄρος ἐπιπαριόντες ἀφίκοντο εἰς τὰς κώμας.

14. τοὺς προτέρους—c. 57, 6.

15. Θέρμη—Thessalonica.

16. προσκαθεζόμενοι—the form does duty as aorist ; cf. c. 24, 7 ; p. 120 l. 5.

20. παρεληλυθώς—' the arrival of.'

22. ἐς Βέροιαν—Beroea is in Macedonia, and seems out of the route. Herbst proposed to read περαιωθέντες ἐκεῖθεν for ἐς Βέροιαν κἀκεῖθεν. The text cannot be regarded as certain. Grote thinks another Beroea, otherwise unknown, must be meant.

ἐπὶ Στρέψαν — this well-known conjecture for ἐπιστρέψαντες suits excellently with πειράσαντες τοῦ χωρίου, which with the MSS. reading gives no sense. The exact position of Strepsa is unknown ; but no objection lies in the fact that it is not mentioned by Herod. iu a list of Greek cities on the Thermaic Gulf (vii. 123), as it may very well have lain outside the limits with which Herod. is dealing.

PAGE 53.

6. πρὸς 'Ολύνθου — ' on the side towards Olynthus ' near Potidaea (=τῆς πόλεως). The other reading 'Ολύνθῳ, is inconsistent with § 3, and as Jowett says, Aristeus cannot have left Potidaea unprotected.

8. ἔξω τῆς πόλεως — the plan of bringing the necessaries outside a city and selling them to troops encamped there was often adopted when it was desirable that the men should not go inside. We hear of it elsewhere in Thuc. and in the Anab.

14. τοῦ 'Αριστέως . . ἔχοντι—ἔχοντα (see crit. note) would be regular before the infin. ; but ἔχοντι is likely to have been altered to this. The dat. is used as if ἔδοξε τῷ 'Αριστεῖ had

preceded. The only exact parallels cited for this are from Homer and tragedy ; cf. Soph. *O. T.* 350 ἐννέπω σὲ . . ἐμμένειν . . ὡς ὄντι. In order to avoid the change, τῷ μέν for τὸ μέν agreeing with ἔχοντι has been proposed ; but the expression so produced (τῷ . . ἔχοντι) is not very probable : we should expect αὐτῷ μέν.

16. τοὺς ἔξω ἰσθμοῦ—'the (other) allies from beyond the Isthmus' (of Pallene). Ἰσθμός is treated as a proper name.

19. ἐν μέσῳ αὐτῶν—i.e. himself being on their north side and the Chalcidians and Bottiaeans attacking them from the city.

24. τοὺς ἐκεῖθεν—cf. c. 8, 2 ; 18, 1.

25. ἀναστήσαντες τὸ σ.—'having broken up the camp' at Gigonus.

PAGE 54.

1. ξυνέμισγον — the battle of Potidaea. It was probably not in this battle that Socrates saved Alcibiades' life ; but in another battle at Potidaea in 430 B.C.

4. λογάδες — for the ordinary ἐπίλεκτοι, not used by other Attic prose writers. (Suidas, s.v. λογάδην.)

τὸ καθ' ἑαυτούς—'the division that faced them.'

5. ἐπὶ πολύ—of ground covered.

7. ἐς τὸ τεῖχος—of Potidaea.

12. διακινδυνεύσῃ—deliberative. χωρήσας with ὁποτέρωσε.

13. δ' οὖν—for MSS. γοῦν : see the same correction at c. 10, 5. Here δ' οὖν suggests a hesitation on the part of Aristeus, the details of which Thuc. has omitted.

14. ὡς ἐς ἐλάχιστον χωρίον—i.e. to concentrate his division so that closely united it might force its way.

16. παρὰ τὴν χηλήν—the object is to enter Potidaea from the *south*, as it would have been risky with the enemy in the way to have forced a way in at the north. The χηλή is a mole or break-water running out into the sea, which at low tide is shallow, on the east side of the city.

18. ἀποβαλών—this is used specially of losing men by a *sudden* attack of an enemy.

19. ἀπέχει—sc. Olynthus ; ἀπεῖχε (see crit. note) would be a common use of imperf. in giving geographical details ; cf.

e.g. ii. **13** τοῦ . . τείχους στάδιοι ἦσαν κτλ. ; many exx. from *Anabasis* in Kühner's n. on *Anab.* I. iv. 9. Of course the pres. is also possible, and ἐστι favours it here. (The imperf. is equally used when the fact given implies the result of the writer's observation : so that it is not right to draw a distinction here.)

20. **ἐστι**—sc. the ground between the two cities.

22. **ἤρθη**—to summon the troops from Olynthus.

26. **κατεσπάσθη**—plup. in sense.

PAGE 55.

1. **παρεγένοντο**—ἐν τῇ μάχῃ.

6. **'Αθηναίων δέ**—the inscription placed over the monument of these men in the Ceramicus is in the Brit. Mus. : Hicks, *Manual*, p. 59. The last of the three stanzas is :

<blockquote>
"Ανδρας μὲν πόλις ἥδε ποθεῖ καὶ δῆμος 'Ερεχθέως,
πρόσθε Ποτειδαίας οἳ θάνον ἐν προμάχοις
παῖδες 'Αθηναίων. ψυχὰς δ' ἀντίρροπα θέντες
ἠλλάξαντ' ἀρετήν—καὶ πατρίδ' εὐκλεΐσαν.
</blockquote>

αὐτῶν—Thuc. had not heard the numbers of the allies who fell.

7. **ἐκ**—cf. πρός, which might have been used here, c. **62**, 1.

8. **τεῖχος**—this is deleted by Classen and others ; but the sense is 'they cut off (from communication with the north) the northern *wall*'—of course by building a wall farther north. See below § 3. **ἐφρούρουν** is intrans.

10. **ἀτείχιστον**—not 'unfortified,' which is not true (see c. **56**, 2), but 'not walled off,' ' not isolated' from the south.

13. **διαβάντες**—by sea.

14. **γενομένοις**—the aor., though weakly supported, is necessary, 'if they should *have divided*' being clearly the sense. In vi. **100** we have correctly φοβούμενοι μὴ σφίσι δίχα γιγνομένοις ῥᾷον μάχωνται, because there the sense is 'if they made a practice of.'

15. **ἐν τῇ πόλει**—at Athens.

18. **Φορμίωνα**—the celebrated admiral.

20. **'Αφύτιος**—Ionic gen. of"Αφυτις : cf. e.g. Τήρης Τήρεω ii. **29**.

23. ἀπετείχισε τὸ . . τεῖχος—the bracketing of τεῖχος makes the sense 'walled it off on the south side'; cf. τὸ δ' ἐs τὴν Παλλήνην above § 1 (where, however, τεῖχος may be supplied). But 'walled off the south wall' may very well be the meaning as above in l. 8. Classen retains τεῖχος here and renders 'built across the south line of circumvallation.' This is scarcely the meaning of ἀποτειχίζω.

26. ναυσὶν ἅμα ἐφ.—'with a fleet blockading it.'

PAGE 56.

1. ξυνεβούλευε . . ἤθελε . . ἔπειθε—like ἐκέλευε: such words being often used in imperf. when a speaker is giving advice.

3. ἄνεμον τηρήσασι—cf. τηρήσαντες τὸν πορθμόν vi. 2.

6. τὰ ἐπὶ τούτοις—cf. ὡς ἐπὶ τούτοις vi. 45; vii. 45; 'what was now necessary.' Ar. Eccles. 82 τἀπὶ τούτοις δράσομεν.

7. ὅπως also depends on παρασκευάζειν.

τὰ ἔξωθεν—referring to what he could do for Potidaea when he got outside.

10. Σερμυλιῶν . . πολλούς—Sermyle on the west coast of Sithonia.

11. ἐs . . ἔπρασσεν—'negotiated with'; cf. e.g. πρὸς ὃν ἔπραξαν ii. 7.

12. ὅπῃ = 'as to how.'

13. μετὰ δέ—now begins the costly siege of Potidaea.

18. αἰτίαι μέν—answered by οὐ μέντοι. What follows shows that αἰτίαι alludes only to the dispute about Potidaea—not to the affair of Corcyra as well.

προυγεγένητο — this (προε-), not προσεγεγένητο, is the reading of all good MSS. As the ref. is to Potidaea only we should expect either προσεγεγένητο 'had been added' (to the Corcyrean dispute)—and this is read by many edd.—or αἰτίαι μὲν καὶ αὗται: cf. c. 56, 1 καὶ τάδε ξυνέβη . . διάφορα. But πρου- can stand; for now it is 'Αθηναίοις καὶ Πελοποννησίοις, not merely 'Α. καὶ Κορινθίοις. Thuc. clearly means that the Corcyrean affair did not constitute a ground of war with Pel. in general; and now explains why the dispute about Potidaea was such, though even that was a matter for Corinth on her own account in the first instance. προ- means 'before Sparta took any part.' Cf. c. 67, 1.

25. σφίσιν—with ἐμάχοντο, not as in c. 13, 3 ; 27, 1 ; 61, 1 with ἐλθόντες.

27. ξυνερρώγει—ξυρρήγνυμι.

4. τε—'so.'

παρεκάλουν — 'invited,' not by formal summons, which belonged to Sparta.

6. κατεβόων — with *gen.* 'loudly accuse'; with *accus.*, 'shout down.'

7. σπονδάς—c. 53, 2.

9. φανερῶς—they were dependent allies of Athens.

10. κρύφα—sc. πρεσβευόμενοι.

12. κατὰ τὰς σπονδάς—the thirty years' truce ; nothing is known of this particular clause in it.

13. προσπαρακαλέσαντες—thus supporting the Corinthian invitation. Steup renders 'summoned before the assembly,' holding that the embassies had already arrived in Sparta as the result of the Cor. invitation. This is impossible, unless we alter the text to προσκαλέσαντες : see c. 87, 4.

τῶν ξυμμάχων τε—partitive ; edd. generally omit τε and make τῶν ξυμμάχων depend on εἴ τις (καί='also'). If τε is sound, then εἴ τις must mean any one else in the position of Aegina : no other state outside the Pel. alliance seems to have sent ; see c. 69, 1 ; 87, 4.

14. ἄλλο—besides those wrongs alleged by Corinth and Aegina. Some accept Reiske's ἄλλος with or without the τε. The invitation is to all who hold that in their case Athens had in any particular broken the thirty years' truce.

15. ποιήσαντες—'called.'

20. εἴργεσθαι—see c. 139.

24. ἐπεῖπον—'added ' to what the others had said.

25. τὸ πιστόν—'honesty,' the good faith you show in your public and private life. This is the outcome of the 'Lycurgean' system. Cf. what Xen. says in the *Polity of the Lac.*, of their virtues, which, when he wrote, were a thing of the past : 'They endeavoured to be worthy to lead . . Others would go to Sparta and ask to be led by her against those who

were thought guilty of wrong-doing. . . Nowadays they obey neither God nor the ordinances of Lycurgus.'

26. καθ' ὑμᾶς αὐτούς—'among yourselves.'

27. ἀπιστοτέρους ἐς τοὺς ἄλλους—i.e. ἐς (ἡμᾶς) τοὺς ἄλλους, hence λέγωμεν. Some, however, take ἐς τοὺς ἄλλους ἤν τι λ. together = 'if we bring any charge against others.'

28. ἀπ' αὐτοῦ—i.e. ἀπὸ τοῦ ἀπιστοτέρους εἶναι. It is a mark of prudence or sobriety, but it leads you into more mistakes than you would make if you were less cautious in believing complaints.

PAGE 58.

5. τῶν λεγόντων =(τόδε) τῶν λεγόντων, so that the ὡς clause governs τῶν λεγόντων, cf. c. 52, 3. The gen. is often similarly used with θαυμάζω.

6. τῶν . . διαφόρων—'private interests,' i.e. the interests of their city apart from the interests of the Pel. confederacy. ἰδίᾳ does not mean 'individual' here. For such complaints to Sparta see c. 90, and for the negligence of Sparta see c. 118, 2.

7. πάσχειν—'we begin to . . '

9. ἐν οἷς—(1) some render, 'before whom'; cf. e.g. c. 85; (2) others, after Classen, with οὐχ ἥκιστα, 'and we among them have the best right,' as in viii. 68 ἐν τοῖς ξυγκαταλύουσι . . πρῶτος ἦν. The latter suits the passage better.

10. ὅσῳ—'inasmuch as'; the καί balances μέγιστα with οὐχ ἥκιστα. We should render 'inasmuch as . . , we have also the greatest right.'

15. εἰδόσι—sc. ὑμῖν.

16. μακρηγορεῖν, ὧν — most edd. supply ἡμᾶς (=τοὺς ξυμμάχους). And τοὺς μέν is then explained as Aegina; but how can Aegina be included under the ξύμμαχοι of Sparta? See c. 67, 3 εἴ τις. It is on all grounds better to understand ὧν as for ἐπεὶ ἐκείνων (i.e. τῶν Ἑλλήνων from τὴν Ἑλλάδα) with Conradt who is followed by Steup. Thus τοὺς μέν naturally refers to the subject allies of Athens, against whom it was a constant complaint that she 'enslaved the Greeks.'

18. ἡμετέροις ξ.—Potidaea and her allies in Chalcidice: since they had revolted from Athens, they are reckoned as allies of Corinth.

19. προπαρεσκευασμένους—the relative is now lost sight of.

I

I

πολεμήσονται—pass., 'shall become involved in war.'

20. ὑπολαβόντες—a gross misrepresentation.

23. ἀποχρῆσθαι—'to make full use of (as a base of operations) in dealing with . . .' (Poppo's view that αὐτοῖς = τοῖς
ἐπὶ Θ. is to be supplied to ἀποχρῆσθαι is clearly wrong.)

27. κρατῦναι κτλ.—see cc. 90 and 107.

28. ἐς τόδε = μέχρι τοῦδε.

PAGE 59.

1. ἀποστεροῦντες — a good ex. of the proper meaning,
'withhold' what belongs to another.

τοὺς ὑπ' ἐκείνων δ.—the subject allies of Athens; see c.
68, 3. Sparta in the Pel. War claimed to be the 'liberator of
Greece.' She had gained the reputation by her opposition to
the τύραννοι.

2. τοὺς ὑμετέρους - the plain meaning is that A. has begun
to act aggressively towards Megara and Corinth. (Perhaps
ἡμετέρους used loosely as in c. 68, 3 is right here—see crit. note
—or ὑμετέρους should be read there.)

5. αὐτὸ δρᾷ—c. 5, 2.

τὴν ἀξίωσιν . . φέρεται—'enjoys a reputation for generosity'
—lit. 'that, i.e. her, reputation . .,' gained by such actions.

7. μόλις δὲ νῦν γε — see crit. note. If we assume a
transposition for ἀλλὰ νῦν τε μόλις ξυν. καὶ κτλ. the τε might
stand ; but γε is certainly idiomatic here.

8. ἐπὶ φανεροῖς—'with a clear issue before us.' χρῆν γάρ
explains this clause.

10. οἱ γὰρ δρῶντες κτλ.—a notoriously difficult sentence.
The transl. 'for they who act advance with plans already
formed and without delaying, against men who have not made
up their minds,' in ref. to Athenian energy, is simple ; but the
statement is not true when made universal, and we certainly
look for a direct ref. to the Athenians (hence the conjectures
οἵ γε, οἵπερ, οἱ γὰρ Ἀθηναῖοι for οἱ γάρ). Classen rendered οἱ γάρ
as 'for they,' like οἱ δέ, i.e. the Athenians, but himself doubted
it ; there is no prose ex. of ὁ before γάρ as pronoun, and more
important, it is very artificial to separate δρῶντες. I should
like to refer this general statement, with the transl. given above,
to the conduct of the Lac., so that the general sense is 'men
of action (which you are not) take immediate steps, with their

minds made up before their opponents are resolved on their course.' The Athenians have not yet decided *on war*, and now is your time σκοπεῖν καθ' ὅ τι ἀμυνούμεθα. It is a ca-e for τὸ προεπιβουλεύειν, not τὸ ἀντεπιβουλεύειν. I think that οἱ Ἀθηναῖοι in the next sentence strongly favours my suggestion, as we then get a proper antithesis.

12. οἴᾳ ὁδῷ . . καὶ ὅτι κατ' ὀλίγον—the two clauses after ἐπιστάμεθα are differently expressed : we should say rather, 'we know that the A. are encroaching on others and how they do it.' (The sentence is awkward : Cobet bracketed καὶ ὅτι. Possibly something is lost after Ἀθηναῖοι.)

15. οἰόμενοι—'while they think,' as they do at present. When they conclude that you know, but do not care, 'they will press on with determination,' and no longer κατ' ὀλίγον.

19. τῇ μελλήσει—'intentions'= τῷ μέλλειν ἀμύνασθαι.

21. διπλασιουμένην—see c. 123, 6 ; mind the *tense*. δύναμιν is evidently a gloss on the unusual αὔξησιν, for which, as applied to Athens, see c. 89, 1.

22. ἀσφαλεῖς—'sure,' though slow ; cf. Soph. *O. T.* 617, cited in L. & S., φρονεῖν γὰρ οἱ ταχεῖς οὐκ ἀσφαλεῖς. (In all other places in Thuc. ἀσφαλής = 'secure,' but that is no reason why it should not mean 'sure' here : he must have known of this meaning !)

ὧν = ἀλλ' ὑμῶν.

ὁ λόγος τοῦ ἔργου ἐκράτει — so ii. 42 οὐκ ἂν πολλοῖς . . ἰσόρροπος . . ὁ λόγος τῷ ἔργῳ φανείη, 'there are but few cases in which report does not outweigh fact.' ὁ λόγος ὑμῶν = 'the report about you,' your reputation ; cf. p. 52 l. 7.

24. ἐκ περάτων γῆς—proverbial of remote countries.

πρότερον ἤ with infin., a rare constn. except in Herod. Thuc., Antiphon.

25. τὰ παρ' ὑμῶν—'your forces.'

28. ἐπελθεῖν αὐτοί—together : so βούλεσθε μᾶλλον.

PAGE 60.

1. ἐς τύχας κ.—'expose yourselves to the chances of war.'

2. δυνατωτέρους—sc. than they were.

3. περὶ αὑτῷ . . σφαλέντα—cf. vi. 33, 5 κἂν περὶ σφίσιν αὐτοῖς τὰ πλείω πταίωσιν : Aristoph. *Pax* 905 περὶ ταῖσι καμ-

παῖς . . πεπτωκότες : Soph. *Ajax* 828 πεπτῶτα τῷδε περὶ νεορράντῳ ξίφει.

4. τὰ πλείω—sc. than through you.

5. ἡμᾶς—we, your allies. Thuc. is referring to the thirty years' truce, which was a set-back to Athens for the time being.

7. ὑμέτεραι—'in you,' of help from you.

8. καὶ ἀπαρασκεύους—καί is explained by its correspondence with διὰ τὸ πιστεῦσαι : because they had confidence in Sparta, they remained *also* (as a consequence) unprepared (E. Chambry).

9. ἔφθειραν—gnomic.

10. ἐπ' ἔχθρᾳ τὸ πλέον ἢ αἰτίᾳ—'to show our enmity, but rather to complain.'

12. φίλων . . ἐχθρῶν—objective. αἰτία in this second sentence = τὸ ἐπ' αἰτίᾳ λέγειν, but ἔχθρα is not equivalent to τὸ ἐπ' ἔχθρᾳ λέγειν, so Thuc. substitutes κατηγορία, which is. The habit of defining terms, common in Thuc., is, as Croiset remarks here, derived from Prodicus of Ceos, who gives a well-known specimen of his skill in this line in the *Protagoras*. Demosth. imitates this passage, *Androt.* 22.

ἁμαρτανόντων—milder than ἁμαρτόντων.

14. ἄξιοι—'have a right.'

16. ἄλλως τε καί—this clause must give a reason for the claim just made, and this can only be if διαφερόντων here = 'the interests' at stake, and not 'differences' between you and Athens. But διαφέροντας presently has the other sense.

20. ὑμῶν with διαφέροντας.

καὶ ὡς—καί is 'nay' or 'in fact.'

21. νεωτεροποιοί κτλ.—we have echoes of this famous comparison in Demosth.

22. ἐπινοῆσαι ὀξεῖς—cf. Dem. *Ol.* 3, 15 γνῶναι πάντων ὑμεῖς ὀξύτατοι.

24. σῴζειν—sc. ὀξεῖς, sarcastic.

ἐπιγνῶναι—'adopt further measures' beyond a resolution to preserve what you have got.

οὐδὲ τἀναγκαῖα—contrast ἐπιγνῶναι μηδέν. The last clause = καὶ οὐκ ὀξεῖς ἐστε ἔργῳ οὐδὲ τ. ἐξ. By τἀναγκαῖα he means 'what will just do.'

26. παρὰ γνώμην—γνώμη here and below prob. = 'judgment,

NOTES 209

forethought': the A. are ever taking risks that their judgment forbids them to venture on; you hesitate to follow the sure indications of your judgment. There is an evident allusion to the favourite contrast between γνώμη and τύχη.

28. εὐέλπιδες—in Ar. *Av.* Euelpides personifies the venturesome character of Athenians.

PAGE 61.

4. καὶ μήν in oratory draws attention to a new and striking point, 'then again.'

5. ἐνδημοτάτους—a marked trait in the Spartan character which was much modified by the Pel. War; though for a long time S. was deficient in vigour in the war.

7. τῷ ἐπελθεῖν — 'aggression.' There is no need to read ἐξελθεῖν; cf. § 7, and the contrast is as old as the *Odyssey*; π 27 οὐ μὲν γάρ τι θάμ' ἀγρὸν ἐπέρχεαι . . | ἀλλ' ἐπιδημεύεις.

9. ἐξέρχονται . . ἀναπίπτουσιν—explained (by Bonitz) as a metaphor from boxing : to follow up an advantage)(to be forced back—*celerique elapsus vulnere cessit*, *Aen.* v. 445.

10. τοῖς μὲν σώμασιν . . τῇ δὲ γνώμῃ—the points of this rhetorical passage are two : (1) the A. give their lives just as much as the S. for their city, but the A. regard their lives as of little worth, while the S. devote themselves entirely to the care of the body as the most precious thing they can offer to their city ; (2) the A. use their intelligence in the service of their city, and for that end they cultivate their minds, whereas the S. neglect them. Thuc. has obscured his meaning by introducing a contrast between ἀλλοτριώτατος 'not their own' (but of course belonging to their city) and οἰκειότατος 'nearest and dearest to them.' The Spartans too gave their lives for their city, *but* they regarded them as οἰκειότατος.

13. ἃ μὲν ἄν—i.e. when they do not carry out a new plan they have hit upon, they regard the failure as a *loss* of something that belongs to them.

15. πρὸς τὰ μέλλοντα—'in comparison with what is to be done.'

16. τυχεῖν πράξαντες—'that in reality they have done,' a very common meaning of τυγχάνω. : e.g. Plat. *Gorg.* p. 468 D οἰόμενος ἄμεινον εἶναι, τυγχάνει δὲ ὂν κάκιον.

του καὶ πείρᾳ σ.—'if they fail too in anything they attempt.' καί (in ref. to ἃ ἂν ἐπελθόντες κτήσωνται) emphasises the *phrase*.

17. **ἐπλήρωσαν**—iterative.

18. **μόνοι γάρ**—possession and desire, 'have' and 'hope' overlap, so impetuous are these Athenians.

20. **καὶ ταῦτα κτλ.**—imitated by Demosth. *dc Cor.* 203 (Athens) ἀγωνιζομένη περὶ πρωτείων καὶ τιμῆς καὶ δόξης κινδυνεύουσα πάντα τὸν αἰῶνα διατετέλεκε. (A misuse of the poetical *αἰών* is that of Polus τέχνη ap. Plat. *Gorg. init.*) It is a fine stroke of style that at the end of the contrast here, the antithesis is dropped and Athens alone is spoken of.

24. **ἑορτήν**—predicate. It is not likely that there is any ref. here, as the Schol. who is followed by some edd. supposes, to the refusal of Sparta to set out for war during festivals. The passage is hyperbolical, and is spoiled by making it too precise. **μήτε** and **τε** correspond.

25. **οὐχ ἧσσον** . . **ἤ** = μᾶλλον ἤ.

PAGE 62.

1. **ἐᾶν**—sc. ἡσυχίαν ἔχειν.

3. **ταύτης**—subject ; τοιαύτης πόλεως pred., lit. 'this (city) that is opposed to you being such a city.'

4. **διαμέλλετε**—'persist in . . .'

5. **οἴεσθε κτλ.**—'you think that peace lasts longest not for those who in using their forces confine themselves to what is right, but (none the less) by their resolution show that, if wronged, they will not put up with it : instead of that, you deal out fair treatment with the object of not annoying others and, where you defend yourselves, of avoiding harm to yourselves.' (1) τὸ ἴσον νέμετε represents δίκαια πράσσετε with slight modification : 'fair treatment to you means (*a*) not provoking others and (*b*) overlooking a wrong if you find that self-defence will entail suffering on you.' (2) ἐπιτρέπειν as practised by Sparta is explained as an attempt μὴ λυπεῖν τε . . βλάπτεσθαι. (All other explanations seem (1) to render ἀμυνόμενοι μὴ β. as if it were μὴ ἀ. β., (2) to strain the meaning of τὸ ἴσον νέμετε : νέμω is not 'control' here ; cf. p. 103 l. 25.

9. **ἀλλ' ἐπὶ κτλ.**—there is anacoluthon here, since strictly we ought to have ἀλλ' (ἐκείνοις) οἳ ἂν . . νέμωσι corresponding to οὐ τούτοις κτλ. But the change greatly heightens the effect.

11. **μόλις δ' ἄν**—even if A. were as conservative as you, it would be almost impossible μὴ λυπεῖν τε ἄλλους καὶ αὐτοὶ ἀμυνόμενοι μὴ βλάπτεσθαι.

12. **νῦν δέ**—'but in fact.'

14. **πρὸς αὐτούς**—'as compared with theirs.'

ὥσπερ κτλ. —full form: ὥσπερ τέχνης ('in an art') τὰ ἐπιγιγνόμενα ('what is new') κρατεῖν ἀνάγκη, οὕτω καὶ ἐπιτηδευμάτων κτλ. τέχνης is *possessive*, with τὰ ἐ.

16. **τὰ ἀκίνητα νόμιμα**—alluding to the conservative νόμιμα of Lycurgus : τάδε . . κατέστησεν ὁ Λυκοῦργος ἐν τῇ Σπάρτῃ νόμιμα Xen. *Lac. Pol.* 7, 1.

17. **πρὸς πολλὰ . . ἰέναι**—'those on whose resources there are many demands need constantly to think out new devices'; cf. ἐπιτεχνᾶσθαι, plan something *untried before*, Herod. ii. 2, 3 ; 119, 2.

20. **ἐπὶ πλέον ὑμῶν**—'more than yours'; cf. l. 14.

μέχρι . . τοῦδε ὡρίσθω — cf. Aeschines 3, 24 μέχρι τοῦδε εἰρήσθω μοι 'so far and no farther,' 'let this be the limit of.' Strictly we have a fusion of—

        (1) 'So far let your slowness have proceeded,'
        (2) 'Here let your slowness end.'

Cf. on p. 69 l. 26.

22. **ὑπεδέξασθε**—see c. 58, 1.

26. **ἑτέραν**—i.e. πρὸς τοὺς Ἀργείους, says the Scholiast. Such an alliance was formed between Corinth and Argos in 421 B.C.

28. **πρός**—'in the eyes of.'

29. **τῶν αἰσθανομένων**—'intelligent men.' The rendering 'men who take notice of our actions' does not suit the context. All Greece must 'note' an alliance formed by Corinth ; not any special part of Greece ; but ἀνθρώπων τῶν αἰσθανομένων could hardly mean τῶν Ἑλλήνων here. Those who look below the surface of things will not condemn Corinth. αἰσθάνομαι is abs., as in v. 26 αἰσθανόμενος τῇ ἡλικίᾳ. That this limitation of ἀνθρώπων does not stand in the same relation to the noun as τῶν ὁρκίων stands to θεῶν is not a valid objection in Thuc.

PAGE 63.

1. **ἐρημίαν**—'isolation.'

ἄλλοις—in quest of an alliance.

2. **οἷς ἂν ξυνομόσωσι**— the parties to a ξυμμαχία have 'the same friends and enemies' : hence the point.

3. **μενοῦμεν**—'remain *firm*,' pregnant sense fixed by ὑμῶν.

212 THUCYDIDES I

5. **ξυνηθεστέρους** — sc. ὑμῶν (not ὑμῶν προθύμων ὄντων, as with οὔτε γὰρ κτλ.).

7. **μὴ ἐλάσσω**—proleptic. ἐξηγοῦμαι of exercising ἡγεμονία in a league appears to take accus. or dat.

9. **τῶν δὲ Ἀθηναίων ἔτυχε γάρ**—cf. c. 115, 4; viii. 30. The gen. follows the constn. of the clause immediately following, and this produces a confusion of constn. between

οἱ δ᾽ Ἀ. (ἔτυχον γὰρ . . παροῦσα) ὡς ᾔσθοντο and
τῶν δ᾽ Ἀ. ἔτυχε πρεσβεία παροῦσα καὶ ὡς ᾔσθοντο.

The anacoluthon is lessened by deleting καί, but it is only a matter of degree.

13. **παριτητέα**—Thuc. alone among prose writers affects this use of the plur. neut. of the verbal adj.; cf. c. 79 etc.

14. **ἐγκλημάτων** — cf. c. 67, 4. The Athenians saw that their business was to answer the Corinthian's speech. See Intr. p. xxxv.

16. **δηλῶσαι δέ** —if this were expressed as strictly parallel to the μέν clause, we should have δηλώσοντας δέ.

17. **ἐν πλέονι**—of time, like ἐν μέσῳ, ἐν ὅσῳ etc.

24. **προσελθόντες**—to the ephors; contrast παρελθόντες below.

26. **εἴ τι μὴ ἀποκωλύοι**—this is the reading of the Laurentian, and its evidence in such a point outweighs all the other MSS. The confusion between the forms of indic. subj. and opt. is continually met with in MSS.; this passage does not stand on the same footing as vi. 21 where εἰ ξυστῶσιν is the only reading.

PAGE 64.

1. **ἀντιλογίαν τοῖς** — the dat. following the constn. of ἀντιλέγω, as in ἐπίπλους τῇ Πελοποννήσῳ etc.

7. **οὔτε ἡμῶν οὔτε τούτων**—prob. to be taken with οἱ λόγοι. The emphasis is on δικασταῖς: we are not in a court of law.

11. **τοῦ ἐς ἡμᾶς καθεστῶτος**—'the general line of argument that is used against us.'

16. **ἀκοαὶ . . λόγων**—'hearsay.'

18. **εἰ καὶ δι᾽ ὄχλου μᾶλλον ἔσται αἰεὶ προβαλλομένοις**—'even if it will prove an annoyance to you to have them continually brought before you.' προβαλλομένοις, sc. ὑμῖν, is personal pass., cf. c. 126, 11; 140, 1; the act. would be

προβάλλομεν ταῦτα ὑμῖν. (To supply ἡμῖν, as many edd. do, produces a sense inconsistent with what follows, esp. τοῦ δὲ λόγου μὴ παντὸς στερισκώμεθα. There is no need to read προβαλλόμενα with Classen ; and to place the comma after ἔσται, as I formerly proposed to do, is no improvement.)

21. **ἐκινδυνεύετο**—impersonal. 'It was to help the cause that we faced danger '—it was not φιλονικία (νίκη) that prompted us. **ἐπ' ὠφελίᾳ** is intentionally vague, because the speaker is to emphasise the share that the Peloponnesians received ; cf. c. 74, 3.

τοῦ ἔργου—'the reality')(τοῦ λόγου 'the mention of it,' 'reference to it,' when such reference is opportune for us.

24. **μαρτυρίου**—'evidence' (not 'protest').

25. **ὑμῖν** with καταστήσεται.

27. **προκινδυνεῦσαι τῷ β.** — 'stand forward,' 'bear the brunt of battle against,' as a πρόμαχος. Demosth. brings in προκινδυνεύω in the famous oath in de Cor. § 208 μὰ τοὺς Μαραθῶνι προκινδυνεύσαντας κτλ. : he probably had this passage in mind.

PAGE 65.

3. **ἀδυνάτων ἂν ὄντων** — masc. = οἱ (sc. οἱ Πελοποννήσιοι from τὴν II.) ἀδύνατοι ἂν ἦσαν (Mr. Forbes takes ἀδυνάτων ὄντων as neut., like πλωιμωτέρων ὄντων c. 7, εἰσαγγελθέντων c. 116— where see notes—as if we had ἀδύνατον ἂν ὄν. This will not do).

6. **ὁμοίας**—sc. καὶ ('as') πρὶν ναυμαχῆσαι (not 'equal to the Greek').

8. **ἀνεχώρησεν**—cf. c. 118, 2.
τοιούτου κτλ.—cf. c. 71, 1.

9. **δηλωθέντος**—cf. c. 76, 2.

ἐν ταῖς ναυσὶ . . **ἐγένετο**—cf. e.g. Soph. O.T. 314 ἐν σοὶ γάρ ἐσμεν.

13. **ξυνετώτατον**—again of Themistocles in c. 138 ; cf. vi. 39 φημὶ . . βουλεῦσαι ἂν βέλτιστα τοὺς ξυνετούς. τὸ συνετὸν ὁ θεὸς δίδωσιν says Euripides.

14. **ἐς τὰς τετρακοσίας**—'to make up the total of 400.' Herod. gives 378 as the total, Aeschylus (Pers. 339) 310 ; cf. Demosth. de Cor. § 238 τριακοσίων οὐσῶν τῶν πασῶν, τὰς διακοσίας ἡ πόλις παρέσχετο. Herod. also puts the number provided by Athens at 200. There is therefore an exaggeration here. (Some edd. read τριακοσίας.)

I   I 2

15. τῶν δύο μοιρῶν—in fractions when the denominator exceeds the numerator by 1, the larger number is omitted ; cf. c. 10.

16. αἰτιώτατος ναυμαχῆσαι—instead of τοῦ ν., as Antiphon v. 23 ἐγὼ αἴτιος ἦν πεμφθῆναι ἄγγελον. When the Peloponnesians in the fleet wanted to retreat to the Isthmus, Them. sent a false message to Xerxes to the effect that now was his chance to destroy the Greeks. The king then attacked the Greeks from the south. See on p. 121 l. 23.

17. καὶ αὐτόν—διὰ τοῦτο = δι' ὅ after ὅπερ : see c. 10, 3 (or αὐτοί—see crit. note, 'you yourselves admitted how great a service he had rendered'). Cf. Herod. viii. 124 of the visit of Them. to Sparta, μοῦνον δὴ τοῦτον πάντων ἀνθρώπων . . Σπαρτιῆται προέπεμψαν.

18. ἄνδρα ξ.—'though . .' τῶν . . ἐλθόντων with μάλιστα. Them. was presented with an olive wreath and a chariot at Sparta, and was escorted to the frontier by 300 mounted Spartans.

20. οἵ γε—quippe qui.

22. δουλευόντων—Greeks used δοῦλοι esp. of the subjects of the Great King.

24. μηδ' ὥς—c. 44, 2.

PAGE 66.

2. τούτου—sc. τοῦ ὑφ' ὑμῶν ὠφελεῖσθαι. οὐχ ἧσσον . . ἤ = . . μᾶλλον ἤ.

ὑμεῖς μὲν γάρ—the ref. is to the tardy dispatch of the Spartan army under Pausanias to Boeotia in 479 B.C.

3. ἀπό τε οἰκουμένων—'from your cities that were undisturbed')(ἀπὸ τῆς οὐκ οὔσης ἔτι (πόλεως): ἐπὶ τῷ τὸ λοιπὸν ν., ' with the object of occupying them in the future')(ὑπὲρ τῆς . . οὔσης, 'which there was but little hope of recovering.' (Some following the Schol. see in πόλις a reference to the Athenian navy ; this is only artificial and does not give a clear antithesis to ἐπὶ τῷ νέμεσθαι.)

9. τὸ μέρος—cf. c. 127, 2, like τὸ σὸν μέρος, τοὐμὸν μέρος in tragedy. ' Did our part in rescuing you as well as ourselves.' The emphasis is on ὑμᾶς, and there is a contrast with ὑπὲρ ὑμῶν καὶ οὐχ ἡμῶν τὸ πλέον of l. 5.

11. ὥσπερ καὶ ἄλλοι = ὥσπερ καὶ ἄλλοι δείσαντες προσ., ' as others did.'

13. ὡς—'regarding ourselves as.'

οὐδὲν ἂν ἔδει ἔτι—because it would have been of no use.

15. καθ' ἡσυχίαν—'without interference.'

17. ἄρα = nonne.

18. γνώμης—'resolve,' sc. τῆς τότε : the gen. is governed by ξυνέσεως.

19. ἀρχῆς depends on ἐπιφθόνως διακεῖσθαι = φθονεῖσθαι. For the point see c. 96.

23. παραμεῖναι πρὸς τὰ ὑπόλοιπα τοῦ β.—'remain at your post to attack what was left of the power of the Persians.' See c. 95, 7 ; 96, 1 ; Herod. vii. 107.

26. ἔργου—the fact of accepting the ἡγεμονία.

27. ἐς τόδε—cf. c. 144, 4.

28. ὑπὸ δέους—fear of the Persians. τιμῆς—the honour enjoyed by Athens when she had once accepted the ἡγεμονία. ὠφελίας—'interest.'

PAGE 67.

1. καὶ οὐκ ἀσφαλές takes up τὸ πρῶτον : when we had acquired this power it was necessary to guard it.

2. καί τινων κτλ. = καὶ ἐπεί τινες καὶ ἀποστάντες ἤδη κατεστραμμένοι ἦσαν.

5. ὑπόπτων—there seems to be no advantage in rendering 'suspicious' here in preference to 'suspected.'

6. πρὸς ὑμᾶς—i.e. now that you were no longer friendly to us, our allies would have taken to revolting to you.

8. τῶν μεγίστων πέρι κ.—'when the greatest dangers are involved.'

εὖ τίθεσθαι—cf. c. 25, 1 ; 'to manage well matters that are for their interest.'

9. ὑμεῖς γοῦν—an example of the principle just stated.

10. ἐπὶ . . καταστησάμενοι—referring to the oligarchies ; see c. 19.

12. ἐξηγεῖσθε—governs τὰς πόλεις.

τότε—in the Persian War.

13. ἀπήχθησθε — 'had become unpopular'; cf. c. 75, 2. This is better than ἀπήχθεσθε, 'had been hated.'

14. **εὖ ἴσμεν μή**—μή generally with a verb expressing confident belief impressed on others.

15. **λυπηρούς**—'severe.'

18. **ἀπὸ τοῦ**—like ἀπὸ τοῦ πράγματος Demosth. 24, 6.

19. **διδομένην**—'when it was offered.'

21. **τριῶν**—cf. c. **74**, 1, and so iii. **40**. The conjecture is however scarcely certain, though elegant. See c. **75**, 3.

24. **καθεστῶτος**—abs. like δηλωθέντος c. **74**, 1 (not governed by ὑπάρξαντες), 'it being established by precedent.'

25. **ἄξιοί τε**—the τε joins the clause to what precedes, and does not belong to the καί following.

26. **δοκοῦντες**—imperf.

μέχρι οὖ . . **νῦν** = μέχρι νῦν ὅτε (Croiset) : 'when, while (really) thinking of expediency, you profess to argue from justice.' So in Bk. v. in the Melian dialogue τὸ ξυμφέρον is opposed to τὸ δίκαιον, and cf. the Corcyrean speech. ὁ δίκαιος (ἄδικος) λόγος = 'the argument from justice (injustice)' ; you tell us what we ought to do, but really think of your own interest.

PAGE 68.

1. **παρατυχόν**—'when there was an opportunity'; to **προθείς** supply τῆς ἰσχύος.

2. **τοῦ μή**—cf. c. **10**, 1.

4. **δικαιότεροι ἢ κατά**—cf. c. **37**, 3.

6. **γένωνται** after οἵτινες : if this is the true reading—see crit. note—we have an instance of the epic and Ionic usage. See Goodwin *M. T.* § 540. The only other ex. of pure subj. with ὅς in Thuc. is iv. **17** οὗ μὲν βραχεῖς ἀρκῶσι, which is thought to be from a gnomic poet.

γ' ἂν οὖν = γοῦν ἂν.

τὰ ἡμέτερα λαβόντας = εἰ ἔλαβον τὴν ἡμετέραν ἰσχύν.

8. **ἐκ τοῦ ἐπιεικοῦς**—i.e. ἐκ τοῦ μετριάζειν.

11. **καὶ ἐλασσούμενοι γάρ**—an ex. to show how Athens got a bad name as the result of her moderation. 'For though in suits arising out of contracts against our allies we are at a disadvantage and in our own city have instituted courts for these cases under equal laws (i.e. laws under which they and we are treated alike), we are considered litigious.' **ξυμβόλαιαι δ.**

is probably from ξυμβόλαιον, a contract, and not from ξύμβολον, a treaty; δίκαι ἀπὸ συμβόλων were suits arising out of international treaties; but (1) it is not clear that Athens had such σύμβολα with the ὑπήκοοι, and (2) it is most improbable that in all such suits an Athenian had to sue in the courts of the subject state. It is known that δίκαι ἀπὸ συμβόλων were tried in the court of the defendant's state. If we assume that δίκαι ἐμπορικαί, commercial suits, which were tried in the state in which the contract was made, are referred to, the passage becomes clear. An Athenian litigant in the courts of the ὑπήκοοι is in an unfavourable position, whereas ὑπήκοοι in the courts at Athens are treated exactly like Athenians. Some think that ποιήσαντες τὰς κρίσεις refers to the compulsory jurisdiction at Athens in certain criminal cases, when a subject ally was involved. But even when both parties were ὑπήκοοι such cases were tried at Athens, whereas Thuc. is speaking only of cases in which one party was an Athenian: so supply ἐν ταῖς .. δίκαις in the second clause. In these latter cases the allies considered that they were badly treated. ([Xen.] Ath. Pol. i. 16 τοὺς μὲν τοῦ δήμου σώζουσι, τοὺς δ' ἐναντίους ἀπολλύουσιν ἐν τοῖς δικαστηρίοις. On the difficulties surrounding the judicial arrangements of the Athenian League see Holm, Hist. of Greece ii. 217, Engl. Transl.)

13. ὁμοίοις—contrast with ἐλασσούμενοι. κρίσιν ποιεῖν = institute a trial.

18. διότι—'why.' The reason why others in our position do not go to law is that they use force. Mr. Forbes points out that the Persians, Scythians, and Carthaginians are instanced as ruling powers by Socrates in Xen. Mem. I. i. 11.

19. οἱ δέ—'but they.'

21. παρὰ τὸ μὴ οἴεσθαι χρῆναι—μή with χ., 'contrary to their opinion that it is wrong' that they should be deprived.

ἢ γνώμῃ ἢ κτλ.—'either by a decision (in our courts) or through the power we enjoy on account of our Empire.' This passage refers not only to defeats of allies in the Athenian courts, but to curtailments of their rights (δυνάμει κτλ.).

24. τοῦ ἐνδεοῦς—'at their (slight) inferiority.' The gen. after χαλεπῶς φέρειν as in ii. 62, 3 probably, unless στερισκόμενοι is to be supplied.

25. ἀπὸ πρώτης—cf. c. 15, 3. Perhaps ὁρμῆς or ἀρχῆς originally completed the phrase.

τὸν νόμον—'law' in general.

218 THUCYDIDES I

69 THUCYDIDES I

PAGE 69.

3. βιαζόμενοι—pass. as often in Thuc. and trag.

τὸ μὲν κτλ.—'the one (τὸ ἀδικεῖσθαι) seems to be an act of over-reaching where both are equal, the other an act of compulsion where one is stronger.' The infins. are impersonal. ἴσου and κρείσσονος are neut.

8. εἰκότως belongs only to ἡ δὲ ἡμετέρα κτλ., and is added as an afterthought, the general sense being : 'It is *inconsistent* that they should chafe at our empire when they endured worse from the Persians, but it is *not strange* ; for' etc. The Persian power too was βαρύ, but they had to put up with that.

9. γ' ἂν οὖν—c. 76, 4.

10. ἄρξαιτε—ingressive, 'gain an empire.'

11. εὔνοιαν—'good-will,' which at present they enjoyed as professed 'liberators' (ii. 9, 4).

ἡμέτερον—c. 33, 3.

12. οἷα . . ὁμοῖα—'measures like those of which you gave some examples.' δι' ὀλίγου, 'for a short time.' For the conduct of the Spartans as leaders, esp. for the hatred excited by Pausanias, see cc. 94 f.

14. γνώσεσθε—'are going to adopt.'

15. ἄμεικτα . . τοῖς ἄλλοις—i.e. τοῖς τῶν ἄλλων ν. For νόμιμα see c. 71, 5.

17. ἐξιών—'when he goes abroad.' Xen. *Lac. Pol.* also speaks of the change for the worse in the Spartan when he left home to assume a command.

οἷς with νομίζει=χρῆται, an Ionic use.

19. οὐ βραχέων—'no trifling matters.'

22. πρόσθησθε—'assume,' 'take upon yourselves,' cf. c. 144, 1. 4 ; Eur. *Her.* 146 ἴδια προσθέσθαι κακά.

24. φιλεῖ ἐς τύχας . . περιίστασθαι—'is wont to turn out at last a series of chances, from which we (you and we) are equally remote' (i.e. we cannot see into them).

26. ἐν ἀδήλῳ κ.—'depends on what is hidden.' The ordinary phrase would be ἐν ἀδήλῳ ἐστί, and so we have a compression of ἐν ἀ. ἐστὶ καὶ κινδυνεύεται. For this kind of expression cf. vii. 77 ἐν κινδύνῳ αἰωροῦμαι.

28. τῶν ἔργων—without stopping to think : as Thuc. says elsewhere, at the beginning of a war, men are impulsive. ἔχονται is equivalent to ἅπτονται.

ἃ χρῆν ὕστερον δρᾶν — if ἃ is right (and the Schol. as well as all MSS. has it), we cannot render ἃ 'a thing which,' but must make τῶν ἔργων antecedent : nor is there any objection to this except that Thuc. regularly uses δρᾶν (αὐτό or αὐτά) differently ; see c. 5, 2 : but δρῶ τὰ ἔργα is good Greek, e.g. συννοίᾳ θ' ἅμα οἷον δέδρακεν ἔργον Eur. And. 806.

29. ἤδη—'only when,' with κακοπαθοῦντες.

PAGE 70.

2. ὄντες οὔτ' αὐτοί—strictly this should have been οὔτ' αὐτοὶ ὄντες.

3. λέγομεν ὑ. —'we charge you.'

αὐθαίρετος—i.e. not forced on us by circumstances.

6. λύεσθαι—cf. c. 140, 2 τὰ ἐγκλήματα διαλύεσθαι.

ξυνθήκην—in the thirty years' truce.

8. ἄρχοντας—c. 49, 4.

ταύτῃ ᾗ ἂν ὑφηγῆσθε—'following just wherever you may lead.'

14. πάντας—sc. τοὺς ξυμμάχους καὶ τοὺς Ἀθηναίους.

16. ἐπὶ τὸ αὐτὸ . . ἔφερον--'led to the same conclusion.'

17. ἀδικεῖν—'were guilty.'

24. ὁρῶ – sc. πολλῶν π. ἐμπείρους ὄντας.

25. τοῦ ἔργου—'the thing,' i.e. war.

26. οἱ πολλοί--in contrast with Archidamus and the elderly Spartans.

27. νομίσαντα—parallel to ἀπειρίᾳ.

PAGE 71.

2. Πελοποννησίους καὶ τοὺς ἁ. —i.e. our allies in Peloponnese and neighbours (who are not allies), esp. Argos. (Some see a hendiadys here, but it is unnecessary.)

3. παρόμοιος—'a match for' ; cf. ἀντίπαλος.

5. ἐφ' ἕκαστα—we can strike at any point promptly.

9. ἵπποις καὶ ὅπλοις καὶ ὄχλῳ—the transl. 'cavalry and hoplites and light-armed troops' is possible (cf. e.g. Xen. *Anab.* III. ii, 36); but the simple rendering (ὄχλῳ = population) is borne out by τοῖς ὅπλοις καὶ τῷ πλήθει, c. 81, 1.

12. φόρου ὑποτελεῖς—contrast c. 19, 1.

13. τίνι—neut.

17. ἔνεσται = μεταξὺ γενήσεται (Croiset).

ἀλλὰ τοῖς χ.—ἀλλά in rhetorical altercation, as often (e.g. vi. 38, 5), 'well then.'

18. ἐν κοινῷ—'the treasury.' The want of money at Sparta previous to Lysander's conquests is well-known. After the Pel. War there was a great change; but the money then acquired found its way into private hands, not into the treasury.

19. ἑτοίμως—'easily.' (The Spartans had not yet become conspicuous for covetousness, as after the war.)

20. φέρομεν—as an εἰσφορά.

21. τῷ πλήθει—the king includes the population of the confederate states. It is true that Sparta could pour a far greater number of troops into Attica than Athens could into the Peloponnese.

22. ἐπιφοιτῶντες—'by repeated incursions.' This was the method adopted, and this is probably written after the event.

26. τίς = ποῖος.

PAGE 72.

1. κἂν τούτῳ—'in that case.

2. καλόν—sc. ἡμῖν. In καταλύεσθαι the mid. denotes reciprocity, as in σπένδεσθαι.

3. μᾶλλον—sc. ἢ ἀναγκασθῆναι πολεμεῖν.

7. οὕτως—adeo.

8. φρονήματι—'pride,' 'high spirit.'

τῇ γῇ δουλεῦσαι—'slaves to their land,' so that they will not endure to see it ravaged, but will resist vigorously. Cf. Archidamus to the same effect in ii. 11, 6-8.

11. οὐ μὴν οὐδέ—c. 3, 3.

ἀναισθήτως—with ἐάν; a reply to the Corinthians; see c. 69, 3.

14. **καταφωρᾶν**—properly 'catch (a criminal) in the act'; hence 'detect,' 'discover.'

16. **δηλοῦντας** with πόλεμον implying a threat, and ὡς ἐπιτρέψομεν (for which cf. c. 71, 1) implying an admission; properly 'explaining'; cf. c. 129, 1.

17. **τὰ ἡμέτερ' αὐτῶν**—'our own resources,' both ξυμμάχων προσαγωγῇ and τῷ τὰ αὐτῶν ἅμα ἐκπορίζεσθαι. The καί clause takes a new constn. after the long parenthesis. (Croiset thinks that τὰ ἡμέτερ' αὐτῶν means 'our *home* resources' only, and that τὰ ἡμέτερ' αὐτῶν ἐξαρτύεσθαι is answered by τὰ αὐτῶν (sic) ἅμα ἐκ. which refers to the resources of the ξύμμαχοι. But τε after ξυμμάχων is much against this; and why should τὰ ἡμέτερ' αὐτῶν be limited by ξυμμάχων προσαγωγῇ ?)

19. **καὶ βαρβάρων**—efforts by Sparta (and perhaps Athens) to obtain the support of Persia are already heard of in the early part of the war.

22. **ἐπιβουλευόμεθα**—by attraction to the ὥσπερ-clause.

24. **τὰ αὐτῶν** = τὰ ἡμέτερα αὐτῶν, 'our own' as distinct from those of our ξύμμαχοι. This is awkward after τὰ ἡμέτερ' αὐτῶν above in a wider sense, and the use of αὐτῶν, otherwise common, for ἡμέτερ' αὐτῶν does not occur elsewhere in Thuc. Hence αὐτοῦ (adv.) and αὐτόθεν have been proposed.

26. **ἐτῶν δύο καὶ τριῶν**—cf. δὶς καὶ τρίς, δύο καὶ τρία βήματα : καί ('even') δὶς καὶ τρίς (see crit. note) etc. is also used.

PAGE 73.

1. **ἤδη** with what follows : when they see that while negotiating we are preparing quietly for war and maintaining a firm tone.

6. **μὴ γὰρ ἄλλο τι** — Archidamus argues against invading Attica at once, that as long as it is unravaged it is a hostage for the conciliatory behaviour of Athens in the negotiations ; when once it is wasted, they will know that they have nothing to lose.

7. **ἔχειν** (sc. ὑμᾶς), by an idiom common in Thuc. = εἶναι ὑμῖν.

οὐχ ἧσσον—'the more so.' The cultivation of the poor soil of Attica was necessarily carried on with great care.

12. **ὁρᾶτε ὅπως μή**—the result may be trouble for the confederacy (τῇ Πελοποννήσῳ). There is much difference of opinion about the transl. : Classen says, 'see that it do not turn out for us as regards Pel. in a more disgraceful and difficult

fashion'; Krüger and others, 'see that we may not bring about a more disgraceful and difficult state of things for Pel.'—making πράξομεν trans. and αἴσχιον καὶ ἀ. adjj. : so Sreup, but he renders, 'see that we do not do (something) too disgraceful and awkward for Pel.' Some think that ἢ τῇ 'Αττικῇ is to be supplied to the comparatives, others—but wrongly—ἢ νῦν. I construe 'see that we do not fare in a manner more humiliating and difficult for the confederacy,' sc. than if we refrain from invading Attica now, spurred on by these accusations. These ἐγκλήματα against Athens, it may be said, if we do not take up the cudgels (see next sentence), may involve αἰσχύνη and ἀπορία to the confederacy ; but they can be disposed of by negotiation. To go to war at once may involve us in worse difficulties.

16. ἰδίων—'separate,' or 'individual,' thinking of Corinth and Megara.

18. εὐπρεπῶς—contrasted with αἰσχρῶς καὶ ἀπόρως πράξομεν. θέσθαι—cf. c. 25, 1.

22. χρήματα φέροντες—'and they contribute money.' The Lac. allies paid no tribute.

23. ὅπλων—'is a matter of,' 'calls for.' Krüger compares e.g. Demosth. de Cor. § 190 ἦν ἐκεῖνος ὁ καιρὸς τοῦ γε φροντίζοντος ἀνδρός. The gen. is one of description.

24. ὠφελεῖ—'are of avail.' The dat. with ὠφελεῖ is not very rare in poetry (see Jebb on Soph. Ant. 560), but ἠπειρώταις here belongs to ἔστι as much as to δι' ἥν, etc., 'especially in the case of a land power fighting against a naval power.' Different explanations have been put forward of the meaning: some suppose Archidamus to allude to the necessity of obtaining a fleet (see c. 81, 4), others think that the allusion is to the equipment of large armies to remain in the field ; but this is against the general argument of the speech. In θαλασσίους is included the idea of tribute-paying subjects : the Lac. have no fleet and no subject allies bound to pay for one. (This is a succinct restatement of cc. 81, 4, 82, 1. Archidamus rightly sees that success in a war with Athens depends on getting control of the sea. You cannot conquer a sea power on land, cf. c. 121, esp. 4 and 5, and c. 81, 1, 2. The two things needful to give success to the Pel. are δαπάνη and μελετή.)

28. τῶν ἀποβαινόντων depends on τῆς αἰτίας, 'the greater share of responsibility for the consequences.'

ἐπ' ἀμφότερα—i.e. for good or ill (καὶ εὐκλείας καὶ δυσκλείας says the Schol. on ii. 11 δόξαν οἰσόμενοι ἐπ' ἀμφότερα).

PAGE 74.

1. **τι αὐτῶν** — i.e. τῶν ἀποβαινόντων, 'let us take some thought of them beforehand.'

τὸ βραδὺ καὶ μέλλον — referred to in τοῦτο and αὐτό below; μέλλον is only another name for βραδύ.

2. **ἡμῶν** depends on ᾦ.

4. **παύσαισθε** — 'reach the end.' If we begin in a hurry, we shall not be properly prepared, and the war will be prolonged.

5. **καὶ ἅμα** — the meaning is 'we have always been free and famous, so our βραδύτης has served us well.' This leads naturally to the reflexion that the so-called βραδύτης is really σωφροσύνη.

7. **δύναται . . εἶναι** — when δύναται = 'means' we do not find εἶναι: δύναται μάλιστα εἶναι = literally 'can be on the whole,' i.e. 'may be called.' **τοῦτ'** is emphatic, 'it is just this that.' **ἔμφρων** too is emphatic; hence its position; and the etymological jingle σω-φροσ-ύνη ἔμ-φρων is equivalent to 'true prudence.' For σωφροσύνη cf. c. 68, 1, to which this is a retort.

10. **τῶν . . ἐξοτρυνόντων** depends as objective gen. on ἡδονῇ. There must be here a side ref. to the increasing influence of oratory in the Athenian ecclesia—ἔπαινος, ἡδονή (produced by rhetoric), κατηγορία all show it. The whole of this paragraph is an independent criticism of Athens as well as an answer to the contrast drawn by the Corinthians.

ξὺν ἐπαίνῳ — ξύν of the means is very rare (cf. § 3 and c. 141 ξὺν φόβῳ), but occurs sometimes in Xen., as well as in poetry.

11. **ἐπὶ τὰ δεινά** — cf. c. 70, 2.

13. **ξὺν κατηγορίᾳ** — like the Corinthian speech.

14. **ἀνεπείσθημεν** — for the aorist cf. c. 70, 7.

15. **τὸ μέν** — i.e. πολεμικοί. The meaning is 'we are brave because we have a keen sense of honour, and we have a keen sense of honour because we are moderate.' But Thuc. proceeds in the opposite direction, and says, 'The chief element in moderation (σωφροσύνη substituted for τὸ εὔκοσμον) is honour, and the main ingredient in the sense of honour (αἰσχύνη = αἰδώς) is bravery.' Cf. iii. 83 τὸ εὔηθες, οὗ τὸ γενναῖον πλεῖστον μετέχει.

17. ἀμαθέστερον . . παιδευόμενοι—*causal* partic., 'not so highly as to despise the laws'; see c. **68**, 1, but a different turn is given to ἀμαθία here in the retort.

18. καὶ ξὺν χ.—sc. παιδευόμενοι, which is again to be supplied to the following infinitives.

20. τὰ ἀχρεῖα—thinking on public policy for one's self, for instance, and putting before the assembly what you have thought of.

22. ἀνομοίως—not so well as the fine criticism would lead one to expect.

ἐπεξιέναι—sc. αὐτοῖς, i.e. τοῖς πολεμίοις (Stahl).

23. παραπλησίους—as good as ours.

24. τὰς προσπιπτούσας . . διαιρετάς—'the chances that befall cannot be determined by argument.' The general sense is 'just as we do not despise the intelligence of our enemy, so we know that we cannot see into the future—how war will go —but must depend on our εὐψυχία and σωφροσύνη in preparing.' διαιρεῖν is properly 'to make a gap in.'

26. παρασκευαζόμεθα—see crit. note : αἰεί favours the indic., καὶ . . δεῖ the subjunc. But an exhortation here would come in very awkwardly before c. **85**, where the peroration begins ; and Steup, reading παρασκευαζώμεθα, thinks this whole section (§ 4) properly follows c. **85** § 1.

PAGE 75.

4. ἐν τοῖς ἀναγκαιοτάτοις—'in the most rigorous discipline'; cf. ξὺν χαλεπότητι παιδευόμενοι above. (The rendering of Bonitz, 'trained (only) in what is indispensable,' as distinct from the *useless wisdom* of the Athenians seems to take us far beyond anything that Archidamus has said on the small extent of Spartan education, and a limitation—'only'—does not fit in well with the context.)

12. βουλεύσωμεν—'come to a decision.'

13. διὰ ἰσχύν—i.e. we need be in no hurry, because the Athenians, knowing our strength and that we are not overlooking what they have done (cf. c. **69**, 3), will not dare to take any further step against us in the meantime.

18. πρότερον—before you too consent to arbitration.

20. κράτιστα—this and φοβερώτατα are pred. to ταῦτα (Classen). If Thuc. means καὶ τοῖς ἐν. φοβερώτατα to explain κράτιστα, the first καί must be omitted (see crit. note). The double καί makes two ideas.

PAGE 76.

2. καίτοι—'yet surely,' a common use.

6. καὶ τότε καὶ νῦν—ἦμεν is implied after τότε. The same form of sentence occurs in iii. 40, 2 and vi. 60, 2. But in Plat. *Gorg.* p. 488 B we have ἀλλὰ ταῦτα ἔλεγον καὶ τότε καὶ νῦν λέγω (ἔλεγον del. Schanz).

11. παραδοτέα—for the plur. see c. 72, 2.

12. οὐδὲ δίκαις κτλ.—'nor must we decide by arbitration and words where we are ourselves being injured not in word.' μή is caused by the prohibition of which the whole clause consists.

24. ἔφορος ὤν—'in his capacity as ephor.'

25. ἐς τὴν ἐ.—after ἐπεψήφιζεν.

26. κρίνουσι—decide in the assembly.

PAGE 77.

3. ὅτῳ μέν — the method of taking the division adopted seems to be introduced for this special occasion.

8. ἐγένοντο—'amounted to.'

12. ψῆφον ἐπαγαγεῖν—'put the vote to them.'

13. κοινῇ βουλευσάμενοι—'arrive at a common decision before . .'

18. τοῦ τὰς σπονδὰς λ.—the gen. of definition. Some edd. think these words spurious.

ἐγένετο . . προκεχωρηκυιῶν—lit. 'took place in the fourteenth year of the thirty years' truce when it had lasted (so long, sc. ἐς τοσοῦτον),' i.e. in the fourteenth year of its course.

21. τὰ Εὐβοϊκά—see c. 23, 4 and 114.

PAGE 78.

1. οἱ γάρ—now begins the so-called πεντηκονταετία, or sketch of the growth of Athenian power in the half century between the battle of Mycale (479 B.C.) and the beginning of the war (431 B.C.). This sketch continues to c. 118, 2 ; and

it consists of two parts : (1) to c. **96**—how they obtained the leadership (ἡγεμονία)—or, as he says here, ἦλθον ἐπὶ τὰ πράγματα ἐν οἷς ηὐξήθησαν ; (2) to c. **118**—how the leadership was transformed into an empire—ἐν οἴῳ τρόπῳ κατέστη (ἡ ἀρχή), c. **97**, 2.

4. ναυσί—Salamis (480). **πεζῷ**—Plataea (479).

7. διεφθάρησαν—by Leotychides, the Spartan king, and Xanthippus, father of Pericles.

11. οἱ .. ξύμμαχοι—probably there was no formal treaty, but ξύμμαχοι is used because they were fighting side by side with the Athenians. (There is no need to remove ξύμμαχοι with Wilamowitz.)

14. ἐπιχειμάσαντες—the winter of 479-478 B.C. The history of Herodotus ends with the fall of Sestos.

19. εὐθύς—in autumn of 479.

ὅθεν = ἐκεῖθεν οἷ. Cf. Soph. *Trach.* 701 ἐκ δὲ γῆς ὅθεν | προύκειτ', ἀναξέουσι, 'from the earth *where* it was strewn,' for ὅπου. The omission of antecedent before ὅθεν is not very rare ; e.g. ii. **94** τροπαῖον ἔστησαν ὅθεν ἀναγαγόμενοι ἐκράτησαν, for ἐνταῦθα ὅθεν. The places are Salamis, Troezen and Aegina.

21. κατασκευήν—'stock, goods,' of all kinds.

22. ἀνοικοδομεῖν—in the autumn of 479.

24. βραχέα—'only a small remnant,' of the wall round the city left by the Persians.

PAGE 79.

1. ἦλθον πρεσβείᾳ = ἐπρεσβεύσαντο, the *sociative* dat. as in naval and military expressions ; but there is no other example of this phrase and hence the variant readings.

τὰ μὲν κτλ.—'partly because' etc. **μήτε** not οὔτε because apprehension is implied.

5. τὸ πλῆθος ὅ—see c. **14**, 2.

6. γενομένην—for the order see c. **11**, 3.

8. εἰστήκει—sc. τείχη.

9. τὸ βουλόμενον (= τὴν βούλησιν) **καὶ ὕποπτον**—see c. **36**, 1. ἐς τοὺς 'Α. certainly belongs to δηλοῦντες and means before the *assembly*. For δηλοῦν in this use cf. c. **82**, 1.

11. ὡς δὲ τοῦ β.—'but on the ground that,' still depending on ἠξίουν.

13. ἀπὸ ἰχυροῦ ποθεν . . ὁρμᾶσθαι—'to use any stronghold as a base of operations.' ποθεν by attraction for που.

νῦν—'lately.' Herod. ix. 13 fol. tells us how the Persian general Mardonius made Thebes his headquarters.

15. ἀναχώρησίν τε καὶ ἀφορμήν—'as a place to retreat to or advance from,' abstract for concrete.

24. ἱκανὸν ἄρωσιν—for the pred. adj. cf. ii. 75 ἥρετο τὸ ὕψος τοῦ τείχους μέγα. The aor. (see crit. note) is necessary: the pres. would mean 'so long as.'

25. ἀναγκαιοτάτου—cf. c. 2, 2.

πάντας—on this the Schol. notes αὐτοὺς καὶ γυναῖκας καὶ παῖδας. It is therefore evident that he did not find these words in the text. Mr. Forbes defends the words as 'forcible,' and adds that the note may only mean that the words καὶ . . παῖδας in the text themselves explain πάντας. Steup finds something wrong with their 'force,' rightly saying that καὶ οἰκέτας is missing after παῖδας : e.g. Diodorus xi. 40 says συνελαμβάνοντο τῶν ἔργων οἵ τε παῖδες καὶ αἱ γυναῖκες καὶ καθόλου πᾶς ξένος καὶ δοῦλος : but the details of his account are not drawn wholly from Thuc. The second point raised in defence is not borne out by the scholia to Thuc.

26. τοὺς ἐν τῇ πόλει—cf. c. 64, 2 : in contrast with those away from Attica.

PAGE 80.

3. τἆλλα . . τἀκεῖ—'the rest, namely what was to be done there' : an intentionally vague and mysterious suggestion of cunning, both being object of πράξοι. The order throws emphasis on both. The Athenians liked such oracular remarks from those whom they regarded as ξυνετοί : this style reflected the manner of the Delphic oracle, the gnomic poets, the sages and early philosophers.

6. ἀρχάς—'magistrates.'

11. ὡς—for ὅπως, 'how' (not 'that').

13. διὰ φιλίαν αὐτοῦ—αὐτοῦ objective : the reason of this favour was, no doubt, that Them. was regarded at Sparta as a protector from the Persians : they owed him gratitude for the Athenian fleet ; cf. c. 74, 1.

τῶν δὲ ἄλλων κτλ. — Classen makes ἀφικνουμένων substantival ; and renders καὶ σαφῶς 'quite positively' (ἐπεὶ οἱ ἄλλοι ἀφικνούμενοι, 'visitors'—'arrivals,' as they say—καὶ σαφῶς κατηγόρουν). The contrast to this subject will then be σφῶν αὐτῶν ἄνδρας below. Others render '(all) the other (visitors) arriving and announcing.' In either case there is probably an allusion to τῶν ξυμμάχων ἐξοτρυνόντων c. 90, 1 in τῶν δὲ ἄλλων: these ' others ' were persons afraid of Athens.

15. τειχίζεται—sc. τὸ τεῖχος.

18. οἵτινες χρηστοί—parts of εἰμί are often omitted in short rel. sentences.

24. ἦκον—' were come.'

29. ἐπεστάλη—impersonal.

PAGE 81.

1. τοῖς Λακεδαιμονίοις—i.e. ταῖς ἀρχαῖς (c. 90, 5).

4. εἰ δέ τι κτλ. — a claim to complete recognition as an equal. τι=' in regard to any matter :' ὡς πρὸς κτλ. lit. ' to go in future as to men who could discern both their own interests and the common interests of the Greeks.' ἰέναι depends on εἶπεν in sense of ἐκέλευσεν: ὡς πρὸς δ. is placed early so as to make it emphatic, and the emphasis must be marked in translating. There is no reason for interfering with the text here: προδ- (see crit. note) is only a slip for πρὸς δ.

10. ἔφασαν—sc. the Athenian ambassadors.

11. βουλεύεσθαι—the attraction of the verb of short rel. sentences in O.O. into infinitive is less rare in Gk. than in Lat.: Thuc. has several examples, e.g. ii. 102 λέγεται . . ὅτε δὴ ἀλᾶσθαι. This sentence stands as accus. of respect to οὐδενὸς κτλ.

14. καὶ ἰδίᾳ κτλ.—' and for the Athenians themselves and with a view to (the interests of) the allies in general it would be beneficial.' The position of the allies would be secure in the general council if Athens was strong. (This passage has been much discussed : (1) Classen takes τοῖς πολίταις with ἐς τοὺς π. ξυμμάχους also, and understands, 'would be of more advantage to the Athenians (both) separately and with regard to their relations with the allies.' But it is rightly objected that the advantage of the fortification cannot be limited to the Athenians, who want to prove that it is good for the allies too (cf. c. 91, 4 τὰ κοινά). Steup deletes ἄμεινον εἶναι, and is thus able to transl. the καὶ ἰδίᾳ κτλ. ' both for the A. themselves and

for the allies.' But there is no decisive objection to the text as it stands. It is true that we expect ἰδίᾳ τε or καί ('both') ἰδίᾳ ; cf. τά τε σφίσιν αὐτοῖς . . καὶ τὰ κοινά : but the omission and the unusual ἐς τούς instead of dative serve to make the allusion to 'the allies' a climax ; καί = 'and in fact.')

15. ὠφελιμώτερον ἔσεσθαι—the argument is that this, like the earlier actions of Athens, was done ἐπ' ὠφελίᾳ, not only for Athens but for the Greek allies in general. Cf. c. 73, 2.

οὐ γάρ—this alludes to all the allies quite as much as to Athens : they would feel that the right to strengthen themselves was vindicated by Athens, thus all would be on an equal footing in the common council and their views would be equally respected.

18. ἔφη—Themistocles.

22. γνώμης παραινέσει—sc. ἐπί, 'to recommend a resolution to the Athenian assembly,' i.e. to give advice. τῷ κοινῷ depends on παραινέσει. δῆθεν is of course ironical.

25. τὰ μάλιστα—best taken with ἐν τῷ τότε, 'at that time more than at any other.'

PAGE 82.

4. οἱ γὰρ θεμέλιοι—the upper part of the wall was of brick (πλίνθοι), but there was a lower course of stone. Cf. Demosth. de Cor. § 299 οὐ λίθοις ἐτείχισα τὴν πόλιν οὐδὲ πλίνθοις ἐγώ.

5. ξυνειργασμένων—'shaped for fitting together.'

6. στῆλαι — fragments of some of these belonging to the walls of Themistocles have been found. Hicks, Man. p. 13.

8. πανταχῇ—the extension did not include the SW. side of the city. For μείζων cf. c. 90, 3.

10. κινοῦντες ἠπείγοντο—'disturbed in their haste' : κινεῖν is specially used of things that should not be interfered with.

12. ὑπῆρκτο δ' αὐτοῦ—'a beginning had been made on it' ; αὐτοῦ is neut. = 'the work.'

13. ἐπὶ τῆς . . ἦρξε—'during his office of archon, which he had held for a year at Athens.' It is not necessary to under-stand by κατ' ἐνιαυτόν 'annually,' which complicates the grammar of the sentence. κατά, with words denoting time,

is not always distributive. The year is now thought to be 482 B.C.

15. **λιμένας**—Piraeus, Zea, Munychia.

16. **καὶ αὐτούς**—'and that the A., having once become a naval people, were in a very advantageous position for the acquisition of power.' (Classen understands προφέρειν as fut. in sense.)

18. **τῆς γὰρ δή**—as often, there is an ellipse here; in full the sense is 'he naturally thought of this, for,' etc.

19. **τὴν ἀρχὴν εὐθὺς ξυγκατεσκεύαζεν**—'at once began to help them to lay the foundation of their empire.' This seems, on the whole, better than the version preferred by Classen and others, 'prepared to *begin* (ἀρχήν) the building,' in which ξυν- is left obscure, and is, in fact, variously explained; and ἀρχήν (cf. c. **96**, 2) is strange for ἔργον. The allusion is to the whole period after Salamis.

21. **νῦν ἔτι**—generally supposed to have been written after the destruction of the walls of Piraeus by Lysander in 404 B.C. There is, however, no certainty in the matter; cf. § 2.

22. **δύο γὰρ ἅμαξαι**—this is supposed to mean that wagons *in two rows* drawing up stones from opposite ends met and passed one another *on the wall* (Classen); or, much better—because the idea of Classen could not possibly be carried out in building—the wagons worked from *one* end up an incline, and after discharging their load turned and passed the laden wagons still coming along the wall. (So already Procopius.) It is almost incredible, however, that Thuc. should have intended this Greek to represent (1) *two rows* of wagons (2) passing *along the wall*, and (3) the one set returning *empty*. But I have no other explanation to offer. Some suppose that two wagons worked on the level and deposited stones ready for the building on either side; perhaps this does prove τὸ πάχος τοῦ τείχους.

24. **ἐντὸς δέ**—i.e. the inside was not filled with clay and small stones, but large blocks were cut and fitted and fastened together on the outside by iron clamps.

25. **ἐντομῇ**—'by cutting *into* them,' so that the ends could fit together and overlap. This is much better than ἐν τομῇ, which cannot = 'at the ends.'

28. **οὗ διενοεῖτο**—i.e. ἐκείνου ὃ διενοεῖτο τελεῖν.

PAGE 83.

1. **ἐπιβουλάς**—an ἐπιβουλή would lead to an ἐπιβολή : Thuc. as often gives to the cause the meaning of its effect : there is no need to alter the text, despite the gloss in the Schol.

2. **ἀχρειοτάτων**—in its strict military sense.

16. **ξυνέπλεον**—it is not clear whether this expedition took place in 478 B.C. or in the early spring of 477. The Athenian leaders were Aristides and Cimon.

21. **ἐν τῆδε τῇ ἡ.**—during the command of Pausanias. ἡγεμονία refers to his leadership, not to the Spartan 'hegemony' ; see e.g. c. **128**, 7. The story of Pausanias is given in cc. **128**- **130**. Some, to improve the sense, connect these words with the sentence that follows ; see crit. note.

24. **καὶ ὅσοι κτλ.**—see c. **89**, 2 ; those who had revolted from Persia after Mycale.

27. **γίγνεσθαι**—the pres., if correct, implies that the change could not be made in a minute.

κατὰ τὸ ξυγγενές—they were not *all* Ionians, but the greater number of them were.

PAGE 84.

9. **ἐφαίνετο** — it is not necessary to supply a subject such as ἡ ἀρχή : the lit. rendering is 'an imitation of despotism was apparent (was to be seen)' ; so in ii. **65**, 9 ἐγίγνετο λόγῳ μὲν δημοκρατία, ἔργῳ δὲ . . ἀρχή, 'nominally a democracy was being formed.'

10. **καλεῖσθαι**—before the court at Sparta.

14. **τῶν μὲν ἰδίᾳ . . ηὐθύνθη**—'was punished for the injuries he had privately inflicted on any person.' τινα is prob. masc., the sing. being used for the plur. as elsewhere, e.g. c. **40**, 5 ; πρός τινα, 'in certain respects,' seems flat, and τινα as neut. plur. is avoided where it is ambiguous.

15. **τὰ δὲ μέγιστα**—those against the state : internal accus. to ἀδικεῖν.

17. **ἐδόκει**—sc. τοῦτο.

23. **οἱ ἐξιόντες**—cp. c. **77**, 6 ; the pres. of the succession of commanders.

χείρους—'corrupted.'

27. **ἐπιτηδείους** = φίλους.

PAGE 85.

2. **ἔταξαν**—cf. *Ath. Pol.* c. 23 τοὺς φόρους οὗτος (Aristides) ἦν ὁ τάξας ταῖς πόλεσιν τοὺς πρώτους ἔτει τρίτῳ μετὰ τὴν ἐν Σαλαμῖνι ναυμαχίαν—in 478–77. Trans. 'assessed the contributions both of the states that were to provide money and of those,' etc.—*not* 'fixed which of the states,' which overlooks the technical use of τάσσειν, 'rate.'

5. **ὧν** = ἐκείνων ἅ, gen. of cause.

6. **'Ελληνοταμίαι** . . **ἀρχή** — ἀρχή is pred., 'as an office,' and the verb is attracted into its number. Only Athenians could hold the office. They were ten in number, and were elected annually in the Ecclesia, one from each tribe. See Sandys' note on *Ath. Pol.* c. 30, 2.

9. **ὁ πρῶτος φόρος ταχθείς**—for the order cf. c. 11, 3. The sum is thought, on the evidence of the extant lists of the quota of ¹⁄₆₀th paid to Athena, to be impossibly large; and Classen therefore considered the whole passage interpolated. Perhaps the sum given was assessed, but not realised.

11. **Δῆλος**—the treasury of the league was removed to Athens in 454 B.C.

14. **βουλευόντων**—co-ordinate with αὐτονόμων. ἀπό expresses the method.

τοσάδε ἐπῆλθον—the series of enterprises that are about to be noticed (c. 98–118); τοσάδε διεπράξαντο ὅσα . . ἐρεῖ Schol.

15. **διαχειρίσει πραγμάτων**—'by the management (manipulation) of political affairs.'

16. **μεταξὺ τοῦδε τοῦ πολέμου καὶ τοῦ Μ.**—'between the Persian and Peloponnesian wars.' Greek often proceeds in this manner from the nearer to the more remote.

ἅ—the antecedent is τοσάδε. ἐγένετο stands as the passive of ποιῶ.

20. **τοὺς αἰεὶ προστυγχάνοντας ἐν ἑκάστῳ**—'who in the several incidents came in contact with them' as enemies ('took part with the allies' as some understand προστυγ. does not seem to be supported by the usage of the word; it occurs only here in Thuc.).

21. **αὐτά**—i.e. ἃ ἐγένετο κτλ.

23. **χωρίον**—'period.'

26. Ἑλλάνικος—this is the only instance in which Thuc. names another historian. H. of Mitylene was contemporary with Pericles, and in his Ἀτθίς (here called Ἀττικὴ ξυγγραφή) he included a sketch of historical events, and is said to have carried his work down at least to 406 B.C.

27. βραχέως τε καὶ τοῖς χρόνοις οὐκ ἀ.—Hellanicus must have been very scanty and inexact in the dates for this period, since this description would apply in a considerable degree to the better account that Thuc. proceeds to give. For the probable dates of the events to be noticed see Introd. p. xxix.

29. ἔχει—sc. ταῦτα.

PAGE 86.

1. Ἠιόνα—this place became later the port of Amphipolis. Miltiades is the victor of Marathon.

6. ᾤκισαν αὐτοί—Scyros was parcelled out among Athenian settlers, or 'cleruchs'; sessores veteres eiecit (Cimon), agros civibus divisit, says Nepos.

7. ἄνευ τῶν ἀ. Εὐβοέων — Carystus sided with Persia, but the rest of Euboea was in the league.

8. ξυνέβησαν—the Carystians.

12. τὸ καθεστηκός—not 'recognised principles of right,' but ' the existing arrangement ' which was that the allies retained their autonomy. δουλεία as in c. 8, 3.

13. ξυνέβη—sc. δουλωθῆναι, ἐδουλώθησαν. The Schol. supplies ἐδουλώθη, and acting on this hint Krüger removes ξυνέβη, so that ὡς ἑκάστη (nom.) = 'severally.' This gives a simpler constn., but the text may be sound ; and, as Classen says, ξυνέβη points to the ' varying circumstances under which the loss of αὐτονομία occurred.

16. λιποστράτιον—i.e. failure to furnish any ships as distinct from ἔκδειαι, which means that part only of the number was supplied.

17. ἀκριβῶς ἔπρασσον—'were exacting' in regard to φόρων ἔκδειαι, not quite 'exacted (the tribute).'

18. λυπηροὶ ἦσαν—cf. c. 76, 1 : ταλαιπωρεῖν refers to νεῶν ἔκδειαι καὶ λιποστράτιον.

20. τὰς ἀνάγκας. 'their coercive measures.' Cf. Aesch. P.V. 1052 ἀνάγκης στερραῖς δίναις, and see L. & S. s.v. ἀνάγκη 3.

22. **ἄρχοντες**—'as rulers' they were not popular as they had been at first. **πως** implies the omission of the details.

24. **ὧν**—i.e. ὅτι οὔτε ξυνεστράτευον κτλ.

27. **χρήματα ἐτάξαντο . . φέρειν**—the mid. denotes a reciprocal arrangement. χρήματα is prob. object of φέρειν and τὸ . ἐκ. ἀνάλωμα, 'the sum that fell to them' is in appos. to it.

PAGE 87.

1. **ηὔξετο**—Thuc. never uses the ordinary Attic form αὐξάνω.

10. **ἀμφότερα**—cf. c. 13, 5.

12. **Φοινίκων**—the Persian fleet consisted almost wholly of Phoenician ships.

τὰς πάσας—'in all.'

15. **ἀντιπέρας**—often used of the coast opposite an island, or vice versa.

16. **ἃ ἐνέμοντο**—see notes on p. 2, 11 and p. 44, 3. Here the two antecedents in different number require ἅ, which would otherwise be ὧν.

23. **αὐτοὶ ἐκράτησαν**—in contrast with the 'Ηδωνοί—but the use of αὐτοί here, to which Steup objected, is strange. Notice how the precise sense of οἱ 'Αθηναῖοι shifts in this passage with the different verbs (e.g. πέμψαντες and διεφθάρησαν).

26. **ὑπὸ τῶν Θρᾳκῶν ξυμπάντων οἷς**—all the Thracians who objected, as distinct from the Edonians only. **οἷς πολέμιον ἦν** replaces a τῶν + partic. limiting ξυμπάντων. Poppo's conj. ξύμπαντες, supported by Valla's transl. omnes, brings this passage more into harmony with Herod. ix. 75 and other passages in which the Edonians alone are named as destroying the A. But if Thuc. meant the Edonians only, why should he say ὑπὸ τῶν Θρᾳκῶν ?

27. **τὸ χωρίον κτιζόμενον**—'the founding of the place.'

PAGE 88.

8. **αὐτοῖς**—ethic: it is constantly placed early in this manner.

περιοίκων—the free, but dependent Lacedaemonians descended from the pre-Dorian inhabitants and living in separate towns.

11. **τότε**—'the descendants of the M. of former times who had been enslaved in the war made up most of the helots.'

πλεῖστοι is pred. ; τότε refers to a well-known occasion, as elsewhere in Thuc. (often too, to some event that has been already recorded by Thuc.)—heie to the first Messenian war, after which the Messenians became, as Tyrtaeus says, ὥσπερ ὄνοι μεγάλοις ἄχθεσι τειρόμενοι : δουλωθέντων is epithet, the order being justified by παλαιῶν, cf. c. 11, 3 κατεσχηκότος.

12. ἐκλήθησαν—'came to be called'; cf. c. 2, 4. οἱ πάντες, sc. Εἵλωτες.

16. καθελόντες—this and the following aor. partic. are what are called 'timeless,' i.e. they denote merely the act, not time anterior to the verb. This happens only when the leading verb is in aorist. Cf. the constn. with ἔτυχον ἔλαθον, ἔφθασα.

17. χρήματά τε κτλ.—the order is ταξάμενοι αὐτίκα ἀποδοῦναι χ. ὅσα ἔδει καὶ τὸ λοιπὸν φέρειν (χ. ὅσα ἔδει), and χ. ὅσα ἔδει is the common object and so is put first. Note the aor. of one act and the pres. of a system. (It is certainly wrong to make ἀποδοῦναι depend only on ἔδει and to render καὶ 'also.' This would mean that they were always to pay as much as the indemnity now exacted).

23. ξυμμάχους—in virtue of the alliance under Sparta still formally existing in spite of the Athenian hegemony.

24. οἱ δ' ἦλθον—there was opposition at Athens to the proposal, but Cimon's view was that Sparta on land was as necessary to Greece as Athens on sea: Greece was 'lamed' while Sparta was tied down (Plut. Cim. 16).

27. τοῖς δέ—edd. are divided as to whether this refers to the Athenians who fell short of their reputation, or to the Lac., i.e. whether to transl. (1) 'but in their case (the Ath.) it gradually appeared that there was a deficiency in this (viz. τοῦ τειχομαχεῖν δυνατοὺς εἶναι),' as they did not succeed in taking Ithome ; or (2) 'whereas it was apparent to them (the Lac.) that they lacked skill in this'—so that the full form would be ὅτι (οἱ μὲν Ἀθηναῖοι) . . τοῖς δὲ (Λακεδαιμονίοις). This seems better. The reading τῆς of the Schol. is prob. only a conjecture. ἐνδεᾶ is again the plur. adj. for sing. (=ἔνδεια). Thuc. might have said τοῦτο ἐνδεὲς ἐφαίνετο in the same sense.

PAGE 89.

2. βίᾳ γάρ —'for otherwise (had they been competent τειχομαχεῖν) they would have captured it by assault'—and would not have had to turn the siege into a blockade. Cf. on c. 11, 1.

8. **ἡγησάμενοι**—'considering'; so often in the aor. : they reflected ὅτι οἱ μὲν Δωριεῖς, οἱ δὲ Ἴωνες (Schol.).

μή τι κτλ. — this depends on δείσαντες, the clause between being parenthetical ; a not very common form of constn. ; cf. Soph. *Antig.* 1278 τὰ δ' ἐν δόμοις | ἔοικας ἥκειν καὶ τάχ' ὄψεσθαι κακά, with Jebb's note.

9. **νεωτερίσωσι**—i.e. by joining the helots. This would be an instance of their τολμηρὸν καὶ νεωτεροποιία.

12. **ἐπὶ τῷ βελτίονι λόγῳ**—'for the better reason,' viz. that they were no longer needed. Of course βελτίων implies a contrast with a suppressed κακίων αἰτία viz. τὸ ὑποψίαν τινὰ γενέσθαι.

15. **δεινὸν ποιησάμενοι** = δ. ἡγησάμενοι : but δεινόν (-ά) ποιεῖν = to *declare* a thing intolerable.

23. **δεκάτῳ ἔτει**—this year (see chron. table p. xxx) would be 456 B.C. ; but there are several reasons for thinking δεκάτῳ wrong ; e.g. (1) we know from [Xen.] *Ath. Pol.* that the Messenians were reduced before the battle of Tanagra, which occurred in 457 B.C., nor is it possible that Sparta should have sent a large army out of the Pel. unless this were so ; (2) with δεκάτῳ the chronological order of events is here only in this sketch of the rise of Athens interrupted to notice an event that occurred after events that are still to be noticed. Hence Krüger proposed τετάρτῳ, supposing that Thuc. wrote Δ which was taken for the initial letter of δεκάτῳ instead of the sign for four. Unfortunately, in view of the fact that Cimon was not sent to Sparta until after the capitulation of Thasos, and that then ἐμηκύνετο ὁ πόλεμος, it is doubtful if four years is long enough.

28. **εἶναι**—the infin. in *O.O.* for ἔστω δοῦλος of *O.R.* This infin. is particularly common in the terms of treaties.

PAGE 90.

3. **Ἰθωμῆτα**—Doric ending, recalling the original.

5. **κατ' ἔχθος ἤδη**—closely together, = κατά ('in consequence of ') τὸ ἤδη γεγενημένον ἔ.

ἐς Ναύπακτον — the settlement proved most important to Athens in the Pel. War ; they were expelled from Naupactus by Sparta at the end of it, and lived dispersed until Epaminondas befriended them in 370 B.C.

12. **ἔσχον**—ingressive. The possession of Megara and its

NOTES

ports was of the utmost value to Athens, because they thus blocked the roads from Pel. to Attica and Boeotia.

20. ὑπέρ—'above,' i.e. further inland.

22. 'Αρταξέρξου—the successor of Xerxes.

PAGE 91.

4. 'Αλιᾶς—nom. 'Αλιῆς or -εῖς (cf. Δωριεύς). The object of Athens was to begin a plan of connecting up the coast from the Saronic G. to the G. of Argos.

19. πρότερον with ἐπικούρους.

21. κατέλαβον—the heights command the Megarid.

28. ἐκ τῆς π.—c. 8, 2.

29. οἵ τε πρεσβύτατοι καὶ οἱ ν.—those over fifty or under twenty did not as a rule serve outside Attica : here περίπολοι (18-20) and οἱ ὑπὲρ πεντήκοντα ἔτη γεγονότες, as Classen points out, are meant

PAGE 92.

3. αὐτοί—subj. of ἔλασσον ἔχειν.

6. κακιζόμενοι = ψεγόμενοι (Schol.).

8. ἡμέραις — with ἐλθόντες ἀνθίστασαν. The dat. is much better than accus. taken with παρασκευασάμενοι.

15. προσβιασθέν—'driven to it,' viz. πρὸς τὸ ὑποχωρεῖν (to take οὐκ ὀλίγον as adverbial and qualifying προσβιασθέν with Steup is very forced). Others explain πρὸς τὸ ἐσπεσεῖν κτλ., which on account of διαμαρτὸν τῆς ὁδοῦ ἐσέπεσεν (=pass of ἐσβάλλω) is less likely.

16. ᾧ ἔτυχεν—sc. ὄν.

19. εἶργον—sc. αὐτούς. τοῖς ὁ. is dat. of means.

22. τὸ πλῆθος—'the main body.'

25. τὰ μακρὰ τείχη—these are not the two parallel 'Long Walls' or 'Long Legs' so familiar, but (1) the northern or τὸ ἔξωθεν τεῖχος running to Piraeus, and (2) the wall to Phalerum, τὸ Φαληρικὸν τεῖχος. The third wall, parallel to the northern wall, and called τὸ διὰ μέσου or τὸ νότιον τεῖχος was added some years later. (Steup supposes that all three walls are here meant, the two to Piraeus being included in τὸ ἐς Πειραιᾶ. This is contrary to Andoc. de pace 37 and Plat. Gorg.

I   K

p. 455 E, and in ii. 13, 7 it is not likely that Thuc. means both walls by τὸ μακρόν, esp. as immediately afterwards he uses the plur.)

28. Δωριᾶς—i.e. the territory of the Dorians. The names of the towns in this district are variously given by different authors; but no doubt the three places here mentioned are the most important.

PAGE 93.

3. Νικομήδους — brother of Pausanias. The Lac. must have crossed the Corinthian ('Crisaean') gulf.

9. ἀπεχώρουν—'began to . .'

15. δύσοδος—i.e. the passes are difficult.

20. τὸ δέ τι—τὸ δέ is 'on the other hand' (cf. τὰ μὲν . . τὰ δέ), and τι 'in some measure' (cf. οὔ τι in Plato).

22. ἐπῆγον—'were egging them on.'

25. πανδημεί—i.e. all liable to serve who remained at Athens.

28. νομίσαντες δὲ κτλ.—νομίσαντες and ὑποψίᾳ are the emphatic words (Forbes).

PAGE 94.

8. φόνος . . πολύς — see Hicks, *Man. Gk. Hist. Inscr.* p. 23. Cimon, who had been banished after the return from Ithome (c. 102), was recalled after this defeat on the motion of Pericles. Plato (*Menex.*) and Demosth. speak of the battle of Tanagra as indecisive. Plato also misrepresents the ostracism of Cimon in the *Gorgias*.

11. διὰ Γερανείας—a good proof of the severity of the defeat is that the Athenians did not attempt to hold the passes against the returning Lac.

14. Μυρωνίδου—cf. c. 105, 4.

26. τὸ νεώριον—Gythium. This Chalcis is in Aetolia.

PAGE 95.

1. ἐν ἀποβάσει τῆς γῆς = ἐς τὴν γῆν ἀποβάντες.

5. ἰδέαι—'vicissitudes,' διάφοροι πόλεμοι, οἷον . . νῖκαι καὶ ἧτται (Schol.).

12. ἄλλως—μάτην (Schol.).

19. Προσωπίτιδα—an island formed by one of the mouths of the Nile and a canal.

24. ἤπειρον—sc. ἐποίησε.

27. πολεμήσαντα—there is no need to read πολεμησάντων with Cobet ; cf. such expressions as νοσεῖ τὰ πράγματα : edd. quote Herod. vii. 9 ἐς τοῦτο θράσεος ἀνήκει τὰ Ἑλλήνων πράγματα.

PAGE 96.

3. ἐν τοῖς ἕλεσι—the Nile Delta.

5. καὶ ἅμα—the constn. changes from subord. to principal form : strictly we require καὶ ἅμα ὅτι κτλ.

7. τὰ πάντα ἔπραξε—i.e. τὴν ἀπόστασιν ἐποίησε τῆς Αἰγύπτου (Schol.) ; see c. 104, 1.

11. Μενδήσιον κέρας—one of the Nile mouths named after a town Mendes. κέρας καλεῖ Νείλου τὸ στόμα (Schol.).

12. εἰδότες—after τριήρεις, of the crews, as often ; e.g. vi. 104, 1.

20. βασιλέως—he belonged prob. to the Scopadae, one of the two branches of the royal house of Thessaly.

φεύγων—'living in exile.'

25. ὅσα—sc. κρατεῖν ἐδύναντο. See Jebb on Soph. O.T. 347.

26. ἐκ τῶν ὅπλων—i.e. outside the camp. τὰ ὅπλα is properly the space in front of a camp where the arms were piled : so commonly in Xen.

PAGE 97.

5. Περικλέους—first mention of him (year 454 B.C.).

9. τῆς Ἀκαρνανίας depends on Οἰνιάδας.

15. ἔσχον—'abstained from war with Greeks.'

18. ἀπ' αὐτῶν—out of the 200.

19. μεταπέμποντος—Thuc. often uses this verb in act., while other authors use the mid. : so too μεταχειρίζω, πειρῶ.

22. Κίτιον—in Cyprus (now Chitti)

23. ὑπὲρ Σ.—'off S.,' with ἐναυμάχησαν.

25. ἀμφότερα—see c. 13, 5.

26. αἱ . . πάλιν [αἱ] ἐλθοῦσαι—'which had returned from Egypt.' αἱ is to be omitted.

5. ἐγγενομένου—cf. c. 80, 4.

6. φευγόντων—after the battle of Oenophyta, the democratic party in Boeotia had driven out the anti-Athenian oligarchs. But the exiles had recovered some of their lost power.

13. καὶ ἀνδραποδίσαντες—there is no sufficient ground for omitting these words (see crit. note): that a scribe copied them from c. 98 is very unlikely. It is remarkable that Athens should have taken such drastic measures against a place in the heart of Greece and so near.

14. καταστήσαντες—sc. ἐν αὐτῇ, unless ἐγ- should be read (if Thuc. wrote in the old Attic alphabet, ἐγ would be nearly identical with the last two letters of φυλακήν) ; cf. c. 115, 3.

15. Κορωνείᾳ—in this engagement Clineas, father of Alcibiades, was killed ; and Tolmides himself.

17. γνώμης—i.e. sympathised with the oligarchs.

22. οἱ ἄλλοι—the other Boeotians, as well as those who had been driven out.

26. διαβεβηκότος—the gen. abs. in place of dat., throwing emphasis on the partic. ; cf. vi. 10 σφαλέντων δὲ (ἡμῶν) . . ταχεῖαν τὴν ἐπιχείρησιν ἡμῖν οἱ ἐχθροὶ ποιήσονται : gen. for nom. viii. 76, 4 ; for accus. ii. 8, 4.

9. Θριῶζε=ἐς τὸ Θριάσιον πεδίον (cf. ii. 19) ; Thria near Eleusis.

11. τὸ πλέον—'further.' Pleistoanax was banished from Sparta on his return, being thought to have taken a bribe to leave Attica (ii. 21).

15. ὁμολογίᾳ κατεστήσαντο—arranged their affairs under a convention. See Hicks Man. p. 33.

20. ἀποδόντες—for the aor. cf. c. 101, 1.

28. τὴν πολιτείαν—this is the only case in which νεωτερίζω has an accus. except a neut. pron. (τι, οὐδέν etc.).

PAGE 100.

5. Λῆμνον—Athenian colony.

6. τῶν δὲ Σαμίων—for the constn. cf. c. 72, 1.

8. τοῖς δυνατωτάτοις—'the leading oligarchs' in Samos. ξυμμαχίαν seems to be used somewhat loosely as applied to τοῖς δυνατωτάτοις.

10. εἶχε Σάρδεις—as satrap of Lydia.

13. τῶν πλείστων—'most of them'; the sense is not clear.

16. οἳ ἦσαν παρὰ σφίσιν—this seems to refer to Athenian ἐπίσκοποι who were sent out to superintend the affairs of the new democratic government of Samos.

18. παρεσκευάζοντο στρατεύειν—μετ' αὐτοῦ (i.e. Pissuthnes) says the Schol.; and this note has strayed into the text of CG (see crit. note).

21. ταῖς μὲν ἐκ.—for the article cf. c. 10, 2.

24. τῶν Φοινισσῶν νεῶν—i.e. the Persian fleet that Pissuthnes might be expected to employ.

αἱ δ' ἐπὶ Χίου—Sophocles the poet was στρατηγός of this squadron. See Jebb's Intr. to the *Antigone*.

25. περιαγγέλλουσαι βοηθεῖν—calling for the contingents they were entitled to. Chios and Lesbos were not entirely to be depended upon.

PAGE 101.

6. κρατοῦντες—'being superior.'

τρισὶ τείχεσι—intended to blockade the town on the three sides that did not face the sea. Why they built three *separate* walls is not explained.

10. ἐσαγγελθέντων—cf. δηλωθέντος c. 74, 1, and for the plur. c. 7, 1.

ἐπ' αὐτούς—i.e. τοὺς Ἀθηναίους.

14. ἀφάρκτῳ—i.e. the Athenians had neglected to protect their naval station with a σταύρωμα.

21. πάλιν ταῖς ναυσί with κατεκλῄσθησαν.

23. Θουκυδίδου—it is not known who this Thuc. is, probably not the well-known politician, nor the historian. For Phormio see c. 64: after winning great victories he died about 428 B.C.

Hagnon led the colony to Amphipolis in 437 B.C., and was again Strategus in 430 and 429 B.C. After the Sicilian disaster when an old man he was one of the ten πρόβουλοι.

27. ἀντίσχειν—the advantage of this pres. form over the aor. of ἀντέχω (see crit. note) is that *continuation* of resistance is implied.

PAGE 102.

1. καθελόντες—for the aor. see c. 101, 3.

3. κατὰ χρόνους—at fixed intervals.

9. πρόφασις—see c. 23, 6.

11. ὅσα ἔπραξαν οἱ ῞Ελληνες — in spite of the verbal similarity to c. 97, 1, Thuc. here includes everything related between cc. 89 and 118.

12. ἐν ἔτεσι πεντήκοντα—i.e. between 480 and 431 B.C. Perhaps it is in order to round off the period to fifty years exactly that Thuc. here says μεταξὺ τῆς Ξέρξου ἀναχωρήσεως whereas at c. 89 he began ἐπειδὴ Μῆδοι ἀνεχώρησαν—which is a different event.

14. ἐν οἷς—since the period begun at c. 97. In such a summary as Thuc. here gives we need not look for absolute accuracy in the details : he is giving the useful landmarks in the chronology. Think of the retreat of Xerxes, he says, and think of the beginning of the war, you have just fifty years, and a convenient plan for remembering how the power of Sparta among the allies was lost and that of Athens was gained.

16. αὐτοί—Athens, independently of her empire.

18. ἐπὶ βραχύ—' to a small extent,' cc. 90 ; 107 ; 112 ; 114.

19. ὄντες μὲν πρὸ τοῦ μὴ ταχεῖς—the μή is unusual : 'it is as if he had said ὡς εἰκὸς μὲν ἦν καὶ πρὸ τοῦ μὴ ταχεῖς ὄντας' (Croiset), i.e. Thuc. wants to represent a *general* cause : persons who had been slow before would naturally be slack in such a case : this connexion of cause and effect is well brought out by the μή. Cf. next note but one. (Goodwin, *M. T.* § 685 offers a curious explanation.)

21. τὸ δέ τι—see c. 107, 4.

πολέμοις οἰκείοις — the use of the plur. where only the Messenian War is meant shows that Thuc. is still representing the cause as a *general* one that would naturally have the effect mentioned.

22. πρὶν δή, 'until at length,' with past indic. often introduces the decisive event.

23. τῆς ξυμμαχίας—esp. the Corinthians.

26. καθαιρετέα—fem.

PAGE 103.

1. αὐτοῖς—as distinct from their allies : see c. 87, 6.

5. ἄμεινον ἔσται—formula used in inquiring of oracles, and ἄμεινον often in the metrical replies.

7. αὐτός—the oracle said ξυλλήψομαι αὐτός.

8. αὖθις with παρακαλέσαντες only ; this is the congress referred to in c. 87, 4. The earlier meeting implied is that of c. 67, 3.

18. παρόντες δὲ καὶ τότε—as they had already expressed their views to the allies as well as to Sparta, their presence at this second meeting is specially mentioned. (There is no sufficient ground for rejecting παρόντες. Steup conjectures παροξύνοντες.)

19. τελευταῖοι ἐπελθόντες—cf. c. 67, 5.

21. οὐκ . . ἔτι—the charges (1) that the Lac. were neglecting their allies in not deciding to fight Athens, and (2) that they had not brought the allies together to vote on a clear issue, viz. on the question of war, had been brought by the Corinthians in the earlier assembly (c. 68).

23. ἐς τοῦτο = ἐς τὸ ψηφίσασθαι τὸν πόλεμον.

24. γάρ implies 'otherwise we should blame them.'

25. τὰ ἴδια ἐξ ἴσου νέμοντας—'while attending to their own interests as much as others do.' τὰ ἴδια is the interests of Sparta in contrast with τὰ κοινά, the common interests of the confederates. ἐξ ἴσου = with as much care as others of the confederates (esp. the Corinthians) attend to their own interests. νέμω is here not 'assign,' but 'direct, manage,' as often in trag.: how distinct the two senses are may be seen from Soph. O.C. 237-240 γῆς | τῆσδ' ἧς ἐγὼ κράτη τε καὶ θρόνους νέμω | μήτ' ἐσδέχεσθαι μήτε προσφωνεῖν τινα | . . . μήτε χερνιβός νέμειν. Here νέμοντας τὰ ἴδια has reference to αὐτοὶ ἐψηφισμένοι τὸν πόλεμόν εἰσι, and προσκοπεῖν τὰ κοινὰ to ἡμᾶς ἐς τοῦτο ξυνήγαγον.

26. προσκοπεῖν—not to foresee, but 'to consider before others,' in a higher degree, in contrast with ἐξ ἴσου and corresponding to the προ- in προτιμῶνται.

ἐν ἄλλοις—the Schol. takes this as neut., and so many edd., 'in other respects' or 'on other occasions': but some prefer the masc., and this is better ; 'among others,' i.e. when the Lac. send representatives to a meeting in any allied city.

27. ἐκ πάντων—'above all' (masc. ; some render 'by all,' which is less likely).

28. ἐνηλλάγησαν—only here in this sense, συνέμιξαν καὶ ὡμίλησαν (Schol.). Cities on the coast who have had com-mercial dealings with Athens are meant.

PAGE 104

2. κατῳκημένους—Thuc., like Herod., uses this verb in mid. as well as in act. : but only the perf. and plup. in mid. For the accus. Krüger quotes Herod. iv. 8 κατοικημένον τὴν . . νῆσον. ἐν πόρῳ—'in the track' of trade : this constn. is strange after τὴν μεσόγειαν and prob. τὴν is meant to extend over μὴ ἐν πόρῳ (sc. γῆν).

4. τὴν κατακομιδήν—i.e. for exportation ; πάλιν qualifies ἀντίληψιν ; cf. e.g. ἡ πάλιν κατάβασις vii. 44. τὴν of course goes with both nouns.

8. ποτε with προελθεῖν.

11. βουλεύεσθαι depends on χρή.

13. ἀνδρῶν γὰρ σωφρόνων—in sense subord. to ἀγαθῶν δὲ κτλ.

ἐστιν, εἰ μὴ ἀδικοῖντο—instances of this idiom in Sophocles are given by Bayfield on Antig. 666 ; Goodwin M. T. § 555 ; Spratt on Thuc. iii. 9. This opt. is esp. suited to such γνῶμαι because it puts the case in the most general way possible. Jebb on Soph. Antig. l.c. ἀλλ' ὃν πόλις στήσειε, τοῦδε χρὴ κλύειν.

14. ἀδικουμένους = εἰ ἀδικοῖντο. The speaker impresses on the allies of the interior that they too are involved when those of the coast are wronged. The change of case (ἀδικουμένων might have been written) makes the partic. more emphatic.

15. εὖ δὲ παρασχόν—this clause added to ἀνδρῶν ἀγαθῶν rather than to σωφρόνων shows that the ἀνδρεία meant is not opposed to the σωφροσύνη.

16. καὶ μήτε . . ἐπαίρεσθαι—this clause gives the negative of ἐκ πολέμου πάλιν ξ. and μήτε . . ἀδικεῖσθαι that of ἀδικουμένους . . πολεμεῖν in chiastic form. Thuc. is fond of restating in a negative a point just made ; while his style is brief, there is yet a tendency to redundancy. See Intr. p. xlvii. τῷ ἡσύχῳ τῆς

εἰρήνης is according to the constant habit of substituting the adj. neut. for subst. in giving the quality of a person or thing. The form ἡσύχιος (see crit. note) is rarer, and as τὸ ἥσυχον occurs in vi. 18 and 34, not to be preferred. ἡδόμενον is in the sing. as if τινα had preceded.

19. ὀκνῶν—sc. πολεμεῖν. Some regard εἰ ἡσυχάζοι as a gloss, but if it is tautological after ὀκνῶν so is δι' ὅπερ ὀκνεῖ after διὰ τὴν ἡδονήν.

22. πλεονάζων—ἐπαιρόμενος (Croiset).

ἐντεθύμηται . . ἐπαιρόμενος—the constn. as with οἶδα. Why the θράσος is ἄπιστον is explained in what follows.

23. γνωσθέντα—'planned.'

24. τυχόντα—'luckily finding the enemy more ill-advised' have been brought to a successful issue. It is difficult to choose between τυχόντα and τυχόντων, 'chanced to be,' agreeing with ἐναντίων, but in such a matter the authority of CG is to be preferred (the Schol. read τυχόντα): for the same reason ἄ is best omitted after πλείω.

26. ἐνθυμεῖται γὰρ κτλ.—lit. 'no man by his confidence forms plans in the same spirit (ὁμοῖα = ὁμοίως) as he carries them out,' i.e. a man may be confident when he makes a plan: it does not follow that he does not carry it out in the same spirit. Reiske's ὁμοίᾳ, 'with the same degree of confidence,' makes the construction easier, but is not certainly necessary. ἔργῳ goes so closely with ἐπεξέρχεται that τῇ πίστει just before in a different relation to its verb is not felt to be awkward. The *security* with which the notion is formed gives place to *apprehension*, and so 'we are found wanting.' Hence τὰ καλῶς βουλευθέντα miscarry.

PAGE 105.

3. ἡμεῖς δέ — the application of the general statements in c. 120, 3.

5. ἀμυνώμεθα—aorist (fut.-perf.).

6. καταθησόμεθα—cf. τίθεσθαι c. 82, 6.

7. κατὰ πολλά—'on many grounds.'

9. ὁμοίως πάντας — 'all with equal readiness carrying out the orders given,' i.e. in the field, as usual; and the edd. point out that the allusion is to the κόσμος for which the Dorians

I   K 2

were famous. Cf. v. 66. *ἰέναι ἐς τὰ παραγγελλόμενα* occurs again in iii. 55 in the sense 'to answer to a call.' For *ἰέναι ἐς* of eager action cf. c. 1.

12. **ἐξαρτυσόμεθα**—the reading of C is clearly right : there is no place here for the hortative subj.

τῶν . . χρημάτων—the treasure in the temples. These could only be treated as a loan.

15. **ξένους**—adj., those from the subject allies.

17. **ἧσσον ἂν τοῦτο πάθοι**—i.e. *τὸ ὑπολαμβάνεσθαι μισθῷ μείζονι*, because our men are not paid—it is the service of men, not money, that gives us our strength. **τοῖς χρήμασι** corresponds to *ὠνητή*.

19. **ναυμαχίας**—defining gen.; **ἁλίσκονται** of course is pres. for fut., 'they are lost.' (Some see here a reference after the event to the battle of Aegospotami and the capture of Athens ; but the *τε* shows that the sentence is a *conclusion* from what precedes ; and Aegospotami was not the result of the cause there stated.)

εἰ δ' ἀντίσχοιεν—'supposing they should hold out,' i.e. if they are not defeated at sea after all (meaning 'suppose we are defeated instead '), we shall get the better of them in the end.

24. **ὃ δ' ἐ. ἐπιστήμῃ προύχουσι**—'the advantage that they have in point of skill.' *ὃ* is accus. of measure, and the dat. as usual gives the point of excellence (*ὃ* is not accus. of *respect* ; and as to *Antig.* 208 *τιμὴν προέξουσ'* see Jebb's note). For the superiority of *φύσις* over *διδαχή* see c. 139, 2.

25. **καθαιρετόν**—'we *can* annul': *καθαιρετέον* would mean 'we *must*,' which does not give a good antithesis to *οὐκ ἂν γένοιτο*. Again C alone has the correct form.

26. **ἐς αὐτά**—viz. *ἐς τὸ μελετᾶν τὰ ναυτικὰ ἕως ἂν ἐς τὸ ἴσον καταστησώμεθα.*

27. **ἤ**—'otherwise.'

εἰ οὐκ . . ἀπεροῦσιν . . οὐκ ἄρα δαπανήσομεν—in a bi-membered sentence of this kind, *οὐ* is regularly used in the second clause if the verb is in *indic.*, *μή* if the verb is in *opt.* The first clause is logically subordinate to the second. Cf. Andoc. i. 102 *οὐκ οὖν δεινόν, εἰ ὑπὸ μὲν τούτων διὰ τοῦτ' ἂν ἀπωλόμην . . ἐν ὑμῖν δὲ κρινόμενος . . οὐ σωθήσομαι;*

PAGE 106.

3. **ἄρα**—'we then decide not,' i.e. infer that this is the way to attain our objects.

4. **αὐτά**—this and αὐτοῖς τούτοις refer to χρήματα.

6. **ξυμμάχων τε ἀπόστασις κτλ.**—'such as revolt of allies, which means in the main withdrawal of the revenues that give them their strength, and erection of a hostile fortress in their country.' The first 'way of war' was followed by Brasidas in 424 B.C. : the second was not used until 413 B.C. (Decelea), but the Athenians had then long feared such an attempt. The context makes it clear that ἀπόστασις implies the *bringing about* of revolt.

11. **ἐπὶ ῥητοῖς**—'in accordance with fixed conditions'; cf. c. 13, 1 : the meaning is explained in the following words.

13. **ἐν ᾧ κτλ.**—'and in this case,' i.e. 'and this being so, he who enters on war in a calm spirit is safer, whereas he who loses control of himself over it gets more falls.' The meaning is 'opportunities arise in war and have to be seized as they arise : it is not well for us to get excited now in thinking out plans of campaign—such cut and dried schemes generally miscarry—but what we must do is to enter on war calmly and take opportunities as they occur.' ὀργή means 'excitement,' not anger here ; cf. ii. 11, 7 : οὐκ ἐλάσσω euphemism for πλείω, i.e. probably ἢ ὁ εὐοργήτως προσομιλήσας.

17. **ἑκάστοις**—each *state.*

πρὸς ἀντιπάλους—'with an enemy equal to us' (and not stronger).

18. **οἰστόν**—'the position would be easy,' i.e. there would be no need for us to combine.

20. **κατὰ πόλιν**=(πρὸς ἡμᾶς) κατὰ πόλιν, lit. 'as compared with us separately city by city.' For ἔτι we expect πολύ, 'far more powerful,' since we want a strong contrast after ἱκανοὶ πρὸς ξύμπαντας. ἔτι must be regarded as a meiosis. (Conradt and Steup have proposed considerable changes, but the text appears to be sound.)

21. **καὶ ἀθρόοι**—'not only as a confederacy, but every tribe and every single town.'

25. **ἀντικρυς δουλείαν**—'downright slavery '; cf. viii. 64 ἡ ἀντικρὺς ἐλευθερία ; the adv. qualifies noun though without the art., as in vii. 81 οὐ ξυσταδὸν μάχαις ἐχρῶντο.

248   THUCYDIDES I

26. ὃ καὶ κτλ.—'the very mention of which as a possibility is disgraceful' (Wilkins). ὅ is τὸ δουλεύειν.

27. καὶ πόλεις κτλ.—some edd. make this a second subject to ἐνδοιασθῆναι (Krüger, Classen, Croiset), which gives an excellent sense: but the constn. is simpler if αἰσχρόν is made pred. to this—'and that so many cities should be maltreated by one.' Whichever be right, the ref. must be to the misery of political slavery imposed by Athens; and cannot, in view of the next sentence, and of ἠλευθέρωσαν, p. 107 l. 2)(δουλείαν, apply to the *present* treatment of the confederacy.

28. ἐν ᾧ—'in that case'; cf. § 1 ;= εἰ πόλεις τοσαίδε . . κακοπαθοῖμεν.

PAGE 107.

2. ἡμεῖς δέ—this is in contrast with οἵ = οἱ μὲν γὰρ (πατέρες). αὐτό means τὴν ἐλευθερίαν implied in ἠλευθέρωσαν. ἡμῖν αὐτοῖς of course means for the Peloponnesians: and this clause implies 'much less do we give freedom to *all Greece*': hence there is no difficulty in supplying ἐν τῇ Ἑλλάδι to ἐγκαθεστάναι.

3. τύραννον δὲ . . καταλύειν—'we allow a despotic state to establish itself in Greece; and yet we make a point of putting down despots in any single city.' τοὺς ἐν μιᾷ, sc. πόλει (which possibly has dropped out of the text), μονάρχους is opposed to τύραννον πόλιν ἐν Ἑλλάδι. The *traditional* policy of Sparta is alluded to.

5. ἴσμεν—sc. ἡμεῖς (of the *speaker*). The subject is not identical with that of ἀξιοῦμεν (the confederacy).

6. τάδε . . ἀπήλλακται—'this policy is (=can possibly be) free from'—viz. the policy of allowing an Athens to flourish. As it is not free from all three, it is exposed to at least one: hence there is no need for ἑνός after ξυμφορῶν : see p. 31 l. 5.

8. οὐ γὰρ δὴ πεφευγότες αὐτά—the rendering 'we cannot suppose that you have avoided these evils only to' etc. (Classen, Croiset, Forbes, etc.), meaning by irony 'we suspect that you have,' cannot be right, since the previous sentence distinctly says, 'you have *not* escaped all three of these ξυμφοραί.' Hence we must transl. (with Krüger, Böhme, Steup): 'For it is not the case that you are free from these errors in assuming that contempt which has proved ruinous to so many (δή strengthens πλείστους), and which from its tendency to trip men up, has received instead (sc. from prudent men) the opposite name of folly.' Nothing is gained by preserving the jingle in καταφρόνησις and ἀφροσύνη, because (1) to a Greek writer such a jingle

has some rhetorical merit; in English it is detestable and pointless; (2) though ἀφροσύνη is spoken of as the *opposite* (ἐναντίον) of καταφρόνησις, it is really only *different*, but early Greek thinkers on the meaning of terms often confuse the coutrary with the contradictory. τὸ ἐναντίον ὄνομα is internal accus. to μετωνόμασται.

13. τοῖς νῦν—neut., and so μελλόντων and παροῦσι.

14. περί = ὑπέρ, with ἐπιταλαιπωρεῖν, i.e. προσθεῖναι τὸν πόνον (Schol.).

16. ἐκ τῶν πόνων τὰς ἀρετάς—famous characteristic of the Dorians. Cf. Hesiod, *W. and D.* 289 (Plat. *Rep.* p. 364 D, Xen. *Mem.* II. i. 20) τῆς ἀρετῆς ἱδρῶτα θεοὶ προπάροιθεν ἔθηκαν, quoted by several edd.: in the Funeral Speech Pericles speaks of the ἐπίπονος ἄσκησις of the Spartans.

18. ἐξουσίᾳ.—δυνάμει.

προφέρετε = προέχετε, only used in this way by Herod., Thuc., and poets.

21. κατὰ πολλά—three grounds for confidence are presently given.

22. αὐτοῦ—see c. 118, 3.

24. τὰ μὲν φόβῳ κτλ.—'those who are not yet enslaved by the Athenians fear to be so (φόβῳ); those who are so already hope to regain their liberty (ὠφελίᾳ),' Croiset. ὠφελία, dat. of motive, is, as Mr. Forbes says, here used for the *idea* (desire) of the thing rather than for the thing itself; he compares ἀρετή c. 33 and τιμή c. 75; and so elsewhere.

25. σπονδάς—c. 53, 2.

PAGE 108.

2. κοινῇ—'in the common interest.'

3. εἴπερ βεβαιότατον κτλ.—'inasmuch as the surest ground (for taking common action) is that both cities and individuals have the same interests.' This is the only natural way of taking the words, for the order does not allow καὶ πόλεσι καὶ ἰ. to go with βεβαιότατον, as Classen supposed (Stahl and others alter the text to make this constn. possible). The meaning is explained by οὖσι Δωριεῦσι κτλ.: it is the interest of every city and every individual member of the confederacy that Dorians should be protected from Ionians. (The MSS. have ταῦτα for ταὐτά, and this is transl. 'since it is most certain that this course—to go to war—is to the interest of,' etc.)

7. **οὗ πρότερον ἦν τ.**—in former times Dorians were recognised as superior in war to Ionians. In such a rhetorical statement we need not look for any specific historical reference.

9. **ὡς οὐκέτι ἐνδέχεται κτλ.**—'for it is now out of the question that we should wait (for common action by the confederacy), and that some of us (e.g. we Corinthians) should now be suffering and others . . should shortly have the same experience.' Cf. vii. **42** νομίσας οὐχ οἷόν τε εἶναι διατρίβειν οὐδὲ παθεῖν ὅπερ ὁ Νικίας ἔπαθεν.

16. **αὐτοῦ**—τοῦ πολέμου.

17. **διὰ πλείονος**—of time, in contrast with αὐτίκα.

ἐκ πολέμου μὲν κτλ.—the sentence becomes clear when τοῖς ἐς ἀνάγκην ἀφιγμένοις is supplied from above, i.e. where war becomes a necessity. πολεμῆσαι is ingressive.

23. **διανοεῖσθαι**—cf. c. **1**, 1.

4. **τὸ πλῆθος**—often of the *greater* number.

6. **ἐκπορίζεσθαι . . ἑκάστοις**—as the several states were to carry out a general resolution, it is best with Steup to take ἐκ- as *passive* and ἑκάστοις as *agent*. It is then unnecessary to read ἑκάστους.

8. **καθισταμένοις**—παρασκευαζομένοις (Schol.).

9. **ἐνιαυτὸς μὲν οὐ δ., ἔλασσον δέ**—this certainly emphasises the length of time occupied, in spite of their haste, and not the promptitude of the confederacy; the latter would be inconsistent with all that precedes (c. **71**, 4; **124**, 1, and this section). Thuc. means clearly (it seems to me), 'I was going to say a year was consumed; but no, it was less than *that*'; i.e. it was not much less. (1) In ii. **2**, if the text is sound, we read that the entry into Plataea took place at the very beginning of spring 431, and in the *sixth month* after the battle of Potidaea (see c. **62**); and (2) we are further told that the first invasion of Attica was eighty days after the seizure of Plataea. Hence the whole time between the battle of Potidaea and the first invasion would be less than nine months, and to arrive at the length of time that separates the *resolution of the confederacy* from the first invasion, we must deduct the time occupied by the events narrated in cc. **63-88** and **118-125**, which are:

   1. The Athenians built a wall on north side of Potidaea and garrisoned it.

2. χρόνῳ ὕστερον Phormio was sent from Attica with 1600 hoplites ; and κατὰ βραχὺ προῄει.

3. Phormio built a wall south of Potidaea.

4. The Corinthians called a meeting at Sparta. (At what exact stage of affairs this was done is not clear.)

5. The Spartans sent to Delphi.

6. The general meeting was held at Sparta, and the decision taken.

Hence the time would be *much* less than a year ; and it is probable that the μηνὶ ἕκτῳ of ii. 2 is somehow corrupt.

πρὶν ἐσβαλεῖν—under Archidamus. The account of it is in ii. **19.**

12. **ἐπρεσβεύοντο**—following, as it turned out, the advice of Archidamus ; see c. **82.** He was afterwards blamed for not having been eager to begin the war.

18. **τὸ ἅγος τῆς θεοῦ**—i.e. those who were under the curse of Athena. The chief authorities for the story of Cylon and the Alcmaeonidae are, besides Thuc., Herod. v. **71** (Thuc. differs from him, and is *perhaps* correcting his account), Plut. *Sol.* 12. The *Ath. Pol.* init. shows that the attempt of Cylon preceded the legislation of Draco. ἅγος is a pollution under which a person, a house, or a community labours.

20. **Κύλων ἦν**—two scholia show that the following narrative was admired in antiquity for its clearness and smoothness ; one says ' The Lion laughed here.'

Ὀλυμπιονίκης—in 640 B.C. (see Sandys on *Ath. Pol.* init.).

21. **τῶν πάλαι**—part., 'of his date' (*not*, 'of an ancient family ').

23. **κατ' ἐκεῖνον τὸν χρόνον**—his expulsion is supposed to have occurred in 600 or 590 B.C.

24. **χρωμένῳ**—cf. c. **123,** 1. Both act. and mid. are rare in Attic, the act. sense being given by ἀναιρῶ or μαντεύομαι, the mid. by ἐπερωτῶ.

PAGE 110.

1. **ἐπῆλθεν**—the reading ἐπῆλθον has not enough MS. support to be acceptable ; but in v. **49** all MSS. give Καρνεῖα ἐτύγχανον ὄντα. In two other places in Thuc. all MSS. give plur. with neut. plur. subj.—v. 26 ἁμαρτήματα ἐγένοντο ; vi. **62** ἐγένοντο . . εἴκοσι καὶ ἑκατὸν τάλαντα. In Xen. the plur. is common.

4. τι προσήκειν—'had some connexion.'

7. ἔτι κατενόησε . . ἐδήλου—'had not gone on to consider
. . gave no information.'

8. Διάσια—'for the Athenians too have (their festival of
Zeus) the Diasia, which is called the greatest festival of Zeus
Meilichius,' in contrast with other festivals of Zeus Meilichius.
Of course καί before 'Αθηναίοις does not imply that the Pel.
had Diasia, but Διάσια is a brachylogy for ἑορτὴ Διὸς Διάσια.

10. πανδημεί—by the whole people together, not in separate
demes.

πολλὰ οὐχ ἱερεῖα, ἀλλ' ⟨ἀγνὰ⟩ θ. ἑ.—Pollux i. 26 (2nd
cent. A.D.) says 'spices are also called "incense": Thuc.
calls them ἀγνὰ θύματα in contrast with τὰ αἱμάσσοντα καὶ
σφαττόμενα,' i.e. with ἱερεῖα. Hence ἀγνά is to be read here.
The Schol. says 'cakes made in the shape of animals' are
meant. πολλοί of the MSS. will not do, because it is inconsistent with πανδημεί. (πολλοί without δέ could not=but
many, as the Schol. suggests; and the Schol. cannot have
read here πανδημεὶ ἑορτάζουσι, θύουσι δὲ πολλοί, which Stahl
prints, since those are the very words of his note, and he
would merely have copied out the text · verbatim. Lastly
θύματα ἐπιχώρια, meaning 'cakes' or 'incense,' is not inconsistent with Xen. Anab. vii. 8, where we read that Xen.
had sacrificed holocausts to Zeus Meilichius when at home; this
cannot refer to the Diasia, but must mean another feast of Zeus
Meilichius.)

14. αὐτοῖς—Cylon and his supporters, who had seized the
acropolis.

προσκαθεζόμενοι—this form serves for the aor. as well as
pres.

15. ἐγγιγνομένου—'being spent over the matter.' Cf.
χρόνος ἐνέσται p. 61 l. 17.

17. τοῖς ἐννέα ἄρχουσι—Megacles the Alcmaeonid was one
of them.

18. αὐτοκράτορσι—without reference to the assembly.

19. ἄριστα—adj., sc. εἶναι, like ἄμεινόν ἐστι, for this is
merely plur. for sing.

τότε δέ—the ten στρατηγοί did not as yet exist, and the
archons were appointed (not elected by lot) by the Areopagus.
In the time of Thuc. their duties were almost entirely judicial.

26. τὸν βωμόν of Athena.

PAGE 111.

1. ἀναστήσαντες = ἀναστῆναι πείσαντες, and on this depends ἐφ' ᾧ, for which cf. c. 103, 1.

τῶν 'Αθηναίων—partitive : see c. 9, 2.

5. ἐπὶ τῶν σεμνῶν θ. τοῖς βωμοῖς—'at the altars of the Eumenides,' probably the most sacred asylum at Athens. The shrine stood by the cleft in the NE. side of the Areopagus, where the Furies were established, after being reconciled to Athena. τοῖς βωμοῖς is however probably spurious; the order is suspicious (cf. v. 60 ἐπὶ τὸν βωμὸν τοῦ Διός), and cf. Arist. *Knights* 1311 καθῆσθαί μοι δοκεῖ εἰς τὸ Θησεῖον πλεούσαις ἢ 'πὶ τῶν σεμνῶν θεῶν, and *Thesm.* 224 (θέω) ἐς τὸ τῶν σεμνῶν θεῶν.

6. ἐν τῇ παρόδῳ with καθεζομένους, on the way, while passing from the altar of Athena. It was because they feared they were to be killed that they sought asylum a second time.

7. ἐναγεῖς καὶ ἀλιτήριοι τῆς θεοῦ—cf. Arist. *Eq.* 445 ἐκ τῶν ἀλιτηρίων σέ φημι γεγονέναι τῆς θεοῦ (Cleon to the Sausage-man). ἀλιτήριοι were thought dangerous people to live with (cf. Neil ad l.c.), and so the Alcmaeonidae were all banished, and at first *for ever*, *Ath. Pol.* i. But they returned, and in 508 a second expulsion took place at the instigation of the opponents of Cleisthenes the Alcmaeonid, who were supported by Cleomenes.

12. στασιαζόντων—the party opposed to Cleisthenes and led by Isagoras. Cleisthenes was almost immediately recalled.

13. τὰ ὀστᾶ ἀνελόντες—so *Ath. Pol.* i. ἐκ τῶν τάφων ἐξεβλήθησαν, but the incident is there connected with the *first* expulsion.

17. πρῶτον—'first and foremost.' δῆθεν shows this is sarcastic.

19. κατὰ τὴν μητέρα—the family tree is as follows :—

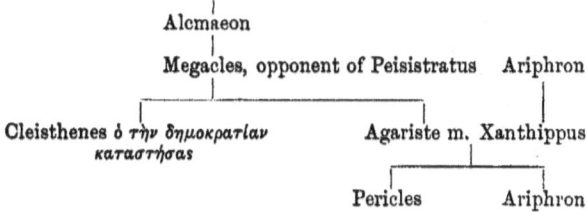

Megacles, the Archon
|
Alcmaeon
|
Megacles, opponent of Peisistratus   Ariphron
|
Cleisthenes ὁ τὴν δημοκρατίαν   Agariste m. Xanthippus
καταστήσας
|
Pericles   Ariphron

20. ῥᾷον ⟨ἂν⟩—the addition of ἂν is necessary ; cf. c. **57**, 5. There is no ex. of pres. in fut. sense after νομίζω (Stahl, *Q. G.* pp. 6 f.).

22. παθεῖν ἂν . . οἴσειν—the aor. with ἂν expresses a contingency, the fut. a certainty. The subject of οἴσειν is prob. αὐτό or τὸ πρᾶγμα supplied in sense.

23. ὡς —'since.'

24. τὸ μέρος—'partly' ; cf. p. 66 l. 9.

26. ἀγὼν τὴν πολιτείαν—cf. ii. **65** of Pericles τὸ πλῆθος ἦγε. In *Ath. Pol.* c. **27** τὴν π. ἄγειν εἰς αὑτούς = ' to get political power into their own hands.'

PAGE 112.

2. τὸ ἀπὸ T. ἄγος —' the pollution resulting from (the affair of) Mt. Taenarus.'

8. σεισμόν—c. 101, 2.

9. Χαλκιοίκου —there was a bronze temple and statue of Athena at Sparta on the Acropolis ; hence the name. The τέμενος covered a considerable space and contained several buildings.

11. τὸ πρῶτον—' for the first time ' ; see c. **95**.

15. Ἑρμιονίδα—of Hermione, in Argolis.

16. ἄνευ—' without the orders of ' ; cf. c. **91**, 5. ἰδίᾳ gives, in the positive form, the same sense as ἄνευ Λ. ; cf. p. 103 l. 16.

17. Ἑλληνικόν—' national,' that against Persia ; if the reading is right the object is to make an antithesis with τὰ πρὸς βασιλέα π., but Ἑλληνικὸς π. generally means ' a war *against*' or '*between* Greeks.' Many edd. accept Μηδικόν (see crit. note).

19. πράσσειν—inf. of purpose ; cf. vi. **8**, 2 ξυγκατοικίσαι Λεοντίνους. The sense of *diplomatic* or *secret* negotiation often underlies πράσσω.

20. Ἑλληνικῆς—' to rule Greece.'

21. ἀπὸ τοῦδε—referring to what follows. For κατέθετο cf. c. **33**, 1.

23. Βυζάντιον—see c. **94**, 2.

τῇ προτέρᾳ π.—dat. of time without ἐν is possible, as παρουσία implies time ; cf. c. **44** ; ii. **20**, ἐκείνῃ τῇ ἐσβολῇ.

26. τότε—' at that time,' viz. τῇ προτέρᾳ παρουσίᾳ : many edd. following Krüger put τότε inside the parenthesis and take

it with ἑάλωσαν, and this seems more likely. τούτων has been conjectured for τούτους: but τούτους refers prob. to βασιλέως προσήκοντες καὶ ξυγγενεῖς, and ἔλαβεν = 'captured,' *not* 'received as his share of the spoil.'

PAGE 113.

1. **τῶν ἄλλων ξ.**—the *exclusive* use of ἄλλος, 'the rest, i.e. the allies.'

2. **Γογγύλου**—he received from Xerxes certain places in the Troad in reward for his treason, and in the time of Thuc. his descendants still possessed them.

5. **αὐτῷ**—βασιλεῖ.

9. **δορί** = μάχῃ, poetical, a remnant of the Ionic in which the original letter was composed.

γνώμην ποιοῦμαι—'propose.' Stephanus altered ἀποπέμπει above to ἀποπέμπω, but the same change from 3rd to 1st pers. occurs in the terms of the Peace of Antalcidas, Xen. *Hell.* v. i. 31.

10. **τὴν σήν**—σήν = 'a daughter of yours' may be right (see crit. note).

17. **ἥσθη τε καὶ ἀποστέλλει**—the co-ordination of historic pres. and aorist is common in Thuc. ; cf. c. **131**, 2.

20. **Δασκυλῖτιν**—Dascylium in Bithynia was the capital of this province, Φρυγία ἐφ' Ἑλλησπόντῳ, or κάτω Φρυγία. The Persian empire was divided into twenty satrapies.

22. **καί** answers τε, so that strictly we should have a second infin., but the constn. of the καί-clause is changed and made independent, as in iii. **94**, 3 ; iv. **3**, 3 ; v. **61**, 4.

23. **ἀντεπετίθει**—'charged him with . . in return'; Croiset compares Demosth. 34, 28 τὰς ἐπιστολὰς ἃς ἐπεθήκαμεν. The infin. follows as with δίδωμι, as if he had said ἀντεπέστελλε.

24. **ἀποδεῖξαι**—i.e. to show to Pausanias, through the messenger, the great king's seal on the letter.

25. **ἑαυτοῦ**—βασιλέως.

PAGE 114.

2. **τῶν ἀνδρῶν . . κείσεταί σοι εὐεργεσία**—lit. 'in connexion with the men . . a service is set down to you in the record for ever.' τῶν ἀνδρῶν is *objective* gen. ; εὐεργεσία is the service

rendered by Pausanias (*not*, as Mr. Forbes supposes, due to him). The benefactors of the Great King were recorded in a chronicle, Herod. viii. **85**. κεῖται is the pass. of κατέθετο, c. **128**, 4. Pausanias had established a right to consideration for himself and his descendants.

6. ἀρέσκομαι—not the Ionic use of c. **35**, 2.

μήτε νὺξ μήθ' ἡμέρα—this and χρυσοῦ καὶ ἀργύρου δαπάνῃ are quite in the Persian style : we can hardly doubt that the letter is substantially genuine.

9. κεκωλύσθω—sc. ὧν ἐμοὶ ὑπισχνεῖ τι. The 3rd pers. is awkward, and κεκώλυσο has been proposed.

12. κάλλιστα καὶ ἄριστα—cf. Xen. *Anab.* III. i. 6 ἐπήρετο τίνι ἂν θύων κάλλιστα καὶ ἄριστα ἔλθοι.

19. σκευὰς Μηδικάς—the dress was the κάνδυς, a long robe with long broad sleeves over a short tunic, ἀναξυρίδες, trousers, and τιάρα, head-dress ; also bracelets (ψέλια) and necklaces (στρεπτοί).

22. τράπεζάν τε—*epulabatur more Persarum luxuriosius*, says Nepos ; cf. the *Persicos odi apparatus* of Horace. The simplicity of the Greek δεῖπνον is notorious.

24. βραχέσι—' small.'

τῇ γνώμῃ—with ἔμελλε, 'he meant to.'

26. ὀργῇ—'temper' in neutral sense ; cf. c. **122**, 1. He made men ' wait before his doors ' as if he were a satrap.

PAGE 115.

4. ἀνεκάλεσαν—plup. in sense.

7. ἐκ τοῦ Βυζαντίου—see c. **128**, 5.

10. Τρῳάδας—adj. =Τρωικάς ; cf. vi. **62** Ἑλλὰς πόλις. The use of such forms as adj. is poetical and Ionic.

14. σκυτάλην—'a secret message.' Plut. *Lys.* 19 gives a complete description : when a general was sent out from Sparta two sticks of exactly the same size were prepared ; the ephors kept one, the officer the other. When the ephors wished to send a secret message, they wrapped a strip of papyrus round their stick spirally and wrote on it. They then sent the papyrus only, and in order to read it, the officer had to wrap it again round the other stick. Both sticks and message were called σκυτάλη.

15. **εἰ δὲ μή**—c. 28, 3.

16. **προαγορεύειν**—depending on εἶπον, but in a different relation ; cf. c. 26, 5.

20. **τὸν βασιλέα** — and Pausanias was only the king's guardian.

21. **διαπραξάμενος**—by some form of negotiation (probably bribery) he was released from prison.

23. **περὶ αὐτῶν**—i.e. τῶν κατηγορημάτων (Schol.) : sc. ἑαυτόν. The other reading περὶ αὐτόν is hardly defended by ἐκ τῶν περὶ Παυσανίαν ἐλέγχων c. 135, 2, for the verb is regularly trans.

26. **ἄν**—with ἐτιμωροῦντο.

PAGE 116.

4. **ἴσος εἶναι τοῖς παροῦσι** — 'to conform to existing conditions,' τοῖς ἤθεσι τῶν Λακώνων (Schol.), or better, 'to the circumstances in which he found himself' as a Σπαρτιάτης. (Various alterations of the text have been proposed here, e.g. ἐν τοῖς παροῦσι, 'in his present conduct' Croiset—or ἐπὶ τοῖς π. Stein—but there seems to be no very definite objection to it as it stands.)

5. **τά τε ἄλλα**—the τε = 'both,' looking as to what follows ; so that we have here an explanation of ὑποψίας . . παροῦσι. (Some edd. insert καί before τά.)

6. **ἐξεδεδιήτητο κτλ.** = ἔξω τῶν . . ἐδεδιήτητο.

7. **τὸν τρίποδα**—this was a golden tripod supported by a bronze stand in the shape of three serpents twisted together (Herod. ix. 81). It was dedicated after Plataea. The gold part was afterwards destroyed by the Phocians in the Sacred War (Pausan. x. xiii. 9), but the stand was removed to Byzantium, and still exists at Constantinople. See Hicks *Man. Hist. Inscr.* p. 11.

10. **τὸ ἐλεγεῖον**—this 'couplet,' which 'he dared to have inscribed on his own authority,' is attributed to Simonides of Ceos. In the Anthology it reads thus :

Ἑλλάνων ἀρχαγὸς ἐπεὶ στρατὸν ὤλεσα Μήδων
Παυσανίας Φοίβῳ μνᾶμ' ἀνέθηκα τόδε.

ἀρχηγός was a title of the Spartan kings.

14. **εὐθὺς τότε**—at the time that the tripod was offered.

17. **μέντοι**—although the offensive inscription was removed.

ἀδίκημα καὶ τότ' ἐδόκει εἶναι—'(this act) was thought even at that time to be a crime.' The subject of ἐδόκει is αὐτό, the act of having the couplet inscribed. τότ' was first adopted by Classen for τοῦτ', and καὶ ἐπεί γε δὴ ἐν τούτῳ καθειστήκει requires it as a contrast of *time*: also there is no point in καὶ τοῦτ', as no other offence of P. in earlier times has been mentioned to justify καί. Stein inserts τοῦτο after ἀδίκημα, but this is not necessary.

18. **ἐπεί γε δὴ ἐν τούτῳ καθειστήκει**—i.e. *now* when he was accused of 'Medism.' ἐπεί γε δή is more emphatic than ἐπειδή.

25. **οὐδὲ τῶν . . πιστεύσαντες**—an explanation of οὐδ' ὥς.

μηνυταῖς—the technical word for an informer who had not full citizen-rights.

27. **εἰώθασιν**—sc. χρῆσθαι.

<h2 style="text-align:center">PAGE 117.</h2>

4. **Ἀργίλιος**—he was a slave from the Thracian town Argilus.

5. **αὐτοῦ . . ἐκείνῳ**—applying to the same person; cf. iv. 73, 4; vi. 61, 7 κατέγνωσαν αὐτοῦ καὶ τῶν μετ' ἐκείνου: Andoc. 1, 64 εἶπον αὐτοῖς . . ἐκείνοις δέ: *conversely* vii. 14 εἰ προσγενήσεται . . πρὸς ἐκείνους χωρῆσαι, διαπεπολεμήσεται αὐτοῖς: Plat. *Rep.* p. 343 c εὐδαίμονα ἐκεῖνον ποιοῦσιν ὑπηρετοῦντες αὐτῷ.

μηνυτὴς γίγνεται, δείσας . . καὶ παρασημηνάμενος . . **λύει**—καί joins δείσας to λύει, which should strictly be λύσας: the constn. is thus changed from partic. to finite verb, as ii. 47 λεγόμενον μὲν . . οὐ μέντοι ἐμνημονεύετο: vii. 13 τῶν ναυτῶν μὲν . . ἀπολλυμένων, οἱ δὲ θεράποντες . . αὐτομολοῦσι. Stein reads ὃς δείσας, but no change is needed. καί does not join γίγνεται to λύει because the clause with λύει is anterior in time to γ. μηνυτής, and such a *hysteron proteron* is without example in Thuc.

6. **κατὰ ἐνθύμησίν τινα** = ἐνθυμηθείς, 'because he noticed.'

8. **παρασημηνάμενος** — 'counterfeiting'; 'for Thuc. says παρασημηνάμενος τὴν σφραγίδα in the sense of παρατυπώσασθαι' Pollux viii. 27. This reading, restored by Hude, is better than παραποιησάμενος, which is probably a gloss on it.

ἢν ψευσθῇ τῆς δόξης—i.e. if his suspicion about the contents of the letter proved false. He could then replace the seal and go on to Artabazus. Did it not occur to him that even in this case he might 'never return,' i.e. be put to death ?

9. ἢ καὶ ἐκεῖνος—i.e. in case Pausanias should ask for the letter back before the messenger left, in order to alter something in it. If the messenger's suspicion about the letter proved false, he would say nothing, but seal up the letter. But suppose the man's suspicions proved *true*, why should he not have contemplated an immediate visit to the ephors, without giving Pausanias time to ask for the letter back? In point of fact this is what the man did. (The text is suspected by some edd.—e.g. Herwerden and Steup—but the confusion of the messenger's motives seems to come from Thuc.)

14. ἐπίστευσαν—sc. that the information they had received from the helots was true.

16. ἀπὸ παρασκευῆς—cf. Lysias 13, 22 εἰ μὴ ἐκ παρασκευῆς ἐμηνύετο, 'by collusion, or arrangement,' here with the gen. abs.

17. ἐπὶ Ταίναρον—the shrine of Poseidon on Taenarus was sanctuary (asylum).

18. σκηνησαμένου—both σκηνᾶσθαι and σκηνεῖσθαι are elsewhere intrans., but here the sense must be trans.: hence Madvig proposed σκευασαμένου, and one inferior MS. gives σκηνωσαμένου: Stein reads ἐς διπλῆν.

19. τῶν [τε]—the τε has no correlative and is no doubt spurious.

23. τά τε .. καὶ τἄλλ᾽ ἀποφαίνοντος—the position of τε shows that ἀποφαίνοντος is added by an afterthought.

24. ὡς οὐδὲν .. παραβάλοιτο—'that he had never hazarded P.'s interests'—a gambling term.

26. προτιμηθείη δέ—ironical: this was all the reward he had got. ἐν ἴσῳ = ὁμοίως.

PAGE 118.

2. πίστιν .. ἀναστάσεως—'pledging his word for his departure from the temple,' sc. in safety. (ἐκ τοῦ ἱεροῦ is perhaps a commentator's note on τῆς ἀναστάσεως.)

4. τὰ πρασσόμενα—the negotiations with the king. The sentence here concluded is a remarkable instance of the partiality of Thuc. for the circumstantial participle.

12. δηλώσαντος—sc. what was about to happen. εὐνοίᾳ is dat. of cause.

19. ἔνδον ὄντα—i.e. making sure that he was in the οἴκημα.

21. ἐξεπολιόρκησαν—the terms are taken from the starving out of a city.

22. ὥσπερ εἶχεν—'as he was,' 'in his present condition,' i.e. shut up in the building; cf. e.g. ii. 46. (In vi. 57, 3 I accepted Krüger's version 'forthwith'; but I agree with Steup that this is wrong.) If he had 'expired' inside, the holy place would have been profaned.

25. τὸν Καιάδαν—the exact site of this ravine called Caeadas is not known: it was in the hills near Sparta. καιατα, crevices produced by earthquake, were so common in Laconia that Sparta is called καιετάεσσα in Homer.

26. οὗπερ τοὺς κακούργους—the Schol. is ἐμβαλεῖν δηλονότι (scilicet). τόπος ὁ Κέαδας ὀρωρυγμένος ἐν Λακωνικῇ, ὅπου τοὺς κακούργους εἰώθασι ῥιπτεῖν. The words of this note have got mixed with the text in the MSS. in several ways, and it is very probable that οὗπερ τοὺς κακούργους is due to the note. (οὗπερ ought to be οἷπερ, but this error—which is common in MSS.—does not count against the genuineness of the words. Volgraff first bracketed them.)

PAGE 119.

2. οὗπερ—the omitted antecedent is ἐκεῖσε.

3. προτεμενίσματι—ὁ πρὸ .. τοῦ τεμένους τόπος (Schol.) until then unconsecrated.

4. ὅ—i.e. τὸ τὸν τάφον κεῖσθαι ἐν τῷ π.

ὡς κτλ.—accus. abs.

7. ἀνδριάντας—not necessarily statues of Pausanias; but symbolic figures consecrated to the gods of the upper world.

15. τοῖς αὐτοῖς—i.e. θανάτῳ.

16. ἔτυχε γὰρ ὠστρακισμένος—when this had happened is unknown; 471 B.C. is generally favoured in spite of the statement in Ath. Pol. that Them. was at Athens in 462 B.C.: the year depends upon other events such as the reduction of Naxos (see c. 137, 2)—of which the date is uncertain. For a discussion see Sandys on Ath. Pol. c. 25.

20. ἄγειν—sc. to Athens.

23. εὐεργέτης—by some official act, probably in some dispute with another state, according to Plutarch with Corinth. In all such decrees of honour conferred on a ξένος a clause giving him ἀσυλία was contained; and on this clause Them. relied.

NOTES 261

23. αὐτῶν—the Corcyreans ; for this idiom cf. c. 34, 4.

26. ἀπεχθέσθαι—ἐχθρὸς (leg. ἐχθροὺς) γενέσθαι (Schol.). The MSS. ἀπέχθεσθαι assumes a pres. form ἀπέχθομαι : similarly in vii. 75 ABEFM give αἰσθέσθαι as from αἰσθομαι, but CG have αἰσθέσθαι : in Eur. Phoen. 300 the MSS. have θίγειν as from θίγω (θιγγάνω). But that these only occur in forms that may be aorists is very suspicious : with other such double forms—e.g. αὔξω beside αὐξάνω—the indic. forms occur.

28. κατὰ πύστιν ᾗ χ.—'in accordance with inquiry as to the road he took.' The opt. is iterative.

PAGE 120.

2. Μολοσσῶν—in Epirus. What the 'difficulty' was that led Them. to one who was 'no friend of his' is not explained.

5. καθέζεσθαι—aor. in sense : the mid. form καθίζομαι is not used.

7. οὐκ ἀξιοῖ—'asks him not to . .'

8. 'Αθηναίων δεομένῳ—Them. must have opposed a request from Admetus for Athenian help.

9. καὶ γὰρ ἂν κτλ.—'for at the present time I might be ill-treated by one far weaker than you (ἐκείνου=ἢ ἐκεῖνος, depending on ἀσθενεστέρου) ; but it is generous (like a gentleman) to take vengeance on equals (not on inferiors) and when equal to them (and not stronger).' This curious form of appeal must be the invention of Thuc. ; and we may doubt whether it would have moved such a king.

13. χρείας τινός—'in reference to,' the gen. of separation parallel to ἐς τὸ σ. σώζεσθαι.

ἐς τὸ σῶμα σώζεσθαι—lit. 'with reference to preserving his life,' i.e. in a matter of life and death. σώζεσθαι is mid. Recent edd. take τό with σώζεσθαι : but it is possible Poppo was right in supposing that in cases like the present the single article does double duty. Cf. Plat. Gorg. p. 489 c μηδενὸς ἄξιοι πλὴν ἴσως τῷ σώματι ἰσχυρίσασθαι. Note that ψυχή below, corresponding to σῶμα, has the article.

16. ἀποστερῆσαι ἄν—'would withhold'; this is the proper sense of ἀποστερεῖν, and hence σωτηρίας is required.

18. ὥσπερ καί—the καί marks the connexion of the two acts, ἀνίστησι—ἐκαθέζετο. ἔχων αὐτόν=μετ' αὐτοῦ. Notice the extreme solemnity of supplication by the life of the child.

19. **καὶ μέγιστον ἦν ἴ. τοῦτο**—parenthetical.

23. **ἑτέραν**—the Aegean.

24. **τὴν Ἀ.**—sc. πόλιν. This Alexander was father of Perdiccas (see c. 57). Thuc. calls the town 'Alexander's' because it lay south of Macedon proper. Its status caused difficulty at various times, for it never fully acquiesced in Macedonian rule till conquered by Philip the Great.

26. **χειμῶνι**—the wind was *north*, and unless the captain tacked would carry the ship right into Naxos.

27. **ὃ ἐπολιόρκει Νάξον**—the accession of Artaxerxes, who had lately ascended the throne when Them. arrived (see § 4) took place in 465 B.C. Hence, to make the dates suit, the siege of Naxos was assigned by Schäfer to 466 B.C.; but, judging from the narrative of cc. 89-90, this leaves too short an interval between the siege of Naxos and the death of Xerxes; for Eurymedon was fought before the latter event, and yet, apparently, some time after the revolt of Naxos. Hence other modern authorities assign the siege of Naxos to 468, 470 or even 473 B.C. But then the narrative here cannot be correct. In Plut. *Them.* 25, where this passage is used, some MSS. have Θάσον for Νάξον: and this would suit here better (see c. 100, 2); but there may be a mistake on Thuc.'s part.

PAGE 121.

4. **τὴν δὲ ἀσφάλειαν εἶναι**—i.e. 'his safety depended on.'

5. **μέχρι**—with μέχρι, μέχρι οὗ and πρὶν Thuc. occasionally uses subj. without ἄν according to the older idiom; but ἕως with plain subj. does not occur.

πλοῦς—'until fair weather came,' in contrast with χειμών above: this and not 'until he sailed' seems to be the sense; πλοῦς = εὔπλοια, as also in iii. 3 πλῷ χρησάμενος καὶ τριταῖος ἀφικόμενος.

6. **ἀπομνήσεσθαι**—the ordinary fut. in Attic is μνησθήσομαι, but Herod. uses μνήσομαι.

11. **αὐτῷ**—for the poetical use of dat. after ἦλθε cf. c. 13, 3. The aor. is pluperf. in sense, and ὕστερον means after his flight. At Athens his goods were confiscated so far as they were found, because he was a traitor.

13. **κάτω . . ἄνω**—as in ἀνά-βασις and κατά-βασις.

15. **νεωστὶ βασιλεύοντα**—for νεωστί with imperf. partic. cf. iii. 20 ἀνδρῶν νεωστὶ πόλιν ἐχόντων.

ὅτι—this convenient form of quasi-oblique speech, where the speaker's actual words follow ὅτι, occurs only in prose.

17. ὑμέτερον—referring of course to the royal family.

18. ἐπιόντα ἐμοί—a fine touch due to self-confidence.

20. ἐν τῷ ἀσφαλεῖ μὲν κτλ.—'when he retreated (πάλιν belongs to ἀποκομιδή) himself in danger, while I was in safety.'

22. γράψας—'referring to'; cf. c. 87, 2, but here the constn. is κατὰ σύνεσιν after ἐδήλου ἡ γραφή.

τὴν ἐκ Σ. προάγγελσιν τῆς ἀναχωρήσεως—Herod. viii. 110 relates that Themistocles sent a message to Xerxes saying that he had persuaded the Greeks not to break down the bridges over the Hellespont, and consequently the king might retreat at leisure. The story agrees with Thuc. here, except that Herod. says the message was sent from Andros, not Salamis. The true object of Them. was to cause Xerxes to retreat rapidly, since Xerxes had been once taken in by a false message from Them. (viz. that the Greeks were about to retreat from Salamis, Herod. viii. 75) and would be sure to assume this one also was false. Them. now misrepresents the object he had had in sending the message. (Haacke and others refer τὴν . . ἀναχωρήσεως to the *earlier* message of Them., viz., that the *Greeks* were about to withdraw from Salamis. By *this* message Them. caused the defeat of the king; by the *later* one he rescued the king. This explanation seems simpler; but it looks as if the parenthesis γράψας . . διάλυσιν refers only to what Them. pretends to have done to *serve* the king.)

24. ἣν ψευδῶς προσεποιήσατο—Herod. says Them. urged the Gk. fleet to break down the bridges, but he was opposed by the Peloponnesians. The Athenian fleet was then willing to go alone, but this Them. successfully opposed. It looks as if Thuc. did not believe in this last part of the story. (Croiset understands 'which he misrepresented,' others avoid the appearance of an inconsistency with Herod.)

25. οὐ διάλυσιν—cf. e.g. iii. 95, 2 τὴν οὐ περιτείχισιν : vii. 34 τὴν τῶν Κορινθίων οὐκέτι ἐπαναγωγήν.

27. τὴν σὴν φιλίαν—'my friendship for you.'

PAGE 122.

4. ὅν—duration of time.

10. τοῦ Ἑλληνικοῦ—'about the Greeks,' but in sense this is object of δουλώσειν.

12. πεῖραν διδούς—so πεῖραν λαμβάνω.

13. ἦν γὰρ . . δηλώσας καὶ . . ἄξιος—the aor. partic. with ἦν is here joined to an adj. with ἦν : the consin. is unusual, and some edd. place βεβαιότατα . . δηλώσας between commas, taking καί as emphasising διαφερόντως τι. Transl. 'Them. was in fact one who showed most convincingly natural powers, and he was beyond all others worthy of the very highest admiration in this respect.' ἐς αὐτό refers to φύσεως ἰσχύν : διαφερόντως τι belongs to θαυμάσαι : for μᾶλλον ἑτέρου cf. c. 84, 2 ἧσσον ἑτέρων.

14. φύσεως ἰσχύν—Thuc. evidently holds with the old view, as against the sophists, that φύσις is superior to μάθησις.

15. ἐς αὐτό—ἐς τὸ ξυνετὸν φαίνεσθαι.

16. οὔτε προμαθών . . οὔτ' ἐπιμαθών—'not aiding it (τὴν ξύνεσιν) by any knowledge acquired before or after,' i.e. either by learning or by experience. (What time is alluded to in the προ- and ἐπι- ? Some say his entry into public life, others, much better, the time when he gave any advice derived from this ξύνεσις—but interpret, 'his opinion was not based on previous knowledge, nor, after giving it,' had he to modify it because he found he was wrong.' Neither verb occurs elsewhere in Thuc. Croiset sees an allusion to Prometheus and Epimetheus.)

18. δι' ἐλαχίστης βουλῆς—'with the least consideration.'

19. ἐπὶ πλεῖστον τοῦ γενησομένου—those edd. who connect these words understand 'to the remotest future,' so that ἐπὶ πλεῖστον refers to time : the objection lies in the sing. τοῦ γενησομένου after the plur. μελλόντων, and so some think it spurious, others join τοῦ γενησομένου to τῶν μελλόντων, which is very forced. But all difficulty disappears if we understand by τὸ γενησόμενον 'the particular event that was going to happen' and take ἐπὶ πλεῖστον of extent, as in ἐπὶ πλεῖστον ἀνθρώπων in c. 1, 2, so that the whole phrase emphasises only the extraordinary accuracy of his εἰκασία : 'his forecasts of the future were the best, in every event proving more accurate th·n those of others.' ἐπὶ π. τοῦ γεν. is lit. 'so as to cover the greatest part (i.e. a greater part than any one else) of just that which was coming.'

20. μετὰ χεῖρας ἔχοι—so Aeschines 1, 70 ἃ νυνὶ μετὰ χ. ἔχετε: = μεταχειρίζοιτο.

21. ἐξηγήσασθαι—'expound his views on it.'

ὧν δ' ἄπειρος εἴη in contrast with ἃ μετὰ χεῖρας ἔχοι = 'that which he took no personal share in.'

22. **οὐκ ἀπήλλακτο**—'he did not fail to,' 'was not without the power'; in later prose we should have τοῦ.—Them. lived before the days of developed oratory.

23. **τό τε ἄμεινον ἢ χεῖρον**—'the advantage or disadvantage' of any proposed step.

24. **τὸ ξύμπαν εἰπεῖν**—parenthetical inf., τό belonging to ξύμπαν.

25. **μελέτης δὲ βραχύτητι**—'with the shortest preparation,' a second way in which he showed his power of hitting on the right thing in a minute. The two phrases are not really quite parallel.

28. **φαρμάκῳ**—the story was that he drank bull's blood: Thuc. evidently thinks it a foolish tale, Aristoph. *Eq.* 83.

PAGE 123.

4. **ἄρτον . . οἶνον . . ὄψον**—according to a Persian custom: cf. Plat. *Alc.* i. p. 123 B 'he said (the person meant is perhaps Xenophon) he passed a district which the inhabitants called ζωνὴν τῆς βασιλέως γυναικός: and another called "the mirror" . . καὶ ὀνόματ' ἔχειν ἑκάστους τῶν τόπων ἀπὸ ἑκάστου τῶν κόσμων.' Lampsacus and Myus belonged to the Delian League, so Them. cannot have actually enjoyed their revenues.

8. **οἱ προσήκοντες**—Cleophantus, a son of Them., lived at Athens. In later times the grave of Them. was located at the entry to Piraeus.

21. **προὔλεγον . . μή**—in the terms of an ultimatum it is not surprising to see μή where οὐ would be ordinarily used: προλέγω contains a meaning of *advice* or *warning*. For the Megarian decree and Aegina see c. 67.

27. **ἐπεργασίαν**—ἐπι· denotes encroachment, as in ἐπινέμομαι.

τῆς ἱερᾶς—'he means the land between Megara and Attica consecrated to the Eleusinian goddesses' (Schol.).

28. **τῆς ἀορίστου**—as Mr. Forbes says, this seems to be distinct from τῆς ἱερᾶς, and may mean an undefined or neutral strip of land.

ἀνδραπόδων ὑποδοχήν—this matter is parodied by Aristoph. in *Acharn.* 325 f.: runaway slaves from Attica found a refuge in Megara.

6. ποιήσαντες—'having called' through the officials.

7. γνώμας σφίσιν αὐτοῖς προυτίθεσαν—'opened a debate,' a technical phrase applying properly to the president of the ecclesia (ἐπιστάτης), who allowed the discussion.

10. ἐπ' ἀμφότερα γιγνόμενοι—'ranging themselves on both sides,' i.e. some taking the one view, some the other.

11. ὡς (χρὴ) μὴ ἐ.—generally ἐμπόδιος takes dat. of person.

14. λέγειν τε καὶ π. δ.—this explains πρῶτος, and always denotes capacity for public affairs.

19. ὀργῇ—'spirit'; their ardour cools when they have to carry out their resolution.

21. τὰς ξυμφοράς = τὰ συμβαίνοντα, 'events'; so below.

τρεπομένους—passive.

22. ὁμοῖα καὶ παραπλήσια—these occur together several times, without substantial difference of sense.

24. τοῖς κ. δόξασιν—fut. perf. in sense = ἃ ἂν δόξῃ.

27. τὰς ξυμφορὰς τῶν π.—' the issues of things (lit. "events following from affairs") can be as incomprehensible in their course as man's thoughts,' so that failure is no proof that a resolution was wrong.

29. ὅσα ἄν—'whenever anything' = (ἐν πᾶσιν) ὅσα ἄν.

3. εἰρημένον—in the thirty years' peace.

δίκας διδόναι καὶ δ.—cf. c. 28, 2. The best MSS. give διαφορῶν from διαφορά: the parallel passages, as cc. 56, 1 and 78, 4 favour διαφόρων from διάφορος, but cf. cc. 23, 5, 146.

8. διαλύεσθαι—middle.

12. τελευταῖοι—pred. with ἥκοντες.

15. περὶ βραχέος—'about a trifle'; cf. c. 78, 1.

16. ὅπερ—accus. de quo, becoming the subject of καθαιρεθείη. προύχονται = προφασίζονται.

18. ὑπολίπησθε—after the war has begun.

20. ἔχει—'involves': ὑμῶν depends on γνώμης: 'the con-

firmation and trial of your resolution' are explained in chiastic order by the two clauses that follow.

21. **oἷs**—masc. = ἐκείνοις γάρ.

24. **σαφὲς ἂν κ.**—'make it clear to them' that they must deal with you on an equal footing rather than as superiors.

28. **καὶ ἐπὶ μεγάλῃ καὶ ἐ. β. π.**—'be the reason great or small' for yielding. The constn. changes from infin. ὑπακούειν to partic. εἴξοντες . . ἔξοντες, 'with the intention of not.' It would be more usual, but it can hardly be necessary, to have ὡς after προφάσει.

PAGE 126.

3. **ἀπὸ τῶν ὁμοίων**—masc.

4. **πρὸ δίκης**—'before,' meaning instead of proceeding by arbitration. Cf. Dem. 23, 28 ἂν ἀφέληταί τις . . μὴ βουλόμενος πρὸ δίκης ἐκδοῦναι.

τοῖς πέλας—cf. c. 32, 1.

5. **τὰ δὲ τοῦ πολέμου κτλ.**—object of ἀκούοντες, but its position gives it the effect of an accus. of respect.

8. **αὐτουργοί**—δι' ἑαυτῶν τὴν γῆν ἐργαζόμενοι σπάνει δούλων (Schol.).

11. **βραχέως**—'only for a short time.' The object of ἐπιφέρειν is πολέμους.

13. **ναῦς πληροῦντες** = ναῦς ἃς πληροῦσιν. Several edd. accept the conjecture πληροῦν, which is very probable. In Plat. Gorg. p. 494 c πληροῦντα is probably a corruption of πληροῦν. Apart from the awkward constn. here there seems to be no point in πληροῦντες.

15. **ἀπόντες**—the three particc. are causal, and the full meaning is 'since to do that (ναῦς . . ἐκπέμπειν) involves to them (1) absence from their lands'—(cf. the opposite ἐπὶ τῶν ἰδίων εἶναι Ath. Pol. c. 15), (2) paying the expenses out of their own money instead of getting it from the state, and (3) being chased off the seas by the Athenians.

16. **αἱ δὲ περιουσίαι**—this sentence has direct reference to the financial condition of Athens. The policy of Pericles was to accumulate a reserve, so that the εἰσφορά — war-tax on property—was seldom levied ; but the Pel. would depend on such a tax ; see c. 121, 4. **βίαιοι** (like βέβαιος always of two

termins. in Thuc.) is a descriptive epithet to εἰσφοραί in general : they are not free gifts (ἐπιδόσεις).

18. σώμασι—cf. c. 121, 3.

20. τὸ μὲν κτλ.—τὸ μὲν . . τὸ δέ apply to σώμασι . . χρήμασι, πιστόν and βέβαιον being pred. : lit. 'having in the one a possession they can rely on—viz. that it may come safe out of the dangers ; but in the other a belonging for which they have no security that they will not spend it before the war ceases.'

26. μὴ πρὸς ὁμοίαν ἀ. — 'against a power differing in character' from theirs. The μή under the influence of the infin.

ὅταν—'so long as' ; cf. c. 142, 1.

PAGE 127.

1. οὐχ ὁμόφυλοι—not all Dorians : of course the Athenian allies were not ὁμόφυλοι (ii. 9, 4), but they were all under the guidance of Athens.

τὸ ἐφ' ἑαυτὸν ἔ. σπεύδῃ—the verb attracted to ἕκαστος : τὸ ἐφ' ἑ., 'what concerns himself' is object of σπεύδῃ. But generally τὸ ἐπί and accus. (1) is adverbial, (2) means 'as far as concerns,' or 'depends on.'

2. μηδέν belongs to the inf.

5. ἐν βραχεῖ μὲν μορίῳ—sc. of the whole time spent in the meeting. ἐν extends over τῷ πλέονι.

7. παρά—'owing to' ; this use is common in Demosth., and cf. Aeschines ii. 80 παρὰ τοῦτο διαφθαρῆναι, ὅτι . . : iii. 80 παρὰ τοῦτο οὐκ ἦλθεν, ὅτι . .

8. βλάψειν—sc. τὰ κοινά.

9. ὑπέρ—'in place of.'

12. μέγιστον = ὃ μέγιστόν ἐστι.

15. μενετοί—act. ; Aeschines 3, 163 ῥητορικὴν δειλίαν δημόσιος καιρὸς οὐκ ἀναμένει : Demosth. 4, 37 αἱ τῶν πραγμάτων οὐ μένουσι καιροὶ τὴν ἡμετέραν βραδυτῆτα.

17. τὴν μὲν γὰρ κτλ.—this is taken in two ways : (1) τὴν μέν object of παρασκευάσασθαι and πόλιν ἀντίπαλον in apposition = ὥστε γενέσθαι πόλιν ἀντίπαλον (Krüger etc.) ; (2) τὴν μέν accus. of respect, 'as regards the one ' (Shilleto, Classen, etc.). The sense is clearly given by Arnold : ' Pericles is distinguishing

between two different methods of ἐπιτείχισις, the one by founding a city in the neighbourhood of Athens strong enough to interfere with her trade and be a check on her power, πόλιν ἀντίπαλον : the other by merely raising one or two forts in Attica, as strongholds for plundering parties to keep the country in constant annoyance and alarm, φρούριον.' The only difficulty is that ἐπιτείχισις is nowhere found of a rival city founded in *time of peace* ; hence (2) is probably the constn. intended.

18. ἦ που δή—'of course,' then, sc. χαλεπόν ἐστι.

19. ἐκείνοις ἡμῶν ἀντεπιτετειχισμένων—this seems to refer to the certainty that Athens would reply to an ἐπιτείχισις by taking similar measures in Peloponnesian territory (Pylus, Cythera) : hence we look for a future ; and ἀντεπιτειχιουμένων, ἀντεπιτετειχισομένων or the insertion of ἄν has been proposed. Another view is that Athens herself is meant ; she is already standing as an ἐπιτείχισις threatening any post that Sparta might establish in Attica. Since an ἐπιτείχισις always occurs in an enemy's country, this could only be justified by supposing that Pericles uses the term loosely for the sake of the antithesis. But it certainly looks as if something to be done by Athens is meant.

22. αὐτομολίαις—by encouraging the slaves in Attica to desert to them. This actually happened in the case of Decelea in after years.

25. πλέον γὰρ ἔχομεν κτλ.—ἐμπειρίας depends on πλέον ἔχομεν, 'we have more experience of land operations through our naval experience than they have in naval operations from their service on land.' Pericles alludes to the use of Athenian fleets on hostile coasts in connexion with descents on the land (ἀποβάσεις). The knowledge of the Pel. coast-line would enable them to choose the right point for an ἐπιτείχισις.

28. τὸ δέ—the δέ answers the μέν of § 3.

PAGE 128.

2. αὐτό—τὸ ναυτικόν.

6. ἐφορμεῖσθαι—'being blockaded.'

9. ἐν τῷ μὴ μελετῶντι—ἐν = 'owing to,' as often ; for the neut. partic. with art. as subst. cf. τὸ δεδιὸς αὐτοῦ c. 36, 1.

13. ὅταν τύχῃ—'as occasion arises,' i.e. casually.

ἀλλὰ μᾶλλον—sc. δεῖ.

I   L

15. **κινήσαντες**—cf. c. 93, 2.

19. **ἐσβάντων**—'in case we embark.' The two highest classes of citizens—ἱππεῖς and πεντακοσιομέδιμνοι—served on board only on occasions of great danger. The citizen crews consisted ordinarily of ζευγῖται and θῆτες.

20. **τόδε**—i.e. τὸ ἀντιπάλους εἶναι κτλ.

21. **κυβερνήτας**—pred.

22. **ὑπηρεσίαν**—'crews,' collective, hence the plur. in agreement.

24. **τήν τε αὐτοῦ**—he would not again be able to set foot in his own city since it was part of the Athenian empire.

26. **ἕνεκα** governs δόσεως : ὀλίγων ἡμερῶν depends on μισθοῦ. Pericles assumes that the Pel. fleet would not be able to keep the sea for any considerable time.

PAGE 129.

3. **οὐκ ἀπὸ τοῦ ἴσου μεγάλα**—lit. 'other important things (μεγάλα) on a greater scale,' i.e. 'have the advantage of them in other important matters.' This refers back to what has preceded, and is not further explained, for Thuc. does not here want to give a detailed account of the Athenian position : this is done in the second book. The ref., as Steup says, is especially to the fleet.

6. **οὐκέτι ἐκ τοῦ ὁμοίου**—'then it will turn out that it is much worse.'

13. **ὅτι ἐγγύτατα τούτου**—i.e. putting ourselves in thought as nearly as possible in the position of islanders.

14. **οἰκίας**—those outside Athens. During the invasions the population of Attica had to crowd into the city, as Athens could not bring into the field an army strong enough to oppose the Pel. invading force.

17. **ὀργισθέντας**—we must not let our indignation at our losses drive us into a decisive action with a superior enemy.

20. **προσαπόλλυται**—for the pres. in fut. sense cf. c. 121, 4 ἁλίσκονται.

ἡσυχάσουσι—sc. οἱ ξύμμαχοι : they will join the enemy.

25. **κτῶνται**—'gain,' meaning with ἄνδρας 'produce.'

PAGE 130.

1. **ἐς ἐλπίδα**—*ἐς* is properly 'bearing on,' 'tending to,' as in λέγειν τι εἰς τὸ πρᾶγμα (Demosth. 57, 7) etc.

2. **ἢν ἐθέλητε**—all this is prophetic, if, as is almost certain, it was really said by Pericles and not put into his mouth by Thuc. after the event.

7. **ἐκεῖνα μέν**—i.e. advice as to the conduct of the war, which is best given during the war itself. For the present (νῦν δέ) our course is clear.

11. **ξενηλασίας**—these expulsions took place from time to time, no doubt by order of the ephors. Plato suggests ironically that the Spartans used them when they wanted privacy for the study of philosophy ; Xenophon says they feared corruption of the traditional character by contact with ξένοι. ποιῶσι, of course, 'enact' in their laws.

12. **οὔτε γὰρ ἐκεῖνο κωλύει**—οὐ κωλύει 'there is no hindrance to' stands for οὐδὲν κωλύει in Aristoph. *Av*. 463, and in two or three passages from later authors. Hence there is probably no need to insert οὐδέν here. **ἐκεῖνο . . τόδε**=the ξενηλασίαι and Μεγαρέων ψήφισμα—there is as little to forbid the one as the other in the thirty years' truce.

16. **σφίσιν ἐπιτηδείως**—see c. 19 ; alluding to the form of constitution. The Schol. says he thinks τοῖς Λ. is a gloss on σφίσι.

18. **αὐτοῖς ἑκάστοις**—sc. ἐπιτηδείως.

20. **ἄρξομεν, ἀρχομένους**—'we will not be the first to fight, but if they enter on a war, we will retaliate.' The difference between ἄρχω and ἄρχομαι is not important to the sense, but it has a rhetorical effect.

PAGE 131.

2. **γνώμη**—'insight': frequently contrasted with τύχη.

4. **ἐς τάδε προήγαγον αὐτά**—'brought our empire to this' ; repeated almost in the same words by Alcibiades in vi. **18**. ὧν = τῶν πατέρων.

13. **τὸ ξύμπαν**—in contrast with καθ' ἕκαστα ὡς ἔφρασε.

15. ἐπὶ ἴσῃ καὶ ὁμοίᾳ—c. **27**, 1.

17. αἰτίαι δέ—taking up c. **23**, 5.

22. ἀκηρύκτως—there could be no communication without a herald after war had begun. At ἀκηρύκτως, with which strictly the sentence should end, Thuc. suddenly adds a qualification.

GREEK INDEX

✱✱✱ The reference is to the page on which the note appears.

A

ἀβροδίαιτος 145
ἀγνὰ θύματα 252
ἄγος 251
ἀγώνισμα 170
ἀδεής 'not feared' 184
ἀδικεῖν 219
αἰεί with τις and adj. 135
αἱρεῖν 'defeat' or 'capture' 154
αἰσθάνεσθαι 'be intelligent' 211
αἰτία 171, 203, 208, 272; ἐν
    αἰτίᾳ ἔχειν 182
αἴτιος with infin. 214; αἴτιον
    as subst. 153
ἀκίνητα νόμιμα 211
ἀκρίβεια 169
ἀκριβῶς πράσσειν 233
ἀλιτήριος 253
ἀλλά in altercation 220
ἀμαθία 224
ἄμεινόν ἐστι 243, 252
ἀμύνεσθαι and ἀμείβεσθαι 190
ἀμφότερος 158; ἐπ' ἀμφότερα
    222; κατ' ἀ. 159
ἀνάγκαι 'coercive measures' 233
ἀναγκαῖος 137, 208, 224
ἀνακαλῶ 141
ἀναχώρησις 'place of retreat'
    227

ἄνεμον τηρεῖν 203
ἀντειπεῖν 'propose in opposi-
    tion' 189
ἄντικρυς 247
ἀντιλογία 179, 212
ἀντίπαλος 'only equal' 247
ἀξιολογώτατος τῶν προγεγενη-
    μένων 133
ἀξίωσις 'claim' 185; 'reputa-
    tion' 206
ἀπέχει and ἀπεῖχε 201
ἀπεχθέσθαι and ἀπέχθεσθαι
    261; ἀπήχθησθε and ἀπή-
    χθεσθε 215
ἀπηλλάχθαι 'lack' 265
ἀπίστως for ὥστε ἄπιστα εἶναι
    168
ἀπό: ἀ. τοῦ ἴσου 270; ἀ. τοῦ
    ἀνθρωπείου τρόπου 216; ἀ.
    παρασκευῆς 259; ἀ. ἐχυροῦ
    ὁρμᾶσθαι 227; ἀφ' οὖ 145,
    160; ἀφ' ὧν 156; ἀ. πρώτης
    217
ἀποβάλλειν 201
ἀποδασμός 156
ἀποδεικνύναι 'point to' 175
ἀποξῆν 136
ἀπολαμβάνειν 146
ἀπομνήσομαι 262
ἀπόστασις 189

273

ἐκνικᾶν 168
ἐλασσοῦσθαι 'be at a disadvantage' 216
Ἑλληνοταμίαι 232
ἐλπίζω 133
ἐν ἀδήλῳ κινδυνεύεσθαι 218 ; ἐν ἀπόρῳ ἔχεσθαι 173 ; ἐν ἴσῳ 259 ; ἐν τοῖς πρῶτοι 144 ; ἐν πόρῳ κεῖσθαι 244 ; ἐν οἷς 'before' or 'among whom' 205 ; ἐν πλέονι, of time 212
ἐναγής 253
ἐναλλαγῆναι 244
ἐνδεές, τό 217
ἐνεῖναι 220
ἐντομή 230
ἐντός, of place 162
ἐξαρτυσόμεθα and -ώμεθα 246
ἑξῆς with πᾶν 166
ἐξιέναι, Ionic use of 192
ἐπάγειν ψῆφον 225
ἐπειδή after χρόνος 145
ἐπελθεῖν 209
ἔπεσθαι 190
ἔπηλυς 148
ἐπί : ἐ. μακρότερον 135 ; ἐ. πολύ, of time 137, 145 ; of space 140, 163, 201 ; ἐ. τὸ μυθῶδες 'in the direction of' or 'into the region of' 168 ; τὸ ἐφ' ἑαυτόν 268 ; ἐ. τῶν σεμνῶν θεῶν 253 ; ἐ. φανεροῖς 206 ; ἐπ' ὠφελίᾳ 140, 213 ; ἐ. μεγάλῃ προφάσει 267 ; ἐ. τῇ ἴσῃ καὶ ὁμοίᾳ 175
ἐπιβουλή and ἐπιβολή 231
ἐπιγνῶναι 208
ἐπιδημιουργός 198
ἐπιεικές, τό 216
ἐπικράτησις 189
ἐπιμαχία 192
ἐπιμιγνύναι 136
ἐπιπαριέναι 200
ἐπιστρέψαντες and ἐπὶ Στρεψάν τε 200
ἐπιφοιτᾶν 220

ἐπιχρῆσθαι 189
ἐρωτᾶν τὰς πύστεις 143
ἐς : ἐς ἴσον καθιστάναι 187; ἐς τὸ παραχρῆμα ἀκούειν 170 ; ἐς τὸ φανερόν 146 ; ἐς τὸ σῶμα σῴζεσθαι 261
ἐσβάλλειν 193
ἐσγράφεσθαι 179
ἕτερος with gen. 176
ἑτοίμως 220
ἐτῶν δύο καὶ τριῶν 221
εὐεργεσίαν προυφείλειν 179 ; εὐεργεσία κεῖται σοί 255
εὐεργετεῖν 260
εὐθὺς ἀπὸ παλαιοῦ 139
εὐνομεῖσθαι 163
ἔφοδος 'intercourse' 144
ἔχειν ἐν θεραπείᾳ 197 ; ἐ. τὸ πλέον 191 ; ἔσχον 'refrained from' 239 ; ἔχεσθαι ἐν ἀπόρῳ 173 ; ἔχεσθαι 219

Z
ζευγνύναι 177

H
ἡγήσασθαι 'consider' 236

Θ
θύματα 252

I
ἰσθμός 201
ἴσος εἶναι τοῖς παροῦσι 257 ; τὸ ἴσον νέμειν 210 ; οὐκ ἀπὸ τοῦ ἴσου 'on a larger scale' 270

K
καθαιρεῖν 'crush' 142
καθαιρετός and καθαιρετέος 246

ENGLISH INDEX

279

R

relative 151 ; not repeated 183
repetition of statement in
negative form 244
rhetoric obscuring the sense
209

S

sacrifice, ceremonies of 174
Salamis, numbers of Greek
fleet at 213
Sparta, poverty of 220 ; out-
ward appearance of 150 ; relation of, to tyrants 163,
248 ; expulsion of strangers
from 271 ; dilatoriness of
250
Spartan character 204, 209,
218
strategi, number of 199
subject, divided 141 ; modified 164
Sybota 197

T

text 134, 138, 141, 142, 148,
149, 153, 154, 155, 161
Themistocles 214 ; walls of
229, 230 ; his natural powers
264 ; his oratory 265 ;
mysterious manner of 227 ;
messages of, to Xerxes 214,
263 ; at Sparta 214 ; in
Epirus 261 ; gift of towns
to 265 ; his grave 265
Thirty Years' truce 208
tripod dedicated after Plataea
257
Troy, siege of 153, 154
tyranny in Greece 157

V

villages, early Greek 138

Z

Zeus Meilichius 252

THE END

PRINTED BY R. & R. CLARK, LTD., EDINBURGH

www.ingramcontent.com/pod-product-compliance
Lightning Source LLC
Chambersburg PA
CBHW032239010726
47494CB00002B/553